ICARUS

BOOKS BY

Max Crawford

Icarus (with Michael Köepf) 1988
Six Key Cut 1986
Lords of the Plain 1985
The Bad Communist 1979
The Backslider 1976
Waltz Across Texas 1975

Michael Köepf

Icarus (with Max Crawford) 1988
Save the Whale 1978

DO NOT REMOVE
CARDS FROM POCKET

ICARUS

Michael Köepf
and
Max Crawford

NEW YORK ATHENEUM 1988

This is a work of fiction. Names, characters, places, and incidents are either the product of the authors' imagination or are used fictitiously. Any resemblance to actual events or persons, living or dead, is entirely coincidental.

Copyright © 1988 by Michael Köepf and Max Crawford

Atheneum
Macmillan Publishing Company
866 Third Avenue, New York, N.Y. 10022
Collier Macmillan Canada, Inc.

Library of Congress Cataloging-in-Publication Data
Köepf, Michael.
  Icarus.
  I. Crawford, Max,   II. Title.
PS3561.Q338T24 1988   813'.54   87-31928
ISBN 0-689-11912-7

10 9 8 7 6 5 4 3 2 1

Designed by Jack Meserole

PRINTED IN THE UNITED STATES OF AMERICA

For
D. B. Cooper

1

THE PLANE circled high over the lake. A silver knife in the sky. The crash, the Super Cub's nose ripping into the ice, had put me out. Not long. Couple minutes maybe. I didn't know if St. Cloud had died in the crash or been dead, frozen, before the busted ski had snagged the snow-covered beaver hutch, the downed tree, whatever had flipped the Cub nose into the ice. Only that St. Cloud was dead. Hunched stiff in the right seat, his rotted fingers still curled around the wheel. The forgotten gas cap that had brought us down in his jacket pocket.

I had walked to the west end of the ice lake. To think how I would kill Blackmuir when he landed. A green bruise spread over the center of the lake. But Blackmuir would see the thin ice. Land the Cessna along the lake shore, far side, sit in the warmed cabin till the sun dropped behind the rock wall at the west end of the lake. Then, with the light going—cold, growing colder—he would circle the bad ice and come for me. I had the .45, but Blackmuir would never come within its range. If he wanted to shoot me, he had the 7mm Remington, its 175-grain slug dropping a couple of inches in two hundred yards—he had told me all about it at Kill Devil Ranch—but that wasn't his style. Something with some torment to it—that was his way of killing. He would stay in the Cessna, engine running, and wait for me to freeze. I could go into the woods. Lure him into the trees. Lie in ambush. Maybe he would come within the .45's range. But as I drew near the shoreline, I saw the drifts in the trees were three, four feet deep. And there were no snowshoes, skis in the Cub. Blackmuir would track me through the deep snow. Shoot me as I crawled up a bank. Or just watch, such suffering in his eyes, as night came and I drifted to sleep. Blackmuir was good at tracking animals in the snow and the mountains. He had told me that at the ranch. Years of killing in the cold.

I stood on the ice lake. Helpless. No plan that would work. I looked back at the Cub, its tail silver, bright in the sun. The shadows were like night where I had come, the ragged outline of the west wall creeping across the lake. In fifteen, twenty minutes the plane would be dull, dark. I looked up to the west wall. My eye went down from the summit, to the ridge that ran up to the peak, and the snow cornice hanging from the ridge. How Dutch had died. Forced out on a cornice platform, the cornice collapsing under his weight.

I went back to the Cub and looked at the cornice again. The snow was deep, heavy, cantilevered twenty feet over the ridge. A hundred tons of snow and ice waiting to come plunging down the mountainside. Maybe it would take us both to our deaths, but it was there. Waiting. It would kill when I could not.

I took the .45 from St. Cloud's jacket and went back toward the west wall. I had made the shoreline, the heavy snow, just as the Cessna skimmed the trees at the east end of the lake. The plane gliding toward a landing on the ice.

2

*I*T BEGAN a couple months short of a year ago. Well past midnight, our 727 stroking along at four hundred knots, thirty-two thousand feet, a little south of Casper, Wyoming. Fifty-five minutes with the headwind left on a vector for Smith Field at Salt Lake City. Denver had just passed us on to Salt Lake control when Max Hubbard, my copilot, returned from the passenger cabin to share his plans for the coming weekend in L.A. with me and the green flight engineer that neither of us had flown with before and, the way the company was shuffling crews around, would never fly with again. We were flight 804—a two-legged, red-eye dog, as Max called these night runs—out of Minneapolis. A touchdown in Salt Lake, now fifty minutes away, and then on to L.A. with the California dawn. Except for a handful of 3M software salesmen crumpled across their stuck armrests, the box office was closed. The passenger deck lights were dimmed, the stewardesses dozing in vacant seats. A canopy of stars shivered over us, while below the string of villages down I-15 gathered our civilization in its own galaxy, with the great prairies and mountain ranges of central Wyoming sleeping dark and primitive to the northwest. We eased toward the approach plate to Salt Lake and I did my best to chew out my first officer as he slid back in his chair. I had already dialed in four dit-dah-dit frequencies as the aircraft passed along our navigational aids. But with the Rockies cropping up below, the nocturnal ionosphere spreading over us, who knew how much distortion had crept into our planned flight path. With forty-eight instruments on the forward panel, thirty overhead, one hundred toggle switches front, fifty-six top and thirty-four on the pedestal between us, we would be in trouble without Max to help bring us down.

Max and I made an odd pair—friends since we had flown together in Southeast Asia. Max stood lean and rangy, hair blond going a little long, against my, shall we say, stocky build and graying military clip. Not more than a couple years my junior, Max at times looked, acted, like a kid brother. Never married, he liked booze, women and gambling, while I was the good husband. A family man, even if my wife and I had no children. As pilots, Max was one-eighty off the detailed flier I had become. No matter how much the company harassed him, he never flew by the book. He was a better pilot than I would ever be and I counted myself lucky to have him as my first officer.

But it was stepping down from the cockpit that Max and I truly went our own ways. In flying, the first step to a crash is often a simple error—a misread altimeter, disbelieved stall warning, the speck on the windshield that in seconds becomes an F-101 coming at seven hundred knots. And so it was with the wreckage of my life. I ignored the klaxon wails from my judgment and believed that Max Hubbard and I were brothers.

Back on the flight deck, strapped in and at the wheel, Max took to entertaining the rookie flight engineer with what I hoped was fantasy. Bullshit or not, the flight engineer lapped up Max's story of the little stewardess' freckled backside perched on the aluminum washstand. Not being known as Quiet Cox for nothing, I kept my mouth shut, hand on the pedestal, and flew the plane.

I was a careful man and a careful pilot that night last spring. I had reason to be. It had taken me seven long years to become a captain with the company, sideslipping into commercial flying long in tooth, age thirty-two, after more than a decade of driving every multiengine kite the Air Force could wheel to the runway, and now I promised myself that no unseen fluctuation of an oil-pressure gauge, no missed compass reading or static-garbled weather report, no unstudied glide path or miscalculated payload/runway ratio, no hot-rod pilot with a pistol for the stewardesses was going to take it away from me.

I made a commander's growl and Max went through a sham search for his flight approach plate for Salt Lake. Max could have taken the 727 into Smith Field blind. "Cabin announcements and communications, check, Cap'n. Pack cooling door open. Airspeed three zero zero knots. Altitude eighteen thousand descending. Checklist. Attitude straight and narrow. Rubber band winding down. Runway in sight, sir."

Landing and taking off we earned our money. We were at it again, for twenty minutes, after leaving Salt Lake's Smith Field. A precision team, checking, double-checking, triple-checking and checking again each and every one of the six hundred gauges, dials, toggle switches, circuit breakers and warning lights in the cockpit. Then at cruising altitude, forty minutes out of Salt Lake, on the home stretch to L.A., we eased back in our seats. Monitored the weather radar, gazed through the windshields for traffic our ground scanners might have missed, and let the flight engineer and the auto control do the rest. Another twenty minutes I sent the flight engineer on a made errand, told him we'd handle the office till we made the Sierras, and tried to have a word with Max. Though this F/E was a good lad, some were company men and when a first officer talked out of school, there was a report on a supervisor's desk in Seattle.

Max listened but he was having none of it. "The hell with Northfuckingwestern, Coxie." Max glanced at his wristwatch. The cockpit tape was well within the thirty-minute erase cycle. "Paid and laid Hubbard, that's what you think of me, right?" Max was silent. "Yeah, well, maybe you are right. Everything I get is going to be got between now and the day one of these crates decides to drop. You know what I want, Dan? I want my life back. Right now I'm a glorified bus driver half scared to death of buying the farm. That someday I'm going to forget to stick a coffee cup over the mike and have some desk jockey in Seattle revoke my pension. What have I got to look forward to?" He looked around the instrument-crammed flight deck, looked back. "I want off, Dan. And I'm getting off."

"What bank you going to rob, Max?"

"You want to look at some land with me?"

"I got some free time next week."

"Nah, not next fucking week. Right now. You want to blow radar control's brains? Take our blip and head for the Canadian border."

I laughed. Max didn't.

"You ever thought about that, Dan? Taking a right at Rock Springs some night and flying up into Big Sky country? I mean it. Have you ever thought about flying one of these tubs where *you* want to go?"

We both fell silent for a time, then our talk turned technical as we approached descent into the L.A. basin. But before the flight engineer had come back to the flight deck, Max had reached up and held a checklist binder to the CVR mike that recorded all flight-deck talk the last thirty minutes of approach. Just in case the 727 strayed through the leader of a hundred-million-volt lightning tree or was flipped on its back by a two-hundred-knot wind shear or was grazed by some little old lady's Mooney, and we had any last messages to set down for our loved ones.

"You ever know my old pal Flaps Gallagher, Dan? The guy who broke me into 727s with the company." Though he had been one of the most senior pilots with the airline, I hadn't known Gallagher even by sight when his jet, seventy-two passengers and seven crew members, had dropped from the sky on approach to Reno, Nevada. No survivors. "Only four people in the world know what I'm telling you. Me, his old lady, another man and the family doc. We never told anybody. Not the airline or the FAA or the insurance cops. Nobody. Flaps tried to kill himself three weeks before the crash. His old lady was fucking another pilot. We made Flaps ground himself. We promised him we wouldn't tell the company. But he slipped back to work without any of us knowing it. He called me up the week before he took the plane down. Told me he was still grounded. That he was never going up again. Don't ever let it get that bad, Dan. Don't ever think that any of us can't crack." Max leaned back and tipped his cap over his eyes. "We're going to make a great team, Coxie. You dig the dirt. Kat and I'll stack the dough." He grew pensive as we came over the squared blaze of L.A. "You know, you are going to love this spread, Dan. Montana. Air clear as glass—OK, a splash of whiskey in it."

The land was a fifteen-hundred-acre ranch along the west bank of the Bitterroot River, eighteen miles south of Missoula, Montana, the closest civilization a well-ghosted village called Victor. My wife, Kat, was on a run to Dallas the weekend Max and I deadheaded out of Portland, flying over the Fourth of July Pass, the Idaho panhandle and Coeur d'Alene, gliding down into western Montana and the Missoula Valley where the waters of the Bitterroot, the Jocko, the Blackfoot and the Rattlesnake rivers converge and spill into the Clark Fork of the Columbia. The air was like fall, crisp, light and brittle as dried leaves, as we drove with the real estate agent south of town into the Bitterroot Valley, snow still heavy on Lolo Peak this late in May. The sky south toward the Big Hole put on a dazzling light show for us. Thunderheads reared fifty thousand feet, their black-based columns cracked with lightning storms so distant we couldn't hear the thunder. Throughout the afternoon, rain squalls swept off Lolo Peak like pirate galleons raiding the valley, hurrying on to the Anaconda Range, to break against the reefs of the Continental Divide. By the time we turned off the highway the sun had fallen behind the ragged teats of the Bitterroots. Looking back toward the valley we saw the windows of Victor afire with the sunset's reflection.

The real estate agent was a buffalo-headed man attired in a western-cut corduroy suit and blood-red cowboy boots. He sipped whiskey from a foam cup as he herded the agency Blazer up the gravel road to the ranch homestead, a weathered rambling house of lodgepole pine constructed, the agent said, about the turn of the century. By the looks of the place—crumbling mortar chinking, a tottering stone chimney, outbuildings that weren't far from being wood piles—not much maintenance had been done since. While the agent and Max talked through the door to the old woman selling, I hiked up a native grass ridge, broken finally by the riprap spill of the Bitterroot Mountains. I stood looking up at the slathering stone wall. Tendrils of drumroll clouds reached out as the cold mountain air pushed over the warmed valley. A storm tonight, but for now a Western 707 bound for Spokane traced its false constellation across the sky. When I turned back, looking down the length of the valley, the Bitterroot River meandering like a fat brown snake through the patchwork of yellowing hay stubble and summer-fallowed fields, I knew I had found my place on earth. I had never wanted anything so bad.

That night after dinner with Max and the agent at a flagstone-and-cedar motel cantilevered over the Clark Fork, I called Kat and told her about the ranch house and the acreage and the access, the tax and the rainfall and the drainage. I told her about the improvements and the water table and heads per acre, when what I wanted to tell my wife was about the pocket plateau I had found shelved at the base of the mountains, how our bodies would burn from the mountain daisies and bear grass and lupin, all enclosed by a wall of fir and black pine. But Kat was not the woman for such talk. Her needs were practical. Physical and fiscal. She wanted to know the price we would have to pay for our Shangri-la.

That price was going to be heavy. We would have to bring with us the world we were trying to escape.

As a captain with over ten thousand hours' flying time with the company I made a decent salary—fifty-five grand a year—and Kat pulled in another twenty as a senior stewardess with Delta. Maybe we owned a house in San Mateo, two vehicles that moved, an outboard, part of a twenty-eight-foot sailboat, and every third weekend of a Cessna we never had the time or interest to fly, but we were like most Americans of our age and class. We lived by dispensations from the bank. But like witch doctors plotting against the high priests, Max and the real estate agent—some distant cousin, it turned out— had plans to make their own magic. Not only could we finance the ranch purchase, we would make a buck as well.

"So what if we build a goddamn Foster City down by the highway?" Max said, overriding my objection. "Up at the ranch house you won't even smell the city slickers. Look, Coxie, if we don't do it, somebody else will. And if it gets too smoggy here, we can sell out and do it right in Canada." He turned to the cousin. "Right, Richie Kay?"

The arithmetic sounded all right, but then facts and figures are the small-timer's rain dance. The drumbeat of the ledger sheet giving us something to jump to while our crops stand dry and burn.

"Take the prime two hundred yourselves. Then thirteen hundred acres divided into twenty-acre sites comes out at sixty-five dream parcels at twenty thou a throw," said the agent, a blend of revivalist, crapshooter and streetcorner poet. "That's a million plus—not counting the interest saved if you and the old gal can work out carrying the paper amongst yourselves. You boys are *lucky* the banks won't touch a deal like this. See, they still think three hundred bucks an acre is stiff. Got their heads stuck back in the fifties. All that tight-ass Republican money. Now I've got the old gal to carry the loan herself, you want it. At six percent. No shit. All you need to get in is sixty, seventy thou. Then the son and daughter can cart the old gal over to a nursing home in Missoula. Look, everybody wants it that way. Fellas, it's an opportunity of a lifetime. California, Oregon, Washington—sucked dry. Better get a piece of Montana quick."

It wasn't easy convincing Kat. On the phone she multiplied acreage times price per and all but hung up. But when we all gathered back in California, student riots up and down every street, her resistance began to wear down. I was on reserve the next weekend and got called onto the milk run to Denver when a young pilot went haywire. When I got back home I found that Max had reined in and turned my hard-mouthed wife. We took out a mortgage on the San Mateo house, sold our interests in boat and plane, and had fifty thousand of Crocker National's finest in hand. With Max's fifteen grand from his savings the three of us formed a small corporation called Lolo Limited and were in business. Max and I put in for an opening on the Seattle-Portland hop—more to have time off together than to fly the same crew—and two weeks later we were signing paper in Montana. An ecstatic Kat met us on our return to San Francisco International. Cousin Richie Kay, she said, had just sold options on the first four parcels, at four thousand each, with half a dozen more buyers sniffing bait. All we were waiting for now was a survey party to finish sectioning up the downhill slope of the old ranch. The high ground was ours.

The honeymoon lasted two months. And when the trouble came it came out of the past. A past I thought was dead and gone.

I had bowed out of the coast flight with Max, hooked onto the Seattle-Spokane-Chicago run, changed domicile to Seattle with a little help from my friends in route assignment, and began spending every free hour I had at the land. During that two months I spent only one weekend in San Francisco and those two days only to sign more papers. My life was in the Bitterroot Valley now. Kat bitched at first, but she flew up to Missoula a couple of times and, though we never got around to making love in the sanctuary I had scouted that first day, I could see her warming to the land. As a place to be, not just another investment. Sitting before the fire in the old house—chinking restored, chimney repaired—she would stare into the flames for hours, her reverie broken only by our lovemaking. We had never had it better, I thought. I did not dream that she, the land, everything, even my name, would be taken from me in a matter of weeks.

I didn't connect St. Cloud and Johnny Kono with me or Max or Kat or the land. They didn't even look like trouble that early September morning I saw them prowling through the topographical maps in the Missoula sporting goods store. But then I had been blinding myself to any connection the land might have with the real world. The survey crew, backhoes and dozers that had begun prowling the lower half-section of our property. I let Max and Kat take care of those payments. I tilled a garden, rebuilt fence, tore down the barn and laid the foundation for a new one, creosoted the lodgepole pine, painted the trim forest green, I even started whitewashing a rock-lined path to the front gate. In flying terms it was like saying to a copilot: "My wing's up. How's yours?"

If St. Cloud had a first name no one ever used it, and no one ever called Johnny Kono anything but J.K., not even his mother if he ever had a mother. I had known them both since Vietnam. They were the new generation cutting their teeth on F-4s, while I had already retroed into a C-130—hauling ammo and supplies forward, body bags out—so it was something of a fluke we ever got to know each other. The first night I came on the pair in the officers' club in Da Nang they looked as green as I had in Korea. Not that I could tell these two twenty-year-olds anything about flying—the pilots who first drove F-4 Phantoms in Nam were among the best the world has ever known—but after hours, on R and R in Hong Kong, the old man of twenty-nine took them under his wing. I never got to know Johnny Kono well enough to be anything but afraid of him. But at one time I felt St. Cloud was the way I had been. A kid thrust into killing from a plane. It didn't take long for me to see my error. St. Cloud did leave the Air Force, not long after I did. But not to escape the killing—because the killing had stopped.

I could have walked away from the sporting goods store that morning, just as I had walked away from the Air Force in Vietnam. But I hung back for an instant and Johnny Kono looked around, smiled, and sighted me through a rolled map. St. Cloud looked up lazily. Like he had been waiting for me ten minutes rather than ten years.

Our talk was brief, casual. St. Cloud and Johnny Kono knew about my last decade becoming respectable with Northwestern and I knew more than enough about Vietnam and the so-called transport company—Air America—they had worked for in Hong Kong and Singapore and finally Saigon. We talked about being in Montana. I mentioned some land and they said something about flying hunters into the Selway. We agreed to meet for a drink sometime and left it at that. They weren't interested in hanging out with bus drivers and I wanted no more truck with spooks. Retired or not.

The encounter cast a shadow over me I couldn't shake. Driving back to the land, I found myself watching for St. Cloud and Johnny Kono in the rearview. But trouble wasn't behind me. It was waiting at home.

The day before I would have driven right by the development being sketched out on the lots near the highway. Today I stopped. The survey crews were gone, the machines idle; the billboard that Cousin Richie Kay had put up had been knocked down. The real estate agency's Blazer stood in the drive. Max's cousin leaned against the fence I had built last week, gazing out over the valley, chewing gum like he was tasting the bad news.

It was the newcomers who always fucked things up, the agent said, considering me an old settler, I guess, for wanting to make a buck. "These city jerks who want to keep things the way things never were before they got here," he drawled. "That's who fucks things up. They want to bring all that money into this valley and then keep it all to themselves. Just one big happy family of peasants herding cattle and chopping up trees. Buncha goddamn eastern conservation jerks," the agent said as we took the Blazer that night and drove toward the airport to meet Max's flight from Denver. "Hell, I *want* to be Californicated!"

At the time Max and Richie Kay had cooked this deal, the land had been zoned rural-agricultural-ranching. The previous fall Richie Kay's first wife's tennis partner's fiancé had got himself elected to the U.S. House and Richie Kay had thought it would be no big matter to have several select ranches in which this congressman had, or would soon have, an interest rezoned to recreational-home. Richie Kay hadn't been too worried anyway. The majority of the county board of supervisors were real estate men or married to their exes, and, what with the new congressman being ever so thankful for all the Missoula Jaycee votes, tinkering with a few antiquated zoning laws seemed like child's play. "Most of these nuts writing letters to the *Missoulian* are only screwed on finger-tight anyway," the cousin said. "But then along comes this eastern monkey wrench the name of Norman Pendergast and he gets in bed with this loony old sheep rancher who come out of his mama on a toot and then one of our boys on the Planning Commission, he shoots himself sighting in his deer rifle—nice .270 I can't get you a price on—and well, fellas," said the cousin, spreading his arms over the riverside restaurant he, Max and I had taken our troubles to, "there's a fifty-fifty standoff on the Planning Commission as of last night. The goddamn ranch is still stuck zoned ranch. Two buyers have filed civil suit implying possible criminal fraud, and this afternoon four sales in escrow folded. With maybe more litigation to come. Can I shake you boys for a drink?"

My head thundered with these reasonable, economic words—escrow, litigation, amortization—while Max and the agent turned to local politics to crush our tormentors. After all, they said, government, especially

local government, existed for men like us. Little guys
trying to make it big. "Everything's going to come out in
the wash," the cousin said, putting the round on a
delinquent tab. "The problem we got is the wash ain't
going to spin dry till November." The agent sucked on
an ice cube. "What's going to happen in November?
November is when the vacant seat on the Planning
Commission is going to be filled by what in cases like
this I like to refer to as the democratic process. Election
day. Say, could either of you boys possibly buy *me* a
drink?"

According to the cousin, the Downtown Association,
funded by every free nickel of real estate change in
western Montana, would come down like a hammer on
Pendergast, the dipso sheepherder, the redskins who
claimed divine right to anything that had dirt spread
over it, and last but not least the goddamn college kids
who hated their own country and had chain-sawed down
Richie Kay's new five-hundred-dollar billboard. All we
reasonable, democratic men needed now was time. Two
months max. Something to stop the lawsuits, to hold
buyers to their escrows, to keep those survey parties
stretching string till we fixed these commies' little red
wagons nice and legal.

Time, like everything else, maybe more than everything else, cost money. We were going to have to buy it.
But Max had that figured. He had been offered a little
job, he told me after Richie Kay had left the restaurant
for some bar built in a parking lot. Just a quick hop to
Mexico. Twenty thousand bucks—and nothing illegal.
Max promised.

I watched Max across the table. We were near alone
in the restaurant now. Waitresses and busboys were
clearing tables and dividing tips. "It's just flying,
Coxie," Max said. "A little fishing trip to Mexico."

"What fisherman's going to pay twenty grand to get laid, Max?"

Max picked up his brandy glass. He sniffed the brandy and put it back on the table. "Dayton."

Now everything—the land, Max, St. Cloud, Johnny Kono, our old boss, Dub Dayton—it all tied together.

We sat for a while not speaking. Max cradled his brandy in his palm, gazing through the plate glass at the black Clark Fork rushing by. The same river, maybe, but we'd be in different water when we met here again with Dayton and the team.

Sitting in the same restaurant three nights later, Dayton in the chair where Max had been, I thought back to the hundreds of times I had seen us here, the pilot and the buyer, in the plush bars of Acapulco and San Juan and Singapore, the cool satisfaction in the buyer's face as his corruption worked on the pilot. And every time, the way I had seen it, the pilot had walked away from just another hop, twenty grand, couple days in Mexico, nothing you couldn't write Mom about. No headlines for that pilot. No wrecked planes, no impounded guns or dope, no jail terms or ruined careers or destroyed families. Not for the pilot I had seen sitting across from Dayton. Just no-thanks and a hike. But tonight the pilot didn't get up from the table. Didn't walk away from the easy twenty K, the hop to Mexico. Tonight the honest pilot stayed stuck to his chair and listened to the buyer buying him out.

Dayton was nursing a whiskey and water when Max and I joined him at the bar table overlooking the sluggish autumnal Clark Fork. It was turning dark in western Montana, the sky to the south, over the Bitterroot, an electric-blue frost on the windows. Across the river lay the state university, the dumpling of a mountain above the campus wearing a huge white M like a fraternity pin a fat girl has won for sex. Dried spidery leaves crawled over the rocks left bare by the falling river.

With Richie Kay's head popping through the restaurant door every few minutes, the bar TV news scanning a line of cars stacked up in Tijuana by the President's new drug enforcement campaign, the cold waters of the Clark Fork rushing silently beneath the plate glass, I studied Dayton. Tried to see him as one would have had one walked into the bar that night. Dayton was perfectly in place in this sleek California lounge set in the middle of Nowhere, Montana. A soft, wrinkled man with weathered skin, narrow sun-closed eyes, well-worn cowboy suit and boots, turquoise belt buckle and string tie, work-thick hands, trimmed silver hair—a Montana rancher who had made good dismembering his homestead.

But as Max left the table, leaving Dayton and me to ourselves, and Dayton began to talk, poker talk, talking around what he wanted to say, everyone in the bar could see, must have seen, that Dayton was no third-string hustler, no rancher selling out. That there was something wrong with Dayton. Something askew. Like walking up to a dog and having it purr and arch its back and rub against your leg. Dayton no more belonged in this little real estate scam than the two figures who had just come into the lounge, joining Max at the bar. The Bob Mitchum and Lee Trevino stand-ins, their loose flowered shirts light for a Montana September night. It was then, with St. Cloud and Johnny Kono standing with Max at the bar, the three of them pretending not to see Dayton or me, that I went back ten years. To Laos, a dirt landing strip cut between poppy fields. The moon full.

*   *   *

The last time the five of us had been together. Seventy-five clicks east of Luang Prabang. Max and I in the C-47 cockpit, St. Cloud and Johnny Kono down on the ground with nine other team members. Faces blackened with burned cork, black fatigues, black knit caps, their eyes shined as they loaded a half-dozen thin pale yellow men into the belly of the worn C-47, its twin engines a good thousand hours past an overhaul—Air America's best. Then another figure came onto the strip. He stood below us, gave Max a sign and called for the loading door to shut. I eased the transport forward, braked left and turned into the wind and moon. And then, as we were revving for takeoff, I looked back and saw the figure, dressed in black like his team. The team leader, that's what we called Dayton then. He smiled and raised an arm— a macabre tour guide bidding his doomed clients bon voyage. We took the C-47 down the moonlit ribbon of the Mekong, made a hard right at the Cambodian border, bearing toward a secret strip near Prachin Buri. Then later that night, when we touched down at Prachin Buri, I went back and opened the cargo doors. Our round-eye team was still onboard. The pale yellow passengers had somehow been lost along the way. And this team member had had enough.

We had been sitting at the bar table a quarter hour, Dayton still talking about everything but what there was to talk about, me still thinking about that no-thanks and a walk, when our attention was drawn to the entrance of the bar. A group of people, ten, twelve men and women, had come into the bar from the motel lobby. They were old and young, fine and faded, sleek and lumpy. Easterners dressed down-home, westerners fitted out to go uptown. A Hollywood crowd taking their Montana ranch hands out for the night.

When this group had passed our table, moving through the bar toward the restaurant beyond, I saw Dayton look back toward the bar. The way the group had come. A man and two women had broken off from the group. They had stopped now, by Max and St. Cloud and Johnny Kono. The three pilots had turned on their barstools to face the man and the two women. One of the women leaned toward Max, touched his arm and spoke in his ear. The woman was my wife, Kat, her Delta flight, so far as I knew, just now touching down in Denver, seven hundred miles away.

Kat drew back from Max, to stand at the side of the man, and the group, the six of them, laughed. The man touched the arms of the women flanking him and the three turned away from the pilots at the bar and came toward Dayton and me.

"Blackmuir," Dayton said, looking toward the second woman, whose arm, like Kat's, was held lightly by the strange man whose eyes had fixed on me.

Lane Blackmuir was a tall man. Kat, five-ten, more in heels, had to look up at Blackmuir, smiling at whatever he was saying as they came. Blackmuir was fifty-five, sixty maybe—there was his silvering hair, the deep lines around his mouth, crossing his brow, at the corners of his eyes. He wore a sharp dark suit cut western—Savile Row on a wrangler, a banker striding across a corral. Blackmuir's eyes didn't belong on his craggy, confident actor's face. Large, uncertain, wandering—there was something torn in Lane Blackmuir's eyes. Something dangerous. When he laughed, as he was now, they didn't laugh with him.

A few feet from our table, Kat broke away from

Blackmuir and the second woman and came toward me, quickly. My wife bent to me and spoke in my ear: "Happy birthday, darling. Surprised? Forget?"

Kat straightened without waiting for a reply. She turned toward Blackmuir and the woman with him, her hand staying on my shoulder till she spoke. Kat made the introductions—between me, Blackmuir and the woman, Kat said her name was Thea. Blackmuir stood before the table, with those soft questioning eyes, but what he said was cold, smooth:

"Let's join the others. I believe we're expected to eat."

One of the women who had arrived with Blackmuir's early crowd—a banker's wife from Livingston, a small town near Blackmuir's Montana ranch—said to me, "What do *you* think of the candidate's chances, Captain Cox? Are you a supporter?"

The candidate, the talk of our end of the table at least, was a man named Gerald Stokes. Some grass-roots congressman from Missouri running for President on some self-hewn platform, heading some independent party of one. Himself.

I drained my birthday martini, third, fourth, I couldn't count that high. "Tell you the truth, ma'am, I don't follow politics that close."

The banker's wife laid a light fat hand on my arm. "Well, who did you vote for in the last election? If you don't mind my asking."

"I'm afraid I didn't vote for anybody, ma'am. Come to think of it, I haven't voted for anybody or anything since I was twenty-two."

Kat sat across the table. Blackmuir was to her left, Dayton on the other side of Blackmuir. Thea, the woman who had come into the bar with Blackmuir, was seated by me.

"That's not very American-spirited, Captain Cox," the banker's wife laughed. "You really should vote again. This November. For Congressman Stokes."

Thea took hold of my shoulder, pulled and spoke past me. "Men like Captain Cox don't vote. Do you, Captain Cox?" She looked across the table at Blackmuir. "They see that votes don't count. Don't they, Daddy?"

Blackmuir looked at his daughter a moment, then looked away. Dayton turned a lump of something in his mouth. He leaned over the table. "Shut up, darling."

Thea flinched and went back. "For now, darling," she said. "For now." She lifted her scotch, her third, fourth, same count as my martinis except hers were big ones, and drained the glass.

Waitresses came and brought plates of avocado mess to the table and the banker's wife's talk fled politics, to range over avocado mess (she was going to eat it anyway), high school football (her son played nose guard for Livingston), and flying (her husband owned a Piper Cherokee). As the banker's wife talked, I studied the women near me. Kat across the table, Thea at my side. They had yet to look at one another.

My wife was a masculine woman, dressed anyway. Tall, tawny and taut, her rusted hair knotted tight at the back of her head, that constriction seeming to form her feline eyes, the blade of her smile. Thea—you could feel something hurting in her. The way she sat, crouched in the chair, it was as if she were in pain, waiting for the pain to return. That night I thought Thea was just another woman, mid-thirties, sliding into alcoholism. Her hair mussed, clothes carelessly chosen, worn without style, her body flaccid, her face, it had been beautiful once, you could still see that, now it was twisted by a drunken, foolish smile.

More food came and Thea continued to drink. When the waitresses stopped bringing her booze, Thea smiled at the men across the table—her father and Dayton—reached into her bag and brought out a miniature bottle of Johnnie Walker. She dumped the whiskey in her glass and toasted the men across the table. She produced two more small bottles, drank them, and began to talk. Low, to herself, at first. Then she began on the banker's wife, the woman still going on and on, her mouth never still, food going in, talk coming out. Then Thea turned on the three across the table—Kat and Blackmuir and Dayton. Then she turned on me. Then she turned on herself. Thea's drunken, disjointed monologue told me she was childless, she was not loved or fucked by her husband, she detested the overdressed country people, the cream of Montana society lined up and down the table, her father, Dayton, me, only slightly less than she detested herself.

For a while I thought this bitter confessional would run itself out, that Thea would fade into a drunken trance, but then a jowly man at the far end of the table—"Husband," the banker's wife whispered in my ear—rose and launched into a roiling speech for Congressman Stokes. The man on horseback his wife had spoken of, a leader who would in a single sweep save the country from the Wall Street lawyers on one coast and the hippies and peaceniks and conservationists on the other. When the banker had finished, there was applause. When the applause had finished, Thea called out to the banker. Her voice carried well:

"Bull burp!"

And I laughed.

And the eyes of the twenty good Montanans and

those dressed like Montanans turned on us. All but the perorating banker. Maybe he hadn't heard, maybe he knew whose daughter Thea was, the banker turned toward our end of the table, his glass raised, and looked to Lane Blackmuir. The man cried out:

"And now I would like to offer a toast to the man who has made Congressman Stokes' impending victory, in Montana anyway, maybe across the nation, possible! Ladies and gentlemen, I propose we drink to the health, wisdom and, certainly not least, financial acumen and generosity of Mr. Lane Blackmuir! Lane!" the banker cried down the table. "Give us the word!" The banker sat amidst heavy applause.

Blackmuir smiled and raised his glass to the banker and pushed his chair away from the table—but it was his daughter, at my side, who came to her feet. Thea lifted her empty glass in mock salute and spoke down the table:

"I drink to you, fools. Don't you know your candidate would be gone bye-bye now if he hadn't changed his schedule? They were waiting for him in Billings." She turned to face her father and Dayton. "Weren't you?"

Dayton had come on his feet. He leaned across the table and struck Thea's forehead with the butt of his hand. Not a blow to cause injury or pain. Just humiliation. Something like the thump you give your head to jog your memory. Thea fell into her chair, said something I couldn't understand. Drew her head down into her shoulders and closed her eyes, as if she were going to be hit again.

And I went across the table for Dayton.

I don't know where they came from—Max and St. Cloud and Johnny Kono—they couldn't have come all the way from the bar that quick, but before I could hit Dayton a second time, the three of them had my arms and head locked, one each, and I was dragged from the table. Out of the restaurant, through the bar, the motel lobby, and pitched onto the sidewalk outside the motel entrance. All the while I was trying to tell them, if only Johnny Kono had let up a little on my neck, it wasn't necessary, all these arm locks and strangleholds—I wasn't going to hit Dayton, or anybody, again. I hadn't hit anybody since the eighth grade. And I certainly wasn't about to go toe to toe with one of America's premier hit men.

I sat on the concrete awhile, feeling better when I started to breathe, while Max herded the waiters and St. Cloud and Johnny Kono back into the restaurant. My old buddy could handle things from here on.

Max came back, lifted me to my feet, dragged me around the corner of the motel, away from the gawking travelers and bellboys. He put me up against the wall and came close.

"For Christ's sake, Cox, don't you know better than to get mixed up in some husband-wife squabble?"

"His *wife*?" I found myself laughing, wiping tears from my eyes. "You're telling me that poor, pathetic woman is Dayton's *wife*?"

Max turned away. "Jesus, Cox, how much juice have you sucked up tonight?"

I pushed away from the flagstone wall. I went back against it. I didn't feel like laughing anymore.

"So Dayton has a wife. I didn't think team men had wives. At least not daughters of men like—what would you call Blackmuir anyway, Max? Some spook banker's banker?"

Max kept his head back, like he was looking at the stars. "Cox, shut up."

I came away from the wall and stayed away. "What

about Daddy? He so much into Dayton he's going to sit on his hands while Dayton thumps his daughter?"

Max turned to me. "He doesn't give a shit, Dan."

OK, maybe I was a little drunk. I went back against the wall and breathed in the cool mountain air. "Yeah, well, at least I saved your ass tonight, Max. Popping Dayton, fucking up your little Mexico trip."

Max spoke quietly, his anger played out. "You haven't fucked up anything, Dan." He turned back, looked at me, cool and easy. "We're still flying. Both of us."

Max came and leaned against the flagstone wall. He shook a cigarette out of a pack, offered me one.

I pushed the pack away. "I quit, Max. Back a long time ago."

Max lit the cigarette and blew smoke. He looked down toward the river. "Yeah."

I waited. "What's going on, Max?"

Max lowered his head. Studied the toe of his shoe. "As far as I know we aren't bringing anything back."

"As far as you know."

"Just what I been told, Dan."

"This a team flight? Like the old Bangkok hop?"

Max blew smoke into the dark. "The team is dead."

"Hell of a resurrection tonight, Max."

Max looked at the cigarette, took a drag and spun the cigarette into the dark, toward the river. "I got to quit too. Things are killing me."

"What have we got to do, Max?"

"We're on call. Mexico. That's all I know."

"Sometime before the election."

Max shrugged. "Could be."

I waited. "Nice little surprise. Bringing Kat up for my birthday."

"It was her idea."

"Yeah." I waited. "Blackmuir the honcho?"

"Dayton," Max said.

"How much up front?"

Max hesitated. "All of it."

"When?"

"I got it on me."

"No no's in this game, Max?"

Max shook his head. "Look, Kat and I've got to catch the last Frontier flight to Denver. Got to get back tonight." He looked at his watch. "You want to ride us out to the airport?"

"You two wouldn't mind catching a cab, would you, Max?"

Max pushed away from the wall. "I've got to go back in." He looked at me. "You going to make an appearance?"

"Think I'll pass tonight, Maxie."

Max looked away. "When you coming back to the Bay Area?"

"Couple days."

"All right. See you then."

Max started toward the corner of the building, toward the front of the motel. I called out: "You hear what she said, Max?"

Max stopped at the corner of the building. He looked back. "Hear what who said?"

"Dayton's wife. She said something. It was why he hit her."

"I didn't hear a thing, Coxie. I wasn't there," Max said and disappeared around the building.

Two weeks after the restaurant fracas I learned we were getting more than money for the Mexico trip. The night Richie Kay called from Montana. All worked up over the

courthouse fire that would save our ranch. "Goddamn,
boy, we are outta the shithouse now! Conflagration
started in the coffee shop downstairs, spread faster'n
clap on a three-day pass! Do you know what I'm saying,
Danny boy? The coffee-shop ceiling is the Planning
Commission floor. One burns, both burn. You know
what this means, boy?"

It meant the parcel maps and parcel descriptions and
deeds and zoning codes and Planning Commission minutes had gone up in smoke. The record swept clean by
fire. At sunup Richie Kay would hightail it over to the
nursing home and take a deposition from the old woman
from the Bitterroot Valley. He had already talked to the
son and daughter: the old woman would sign anything
they put in front of her. The land had never been zoned
anything but woodland, the old woman would swear,
never been specifically set aside for agricultural/ran-
ching. The old woman's affidavit would read she had
filed a declaration of intent to rezone recreational with
the County Planning Commission before she sold the
ranch to us. All this might not stick in court, the real
estate cousin said, but by that time the democratic
process would have us home free.

Except, of course, for the bill for our good fortune,
which came two weeks after the courthouse burned.

Max met my Montana flight in San Francisco the last
week in September. Oh yes, the good times were just
beginning, Max said as he pushed his yellow Porsche
past eighty on the new section of I-280. Back from one
vacationland, he and I were going straight to another.
"We got it cheap, Dan," Max said as we drove down to
San Carlos where the rented twin-engine Cessna 310
waited. "Four days in Mexico. Two straight airline
jockeys on a lark. That's it. No funny stuff. You in,
Coxie?"

I asked to see the flight plan.

Dayton was waiting for us at the field, sitting in the cockpit, warming up the twin Cessna. He handed us a manila envelope—overlays that would be fixed on maps we'd pick up in Mexico—exchanged a few words with Max I couldn't hear for the warming engines, and then the three of us shook hands. No sign anywhere of the tiff in the restaurant. A quarter hour later my copilot and I were airborne. Max was beat from a night out and I flew the first six-hour leg, clearing Mexican customs at Mexicali, making Hermosillo later that night. The next day we flew into Guadalajara and checked into an old colonial hotel a few blocks off the *zócalo*. I walked the streets of the *centro* till past midnight. Even when I returned to the hotel, I didn't sleep.

Our Mexican contact called for us at the hotel the following morning. Señor Ruiz, a bulky, affable thug in a double-breasted powder-blue suit, joined us at breakfast. After working his way through some green enchiladas and red eggs, Ruiz took us to a warehouse east of Guadalajara. The area was a jungle of a factories and crumbling warehouses and building projects that were falling down faster than new projects could be thrown up. That morning as we drove out of town hordes of workers were swarming into these factories and warehouses like packs of attacking rats. When we returned that evening the same insane rush was taking place in reverse, the workers scattering to the garbage dumps of sheet-tin lean-tos they called home. At the end of that day in east Guadalajara, I didn't care why Max had paid Ruiz fifteen thousand dollars for two thousand thirty-liter aluminum cans, even if, as Max assured me, they didn't have anything to do with our flight. That night I sat alone in a dark corner of the Hilton bar and put down as much tequila as I could hold. I felt the world was a human swamp, no place to land but the ranch in Montana. No matter the price.

Max didn't open our return flight instructions and maps till we were off the ground the next morning. We were going back a different way than we had come. Fly up and along the west coast, check out landing sites for a DC-3 that would be loaded with the two thousand supposedly empty aluminum cans we had bought from Ruiz. We were to make touch-and-gos at two places, three stop landings at strips whose coordinates Max now fitted into the new maps. It was here, only a few minutes north of Guadalajara, with an easy run to Acuna, that I presented my plan to Max. That morning before takeoff I had gone over the Cessna inch by inch. The plane was clean. No stash built in anywhere, not an ounce of anything put on board overnight. What we would take back was waiting for us at one of the landing sites. Why not run past them? I told Max. Claim engine trouble, fabricate bad weather. Something, anything. Maybe, just maybe, I argued, our part in the deal was done. Maybe the milk cans were all Dayton had on his mind.

Max took the wheel and banked the Cessna hard to the west. "Once you've had 'em, you've got 'em. Right, Dan? Shit, Cox, you know you don't get paid in this game till you put the ball in the hole. Know what would happen if we aborted right now? Remember that tree-hugger up in Montana? Pendergast. The guy on the Planning Commission who was fucking up our little party. Well, he skidded his car off into the Blackfoot River. Just found his body Friday. We don't follow through on this, we're going to have to start wearing water wings, Dan."

Max held the Cessna in a steep climb. He pulled the column back till we hit three hard stall buffets—only then did he ease the nose down. Max laughed in my face. He could fly circles around me, we both knew it. "Look, Dan, I'm not in with these guys anymore." Max chewed at the inside of his mouth. "I got out. OK, I stayed on with them for a while in Nam and other humid places after you walked. But then I got out. And I've stayed out." He tipped the wing as we sighted a town on our flight path that had drifted a couple miles too far north. We leveled off at twelve thousand feet. "What do you think these guys are anyway, Dan, some kind of two-bit mafiosi? Shit, Dayton's as good a man as you'll ever be. He's one of us. He was flying Tigers for Chennault when I was riding a trike. You know, they didn't have ammo the first couple weeks of the war. He pulled his guts out his asshole in a three-g dive running a Jap plane into the jungle. He trussed up and didn't report on sick call till V-J Day. Don't tell me a man like that ain't serving his country."

"Yeah, wrap it in a flag, Max. It doesn't change a goddamn thing. Dayton's a fucking hit man. I don't care who or why he's hitting."

Max thumped his knuckle against the altimeter window. "Take it for a while, Dan. Two seven five or thereabouts."

"Fuck off, Max. Come on, break down. Now you can tell me. What are we carrying in? I searched the plane at Guadalajara. We ain't got it yet. What's it going to be?"

Max gave the column a slight jar and the Cessna's nose pitched down, then leveled. "Just money, Dan."

"Just money. And maybe a courier?"

Max covered his face with his hands. Like he was tired, still hungover. He took his hands away from his face. "I'm getting out of airlines, Dan. You ought to be thinking about retiring yourself."

"Believe me, I have been."

Max smiled. The strain of it made him look years

older. "You know the fuckup you made in Seattle last month? It went on the books. They work deep, Dan."

My hands were bone-white, rigid, on the wheel. As they had been during the approach to Sea-Tac, my mind on the land, what I would be willing to do to save it, when I should have been talking my first officer down to a landing. For one moment we had both been flying the plane, me pulling one way, my copilot, not realizing what force he was fighting, pulling the other. Max was right. They did work deep. Nobody but me and the first officer knew about our near-fatal tug-of-war.

Max corrected our course and pulled his cap over his eyes. "Two seven oh, Dan. Wake me up in an hour." He was asleep in minutes.

Our first checkpoint was near a village named Ortiz, seventy-five miles east-northeast of Guaymas. We put down on an abandoned dirt strip once used at a nearby cinnabar mine. As we taxied a dozen or so Mexican children came out of nowhere, the kids running under the wings, begging pesos, throwing rocks at the plane's tail. Max laughed at an old GMC pickup, fenders and roof sandblasted silver, driven at us by some local cop in a handmade uniform, epaulets flying in the wind. Max let the truck get just close enough to drag the Cessna during takeoff.

Two miles above Bahía Kino I dropped the Cessna down to a long, curving beach, cruising it at a hundred and forty knots. Max shook me off when we got close enough to see the wind ripples crawling across the sand like sidewinders. Max crossed off that checkpoint and I twisted the Cessna into a banked climb over the water, turning inland. Fifty miles to the east we sighted a stretch of desert near the abandoned pueblo of Ciudad de la Libertad. We circled the desert till we found a stretch of dust that looked clear of rock, brush and pothole. A bent prop and we'd walk home. We touched down in an explosion of dust, the sweetest landing Max had ever made. Underneath the dust the desert clay was baked hard as asphalt.

We then turned toward our last stop, a saber-shaped island that lay two hundred yards off Puerto Peñasco, a ramshackle fishing village on the Gulf of California. The shoreline on the lee side of the island was ragged, rocky, but as we crossed to the Gulf, Max banked the plane over a gray-black strip of shale sand a mile long, twenty yards wide, not cocked more than a degree or two toward the sea. Max read the warning from Dayton's guidebook: the hard shale was exposed only during low tide. Above the tide mark the sand was soft, treacherous under its crust. Max checked the tide tables. "Minus tide. Let's go down and take a look, Dan."

We touched down on shale packed smoother than L.A. International, taxied the length of the beach, then turned back to our touchdown point. Max wheeled the Cessna around, into the wind, had the throttle under his fist, ready to push it forward, hard, when we saw a car parked on a track that wound through the dunes. An old Chevy, painted dull red, an elaborate taxi name and number lettered on the door. The car's windows were fringed like a surrey top, so dusty you could only make out the forms of three men inside. Two in the back, one behind the wheel. Max held off the throttle and the rear door of the taxi opened. One of the men in back got out, closed the door and came quickly toward us. During the instant the door was open, I had seen the man in the back, his chiseled face, the actor's profile. But that was enough. We were working for Blackmuir.

The man who had left the taxi, his hand stretched up to touch the wing of the plane, now climbing into the Cessna, was lean, lithe, with close-cropped hair, sinewy face and zombie eyes. Once settled in back, he took a .45 out of his jacket and touched it against the base of Max's neck. Max pushed the Cessna down the strip of shale, then, in the air, went into a steep climb. North, toward the Arizona border.

We were flying a killer home.

*I*WOKE in bed. A hospital room. Square and pale. A window to my left, behind me. It was night. Street traffic, car horns and sirens came from beyond the window. There was a door opposite the bed. A cop sat by the door, his chair tilted back. The cop was reading a magazine. An IV bottle hung from a stand to the right of the bed. I tried to turn. A tube from the drip bottle was fastened in my right arm. My left foot was held to the bedstead by a chain.

The cop looked up. He reached back and opened the door and spoke into the hall. "He's with us," he said to someone in the hall, I couldn't see who. The cop closed the door and sat forward, putting the chair's four legs on the floor. He closed the magazine to the cover and tossed it on the floor. He sat looking at me. He didn't say anything else.

A nurse came first. She looked at the chart hanging at the foot of the bed, looked at me, and left. The cop looked at her legs as she went out into the hall. The nurse came back in a couple of minutes. A doctor was with her. The doctor looked at the chart. He looked into my eyes and ears with a small light. The nurse took my blood pressure and pulse. She wrote the figures on the chart while the doctor thumped my chest. He listened to my heart and lungs with a stethoscope. He finally spoke.

"How do you feel?" he said. "How's the head?"

It hurt like hell. Something wrapped tight around my forehead.

The doctor held three fingers before me. "How many fingers have I got?"

"Three."

The doctor took the fingers down. "You've suffered a concussion. Been out eighteen hours. What's the last thing you remember?"

I shook my head. "I don't know. Where am I?"

"In trouble," said the cop from the door. He was standing now.

The doctor said, "You know your name?"

I remembered that. I told him my name.

The doctor looked at me, drew up his mouth, like I hadn't got it quite right. "We're going to keep you quiet till morning. Then we'll do an EEG. No point in an X-ray right now. It won't show much for a week or so. We're going to be waking you every two hours tonight. No solid food till tomorrow. You're probably not that hungry anyway."

"I could use a drink."

The doctor smiled. He took a cup of water from the nurse and gave it to me.

"We'll see how you're doing in the morning." The doctor turned to the nurse. "I would like to have the officer moved out into the hall. The prisoner's not going anywhere."

The doctor and the nurse left the room. The cop went to the door. He watched me. "Convenient," the cop said. "Not remembering anything." He hitched up his gun belt as he went through the door.

A new bunch—four doctors and two nurses—came the next morning. They asked if my vision was clear, sharp, any numbness in my fingers, toes, anywhere, was I sleeping and did I have any insurance.

In a short time a couple of male orderlies and a new cop came into the room. The orderlies were pushing a gurney. One of the orderlies pulled the drip needle from my arm while the cop took the chain from my ankle. The orderlies got me on the gurney and I was wheeled out of the room, down the hall, to a medium-sized room with some electronic gear placed around. The orderlies fixed electrodes and other things to my head. I was told to close my eyes, keep perfectly still. After five minutes or so, one of the orderlies said I could open my eyes. The other orderly was tearing a long sheet of graph paper from a machine. The orderlies unhooked all the things they had put on my head, put me back on the gurney and wheeled me into an adjacent room. The new cop was waiting in the room.

"What the hell were you guys up to, anyway?" he said.

I said I couldn't remember and the cop didn't say anything else.

A couple minutes later a doctor came into the room. Not the one from last night. The doctor put me through a lot of old-fashioned tests. Tickled my feet, tapped my ankles and wrists with a rubber hammer, had me stand, close my eyes, open them, hold my index fingers before me, close my eyes again, open them, grip his fingers with my hands. He had me stand, walk, and when I more or less staggered, put me back on the gurney.

The doctor made some notes on a form snapped to a clipboard. He was still writing when he said, "What do you remember? The last thing before you woke up."

I had had time to think about that while my brain had been making mountains and valleys on the EEG graph. "I was flying. In a plane."

The doctor stopped writing. He looked at me. "Do you remember anything about coming down?"

I said I didn't. It wasn't all lie.

"You made a forced landing. Hit your head against the windshield. What is it—some kind of plastic?"

"Plexiglas."

The doctor looked back over what he had written. "Too bad cars don't have them. I don't know if the concussion would have been less severe, but it kept you from getting cut up." The doctor took the clipboard from under his arm. He took the EEG chart from the clipboard and studied it, marking lines here and there with a pencil. Finally he refolded the paper and put it back on the clipboard. "Looks better than mine," he said and sat back in his chair and crossed his legs. He studied me, then said, "Nothing on the EEG. Of course, something could always develop later. When you're dealing with trauma to the brain, it sometimes takes time for the damage to make itself apparent to our technology." He uncrossed his legs and looked at the cop. "I want to keep him here for another twenty-four hours anyway." He looked back to me with a flicker of a smile. "Then you can have him."

A couple of plainclothes cops and a couple young guys from the D.A.'s office were waiting in my room. A nurse was there too. She got me off the gurney, into bed, and left the room.

One of the cops, a big guy with a burnt-red face and black bushy eyebrows—the top of his head white and clean, looked soft as a peeled egg—came forward in his chair.

"Cox, we don't want any of this crap about not remembering anything. Now tell us—what were you and your pal running in?"

Something was changing in me. Going wrong. I was starting to remember. "I don't know what you're talking about."

The bad-ass cop sat there a second, tense, forward in his chair. "What bullshit," he said and went back.

One of the assistant D.A.s spoke up. A rabbity-looking little guy wearing horn-rim glasses. "What we have to establish first, Mr. Cox, is were you or were you not flying back from Mexico?" The assistant D.A. had a soft voice, but you wouldn't call it rabbity. Just young. "We're having some kind of jurisdictional dispute in this case. With the federal authorities."

The bad-ass cop snorted. "We got you in Mexico three days ago, Cox. Fuck, I wish we didn't. I'd give an eyetooth to bust your ass. A fucking *airline* pilot pulling this shit." That was it, why the bad-ass cop didn't take to me. Fly a 727 and fuck up, it was like a priest gargling holy water. The bad-ass cop went back in his chair. "But it looks like the feds are going to get that pleasure."

The rabbity little lawyer said, "Even if we lose that, Sergeant, we may still have part of him." The assistant D.A. turned to me, turning cold, looking a lot older. "Maybe the best part."

The bad-ass cop spoke again. The extra cop and the extra lawyer still hadn't said a word. The bad-ass cop said, "Yeah. We want to know how your partner died. Remember anything about that?"

Something turned inside me. There was a black wall just behind my eyes. Which was it? I didn't know or just that I didn't remember? "Max is dead?"

The bad-ass cop nodded. "Maybe he died before the crash. Maybe he died later. Now you going to tell us what you know?"

Now I worked at it. Remembered. The island off Puerto Peñasco. The killer climbing behind Max. The gun. Taxiing. The takeoff. The Cessna curling up and north. Leveling off at—what?—nine thousand feet. Two hours, three. No problems. Not a word from the killer in the back. Just flying talk between Max and me. Then a black wall came hard from the northwest, a desert storm rushing across our path. Max wanted to go over the boiling cunimb. He could take the Cessna up high as it took. Better than trying to beat the storm going east, it was moving too fast to head. Going to the west, to come in behind the storm, looked too risky. We couldn't see the end of the storm. To the northwest there was nothing but black. The killer decided it for us. He touched the .45 muzzle to the back of Max's neck. He cocked the gun. We were going through the storm.

We went into the storm. It was black. No night, not

even blindness, was that black. The wind—a hundred knots, one twenty, one forty—the numbers didn't mean anything. The airspeed indicator spun out of control. The VOR needle kicked back and forth like a metronome. Even the gyro was screwed. North, south—we didn't know which way was up. The noise was like being inside a locomotive boiler. Max fought the wheel. Trying to keep the plane forty-five degrees into the wind. It was all he had to fly on. The wind.

We came out of the storm. Were thrown into a heavy gray rain. The plane was buffeted, bad, but now we could feel where the blows were coming from. Up and down made sense again. The gauges, altimeter, airspeed, the needles jerked, swinging crazy, but we could see there was some place on the dial that was right. Then the rain eased, the light paled, and the air grew smoother. The plane straightened and the gauges calmed. Just nervous, jittery now. Then I saw sky and earth and then a mass of rock stretched across the windshield.

The mountain range blocked our path. Beyond the first ragged string of mountains stood the ghost of another range, the peaks white, icy blue in shadow. The first range—a jumble of desert thrusting into the sky— spread unbroken across the northern horizon, but Max turned the Cessna toward it. We would find a way through, go over it. In a quarter hour a break appeared in the wall and Max took the plane into the mountains. I searched the sectionals for the range. I could find nothing like it. The storm had thrown us off course, screwed up the instruments, maybe we had the wrong maps. We were flying lost.

We went for thirty minutes into the mountains. Max followed a maze of passes and canyons and mountain valleys. We flew wherever the mountains let us. East.

North. East again. Then north. There was an hour, hour and a half light left when we came out of the range. A high desert plateau, covered with pine and spruce and juniper, lay before us. Max gave me the wheel and took the sectionals. He studied each plate. Looked down at the terrain, scanned the empty plateau for some butte, ridge, river, anything that would tell us where we were. He put the maps away. We were home. We had crossed the Arizona border a quarter hour back. Max took the wheel and put the Cessna on the plateau deck. We had entered restricted air space. Luke Air Force Range.

The Phantom IIs, a pair of them, dropped on us like hawks. Their turbojets split the air over us. The boom rattled and bucked the Cessna. The Phantoms curled up, turning to come back for a second pass. Max looked to the ground. I missed it, but Max saw something on the desert floor. A road maybe, some forgotten trail, someplace clear and flat that would take us out of the sky.

The Cessna hit the plateau floor hard. The plane jerked up, a couple feet above the scrub juniper. The desert floor wasn't clear, it wasn't flat, but Max went down again. The plane bucked through the scrub, bounding over the ragged, rocky floor. The killer in the back screamed at Max to take the plane up again. He reached over and pulled at the wheel. Then, with Max and the killer fighting for the wheel, the Phantoms making their second pass over us, the plane hit something hard. Metal tore, snapped. The plane hit a second time and went up. Floated. Tumbling tail over nose. Then there was nothing.

The cops and the lawyers placed around the bed watched me, waiting.

"He was alive when we went down," I said. "That's all I remember."

The cops and lawyers looked at one another. The assistant D.A. turned to me. "Your friend wasn't killed in the landing."

The cops, lawyers, watched me. It was the silent cop who said:

"Hubbard's body was found fifty yards away from the plane. Shot in the back of the head. With a .45."

The nurse's face was over me. Strained. Then she smiled.

"I told them they were pushing you too far too soon." She did something with the pillow behind my head. "One of the D.A.s is back. Says he's friendly. Can you handle it?"

Maybe I was hurting. Sick. But I didn't want to be alone. Let the lawyer in. I'd talk to anybody who could tell me what was happening.

The nurse went to the door, let the assistant D.A. into the room. The guy with the specs and the soft voice. The D.A. came to the bed. Quick. He was talking when he got there.

"Look, we don't have long and I don't want any bullshit from you. I'm trying to find out what the hell is going on around here. I may even be helping you indirectly. Now you just listen while I tell you something. Then when I'm finished I want you to tell me something. There's something rotten going on around here. I don't know what. Let's call it a cover-up. I don't like that word, but we've got to start somewhere. Now, do you remember what we were talking about when you went out? Don't say anything. Just listen. A Mexican boy found your plane wreckage a short time after you came down. You in the cockpit. Out. Nobody else around. Then he found Hubbard's body. Fifty, sixty yards away.

Hubbard had been shot in the back of the head. The air police from Luke took the boy into custody. None of us locals have talked to the boy. I've got a friend at Luke. He gave me the story I've just told you. My friend at Luke said this Mexican kid had some money on him. Big bills. Were you bringing money in from Mexico?" The D.A. looked at me. "Is that what you were doing, Cox? Bringing money in?"

"We had a little money with us."

The D.A. watched me. "Was there somebody else in the plane? Besides you and Hubbard. A third man? The courier? They didn't find any kind of gun in the plane, anywhere around. Did this third guy have the gun? Did he shoot Hubbard?"

I waited. "Look, I've got to talk to somebody first."

"The people you're working for?"

"I was thinking of talking to a lawyer."

The D.A. looked toward the window. Light was coming flat through the blinds. Early morning, late afternoon, I had no idea when it was. The D.A. kept looking toward the window, the amber bars of light stretched across the room: "All right. But let me tell you some more funny things. The first day you were found, the day you were out, this place was crawling with feds. FBI, NTSB, Air Force security from Luke. And there were some spooks, nobody knew who they were. We couldn't get to the front door, there were so many of these guys lined up to get to you. Then along about the time you woke up, a funny thing happened. All these spooks disappeared. You were handed to us on a plate. Custody. Security. The feds never talk prosecution, not giving it up anyway, but that was implied in your becoming our prisoner. Now that was fine. We were glad to have you, Cox. What with the word coming from my friend at Luke—the Mexican boy's story, your partner found fifty yards away from the plane, shot in the back of the head with a gun nobody could find—our mouths were watering. The D.A. was thinking about taking the case himself. But then another funny thing happened. We got the official report from Luke. There was no Mexican kid in this report. No body found fifty yards from the crash. No gunshot wound. No money. No nothing. According to a deposition from the ranking AP who first came onto the crash, Hubbard's body was found in the plane. Dead from a blow to the head. Like the blow that put you out for eighteen hours.

"Now, I found this a very strange kettle of fish. So I call Luke Air Force Range. My friend's not in the office. Not working today. I call my friend at home. The friend's wife doesn't want to talk to me. This lady and I have known each other since high school. I introduced her to her husband. Best man at the wedding. Today she hangs up on me. So I call the AG at Luke. Nobody knows anything. The Tucson D.A.'s office would like to have a look at Hubbard's body. The autopsy report anyway. Impossible. Hubbard has been buried. Cremated maybe. Nobody knows for sure. OK, what about this Mexican kid? What Mexican kid? OK, what about the plane wreckage? Impounded by the FAA. Somebody. OK, what about the money? Money? What money?

"Then a third funny thing happens. About thirty minutes later I get a call from the D.A.'s secretary. The boss wants to see me immediately. What the fuck are you up to? the boss wants to know. Who told you to go nosing around out at Luke? This is a federal case. There's no fucking murder. No Mexican kid. No sixty, seventy nice crisp hundred-dollar bills. Get out of this case, the D.A. says. The D.A. himself will decide who, why and when the D.A.'s office prosecutes. If I want to prosecute so bad, the boss says, there's a lot of very real crime going

on in and around Tucson. Some drunk has just run
seventeen straight red lights out on Beechmont. Ain't
that far from where the boss' kids go to school." The
assistant D.A. stopped. He watched me. "Now, have you
got any comment to offer on any of this shit, Cox?"

"Seventeen in a row—must damn near be a record."

The D.A. pulled a card from his wallet, tucked it in
my pajama pocket. "If you change your mind, give me a
ring." The lawyer waited. "I know one guy who's not
quitting. I'm going out to Luke and I'm going to talk to
my friend. Wherever they've got him stashed." The D.A.
went to the door. He turned back. "Ah, like the boss
says, this is probably just an exercise in futility. You've
got a lawyer now. A good one, I hear. Word's going
around he's going to spring you sometime today, tomorrow. Still, if you're curious about how Max Hubbard
died, keep in touch."

The good lawyer was a small elegant man in pinstripe,
with dry silver hair, Bermuda tan—a face you might see
on the society page. He sat relaxed in the back of the cab,
going through papers in an attaché case. The papers the
troubles of the fool airline pilot he had flown in from
Washington to sort out. As the lawyer had said during
our ride to Tucson International Airport, I might not be
out of the woods yet, but from here on it was just a matter
of dealing with bureaucracies—the NTSB, Air Force,
Customs, and Immigration. Paperwork and knowing the
right people. The lawyer would take care of that when
he got back to Washington.

The lawyer took the brief next on his schedule from
the case, closed the lid and snapped the case shut. He
put the attaché case and the folder on his lap.

"You still might have some problems with your

employer—Northwestern?—and the FAA. When I get back, I'll make some calls and see what I can do. I think I can handle the FAA, but sometimes the airlines are, shall we say, overcautious." He smiled. "But then you won't want to be going back to work straightaway in any case, will you?" He glanced at the gauze wrapped around my head. "Maybe we can get part of the suspension laid off to health. I'm not all that familiar with how airlines handle these things. I suppose it differs from line to line. What sort of pay reduction do you expect to suffer, Dan, if you do have to sit out for a while?"

"I really don't know."

The lawyer's eyes flickered. "Well, it will probably cost you something. I'll try to keep it to a minimum." He looked back at me, the manila envelope on my lap. First-class ticket to San Francisco, ten thousand dollars in cash, my wallet and watch—all the luggage I had. "If you don't have enough to tide you over, we can probably come up with something."

"All right."

The lawyer fingered the folder he had taken from the case. "Give me a ring in a couple of days, Dan. After you've talked to your employer and the pilots' association. We should know how the land lies by then."

"All right."

"Just stick to the story as you told it to me. The storm. Wrong maps. The temperamental instrument panel. An accident. Ill fortune. Might sound a touch unlikely on the face of it." The lawyer smiled. "But then the truth often does."

I didn't say anything. The lawyer opened the folder, looked at the topmost paper, closed the folder. He sighed. "It's a terrible shame about Max. For such a young man to die in such a freakish accident." He yawned. "It's possible we may get some kind of settlement out of the Air Force. But we can't count on it. Very tough to argue any sort of liability in a case like this." The lawyer smiled. "When one is defending one's borders against attack, recklessness can quite easily be seen as zeal. Did Max leave any family?"

"No."

"No wife?"

"No. He never married."

The lawyer looked at me. "I see." The cab had come to the airport. The lawyer turned in his seat, toward the terminal building. "What time is your flight, Dan?"

I took my watch out of the envelope. "Forty minutes."

"What time is it now?"

"One-thirty."

The lawyer exhaled, a long breath. "Damn. Two and a half hours to kill. Your flight stop on the way to San Francisco?"

"Las Vegas."

The lawyer shook his head. "Probably worse connections than here. Maybe I could find a nice park somewhere." The lawyer leaned forward. "Driver, do you know of a park in town? One with a telephone?"

The driver looked in the rearview. "A park with a telephone?"

The lawyer leaned back, smiling. "I thought it would be too much to ask." The lawyer watched a willowy young woman come from the terminal. The woman smiled at us, it seemed, and waved, but the lawyer had looked away. A young man in a leather jacket was getting out of a cab double-parked next to ours. "Well, I won't keep you any longer, Dan. You should probably get checked in." The lawyer smiled. "Maybe have the beer the nurse said you were asking about." The lawyer opened the door and put a foot on the sidewalk. So I wouldn't have to get out in traffic. "Anything else, Dan?"

"Yeah. There is one thing." I opened my door to the traffic. "Who hired you?"

The lawyer's eyes flickered. "Your wife contacted me, Dan."

"I see. You know my wife?"

"No. She was put in touch by a mutual friend."

I smiled. "OK. Sorry about that. I couldn't remember if I'd talked to you or not. My memory's not all that good. About what happened after the crash."

The lawyer smiled. "It'll come back, Dan. Everything's going to be just fine." As the cab moved away from the curb, the rear window near me came down. "Call me in a couple of days, Dan," the lawyer called out. "After you've talked to Northwestern and the pilots' association." The lawyer waved out the window and the cab went into the traffic.

I found a telephone in the terminal and dialed Kat in San Mateo. No answer. I stopped at a newsstand and bought the *Arizona Daily Star*. I asked the clerk if they had any back issues of the *Star*. Yesterday. The day before. Something that might have a story about the crash.

"All gone," the clerk said. "We got last Sunday's paper, you want that."

Today's paper was dated Thursday. We had flown out of Guadalajara Sunday morning. I bought the Sunday paper anyway and went down the concourse to the Frontier gate. Checked in, took a chair by the window. The Frontier 727 was being refueled, a line had formed at the gate desk, people checking in for the Las Vegas/San Francisco flight.

I opened the five-day-old Sunday paper. The story was at the bottom of the front page. DARK HORSE PREZ

HOPEFUL TO VISIT TUCSON, the headline read. There was a photograph of Gerald Stokes, the man on horseback, the populist supported by Blackmuir's Montana friends. Then the story, five paragraphs. One about the impending constitutional crisis with Stokes in the presidential race. Stokes had been due to appear in Tucson Monday, the day after the paper's publication, the day I had been unconscious in the Tucson hospital.

I went back to the photograph of Stokes, the men standing around him. Secret Service men, some local supporters, then toward the rear there stood a tall man, partially masked in shadows. The huge head, the chiseled actor's features, you could even make out the suffering eyes of Lane Blackmuir in the grainy newsprint.

I turned to the man sitting next to me. "You from Tucson?"

The man looked up from his paper. "Vegas."

"How long you been in Tucson?"

"Three fucking days."

I held the Stokes photograph to him. "You hear anything about this guy speaking in Tucson?"

The guy from Vegas looked at the photograph. "Nah. I don't follow that crap."

"Nothing? On TV or anything?"

The guy from Vegas looked at me. "Pal, the only thing I read is the betting line. I wouldn't have known if they had shot the son of a bitch."

I tore the photograph from the paper, put it in my pocket and threw the rest on the floor. Unwound the gauze from my head, put my chin on my chest and napped till they called our flight.

4

*T*HE HOUSE was dark. Three, four days' newspapers cluttered the front steps. A trike sat on the sidewalk in front of the house. I paid the driver and after the cab had pulled away, crossed the street. I took the trike and pulled it along the sidewalk in front of a neighboring house. Both cars—mine and Kat's—were in the garage. I gathered up the rolled newspapers—the *Chronicle,* the *San Mateo Times,* Kat liked to keep abreast—and tried the door. Locked. I found the spare key under a cactus pot, opened the door and went into the house. There were no lights on anywhere, but there was something there—as if someone had been sleeping through the afternoon and hadn't waked yet.

Kat was in the bedroom, lying on the bed, facing the wall. I sat on the bed, near my wife. Her eyes were open. She stared at the wall. An empty glass, cigarettes, lighter, an ashtray filled with butts sat on the nightstand by the bed. When I touched my wife's leg, tears came into her eyes. I took my hand away and she closed her eyes. I went into the main room, made a drink and took it onto the deck that overlooked the backyard. I sat in a deck chair, sipped the drink and looked east, where it was already night. Beyond the half-dozen high rises that marked downtown San Mateo, to the Bay and beyond that to the sprinkled lights of Hayward or whatever town lay across the Bay from San Mateo, I had never been sure exactly.

I finished the drink, went into the kitchen, got a bottle, water, a tray of ice, came back to the deck. I made a drink and sat and drank. I had never seen my wife cry before. I hadn't even thought it was possible. But then Max was dead.

It was well dark when I heard movement in the house. A light went on, another. Sounds came from the kitchen—drawers, pantry doors being opened, slammed closed—then the kitchen light went out and the deck was dark again. Kat came to the door behind me, then came out onto the deck, crossed it. She stood by the railing, looking out toward the east. The downtown towers, the San Mateo Bridge, the East Bay beyond, everything was lit now, sparkling. My wife turned to me.

"Have you got any cigarettes?"

"No. I quit—remember?"

She turned away. "Fuck."

"I can go out."

She didn't speak. She lowered her head, held on to the railing. "I'll go. I need to get out."

I waited. "You want a drink?"

"Yeah." She came toward me, took the glass and sat in the second deck chair. She sipped at the drink. She looked around me, at the bottle and water pitcher and ice tray on the deck. "This yours?"

"It's all right. I'll get another glass."

I went into the kitchen, found a glass and went back to the deck. I reached toward Kat, to take her glass. She shook her head, lowered it. It was too dark to see her face anyway.

I drank, then put the glass on the deck. "How long?"

She shook her head. "I don't know."

"Since the land?"

"Before."

"How long before?"

"My God, I don't know."

"Just before." She didn't answer. I waited. "Do you want to go on?"

"No."

"Do you want to talk?"

"No. I don't know. Maybe I do. But not now. Later maybe." We were silent, then Kat raised her face. When she spoke, something had gone out of her voice. "There are some things we have to talk about. But not that."

"All right."

Kat leaned to one side. She put her glass on the deck. She held her body twisted, like a dancer loosening up. "What happened?"

"An accident. We ran into a storm. Lost our position. Our maps were fucked. The instrument panel was fucked. We crossed the border where we shouldn't have. The Air Force buzzed us down. You know the story."

Kat turned in the chair. Straight, still. "I don't know the fucking story."

"Sorry. I thought your lawyer would have told you."

"Lawyer?"

"The lawyer who sprung me from Tucson, you cunt. He said you hired him. Some Wall Street job."

"They just used my name. I didn't know. It makes sense. I don't care."

"You work for them too, Kat?"

Maybe I really expected a no. Kat said, "I used to."

"What did you do?"

"Courier, mainly."

"What did you carry for them?"

"I don't know."

"You don't know."

"There were attaché cases, you fuck. Some of them were heavy. Some of them were light. Anything else, Dan?"

"You work for Dayton?"

She shook her head.

"Blackmuir?"

She didn't move.

"Were you working on this job?"

"No." She waited. "I did some things for Max."

"What things?"

"None of your fucking business." What she told me once when I asked if she had ever slept with another woman.

I moved forward in the chair. I spoke low. Maybe it would pass for care. "Kat, I need to know as much as you can tell me. Look, he's dead. It's just the two of us now. You've got to tell me what you know."

"He never talked about it. Any more than you ever talked about it." She stopped. "He was afraid."

"Afraid of what? Sorry. Foolish question."

Even in the dark I could see her go hard. Small. "Did you kill him, Dan?"

I wanted to laugh, so bad, at the elation surging through me. How miserable can you get, that it makes you feel good to have your wife think you've killed her lover? "Darling, I couldn't even kill the frog in high school biology."

"I bet you loved cutting it up, though." She made some sound. Then: "You're capable of it, Dan."

"If you think that, you don't know me."

"You don't know yourself. You're not any different than they are. You may have to be driven to it, but once you get there, you'll dive right in with the rest of them."

"Max ever kill anybody?"

"Don't be stupid."

"What did he do for them?"

Kat looked at me. Her head erect, shoulders squared. I had never wanted her so badly.

"He flew," she said.

When talk returned, we talked around what was before us. But then I had been put out by the crash, out for nearly twenty-four hours, what did I know? Max had died in the crash. The official line, maybe it was true. That Max had been found fifty yards from the plane, a bullet in his head—just the word of some Mexican kid who had talked to some guy at Luke Range who had talked to some assistant D.A. in Tucson. Why shouldn't I present the official line to Kat? That Max's death had been an accident. At a time like this, what harm could another small lie do? That the truth might save her life—that she might be able to run and hide from Max's killer—hadn't occurred to me. Or had it?

Kat relaxed a bit after this, took another drink and asked about me. My case. What sort of trouble was I in? I gave the lawyer's story. The storm. The busted instruments. The bad maps. Everything an accident. I might have some problems with the airline, maybe some suspension. But I was going to call Northwestern in the morning, the pilots' association, then get back to the lawyer. The lawyer had friends in high places. There didn't seem anything in it he couldn't fix.

Kat said she hadn't seen or heard anything about the crash locally. But then she hadn't been reading the paper, watching TV. I got the stale newspapers, turned on the deck light and took them onto the deck. Not a line about the two local pilots cracking up near the Arizona-Mexico border.

Then there was nothing to talk about but what we were going to do. We started with tonight. Kat didn't want to be alone. But just for tonight.

"I'm sorry, Dan. It's just the last four nights—I don't think I could take another one."

"It's all right. I think I understand."

Kat waited. "What are you going to do now?"

I looked across the Bay. It was true night now. The incoming jets were making a southern approach to SFO, their landing lights crossing the night sky every minute, moving so slow, so close, they seemed bound for collision with the towers in San Mateo. "I think I'm going to get out of flying. I don't know. I'll talk to the pilots' association. See if I can get some kind of settlement. I've got a little from this trip. Maybe we can sell the house. Split it, if you don't want to keep the place." I sat back, looking northeast, as if I could see Montana from the Peninsula foothills. "Then I think I'll go back to the land. I don't know if Max left a will or not. Maybe I can get something there. Buy him out. Make some kind of settlement with you if you want to sell."

Kat had turned her head away as I spoke. Now she turned back. "Dan, I completely forgot. That wild-west cousin of Max's, the real estate man in Montana—he called. Something's gone wrong with the land sale. Really wrong this time. Something about the title. It's not clear. I guess the old woman died and there was somebody else in the will besides her kids. I don't know. You'll have to talk to the agent. It sounded like he might be in some kind of trouble himself." She stopped. "I'm sorry, Dan."

I went to the deck railing. The house was built on an incline, the backyard, where the pool would have been if we hadn't bought the land, falling away. "Any other calls?"

Kat waited. Her voice came thin. As if she were giving somebody over and was sorry about it. "He asked me not to tell you. Dayton called."

I turned, leaned against the railing. "What did he want?"

"He wanted to know when you were getting back."

"What did you tell him?"

"That I didn't know."

"Yeah. You know how I can get in touch with Dayton?"

Kat shrugged. "He's in the book. Atherton."

I turned away and laughed. "Christ. A wife? In the book? *Ather*ton? The fucking guy'll be handing out business cards next." I turned back. "Ah well, Daddy probably bought them the house, right?" Kat didn't speak. "Who is Lane Blackmuir?"

"I don't know."

"Who is he, Kat?"

"I said I don't know."

"Who the fuck is he?"

"The one before Max." Kat picked up one of the *Chronicles* from the deck and stood. "I'm going to bed." She went to the door. "Are you going to stay?"

"I don't know yet."

I waited—there was the sound of Kat banging around the kitchen, the eternal quest for a smoke—then went inside. I found the San Mateo County phone book and turned to the Atherton listings. There was an address and number for E. E. Dayton. I dialed the number.

A couple rings and Dayton's voice came on the line. His voice slow, mechanical. Like a boy reciting in front of class. Dayton on an answering machine. Dayton's voice ended, then came a beep, the tape was rolling. I spoke to the machine:

"Dayton, this is Dan Cox. I just got back from Tucson. Thursday night, about eight o'clock. I want to talk—"

There came a click on the receiver. Somebody at the Atherton spread was listening to calls coming in on the machine.

The bedroom door was closed. I opened it, stood in the doorway. Kat was in bed, still dressed. A cigarette burned in her hand, but she wasn't smoking. The *Chronicle* was laid open on her lap, but she wasn't reading.

"I'm going out for a while. You want me to bring you some cigarettes?"

She turned toward me. "That's all right. I found some."

"Want me to pick up something to eat?"

She shook her head and looked at the paper. "No."

I pushed the manila envelope I had brought from Tucson toward her. I had left it on the bed. Ninety-eight bills left, out of the ten grand the lawyer had given me. My salary. "There's some money here. We can split it. Take what you want."

She looked at the envelope. "All right."

I went to the door. "You mind if I take your car? I think I left mine on empty."

She turned toward me. "Mine's not running right, Dan. Better take yours."

"What's wrong with it?"

"I don't know. It's missing." She waited, then said my name. Just that: "Dan." Then: "Nothing."

I got gas, then drove down El Camino, through the glare and junk and glitter of Redwood City, to the dark seclusion of Atherton. A principality of having it and keeping it.

I came on Dayton's street—Arbor—followed it till I found a wall with the number of his address, parked off the narrow strip of asphalt that ran through the willow-and-redwood forest. An iron gate was set in the wall. Through the gate I saw a tall, graceful structure, its brick painted light gray or blue. The grounds were sheltered by dark close stands of black pine and oak. A drive at the side of the house led to a garage, far back, near the rear of the grounds. A late-model BMW was parked in the drive. The house was dark.

I went through the gate, had near made the front steps when a dog—an old German shepherd bitch, teeth bared, ears back—came from the side of the house. I stopped. The dog stopped. Her ears went forward and she began to bark. The front door opened. Thea stood in the door. I could just see her face in the shadows. Thea called out to the dog:

"Ginny!"

The dog stopped barking. Thea came forward in the door. She looked much younger than she had in Montana. Near her real age, younger maybe.

Thea said: "What do you want?"

"My name is Dan Cox—"

"I know who you are."

"OK. I just called and left a message on your machine. I wanted to talk to your husband."

"He's not here." She shifted a leg. "Why did you come here if you knew my husband wasn't home?"

"I thought somebody was listening to the machine. I thought it was you." The woman didn't say anything. "I want to talk to you, Thea."

"No," the woman said.

I made some slight movement and the dog's ears went down. "Look, couldn't you call off the dog? Let me come in. Just a minute. It's about the trip to Mexico."

"I don't want to know about that."

"All right. It's about something you said when we met. In that restaurant in Montana. Your father and—"

"I was drunk. I didn't say anything."

"You may have been drunk, but you did say something." All I had to do was say Stokes' name. "Look, I can't talk about it out here."

The woman moved. The dog's ears went down.

"All right. Max is dead—"

"I don't know any Max."

"The fuck you don't. I want to know what happened in Arizona."

The woman went back from the door. "I don't know anything about that. I *can't* know. Don't you understand?"

A car stopped on the road behind me. Doors opened, closed. Footsteps approached the gate. I had to say something, I didn't know what. "Thea, I'm alone in this.

I'm not one of them. I need your help. If you won't let me come to you, you come to me."

The woman faded back from the door, the door began to close. "Stay," she said to the dog and the door closed.

A man's voice came from the gate behind me. Even. Hard-edged. "Excuse me, sir."

I turned to the cop. I could see his partner through the gate, flashing a light on the rear of my car. The license plate.

"Is this your vehicle on the road, sir?" the cop at the gate said.

I went toward the gate. "Yeah. It's mine."

"There seems to be some problem, sir." The cop pushed back the gate. "You're losing fuel."

The cop at the back of my car straightened. "No gas cap."

I went through the gate. Spoke to the cop by me: "I just filled up in Redwood City. The kid must've forgotten it. I'll pick it up on my way back home."

The cop and I crossed the street. The cop with the flashlight had gone to the front of the car. He was flashing the light on the SFO parking sticker. He lowered the light. "You work at the airport?"

"I'm a captain with Northwestern."

The cop put away the flashlight. "Yeah? What do you fly?"

"727."

"You ever fly a 747?"

"No."

The cop with the flashlight had gone relaxed now. He leaned against the fender of the car. "The old lady and I were thinking about taking one to Europe. Christmas maybe. Good plane?"

"One of the best ever made."

The cop who had been at the gate wasn't an airplane buff. "May I see your driver's license, sir?"

The plane buff said: "Come on, J.D. The guy's a pilot."

The first cop looked at me, turned toward the squad car. Just as well. I had left my license in the manila envelope in the bedroom. The cop started toward the squad car. "Just remember, sir, to drive carefully till you retrieve your gas cap. It could be a hazard for yourself, as well as other motorists."

The plane buff grinned. "Yeah. Don't do shit for your mileage either." That cop looked at me. "What happened to your head? Nice goose egg there."

"Little accident."

The cop's lips turned down. "Plane?"

"Yeah. Light plane. Rough landing. Believe me, the big ones are much safer."

The cop looked better. He turned toward the squad car, the other cop already on the radio, punching my plate number into the Sacramento computer. The cop made a little salute. "You take it easy, you hear."

I got in my car, pulled away. The squad car followed me for a while, till I got to Redwood City. Then the cops turned back to Atherton.

The garage door was open. Kat's car—missing, whatever the problem was—was gone. I had left the front door locked. Now it was unlocked. The bedroom door was open, the bedside lamp still on. The manila envelope lay on the bed. The money, my driver's license, the credit cards were gone. It could have been worse, I told myself. I still had the change from the two hundreds I'd broken today.

I was pouring a second, very large whiskey when the phone rang. I got to the phone on the third ring.

"Cox?" said the voice on the line.

I knew the voice—a young man's—but I couldn't place it. "Who's calling?"

"Peter Wiley. Is this Dan Cox of 1643 Carmel Drive in San Mateo, California?"

I still couldn't place the voice. Some TV reporter, a stranger you heard talking to you every day. I thought about hanging up, but didn't. If I was going to be an innocent man, I might as well face it now. I said I was Dan Cox. The last time I would use my real name for a long time.

The voice changed. Not professional, cool. Not a reporter. "Where the hell did you get off to today?"

Now I had it. The assistant D.A. from Tucson, not rabbity at all.

"This is Peter Wiley," the lawyer said. "From Arizona. Remember, I talked to you—"

"Yeah. I forgot your name. Left your card in my pajamas."

"Why didn't you check with me before you left town?"

"I didn't know I was supposed to. At least my lawyer didn't say anything about it."

"That guy. I'm not sure he's supposed to be practicing in Arizona."

I looked toward the kitchen. I had forgotten my drink. I didn't think the cord would reach. "Look, I've had a rough day. What's the problem now?"

"You've got to come back to Tucson."

I started walking the phone toward the kitchen. It wouldn't reach. "Yeah, I figured I'd probably have to. What day's good for you?"

"Tonight."

"Look, I'm not coming back to Tucson or anywhere tonight."

"All right. Tomorrow morning then."

"Not tomorrow morning either. I've got too much shit to get through the next couple days—"

"Cox, maybe I haven't made myself clear. I'm not asking you to come back. I'm telling you. You either come back on your own—as soon as possible—or they'll come and get you and bring you back." I didn't say anything. The lawyer said, "Something's come up." He paused. "Couple things."

I waited. "Tell me about it, Peter."

"You've been hit with a smuggling rap."

"Smuggling. That's good. What was I smuggling?"

"Heroin. I don't know how much yet. But it was a lot."

"What crap. I checked the plane out myself. It was clean."

"Well, you didn't dig deep enough. The DEA came in. Went through the wreckage. They found a stash built in the frame. Could be as much as forty kilos. Mexican brown."

"No shit? I thought the plane was flying a little ass-heavy."

"Anyway, there's another reason you've got to come back." He paused. "I've got to talk to you."

"About what?"

The lawyer's voice dropped. "Is your phone OK?"

"As far as I know."

"Yeah, well, mine aren't. OK, the office phone, somebody's listening in more or less all the time. But—I think they've got my home phone bugged now. Sounds like it, anyway. I'm calling from a phone booth. Maybe you ought to get to one, call me back."

I could have flapped my arms and flown before I

could have driven down to El Camino, found a phone booth, called the lawyer back in his phone booth in Arizona. "I think this phone is all right. Listen, could you hang on a second? I got a drink burning in the kitchen."

The lawyer made some move in the booth. Now that he had mentioned it, I could hear traffic in the background. "Yeah. Sure. This won't take long, but—go ahead."

"Be right back." I put the phone down, got the drink, went back to the phone. "All right. What's up?"

The line was silent, then the lawyer's voice came back. "You remember that friend of mine at Luke? Who—well, you remember the story he told about—"

"I remember."

"Well, his wife has called me. She's frightened." He stopped. "She's afraid he's going to die."

I listened to the house. It was so quiet. "What's happened, Peter?"

"Well, my friend was flown to Colorado Springs, day before yesterday, for some Air Force business there. His wife doesn't know what. Well, the guy didn't call from Colorado when he got there. And this guy and his wife are close. He always calls her when he's been flying. When he didn't call, the wife called a friend in Colorado. The guy had been there and gone on. To Washington."

"Washington. All right."

"The guy's been checked into some military hospital. An Air Force doctor called the wife from Washington. I guess the guy has a brain tumor or something. According to the doctor, he'd had it for a while. He wanted to have it checked out before he told his wife. He had the operation this afternoon. He's still out. Condition critical."

"Fuck."

"That's what I've got to talk to you about, Cox."

"Yeah. I understand." I put the drink on the coffee table. "Peter, do you know if your friend told his wife the story he told you?"

"I don't know. That's what I'm going to find out. I'm meeting with her tonight. That's why I wanted you to fly in tonight."

"Yeah. Look, I just don't think I can make it tonight. I'm still hurting. Beat. And I've got things I've got to deal with here at home."

"All right. I'll meet with her tonight. See what's going on. What she knows. Then maybe we can get together tomorrow. Before you surrender."

"All right. That sounds fine. But listen, don't let this woman get involved in any of this shit. I mean—keep her out."

"I'm afraid she may already be in."

"Then get her away from the Air Force base. Wherever they live. Check her into a motel. Not under her name. Get somebody to stay with her if you can. They got any kids?"

"No."

"OK. Try to find somebody to stay with her. Stay with her yourself if you have to. All right?"

"OK." The lawyer was silent. "Cox, I've got a question to ask you."

"Yeah?"

"We are on the same side, aren't we?"

"I hope so, Peter. I sincerely hope so."

"The heroin—do you think they could have planted it on the plane?"

"I don't know. Maybe." The lawyer started to speak, but I cut in: "We'll talk about it tomorrow when I see you."

"All right. But I'm going to want to know everything, Dan."

"I'll think about it."

"OK, but—one of the problems we've got now is some people know too much and not enough."

I smiled. "Yeah."

"You want me to book you into a motel, Dan?"

"Yeah. Put me in the same motel as the wife."

"Under your own name?"

I thought. "With this heroin charge hanging, maybe it'd better be under another name."

"All right. There's a place called the Alhambra. Near downtown. How's Schwartz?"

"That's fine."

"There's a flight leaving San Francisco at seven forty-five tomorrow morning. Gets in Tucson at ten-twenty. You want me to meet you at the airport?"

"No. Just get me the room."

"The Alhambra."

"I've got it."

"I'm going to feel a lot better when you're here, Dan. Maybe I'd better give you my home number, in case anything comes up."

I wrote down the assistant D.A.'s home number on a newspaper clipping in my pocket. The photo and story about Gerald Stokes I had torn from the *Star*. "Listen, Peter, before you go, was there any coverage of the crash in the Tucson papers? Anything on TV?"

"Nothing. They sat on it. But with the heroin, they've let it go. You made the six-o'clock news. Papers in the morning."

"Any pictures of me on the tube?"

"Not at six o'clock."

"OK." I held the photograph of Stokes to the street-light coming through the window. "One more thing,

Peter. There's a guy named Stokes. Gerald Stokes, some kind of far-out candidate for President. He was in Tucson a couple days ago. While I was out. Anything happen while he was there?"

A silence, then the lawyer said: "That was canceled. He's coming in tomorrow. Supermarket-parking-lot show. Then on local TV tomorrow night."

"Any time on the parking-lot appearance?"

"Sometime in the afternoon." Then: "Christ, Dan, we've got more important things in front of us than some kook from wherever he's from."

"Yeah. I'll be on the early flight."

"OK. Tomorrow then."

"Right."

We hung up. I sat on the couch looking at the photograph. The candidate had a particularly evil grin. Maybe I didn't know what I was doing. Maybe the world would be a better place without Gerald Stokes.

I went back to the bedroom. Opened the closet. I couldn't remember what my wife had, but it looked like some clothes, shoes, maybe a suitcase were missing. I wandered around the house for a time. No note, but then Kat never left them.

I went to the phone, dialed Dayton's number. Now there was nothing. No answering machine. Just the phone ringing.

I took a drink onto the deck. Stood at the railing and looked out across the Bay. The jets were still making their southern approach to SFO. 727s, 747s, 1011s, DC-7s, -9s, -10s, some smaller private planes sandwiched between the monsters—their landing lights drifted across the sky every ninety seconds. You could have kept time by it.

*T*HE ALHAMBRA, near downtown Tucson, was a pale stucco compound with some turrets and spires placed around. The front of the motel presented a solid wall but for an arched drive and walk that led into the motel's courtyard—swimming pool, children's playground, parking area. The office sat like a guard shack at the head of the drive. The room doors and all windows large enough for an adult to crawl through faced onto the courtyard. You weren't taking anything larger than a towel or an ashtray away from the Alhambra without the desk clerk knowing about it.

A paper rack sat by the motel office door. The *Arizona Daily Star,* same edition I had tucked under my arm. The rack papers were folded in half, the plane crash/heroin smuggling story not showing. I went into the office and asked for the room being held for Schwartz. The clerk signed me in, gave me a key. The room had been prepaid. Which was good. After the flight, cab and newspaper, I had twelve bucks to my name. The clerk had a copy of the *Star* spread over the desk. Not a bad picture of me. Official airline portrait, taken about seven years ago. The clerk looked at me, looked away. He would have checked Himmler into the Ritz on V-E Day.

"Schwartz," he said, turning back with a memo slip. "Message."

I opened the door to room 33, switched on the light, tossed my flight bag onto the bed and unfolded the message:

"Dan. Call me at home when you get in. If I'm not there, sit tight. Peter."

I dialed the home number Peter Wiley had given me. No answer. I dialed the digits for long distance, then the fancy lawyer's number in Washington. A woman answered. The lawyer would be in court till midafternoon. I gave her the motel's number, then dialed the Tucson district attorney. Peter Wiley was out of the office today too.

I went into the bathroom, undressed, showered, shaved, all things I had forgone that morning in California to make the seven forty-five flight to Tucson. When I came out of the bathroom, Peter Wiley was sitting in a chair by the TV. The blinds had been pulled, the door closed, safety chain latched. Wiley was reading the *Star.* Not the front page. He put the paper down. He had the beginning of a nice black eye.

*   *   *

"Look, Cox, I tried to get Marty, my friend's wife, away from the house at Luke. Check her into a motel. But she won't come out. She wants to stay by the phone. She doesn't want to talk to you. See you, meet you, have anything to do with you. With either of us." Peter Wiley smiled, pressing the damp cloth against his eye. "She's not going to do anything unless she thinks she got the idea herself."

"Did you talk to her? I mean, talk."

The assistant D.A. took the cloth from his eye, studied it, as if he was looking for blood, put it back to his eye. "Yeah, We talked." He took the cloth from his eye, put it on the TV console. He looked at the paper lying on the floor by his chair. "See your story?"

"Yeah."

"What do you think of it?"

"Funny story."

"Yeah." He reached down and picked up the paper, turned to the front page and looked at the story. There was my picture. A shot of Max. Then the head of a man with a question mark for a face. He looked away from the paper, at me. "What about this third man, Dan? Someone in the Air Police leaked it to the *Star*."

"What did your friend's wife say, Peter?"

The lawyer tossed the paper to the floor. "That Jay came home Monday lunch and said that something funny was going on at the base. That there'd been a plane crash at the testing range the day before. That that morning range security had found a man wandering around in a restricted area. That's what he said at lunchtime. When he came home that night he told her to forget everything he had said at noon." He stopped. "You want to see if she'll talk to you?"

"I don't know, Peter. Maybe we should leave her out of this. Maybe you both should get out."

Wiley sat forward in the chair. "I find the timing on this interesting. They found this third man on the range Monday morning. Then a couple hours later the feds drop you. Look, Dan, OK, you don't want to tell me about this mystery man. But whatever your story is, it's not going to hurt to talk to Marty. I'll risk another mouse."

"All right. But it'll have to be right away."

Peter Wiley looked to the Tucson paper spread on the floor. "Going to the Stokes rally this afternoon?"

"It's business, Peter."

The lawyer shrugged. "I've made an appointment for your surrender for five o'clock. Judge Hayes' office in the courthouse. Want to meet there?"

"I'd prefer we went together."

Peter Wiley looked at his watch. "All right. I'm in court till four. Say we meet back here at four-fifteen. It's only a couple blocks."

"Four-fifteen is fine."

"Bond on this is not going to be cheap. What's your cash setup?"

"Not good."

"Property?"

"Some—but let's talk about that later."

"All right. I know a bondsman. If it's not too steep, he can handle it till you get your paperwork done in California." The lawyer stopped. "What time's your Stokes rally?"

"Two o'clock."

"Desert Mall's quite a ways. Take my car." He tossed a set of keys onto the bed. "I'll be at the courthouse all afternoon. Look, I don't want you running around Tucson as Dan Cox." He took out his wallet, tossed his driver's license onto the bed with the keys. "No pictures in Arizona yet. You might be able to pull it off. Just don't break any more laws."

I took up the license and keys. "I don't have my license with me anyway."

Peter Wiley walked around the room, watching me. "Dan, let me ask you—has all this shit got something to do with Stokes?"

"Peter, let's talk about that this afternoon."

The lawyer looked at me hard. Little comic, little serious. "You're not some kind of assassin, are you, Dan?"

I looked at the ceiling. "No."

"All right, all right." The lawyer crossed the room. "I'll give Marty a ring. See if she'll talk to you this morning."

As the lawyer dialed, I took up the *Star* and turned to the story about Stokes' appearance in Tucson. No photograph today.

The lawyer spoke on the phone:

"Marty, it's me. Listen, I've got this guy here I told you about. The pilot from California. He still wants to talk to you." The lawyer stopped. His face went slack. "Oh no. No." He turned away from me. "Oh God, Marty. When?" He waited. "Marty, I can't believe it." He waited. "All right. Yes." He waited. "OK. Look, is there anybody with you now?" He waited. "I'll come out." He waited "No. That's all. Not now." He waited. "Have you called Grace?" He waited. "Look, I'll call her." He waited. "All right. I'll call her from there." He waited. "As soon as I can get there." He waited. "God, I'm sorry, Marty." He held the phone for a moment, then put the receiver in the cradle. "Jay's dead. He died this morning."

*   *   *

Gerald Stokes, I had learned from the paper, took his first steps toward national power in a supermarket parking lot. He had become a representative to Congress from Missouri's 5th District by hanging around outside A&P automatic doors and haranguing stunned shoppers about the price of eggs. Hitting the voters in the breadbasket had become his trademark, and he was still dealing out body blows to the corporate thieves the early afternoon I drove out to the Desert Mall.

I found a sidestreet off the mall complex, parked Peter Wiley's Rabbit—he would go to his friend's widow with her mother, take a cab back to the motel, we'd decide what to do about Jay's death and my surrendering, maybe not surrendering, then—took the sunglasses I had found on the dash, and went toward the Desert Mall on foot. It was now two-thirty, half an hour after Stokes' scheduled appearance, and still the cordoned area of the parking lot was only half filled. Not to put all the blame on Stokes. The supermarkets he hung out in these days were vast. The Desert Mall in Tucson, Arizona—a sprawling interconnected complex of shops and stores and arcades that swallowed up the two grocery chains that had outlets here. The developers had put markers on the light stanchions—B6, C3, G7—so you could find your way back to your car.

I started my search for the killer I had flown home at the back of the crowd, making my way toward the front and the still empty speakers' platform and VIP stands. At the front I turned and went toward the rear, looking into every face in the crowd. A couple dozen true believers here and there, proudly bearing red-white-and-blue Stokes badges and pennants and straw boaters, some gawkers and freaks scattered around, but the majority of the crowd was nothing but curious shoppers on their way to the mall to commit deeds with credit cards that a hundred years ago would have landed them in jail.

I went to the rear of the crowd, saw nothing, was turning to make my way back toward the front, when a wave of excitement passed through the crowd. People began moving forward, straining to see over those in front of them. A murmur of expectation went through the crowd, then there was silence.

A group of twenty or so men came marching in formation toward the speakers' platform. Those who made the outside of the group were big, hard men. Polished suits, empty faces—local hardcore supporters, Chamber of Commerce types who had played football at Arizona State. You couldn't see who they were shielding, those men were short, but a chant rose from the crowd—"Stokes for the folks! Stokes for the folks!"— and those around me surged forward. It was then, when the crowd went away from me, that I saw the lean killer we had flown in from Mexico, the man with the clenched-fist face, on the far side of the cordoned area. Left standing alone by the forward surge of the crowd. Now the man went forward with the crowd, not entering, moving only to stay just behind the crowd.

The Stokes men, the short men with them, had gathered behind the speakers' platform. One of the Stokes men went up on the platform and looked over the crowd. A short man now climbed onto the platform and placed himself behind the speaker's podium. I didn't look, I kept my eyes on the killer, but I knew that the man at the podium wasn't Stokes. You could feel the disappointment passing through the crowd. Some of those at the back were already turning away. The mike whistled, the man's finger tapping the mike was amplified a hundredfold, and the man at the podium began to speak to the crowd. He apologized for the delay. The cancellation. As I came to the killer's back, a man in front of me turned away from the speaker, leaving an opening directly behind the killer.

I took a breath—my chest set hard, as if it was wrapped in concrete—and went behind the killer. I stood there a couple seconds, the speaker reminding the crowd about Stokes' TV appearance tonight, eight-thirty, don't forget, then I leaned to the back of the killer's head:

"Don't turn around. I've got a message I want you to give your boss."

That was all I said. A violent pain hit my stomach. The breath went out of me. My vision dimmed. My legs disappeared. And all I had seen from the killer was a twitch in his shoulder, a slight movement of his arm. As I was going to my knees I saw the killer moving away, still looking forward, toward the speakers' platform. Then everything around me began to go black. I heard a groan, then somebody calling out in many voices:

"Stand back! Stand back! Give him air! We got a heart attack here, folks! Give the man some air!"

By the time the rent-a-medics had treated my heart attack, sunstroke, whatever, the Stokes rally was closing down. The VIP stands were being dismantled, the crowds had gone home, back to the mall to buy more, the parking lot reopened to cars. What the Lord had intended it for, commented one shopper who, like me, had had to park a couple blocks away. Peter Wiley's Rabbit decided not to run right—fuel-injection problems, said a good samaritan with a screwdriver, get a carburetor—

and it was near five, an hour late for my appointment with Wiley, when I got back to the Alhambra.

I had turned into the motel, intending to pass through the arch into the courtyard, when I saw the two police squad cars and the ambulance at the back of the courtyard. I stopped the car, still under the arch, the motel office to my immediate left. The motel courtyard was framed by the arch, like a stage. The ambulance was backed to the door of room 33—the room that Peter Wiley had reserved for a Mr. Schwartz. The door to 33 was open. Two uniform cops stood near the door, looking into the room. Small groups of people were gathered here and there, around the swimming pool, by the playground, watching the door to room 33. Now I saw the unmarked police car. Two cops in civvies sat in the car. One of them was talking on the radio. The motel desk clerk—not the guy who had checked me in this morning—stood on the walk outside the office. The clerk was smoking a cigarette, looking back toward the ambulance and the cop cars. The clerk looked at me, a couple yards away.

"Some guy just hung himself," the clerk said.

I looked toward the rear of the courtyard. A man wearing a suit was coming out of 33. A doctor, somebody from the coroner's office. "What happened?"

The clerk came to the car, leaned down to the window. He looked around inside the car as he spoke: "Something big going on, I figure. Cops all over the place. Roanne, she found the body in the shower. Necktie around the spigot. I called the cops. They come in, look at the guy, cut him down maybe, I don't know. Then they come into the office. Take a look at the register, then they start hustling around. They get on the blower to Roger—the desk clerk this morning. He

checked this Schwartz or whoever in. You been following that plane that crashed out at Luke last week?"

"Read about it in the paper."

The clerk's eyes went over me, everything inside the
car. "The guy in thirty-three—not the guy strung up—
the guy who checked in, he was one of the pilots in that
plane. Smuggling heroin. The other pilot got killed in
the crash." The clerk straightened, looked toward the
ambulance. A white-coated attendant had come out of
33. The attendant climbed into the back of the ambulance. "Something funny going on around here."

"Yeah? Like what?"

The clerk looked back. "I heard one of the cops
talking. He knew the guy in the shower. Not this flying
dope pusher. Not the guy who checked in as Schwartz.
The strungup guy, he was a D.A. One of the young ones.
A couple newspaper boys come into the office. Just left.
They weren't talking suicide. They were talking
murder."

I looked to the rear of the courtyard. The attendant
had come out of the ambulance and gone back into the
room. One of the uniform cops had left the door and was
walking over to the unmarked police car. The plainclothes cop behind the wheel had opened the door. He
had his leg out of the door, his foot on the ground. He
was saying something to the uniform cop as he approached. I put the Rabbit in reverse.

"I guess I better back out of here. Don't want to be
blocking the way when the ambulance comes out."

The clerk gave the Rabbit a look. "Yeah. Better park
it on the street. Ain't room in there for you now." The
clerk grinned. "You want a room for the night? Gonna
have a vacancy in a couple minutes." He held up his
hands. "Just joking. Got plenty other rooms."

I drove four or five blocks and stopped the car. Then I was afraid. Really afraid, for the first time. The conservationist who had skidded his car into the Blackfoot River, Max, the Air Force man who had died under the knife in Washington, now the tough little lawyer hanging in the shower stall—they had cut him down by now. By now they had him wrapped and on the stretcher. They had killed Pendergast, they had killed Max, they had killed the man who liked his wife, and they had killed Peter Wiley. And they were going to kill Gerald Stokes and whoever else got in their way. It was the business they were in.

I pulled the car away from the curb. After a couple blocks I turned on the headlights. It wasn't dark yet, but it would be by the time I got to the airport. The doorway through which I would escape, then hide, wait, and come back for them.

The hat had cost two-fifty at the gift shop. One of those canvas roll-up jobs with a two-inch brim. Pale blue, with a flowered headband. The black tie had been one-fifty. The small canvas shoulder bag—orange, with Frontier's logo on the side—six. Three bucks left. I unrolled the hat, put it on, put on Peter Wiley's sunglasses, and looked in the washroom mirror. Like one of the freaks at the Stokes rally. I took off the hat and sunglasses and put them in the shoulder bag. I took off my jacket, stripped the rep tie from my collar. I put the rep tie in the bag with the hat and the sunglasses and put on the black tie, knotted it, tightened it to the collar. There had been no clean shirts in the San Mateo house this morning and I had worn a Northwestern shirt under my sport jacket. What I wouldn't have given for the uniform jacket as well. The captain's three gold cuff bands, the wings fixed to the jacket pocket. But the dark slacks and the work shirt, the epaulets and the Northwestern logo, were going to have to do. I put the bag over one shoulder, folded my civilian jacket to the lining, slung it over the other and looked in the mirror. I took the sunglasses from the shoulder bag and put them on. As good as it would ever get. I left the restroom and went down the concourse toward the Frontier flight operations office.

I tried not to think. That had been done. When I had arrived at the airport I had first checked the Frontier departure video. FLIGHT 306 LV/SF DEP 8 : 30. No assigned seats. Maybe half full tonight, the check-in clerk said. Continuation from Albuquerque. The check-in clerk had told me how to get to Frontier flight operations office. I had found the door marked NO ADMITTANCE, then gone down the hall to the flight operations office. I chatted with the guy there awhile. I flew for Northwestern, was looking for an old pal, Bernie Reid, flew Frontier out of Tucson last time I knew. The flight operations clerk looked it up for me. Reid was working out of L.A. now. I thanked the FO clerk and went back to the main concourse. Maybe, just maybe, if the clerk saw me again, wandering down the hall, toward the door that led onto the field, he'd think I was still looking for my long-lost buddy. Back on the main concourse, I shopped. Got as good a disguise as ten bucks would buy. Then I waited. In one of the cocktail lounges till the local evening news came on TV. The headline story about Dan Cox, smuggling pilot, wanted for murder. Then I waited in one of the restroom stalls. Watching the minute hand creep around my watch face. I couldn't get to the field too soon. Or too late. The timing had to be exact. Time to get to the baggage barn, take what I needed there, then on to Bay 3 and Frontier flight 306. A continuation from Albuquerque, stop in Las Vegas, then into SFO.

It was seven forty-five when I came out of the restroom. Time to do what I had thought out. The first step. To get out of the passenger section of the terminal, behind the scenes, where the business of flying planes went on. Where I had spent the last ten years of my life. That's all I thought as I approached the door marked NO ADMITTANCE. I was going to work. As I had gone to work thousands of times before.

I went through the door without looking left or right. A group of pilots were standing in the hall, three-quarters of the way down. Not by the Frontier flight operations office, but near it. I walked toward the pilots. As I came to within twenty paces, the pilots, three of them, laughing, talking, turned into an office across the hall from the Frontier flight operations. The last pilot was just going into the office, the door closing, as I went by. As I passed, I saw three more pilots standing at the counter in the Frontier office, talking to the clerk, checking in before they went on to flight planning. I walked on. Nothing happened. Nobody came out into the hall and called me down. Not a word as I went to the door at the end of the hall, turned the knob, pushed the door and went through it. Onto the field.

The strip stretched before me. A vast black plain strung with runway lights—prayer beads, Max had called them—their cowls glowing electric blue in the night. A half mile to the south, my right, just above the tiered landing guides at the end of the runway, a 737 squatted in the air. Settling down to a hundred and twenty knots for touchdown, its landing lights blazing like furnaces. Across the field another jet idled on the lateral strip, waiting for the 737 to touch down before it turned onto the main runway for takeoff. To my left, maybe a hundred yards, stood the passenger terminal, a three-story semicircle of glass bulging onto the field. People in the restaurant, the observation deck, were turning to watch the incoming 737.

To my right—maybe two hundred yards from where I stood—was the baggage barn. A cargo door showed in the terminal building wall. Baggage trains, some loaded, some empty, entered and left the cargo door. The locked strings of baggage cars hurrying about like miniature trains in a park. Bay 3, where I had to go, lay on the far side of the terminal from the baggage barn. Beyond the curved glass wall of the restaurant and the observation deck. Four, maybe five hundred yards of floodlit bays, planes taxiing in, out, standing as passengers deplaned, came onto the waiting aircraft. A quarter mile of being seen from the restaurant, the observation deck, the flight control tower, by ground control and airport security and maintenance and fueling and baggage workers, by the pilots and crews and the passengers on the planes. I went away from the light and confusion surrounding the passenger terminal, toward the dimly lit baggage barn.

I went through the cargo door into the baggage barn. A two-story enclosure, fifty yards deep, thirty across. Another wide, tall door stood at the far end of the shed, open to the night. Baggage trains hurried in one door, out the other. Two conveyor belts looped down from curtained doors high in the shed wall. Jumbles of luggage bumped along the descending belt, bags coming down from the airline check-in desks. Workers on the shed floors sorted the arriving baggage into docks assigned for each flight. The outgoing bags were loaded by other handlers onto waiting trains. Another gang of handlers unloaded incoming trains, tossing luggage on the ascending conveyor belt. The luggage moved up through the curtained doors toward the baggage arrival carousels.

Directly to my left, not five yards from where I stood just inside the cargo door, was a hall that led to the back of the barn—locker rooms, tool and supply rooms, maybe a coffee shop or lounge for the handlers. I turned and went down this hall. Not being seen, so far as I knew, by any of the handlers working the belts and the docks and the baggage trains.

I came on no one in the hall. Found the baggage handlers' locker room. Banks of gray lockers stood against the walls. One bank of lockers extended into the center of the room, dividing it. On the left side of the locker room a man sat on a bench before the lockers. All I could see of the man was his legs and feet. He was tying his shoes. Street shoes—the man was going off work. I went into the right half of the locker room, where no one was.

I went to the first locker without a padlock. Empty. The second locker was empty. The third and fourth empty. Two more lockers without padlocks in the bank of lockers that divided the room. Both empty. I closed the last door, quietly, and waited. The guy on the other side moved about, his shoes scraped the concrete. He was humming something. I could smell his aftershave. I reached down to one of the locks on the doors and rattled it.

"Fuck!" I said.

There was quiet, then the man beyond the bank of lockers laughed. "That you, Stovall?"

I rattled the lock, twisted the dial. "I've forgotten my goddamn combination."

The man laughed softly. "Wish I could forget that fucker." The voice was young, maybe twenty-five.

"Rough night last night. Fucking brain turning to cheese."

The man laughed, didn't say anything.

"It's forty-six something eleven. I got the eleven. I got that."

The man laughed, started humming again.

I rattled the lock hard, kicked the door, waited. I called out over the bank of lockers: "Hey, you got a jumpsuit I can borrow till tomorrow?"

The humming stopped. "Hey man, Charlie'll give you a clean one. That's what he's there for."

"I looked all over for him. Can't find him."

The man laughed. A pair of blue coveralls came sailing over the bank of lockers.

I picked the coveralls off the floor. "Want me to put them back in the morning?"

"Shit," said the man from behind the lockers. "Keep the fuckers."

I turned into the corner of the locker room, took the roll-up hat and sunglasses from the airline bag, put them on. I stripped the black tie from my collar, put the tie and the sport jacket in the airline bag. I stepped into the coveralls and pulled them over my shoulders. I was fastening the last button when the man spoke over the bank of lockers.

"Fit?"

I turned my head. "Yeah, fine. Thanks."

The man laughed, then he said: "Well, gotta run. Catch you later, man." I heard him go to the door, humming as he went down the hall.

I forced the zipper on the airline bag, got it closed, waited another fifteen seconds, then went out into the hall. Back the way I had come.

A man had come into the hall from the barn. A baggage handler, about forty, bald, sour, wearing blue coveralls. He didn't look at me till we had come within feet of each other. Then his eyes cut to me, the flight bag, then away. When I came to the end of the hall, I looked back. The handler was standing at the end of the hall, watching me. I went into the barn. There was a lull in work. The conveyor belts ran empty. The handlers and train drivers were standing around talking, laughing. Somebody had a transistor radio playing jazz. I went through the cargo doors into the night.

I walked through the dark toward the passenger terminal. A 737, maybe the one I had seen landing, had docked at the near bay. Ground-crew teams were swarming around the plane. Ground control setting blocks on the wheels, the driver of the generator truck plugging in the 737's electrical system. A fuel tanker had come under a wing. Everybody hustling. The 737 would be on its way in twenty minutes. The mobile stairs had been set at the plane's forward door, the door was just being cranked open, the first passenger bounding down the stairs as I went into the circle of light around the 737.

I went to the tanker parked under the starboard wing. The tanker driver was on the far side of the plane, checking the port wing fuel tank. I opened the tanker's passenger door, reached in, went through the glove box. Nothing. Nothing under the seat. I went behind the tanker to the generator truck. Opened the door, reached in, found a screwdriver—a small rubber-handled Phillips—in the glove box. Passengers were flooding out of the plane now, shaking the stairs. A new herd stood waiting behind a cordon just inside the terminal.

I turned away from the generator truck and the milling passengers and the hustling ground crew. Then I stopped. An empty baggage train stood just at the edge of the light flooding the bay. The driver of the train, the sour, bald man I had seen in the baggage barn, sat at the wheel of the tractor. He watched me.

I turned away from the train and the driver and went toward the nose of the 737, passed under it and went toward the glass wall of the passenger terminal. As I passed the fishbowl, a couple seated by the restaurant window grinned down at the funny worker in the blue monkey suit, the Bing Crosby hat, sunglasses, going off to set some massive jet right with a lone screwdriver.

I went away from the passenger terminal, into the dark. Bay 3 was three, four hundred yards away. Two bays—one empty, one harboring a Western 727—lay between me and the Frontier bay. Eight o'clock. The Frontier flight from Albuquerque would probably roll into the bay at eight-five, eight-ten. Ten minutes maybe—too much time for ground control, the Frontier ground crew, to look over the guy from maintenance they had never seen before. The clown with the screwdriver. When I heard the baggage train coming up behind me, I turned and faced the sour, bald driver. If I was going to bluff my way by the Bay 3 ground crews, I might as well have a rehearsal.

The driver brought the tractor alongside me and stopped. I slapped the screwdriver against my leg. "How about a lift?"

The driver looked at me, cocked his head toward the seat by him.

I got on the tractor and the driver went off, circling away from the nearest bay. The driver looked at me. "Where you headed?"

"Three."

"I'm going to seven," the driver said and turned toward a dark stretch of apron. Once we made the dark, the driver looked at me. At the screwdriver. "Maintenance?"

"Yeah."

The driver turned the tractor. Making a wide sweep around the Western 727 in Bay 2. Bay 3 next. Empty. Floodlit. Two ground control men were standing back by the terminal wall, waiting for the Frontier flight from Albuquerque. The driver looked at me. "Thought I just saw you in the baggage barn."

"I was looking for a guy."

The driver looked away, turning the tractor. "Who is that?"

"Charlie. Owes me a little money."

"Yeah?" The driver looked back. "I thought maybe you were fuzz."

I laughed. It came out sounding real.

The driver shrugged. "Lot of funny people around the barn these days."

"Some of the boys being bad?"

"That's the word going around." The driver looked at me. "Thought maybe you were a nark."

I bounced the screwdriver handle against the tractor dash. "Believe me, pal, I ain't a fucking nark."

The driver looked at me. "You coulda passed." He waited. "Some straight guy wearing sunglasses at night and that fucking hat."

"Listen, I don't play for either side. Don't use the shit myself. Don't care who does."

The driver looked at me. Looked away. "Yeah. Same here."

The driver turned the tractor in a circle toward Bay 3. As he drew near the bay, he turned another circle, drawing the baggage train up just inside the blazing lights of the bay. The ground control men were looking toward us. The driver looked straight ahead, into the dark. "Bay three."

I got off the tractor. "Thanks for the lift."

The driver didn't say anything, let the clutch out, and the baggage train disappeared into the night.

I walked across the floodlit bay toward the ground control directors. They watched me come. I went easy, walking at five bucks an hour. I went up to the ground control men and stood with them. Turned to look across the lit bay toward the dark runway. "On time?"

"Just coming in," the guy near me said. The second guy turned and looked out at the dark field. The second guy had the guide sticks. He lit them, two glowing orange batons, two and a half feet long. The first guy looked at the hat, the sunglasses, the screwdriver, the flight bag. "What's the problem?"

I held the screwdriver up. "You wouldn't believe it. Some fucking company big shot on this flight. Found a screw loose in one of the crappers. Had the captain radio in. One fucking screw loose."

The guy next to me shook his head. "I believe it."

The guy on the far side said: "Some of these heaps got more'n one screw loose." He took the ear mufflers from around his neck, put them on. "We sent one out last night I wouldn't drive down to the corner grocery for a loaf of bread."

The guy next to me didn't say anything. Now he was looking out, like the other guy, toward a 727 that had just landed and was running down toward the end of the strip. When the plane came to a halt, wheeled around toward the lateral strip, the guy with the guide sticks went away from us. He crossed the floodlit bay, toward the plane. The guy by me didn't move. He stood looking out toward the taxiing plane.

I dropped the screwdriver rubber handle first to the asphalt. It bounced in the air. I bent and picked it up. "What the hell's going on over in baggage, anyway?"

The ground control director looked at me. "Better ask them."

"Guy I know told me they got some kind of nark working over there."

The ground control man turned behind him. He picked up a couple of wheel blocks. He clapped the blocks together, still watching the plane come up on us. The guy with the sticks stood in the center of the lit bay. He had the sticks raised high, guiding the 727 straight in. The guy near me said: "Far as I'm concerned, they can clean that fucking place out and start over." He put his ear mufflers on, clapped the blocks together and moved away.

I went back against the concourse wall and covered my ears. The nose of the jet came into the floodlights, its three Pratt-Whitneys screaming. The captain's face showed in the cockpit window. A middle-aged guy, regular face, maybe going a little gray at the temples, grinning at the ground control director guiding him in. Me, a week ago.

The 727 came forward, slow. Looming over us like a great metallic bird coming to nest. The jet made the center of the bay, its wings and fuselage glittering in the floodlights. Its engines shut down, a mournful rushing sigh, and the ground team converged on the plane. One ground control director blocked the nosewheel, while the guy with the guide sticks dropped larger aluminum blocks from a compartment under the wing and blocked the starboard wheels. A generator truck came into the bay from the dark, swept up in front of the port wing and stopped. The driver jumped out of the truck and began fitting the generator cable to the power inlet in the 727's nose. A fuel tanker came from another direction, stopped on the far side of the cockpit. The first officer slid back the cockpit window, said something down to the tanker driver, then closed the window, stood and disappeared from view. The tanker driver went to the starboard wing, dropped the cover to the fuel fittings, then went and stood by the tanker, waiting for the passengers to de-plane before he began refueling the aircraft. By now other members of the ground crew had wheeled the stairs to the port door, were locking the stairs in place. At the rear of the 727 the ramp stairs were being lowered from the tail. One of the ground crew ran up the forward port stairs. He pounded on the port door, laughing as the door opened. A stewardess appeared at the door. She was laughing too, and the guy from the ground crew went into the plane. A couple seconds later, another stewardess took a position by the port door, smiled back at someone inside the plane, and the first passenger came out the door and went down the port stairs. Seconds later, the first passenger showed on the tail ramp stairs. I went toward the plane, toward the tail ramp, away from the port door, the front of the plane where most of the crew and the ground team members would be gathered.

Almost twenty passengers were making their way down the port stairs. Another half-dozen leaving the plane by the tail ramp. I went to the foot of the ramp stairs, not looking up at the stewardess at the tail door. Not yet. I waited till the last passenger had cleared the stairs, then went up toward the stewardess at the tail door. Grinning, holding the screwdriver as if I had come to fix something loose on the stewardess. The stewardess laughed, let me past, then she turned back, to wait for the rush of Tucson passengers.

I went into the aft toilet, latched the door behind me.

I took off the hat and the sunglasses and shoved them into the waste bin. I stripped off the coveralls, forced them into the bin. I yanked the zipper of the flight bag, took out my sport coat, shook out a couple of wrinkles, put the coat on. I took my rep tie from the flight bag, slipped it under my collar, knotted it. I stuffed the flight bag into the waste bin, then the screwdriver. I looked into the mirror. A little pale, haggard, frayed around the edges—a small businessman, his small business in trouble. When I heard the rumble from beyond the toilet door, the tail ramp stairs shaking as the Tucson passengers charged the plane, I unlatched the door and went into the passenger cabin. I fitted in third from last in the string of Tucson passengers filing onto the plane. A dozen or so of us moving down the aisle, looking for a seat by somebody nice or naughty. Whatever was on our minds.

*I*T WAS my second day shuttling cars for Hertz, looking for anything to cut the boredom, that I found the runway freaks. I went off the freeway at the South San Francisco exit, but instead of turning south past long-term parking to the Hertz storage lot at SFO, I went east. Into a small industrial area tucked behind Bethlehem Steel, a quarter-mile bulge of landfill extending into the Bay. Beyond some welding sheds, a cut-rate car-rental outfit and a forklift dealership lay a vacant stretch, nothing but rutted gravel, marsh grass and litter, its shore bounded by a chain-link fence. A dozen or so cars were parked nose in to the fence. Some of the runway

freaks were standing out by the fence, some perched on
their car fenders. Some had binoculars, some clipboards,
notebooks, all of them scribbling away like students on a
field trip. Plane watchers, ever turned south, looking
across the Bay toward the north end of SFO's west
runway, watching the jets come and go. For the week or
so I shuttled for Hertz, whenever I felt I could spare an
extra ten minutes, I joined the freaks. As close as I could
get for now to flying.

My two and a half weeks as a new man hadn't gone
all that bad, all things considered. Stowing on the
Frontier 727 back to San Francisco had gone without a
hitch. If the stewardesses had counted tickets and passengers and come up one off they had said the hell with
it. No problem leaving the plane, going through the SFO
terminal. Not a cop, no airport security in sight. I left my
car in the parking deck and took a bus downtown. I
hated to give up the old Dart, but if the car wasn't staked
out already, they'd have a plate number at the top of the
computer printout by morning. I had had a couple
bourbons, as relaxants, on the Tucson flight, so when the
bus dropped me in the Tenderloin there was all of
eighty-five cents in my pocket.

I spent the first night on the streets. The next
morning I got on a panel that delivered supermarket
fliers door to door around town. I hung paper, as the
regular carriers called it, for about a week, found a pretty
good three-buck-a-night hotel, the Regent on Taylor,
and began accumulating capital for my comeback. As
one of the old boys I had met my first night out had said,
I wasn't ready for the streets full-time. A little trouble
with a woman, the job, money, maybe a scrape with the
law. I'd come down to the streets to get it all straightened out. Once I got it straightened out, I'd be going
back, to the world where people lived in rooms.

Despite working every day hanging paper, doing odd jobs at the hotel, shoplifting—no longer against my principles—and practicing various economies, after a week I saw I was going nowhere. Just staying afloat. One evening after a day of seeing that every resident on 41st, 42nd and 43rd avenues between Golden Gate Park and Quintana had been made aware of the weekend specials at CalMart, I told the Regent night clerk I wanted to be moving up in the world. Anything that wasn't walking. The clerk thought it over, said something about shuttling Hertz rental cars from their downtown garage to the airport. There was going to be just one hitch, the clerk said. I was going to have to have a driver's license. I had one. The problem was that the license belonged to the man just about every cop west of the Mississippi thought I had murdered. I took the photograph that had accompanied the *Chronicle* story about Daniel Cox, Northwestern pilot wanted in Arizona for murder, smuggling, you name it, and compared it with what I saw in the flophouse bathroom mirror. The soft, successful airline pilot and the lean, sunburned loner whose mustache already looked respectable after a week's growth. I decided to give it a shot.

The next day I passed the driving test with flying colors. The Highway Patrol examiner glanced at Peter Wiley's Arizona license—a guy twenty-nine, five-eight, one-sixty—and gazed off forlornly at the string of Vietnamese refugees waiting to be tested. From the DMV office I went down to the Hertz garage on Turk and, with the night clerk's recommendation, was signed on as a shuttle driver.

The next week went quiet. Too quiet. I shuttled cars for Hertz. Became their ace driver. A little slow maybe, compared to some of the other shuttlers, but the nice shiny pieces of shit I took out of the Turk Street garage reached the Hertz lot at SFO still nice and shiny. Then, on the sixth day with Hertz, one of those days that I joined the runway freaks at the fence every trip I made to the airport, I decided I was going to have to make a move. Do something, even if it was wrong.

It didn't take me long to become a regular with the runway freaks. I knew when somebody was coming in high, short, too fast, drifting a little. I looked somewhere else when a Korean Air 747 banged hard on the asphalt, blew a tire. Smiled a little when a BA jumbo was put down as gently as the captain would cover a sleeping child. Whoever I was, whatever I was doing by the fence, I knew flying. Another runway freak.

I got to know two other regulars. One a tall, rangy cowboy type called Clyde. About the same age as me, soft Oklahoma accent he didn't use much. Clyde didn't have glasses or carry a notebook or pen. He just watched, gazing out at the planes, eyes narrowed against the light. The other guy was Herbie, from somewhere back east—not New York, Herbie made it clear. Herbie had all the gear. Binoculars, charts, logbooks, airline schedules—the back of his car was like an office, crammed with flying data and instruments of observation. Herbie knew runways all around the country. The weather and wind and topography of every field. The airlines that served them, the routes coming and going. He knew the manufacturers and their problems with unions and finance. He knew their planes and the planes' specs and capabilities and their modifications. Herbie knew the economics, politics, geography and history of flying. And of not flying. No matter how much Herbie talked and studied and watched flight, he was like a lot of the other runway freaks. He was out on that spit of landfill day after day to see a plane fall and crash.

Clyde was another matter. Whoever Clyde was, whatever he was doing here, he was like me. He still wanted to see them in the air.

It was the day I decided to do something even if it was wrong that I saw a plane I knew. Like being back in the embarkation center in Vietnam, seeing a man fifty yards away and knowing, among all the other men in fatigues, that it was a guy I had grown up with, we'd played basketball in high school. When the Northwestern 727 was still in its approach, looking like all the other Northwestern 727s I had seen the last week, I asked Herbie for his glasses and followed the plane in to touchdown. 3226—the 727 Max and I had been flying the night we had first talked land and Montana somewhere over Wyoming.

"Pretty good landing," Herbie said, taking his glasses back and focusing on the plane. "In from Portland. Near full, I'd say. The way it touched down. What do you say, Clyde? Pretty full?"

But Clyde wasn't watching the plane. He was looking at me. Clyde didn't say anything, but then he didn't have to. Don't get like him, another busted pilot standing at the fence, watching planes you had once flown. Whatever it took, get back in the air.

My chance to fly again came the next day. I shuttled my first car to the airport about nine, parked in the lot, checked in and was about to hop the Hertz van back downtown when the supervisor called out. Told me to hang on a minute. He had a Caddy to go to the downtown Hilton. VIP. At the door, ten sharp.

I took the Caddy out of the lot, but when I got to the freeway, instead of bearing right, going onto 101 north, I stayed on the overpass and went south. Down to San Mateo, off the freeway at the Maple Street exit. I went through San Mateo city center, up Orlando into the foothills to Carmel Drive, then six blocks to 1643.

The house looked the same. Still a little the worse for wear. But the grass had been mowed, they'd even done a trim around the sidewalk. A realtor's sign was planted in the front yard. A moving van parked tail-in in the drive. The front door was open. I stopped a couple houses down the street and waited. Two movers came out of the front door. They went up the tail ramp into the van, came out with a couch, and carried it into the house. The bank was moving fast. The realtor hadn't even had time to slap a SOLD sticker over their sign.

I went back to El Camino, south to Atherton. I parked the Caddy so I could see the front of Dayton's house through the gate in the wall. The house looked even more graceful in daylight. The bricks of the facade were long and narrow, painted a soft gray. In morning shadow the house looked as if it were draped in velvet.

I saw the dog—the old German shepherd bitch— through the gate. The dog was frolicking, its ears back, its forepaws flat to the ground. The dog bounded forward, then back. Then Thea came into the frame made by the gate. Thea had her hands on her knees. Bounding toward the dog as the dog had bounded at her.

I crossed the street and stood on the brick walk outside the gate. Thea had backed the dog onto the drive. I said her name and she turned to face me. The dog came to her side, her ears forward.

"Stay, girl," Thea said. She smiled. "Yes?"

I took off my sunglasses, lifted from Walgreen's.

Thea leaned forward, peered through the iron bars. She moved back. "My God, it's you."

"Yeah. It's me."

She shook her head. "I didn't recognize you. You look so different. You've lost so much weight."

"Regular exercise, lot of fresh air, and I've started smoking again."

"I see." Thea looked down to the dog, stroked an ear. She wasn't how I had first seen her either. There was something about her eyes—she was off the sauce. Maybe even getting laid. I said she looked different too and Thea hitched up her shoulders. "Not as different as you." She stopped and looked very serious. "I sort of liked you better"—she shrugged—"fat."

I laughed, put the sunglasses on. Thea's eyes hardened. I probably didn't look like a nice man thin. Maybe I wasn't.

"Thea, I'm in trouble. Bad trouble. Do you know what kind of trouble I'm in?"

She looked down at the dog. Her hair fell across her face. "Yes," she said without looking up. "You're wanted for murder. Among other things."

I waited. "Yeah. Well, I didn't do it. Not any of it."

She looked at me. "I know." She kept looking at me.

"All right." We waited. "Thea, I want to talk to them."

She shook her head. "It won't do any good. I've tried that."

"All right. You tell me. What should I do?"

She shrugged. "You look so different. Just go away." She shook her head. "I don't know."

"Look, in the last couple weeks I've lost friends, people who would have become friends if they'd gone on living. This is aside from all the shit they're pulling on me."

She looked down. "I understand."

"Do you?"

She nodded. "Yes, I do."

I waited. "Is Dayton around?"

"No."

"Where is he?"

"I don't know." She looked at me. "I really don't. He's working."

"All right. How about your father? Is he working too?"

"Don't go to him."

"Why not? He'd like me."

She shook her head. "Just don't."

"Can you tell them I've been here? That I'm looking for them?"

She didn't speak.

"Will it cost you anything if they know I've talked to you?"

"I dont' know. I think I'm all right."

"You are the one's wife and the other's daughter. Right?"

She looked at me. Afraid. "Yes, I am."

I looked at my watch. Three bucks from a hustler at the Powell Street turnaround. A Market Street hock shop had given me twenty bucks for the old Waltham I had had since I started flying. It had gotten me through the first couple days on the streets. It was two minutes to ten. "All right. I'll see if I can find them myself."

"They'll find you. If they want to."

"I'm sure they will. But we don't have much time. The election's Tuesday week."

"Is it?" She looked out toward the street, the Hertz Caddy. "You have a nice car now."

I turned to the street. "Yeah." I turned back. "If it comes up in conversation, I'm at the Regent Hotel. On Taylor, in the city."

"All right."

I waited. "I don't guess it would do any good to tell you I'd like to see you again."

"No. It won't do any good." She looked down at the dog. "I really would like to help you. But I can't think of anything to do."

"All right. I've got to go."

She shrugged, looked at me. "I like your mustache."

"Thanks."

I went back across the street. When I got into the Caddy, I looked back. Thea was standing as I had left her, looking down at the dog, stroking an ear, her hair falling over her face.

I drove into Redwood City, found a phone booth and called the Hertz office in San Francisco. I asked for Cosmo, the guy who had hired me. Another man who had had trouble with a woman, the job, money, a scrape with the law, and was coming back. A minute or so, Cosmo came on the line:

"Yeah?"

"Cosmo, it's Pete—"

Cosmo's voice went up. "Pete! Where the fuck are you?"

"Daly City. I had a flat—"

"A flat? You telling me it took you nearly forty fucking minutes to get to Daly City and have a goddamn flat?"

"Cosmo, relax. I had it fixed. It's all right. I'm on my way now."

Cosmo groaned. "You had it fixed—Christ. What the hell do you think we got this goddamn fleet of break-down trucks for? You know you're supposed to call in anything goes bust, Pete. Shit." Cosmo turned away from the phone, called out to somebody, Marvin, the garage dispatcher. "It's Pete. He's all right. Yeah. Yeah."

Cosmo came back to me: "OK. Look, just get your ass back here. They've got another car going over to the Hilton. Man, have you fucked things up." He let out a breath. "All right, just get back here. I think Marvin has already called the cops. That fucking Jackie"—the Regent night clerk who had gotten me the job. "All right. Come on in. I'll see what I can do," Cosmo said and hung up.

I drove back to San Francisco, parked the Caddy in the lot across from the garage, and had my ass chewed by Cosmo. Then Marvin. They were short three drivers today, so I got another car to shuttle to the airport. Cosmo walked me out to the lot. He leaned down to the window.

"I think it's going to be OK, but I don't know. Marvin's on the rag today. Just keep your nose clean. Maybe he'll be on the rag about something else tonight. The guy at the Hilton overslept anyway, so—I don't know. We'll see." Cosmo straightened and went back across the street to the garage.

I drove the car to the airport, made four more shuttles that day. Didn't have a chance to go back and tell Herbie and Clyde goodbye. Just kept my head down and moved cars. But at the end of the day, when the van pulled into the lot across from the Turk Street garage, I saw Cosmo standing by the office door, an envelope in his hand. Marvin was in the office behind Cosmo. Two guys in suits were in the office with Marvin. The three were leaned over the desk, looking at something. Cops and my job application. Johnny Kono and St. Cloud I had been expecting for days and had plans to deal with them, but cops—with murder and smuggling warrants—and I was finished.

Cosmo left the garage without the trio in the office seeing him, crossed the street to the lot. He came up, gave me the envelope, turned and started back to the garage. He talked like he was talking to himself:

"Go on. Just walk. Get the fuck outta here."

I made my way through the cars in the lot, went over to Taylor, down Taylor to the Regent. The day desk clerk looked at me funny. The way the CO had looked just before he told me my mother had died.

"Two guys in here looking for you, Pete. About an hour ago."

"Yeah, I know." I tore open the envelope. A check for a hundred and forty bucks. Made out to Peter Wiley. "You cash this for me, Larry? Take my rent out."

The day clerk looked at the check. He turned the check over, put it on the counter. "Sign it to the hotel."

I endorsed the check to the Regent. "I got to get a few things from my room."

Larry was already under the counter, twirling the safe dial.

I went up to my room, stripped off my work clothes, put on the dark trousers, airline shirt, the jacket I had worn to Arizona. I took the stash from under my mattress—little over thirty bucks—and went back downstairs. Larry had come out from behind the desk. He had some bills in his hand.

"They're across the street. You want to go out back?"

I moved to the front window. Across Taylor was a yellow Trans Am. Two men sitting in it. A big white guy behind the wheel, busted nose zig-zagging down his face. The man in the passenger seat was squat and dark. Wearing sunglasses, a Hawaiian shirt. Sitting low and looking toward the hotel.

I took the cash from the day clerk and put it in my pocket. "It's all right, Larry." I went to the door. "They're friends. Of a sort."

The day clerk was back behind the desk. He shrugged.

I opened the door, went out, crossed Taylor to the yellow Trans Am. Johnny Kono got out of the car, pulled the seat forward and pushed me in the back.

Lying in the back of the Trans Am, eyes shut tight like a good boy, I could hear the killers grinning. How they sure were fooling me.

St. Cloud went up to Post, down Post, right on Stockton, crossed Market to Fourth, then to the bottom of Fourth where 280 started. On 280 about four miles, to the Allemany Interchange. So far Hertz's recommended route to the airport. At the cloverleaf St. Cloud curled back on 101, north, got off the freeway quick, at the Army Street exit, took Army west for ten, twelve blocks, then turned north again, probably on Folsom or Capp. Another dozen blocks on Folsom or Capp, then the car turned, went half a block and stopped.

When I was told to open my eyes, get out of the car and not make a fucking peep, I saw we had come to a dead-end alley, warehouses packed tight along the alley. The air was sweet with the smell of baking bread. If I ever had reason or the opportunity to come back, it wouldn't be too hard to find.

St. Cloud led us up a flight of rickety stairs slotted between two warehouses, unlatched a padlocked door and pushed me into a top-story loft. St. Cloud walked me across the loft, Johnny Kono at my back. When we got to the far wall, St. Cloud grabbed my wrist and snapped a handcuff around it. The other cuff was locked around a pipe that ran along the wall the length of the loft. St. Cloud stepped back, opened his mouth and yawned.

There was a low bench against the wall. I sat on the bench.

The only light in the loft came from a window by the door we had come in. A fine dusty haze from the late fall evening spread over the floor, pretty much played out by the time it reached me bound against the far wall. The loft was divided in two by an interior wall, a sheetrock partition that fell a couple feet short of reaching the ceiling. St. Cloud and Johnny Kono went into the back room made by the partition and closed the door. A light came on in the back room. Light showed over the partition, under the door, through the keyhole and through the hole cut in the sheetrock around the pipe I was fixed to, the pipe running the length of the loft. For a while St. Cloud and Johnny Kono talked low in the back room. I could have slid the cuffs along the pipe to the partition and maybe heard what they were muttering about, but decided I probably didn't really want to know what they had in mind for me. Not during the first act anyway.

In a couple of minutes St. Cloud and Johnny Kono came out of the back room. They left the light in the back room on, the door open. The light spread toward the front of the loft. There was a small living area against the front wall of the loft—bunk bed, table, chairs, a sink, stove, cabinets.

St. Cloud came toward me.

"Look, Danny, don't know how long we're gonna have to keep you here." He tapped the pipe I was fixed to. "Can't afford to let you out on the street at this stage of the game. We're working on a tight schedule here. Can't afford to have any delays." St. Cloud looked around the loft. At the door to the back room, at the living area against the front wall, at Johnny Kono standing in the center of the room, watching us. St. Cloud turned back. "Anything you want, Danny boy?"

"I wouldn't mind having something to eat. And something to drink."

"Something to eat. Something to drink." St. Cloud looked around. "That do it?"

"And something to piss in."

Johnny Kono half turned away. "Christ."

"Fuck, J.K., I don't know how long you goons are going to keep me strung up here."

St. Cloud raised his hands. "I'll find you a bucket somewhere. See if I can get you some chicken or shit. What you want to drink?"

"If you can find me a bucket, I'd like a beer."

"OK. Beer and a bucket." St. Cloud turned to Johnny Kono. "You know, you could look around and find a bucket, J.K. You ain't done shit today."

"Let the son of a bitch piss on the floor. We're gonna need the bucket we got."

St. Cloud turned to me. "All right. I'll be back in a couple minutes. Got to make a phone call. See what the hell is going on."

I lay on the bench. The boards had some spring and the pipe my hand was fixed to wasn't more than a foot above the bench.

St. Cloud and Johnny Kono went to the exterior door. They stopped there and had a few words. They spoke quietly; maybe they thought I couldn't hear.

"I still think we oughta get our thing started tonight, J.K. We don't know when their thing's gonna come down. Hell, they could be hitting the guy right now."

"Look man, I already explained it to you. The stiff's gotta be fresh. We don't know when they're gonna hit the son of a bitch. *They* don't even know. We can't have a fucking stiff up here a couple days stinking up the place."

"Hey, we could get a live one. Finish him off when we get the word."

"And have two assholes up here squawking for buckets to piss in? Fuck that."

"OK, J.K., OK. Just thinking things out. We gotta get it right, boy. Details. This has gotta look good. Not only we got to get the stiff, we got to get the equipment lined up. You think this is all a fucking cakewalk, J.K., because you ain't doing any of it."

"Listen, St. Cloud, you're in charge of the stiff *and* the equipment. I'm doing the beauty work. Now I'm staying here with Cox and I'm getting a little rest. And I ain't going out till it's time to bring the stiff in. You do what you want to do, man, but I'm telling you, if they pry open that plane and find somebody three days ripe in there, your ass is going to be in a sling. Know what I mean?"

"Yeah, yeah. Maybe I'll ask Dayton. See what he says. Fuck, I'd like to get this thing over with tonight. Jesus, I hate this job."

"Relax, man. I got some blow. You ain't going to feel a thing."

"Yeah. Yeah. That's good. OK. OK. I'll go call Dayton. See what's happening. Things are stepping up. Might even be coming down tonight."

"There you go. Give Dayton a ring. And calm down. Everything's gonna come out just fine. I promise you, the son of a bitch is gonna be a work of art."

Johnny Kono had opened the door to the stairs. The light outside was blue-black, the air cool. St. Cloud stood in the door. "OK. I'll be back in a couple minutes. You want anything?"

"Bottle of Beam. That's it."

"How about a pack of cigarettes," I said from the bench. "I feel like having a smoke."

"Cigarettes. All right." St. Cloud said vaguely and went down the stairs, the old warehouse creaking from his weight.

Johnny Kono waited till St. Cloud made the bottom of the stairs, then he closed the door and came across the loft to me. He pulled a .45 from under his Hawaiian shirt and leaned down to me, like a father tucking his kid in. He rested the .45 muzzle on my temple and said real quiet:

"Cox, if you say one more word or move a singlefuckingmuscle I'm gonna blow your brains out. ¿Comprende?"

My Spanish wasn't all that good, but I understood.

Johnny Kono went to the door to the back room, looked around the room, turned off the light and closed the door. He crossed the loft to the living area against the front wall. He lay out on the bunk bed, holding the .45 across his chest like a prayer book. He was snoring in a couple of minutes.

I lay in the dark, drowsed for a while, half sleep, half awake, considering things like stiffs and equipment and beauty work, then went to sleep. Seven o'clock, the last time I checked my watch.

The old wooden warehouse shaking—someone coming up the outside stairs—waked me. The door swung back, St. Cloud came into the loft. Johnny Kono only moved to take the .45 off his chest and train it on the door. When he saw St. Cloud, he put the .45 back on his chest.

St. Cloud came across the loft, exercised. "We're in business, J.K., boy. It's come down! They fucking got him!" St. Cloud was carrying two large cardboard boxes.

He went to the living area, put the boxes on the table. Then went and sat on the bunk by Johnny Kono. "Things have changed a little though, J.K." He jerked his head back to me. "We're going like before, but now I think they got something else"—he jerked his head again—"in mind."

Johnny Kono yawned and moved back in the bunk bed. He rested his head against the wall. "Fine with me."

St. Cloud settled his ass on the mattress. "I got the equipment. Everything we're gonna need." He reached out and waggled Johnny Kono's foot. "Fucking Dub's come through. The stiff's all lined up. Fresh as a daisy. Right size. Everything. And only five hundred bucks. We're coming in under budget, boy!"

Johnny Kono called out in the dark, "You awake, Cox?"

"Yeah."

Johnny Kono swung his legs off the bed. He looked at the boxes on the table. "Let's take a look at what you got."

St. Cloud got up, went to the table. He picked up the boxes. "It's ready for us right now. All we got to do is make a call. We might even get this thing moving tonight."

Johnny Kono sat on the bed. He scratched and yawned. "What time is it, anyway?"

"Eight o'clock," I said.

"Shut the fuck up, Cox," Johnny Kono said. He stood. "Let's take a look at what you got." The two killers took the boxes, crossed the loft and went in the back room. The light there went on, the door closed. There came the sound of the boxes being unloaded. A half-dozen heavy metal objects striking the table. In a couple minutes St. Cloud and Johnny Kono came out of the back room.

They crossed the loft to the living area. They didn't turn off the back-room light, they didn't close the door. They sat at the table. Johnny Kono took a small bottle from his pocket, unscrewed the top and dipped his little finger in the bottle. He brought out his finger, white powder cupped under the nail. He snorted one nostril, then the other. He handed the bottle to St. Cloud. Johnny Kono sniffed, snorted and blew his nose. "You bring the whiskey?"

St. Cloud dumped the powder on the table top. He did both nostrils with a rolled bill. He breathed deep and leaned back. "Fuck, I forgot, J.K. We'll get something on the way."

"How about my cigarettes?" I said from the bench.

"Shut your mouth, Cox," Johnny Kono said. He scooped up powder with the nail of his finger.

After a couple minutes, Johnny Kono got up from the table. St. Cloud went on pushing his nose through the coke. Johnny Kono patted St. Cloud on the head. "Save a little for later, man."

St. Cloud stood. He laughed. "Shit, we're moving this thing tonight, J.K. I promise you that."

"Maybe." Johnny Kono crossed to the exterior door, St. Cloud behind him. "You got the flight plan and maps and everything all in one place?"

"In the trunk. Dub's got the whole package. Everything set. Plane's ready. Everything."

Johnny Kono opened the door. He went out on the stair landing. "Who's he got to drive Cox down to the strip?"

St. Cloud went out on the stair landing. He laughed high and crazed. "Fuck, boy, Dub's got *that* all set up. You ain't going to believe it. Guy's got class. Keeping it in the family." They started down the stairs. "Hey, J.K., remember that time in Quang Thut, Dub put the baby's arm in the stew? Had fucking Chacon convinced it was off a rubber doll till he got down to the bone!"

"Nah, man, you got it the wrong way round. Chacon was freaking cause it didn't have a fucking bone. Laid rubber for a week."

"No shit? Nah," St. Cloud said, making a hideous laugh as he and Johnny Kono went down the stairs. The old warehouse shuddered like it had had enough.

The Trans Am roared in the alley below, tires squealed, then there was silence. I got off the bench and slid the cuffs down the pipe to the sheetrock partition. I looked through the cut made around the pipe. All I could see was the corner of a steel-top table. On that corner of the table sat a blowtorch. Near that was the wooden handle of a hammer or a mallet or a hatchet. I slid the cuffs back down the pipe. I lay out on the bench and waited.

The Trans Am came back into the alley about an hour later. Quieter than it had left. Doors slammed, silence, trunk lid slammed, then the shuddering warehouse. The two came up the stairs, climbing heavy. They kicked open the door, carried a long object wrapped in a plastic sheet into the loft. They carried the body into the back room and slammed it on the metal-top table, knocking a hammer, maybe a crowbar from the sound of it, onto the floor. Some deep breathing, muffled talk. Then St. Cloud came out and checked the cuffs. He didn't look happy. He went to the table in the living area and snorted. He went back to the back room. He closed the door.

The next couple of hours were given over to cosmetics. A lot of pounding, crushing sounds, St. Cloud gagging, metal objects rattling around, being dropped on the floor. St. Cloud came into the front room every now and then to puke in the sink, wash his hands and face, sip water from the tap, snort, and check on me. Johnny Kono stayed with it without a break. After the corpse, if whoever it was had been dead when they brought him in, had his face and teeth and any other distinguishing features beaten out, the blowtorch was fired up. There came some sizzling. Flesh and hair burning. St. Cloud came into the front room and stayed there awhile. The acrid, musky odor of charred meat and singed hair hung thick throughout the loft. St. Cloud paced around the loft, not looking well. When the blowtorch went off, St. Cloud went back into the back room. There ensued an argument. They had forgotten a mole under the guy's arm. Was it going to be fire or the blade? Fire won and St. Cloud came out of the back room. He really couldn't take the heat. When the torch shut off, St. Cloud went into the back room. From the silence, the two artists were standing around viewing their work.

While Johnny Kono was putting on a few finishing touches, St. Cloud came out and told me to take my clothes off. I shook the cuff against the pipe. St. Cloud cursed and went into the back room. He came out with a key and a pile of clothes. He unlocked the cuff, tossed the clothes at my feet and watched me undress.

"I don't think it's right you having to wear this shit. I'll get you something else in the morning." St. Cloud picked up my clothes and went into the back room. I put on the dead man's clothes. They didn't fit that bad, smelled fairly fresh considering. St. Cloud had forgotten to put the cuff back on my wrist. I did it for him. Didn't want to get them more upset than they already were. Another quarter hour of dressing the corpse, wrapping him in the plastic sheet, tying up the bundle, then the light in the back room went off. The two killers came into the front room. There wasn't any more talk of getting the job over with tonight.

The rest of the night went quick for Johnny Kono, mixed for me; it must have passed like centuries for St. Cloud. First, St. Cloud said he had to get out of the loft. The stink of the barbecue was driving him crazy. Everybody wanted something—whiskey and something to eat for Johnny Kono, cigarettes and beer for me, St. Cloud said he was going to get some Pine-Sol—so St. Cloud was sent out shopping. He came back shortly and each of us ate or smoked or sprayed bathroom deodorant in the air, as he liked it. After that, near midnight, we settled in for the night. St. Cloud relinquished the bunk without a word and Johnny Kono settled down, .45 on his bosom, and went to sleep. St. Cloud's pacing and muttering— the best line being something about turning to tofu after tonight—kept me awake for a couple hours. Then I went to sleep. I didn't wake till after daylight. St. Cloud was still pacing the floor, coming down hard from the coke, Johnny Kono still snoring on the bunk. His grip on the .45 had loosened a little.

My waking set St. Cloud in a fury. He paced hard, sat at the living-area table with a vengeance, wildly scraped the tabletop with his fingers, massaged his gums. Then he leaped up to pace the floor some more. He finally snapped and went over and kicked the bunk. Johnny Kono's hand tightened around the .45. He went on snoring. St. Cloud was taken by rage. He started moaning that anybody who could sleep at a time like this was heartless. "I mean fucking *without a heart!* Like a snake," St. Cloud said, wild-eyed, probably still not understanding why he had flunked high school biology.

St. Cloud went and kicked the bunk again— nothing—went to the sink, drew a glass of water, looked at the .45 on Johnny Kono's chest, and poured the water in the sink. He then went and sat on the bed and went berserk. He leaned his head back and howled. Something like a shut-in dog. It had its effect. In a couple minutes Johnny Kono stopped snoring. His eyes opened. For some inexplicable reason, since I had been quiet as a mouse, he aimed those black, hooded eyes across the loft at me.

Now it was time for Johnny Kono to go out. Get something for breakfast, a newspaper—both killers were anxious to see the morning paper—some cigarettes, make a phone call. Johnny Kono washed his hands and arms, rinsed his mouth with whiskey and went out. St. Cloud stretched out on the bunk and twitched awhile. By the time Johnny Kono got back, St. Cloud was asleep. Johnny Kono looked at St. Cloud, at me.

"Takes it hard, don't he?"

Johnny Kono crossed to the table, put down the paper bags he was carrying and unloaded them. Coffee, doughnuts, more cigarettes, a *Chronicle* he kept folded so I couldn't see the front page. Johnny Kono looked at me. "You hungry?" I said I'd have some coffee. Johnny Kono brought me a cup of coffee. He went back to the table, pried the lid off a foam cup, dunked and ate four doughnuts while he read the paper. He kept the paper flat on the table when he turned from the front page to the continuation on the back. When Johnny Kono finished reading the article, he looked at me and grinned. Then he read the sports page.

St. Cloud waked in the early afternoon. He looked bad. He sat on the bunk and shook. When he could keep water down, Johnny Kono gave him some pills. St. Cloud shook some more till the pills kicked in. Then he held his head under the tap, dried off, and he and Johnny Kono went into the back room. They took the newspaper with them. They stayed in the back room awhile, talking low, then they came out. They had left the paper in the back room. More pills and St. Cloud went down to the alley. He came back up the stairs carrying a large manila envelope packed tight with papers. Johnny Kono dragged the living-area table and a couple of chairs over to my bench. St. Cloud and Johnny Kono took the chairs. St. Cloud opened the envelope and spread out the plan for that night on the table.

The Cessna that Kat and I had once been part owners of was waiting in a back hangar at the San Carlos airstrip. The boys had somehow managed to get the keys off one of the present owners. Whoever that was was out of town, so there wouldn't be any trouble there. It would look as if Kat and I had kept a spare key when we sold the plane and I had in desperation returned and stolen the plane. Johnny Kono drew a rough map of the San Carlos airport and marked the hangar where the Cessna was parked. Johnny Kono gave me the map. I would need it to find the plane. Everything else—the key, flight maps, jumpsuit, chute, lights, gasoline, everything else I would need—would be on the plane when I got there. The corpse too. After dark tonight, Johnny Kono and St. Cloud would take the body wrapped in the plastic sheet down to the San Carlos strip. The body would be right by then. Dressed in the clothes I had last been seen in before I disappeared, with all the old Dan Cox papers—driver's license, credit cards, wallet that Kat had taken and were now being returned—and the ninety-eight hundred-dollar bills I had left from the lawyer's payoff stashed on the body.

After Johnny Kono and St. Cloud had loaded the body into the Cessna, they would take the Trans Am up into the Sierras. That would take about four or five hours. They would have to wait till dark to get the body out of the loft, so it would be eight o'clock at least before they got the body to San Carlos and into the plane and were on the road to the mountains. I was to leave the loft no earlier than midnight. And under no circumstances was I to take off from San Carlos before one a.m. No way were they going to have me getting there early. A dead man wandering around hitchhiking in some Sierra canyon.

We went through the timetable a second time. Then St. Cloud spread the flight maps out on the table. From San Carlos I was to take the Cessna across the Bay and make for Modesto. From Modesto I'd fly to the next checkpoint at Sonora, a small town fifty miles into the Sierra foothills, elevation eighteen hundred plus. St. Cloud pulled a photograph from the envelope. A night aerial shot of Sonora. He had me memorize the pattern of lights made by the village streets. I had to get this checkpoint dead right. Get the wrong mountain village and I'd be driving the Cessna up a cliff. After I had got nighttime Sonora fixed in my mind, we went back to the maps. St. Cloud led me through the next-to-last leg of my last flight as Dan Cox:

"Out of Sonora you go sixty degrees east-northeast. There'll be a two-lane highway leading into high country. Use it as a reference. Be just like moonlighting down the Mekong. Now, you climb quick as you can to ten thousand. That'll keep you out of trouble if you wander off course. Once you make ten thousand, you level off and keep the Cessna at one five oh knots, still sixty dead even on the compass. Write that down. At Sonora you set your watch—that son of a bitch keep time?"

"It's a little fast."

St. Cloud looked at my watch. "What happened to that hack watch you had?"

"I hocked it."

"Shit, I wanted to put it on the stiff. All right. Now, we don't know what kinda winds you're gonna run into up there, so we ain't sure, but we figure between forty and fifty minutes after leaving Sonora you're gonna see Highland Peak here." He spotted the mountain on the map. "Three red lights topped by a white. Eleven thousand feet. Should be dead ahead of you if you ain't drifted off course." St. Cloud traced a line on the map from Sonora to Highland Peak. "From the time you see the three reds and the white, you got ten minutes before you get in trouble. And if you ain't at ten thousand, you're gonna be in trouble before you see the lights. Mountains rise real quick up there. The forecast says we got fine flying weather in the Sierras tonight. Clear. Never know about the wind up there, but it shouldn't be too bad. Even a little moon. But now listen, Cox, you do have any trouble, Highland Peak's socked in, bad winds, if there's anything that ain't gone perfect or fucking near perfect fifty minutes out of Sonora, you turn around and fly right back to San Carlos. We'll have somebody there all night, just in case. No heroes tonight, Danny boy. All right?"

"All right."

St. Cloud went to a section of the map just south of Highland Peak. "Now, everything goes all right, you make the Highland Peak lights, you're lined up sixty-five degrees, there ain't no freaky winds, you're eyeballing everything, you got a go. And this is where you're gonna be going." St. Cloud tapped the map, turning it to face me. "Just south of Red Mountain, which is just south of Highland Peak—watch for the snow cap." St. Cloud drew a long hatched line south for what looked like ten miles on the map, then took the line ninety degrees right to the east. He ran his pencil over the L hatched on the map. "That's Sonora Pass. One of the light-plane routes through the Sierras. You know it?"

"I've never flown it."

St. Cloud leaned over the map. "Yeah, well, most people in their right minds ain't. You heard of Devil's Gate Canyon?" He took the pencil and extended the due-south part of the L beyond where the hatched line turned sharp to the east. "It's a killer. You miss the turn here to Sonora Pass"—he moved the pencil over the hatched line running east—"you keep going into Devil's Gate Canyon"—he made a dark box on the line he had drawn extending due south—"and you're a dead man. Really dead. Five minutes past Sonora Pass and Devil's Gate Canyon narrows real quick to about three hundred feet. The canyon floor comes up at about forty-five degrees. Too tight to turn around in, not enough space to make the twelve thou to get you over Mount Wheeler at the head of the canyon. And no place to land but a wall." St. Cloud looked at Johnny Kono. "How many light planes eat it in that rock closet the last twenty years, J.K.?"

Johnny Kono looked at me. "A lot."

St. Cloud leaned back, clasped his hands behind his head. "Well, as of tonight, there's gonna be another one. Devil's Gate Canyon, Danny boy. That's where you buy the farm." St. Cloud opened his mouth and grinned.

At that point Johnny Kono took over the map and sketched out the last stage of the flight. Johnny Kono being in charge of the body and the drop and ground operations in general. When I got to San Carlos tonight, I would find the body in the back seat of the Cessna. Still wrapped in the plastic sheet. And that was the way the body was going to stay—in the back, packaged—till I made the lights of Highland Peak and turned into Devil's Gate Canyon. Couldn't take the chance of unwrapping the stiff, propping him up in the pilot's seat, on the ground. Might be seen. Might run into some weather and have to turn around and fly back to San Carlos. Everything—pulling the body from the back into the pilot's seat, stripping off the plastic sheet, checking to be sure the ID and the money were in place—that all had to be done from the foot of Devil's Gate Canyon to the jump point. I'd have about ten minutes. Plenty of time, Johnny Kono said, if I didn't lose it. In the back with the body would be a parachute, a black skydiving rig that Johnny Kono had packed himself, and a plastic jug filled with gasoline. After the body was fixed in place in the pilot's seat, I was to bring the parachute forward, strap it on, buckle up. Then I was to splash half the gasoline in the back of the plane, and douse the body with the remainder of the gas. That was important. Gas on the stiff. Couldn't take a chance he'd be thrown clear of the plane on impact and not get a proper cooking. All this time I was to be flying the plane. Nothing to it, Johnny Kono said. Once he had flown a L20 over the Quang Ngai Mountains bound for Hue, steering with his feet while he banged a mama-san girl in his lap.

Then, with the stiff in place and gas splashed, I was to toss the plastic sheet and the plastic bottle. Couldn't take any chance of anything being found on the plane. Bears eat plastic, Johnny Kono said he'd heard that somewhere. No evidence. With the bottle and the sheet overboard, I was to check my position. When I saw Devil's Gate Canyon dead south, I was to get in the door, toss a flaming lighter in the back, grab my nuts and jump. The burning plane would fly on another three, four minutes and crash in flames against the granite walls of Devil's Gate Canyon. I'd float to the bottom of Devil's Gate Canyon, make an easy landing somewhere in Kennedy Meadows. Johnny Kono and St. Cloud would be waiting there on an access road. They'd pick me and the chute up and I'd be alive and dead.

Johnny Kono went over everything again, then looked at me. "Got it?"

"Got it."

"Ever jump before, Cox?"

"Plenty." Which was entirely true. The one time I had been kicked from a C-119 had been enough to last me for a lifetime. Though I would be forced to admit, ten hours later, clinging desperately to the Cessna's wing strut with one hand, trying to steer the plane away from a sheer canyon wall with the other, still gagging from gas fumes and the sight of the body the boys had fixed up for me, flames tearing through the back of the cabin, waiting below a five-hundred-foot fall, two-hundred-foot float and a fifty-foot ponderosa—at that point I would find myself longing for eight weeks in jump school.

But for now I said there would be no problem with the jump.

St. Cloud came from the outside landing. He had been pissing between the warehouses. Was zipping up. "You tell him about the money?"

Johnny Kono leaned back in the chair. "Tell him again."

St. Cloud sat at the table. "You can't fuck with any of that money, Cox. It's all gotta go down. The feds got the serial numbers on the bills. The chief had that fixed. They already picked up the two you broke. The other ninety-eight ride down. Just in case the plane don't burn right."

I promised not to touch a thing.

St. Cloud looked at Johnny Kono. "Guess that's it."

Johnny Kono yawned. "Want to go over it again?"

I shook my head. "I think I've got it." I took a cigarette from the pack. "I do have one question."

St. Cloud leaned back in his chair. "Shoot."

"This parachute—is it going to open?"

St. Cloud came forward. "Sure it's going to open. Why shouldn't it open?"

"Well, no insult intended—but what I thought you might have in mind was killing me. Like you killed Max, Peter Wiley, Pendergast, the Air Force guy in Washington—have I left anybody out? It was just wondering why you're going to all this trouble. Bodies and flaming planes and parachutes. When you could just take out a .45 and put a bullet between my eyes."

St. Cloud looked at Johnny Kono. "We got any plans to kill him?"

Johnny Kono sneered, didn't say anything.

St. Cloud looked back. "Hey, we ain't going to kill you, you fuck. We're going through all this shit to give you a new start in life."

"Why?"

Johnny Kono yawned. "Because that fucking fairy Creesy killed the wrong pilot in Arizona."

St. Cloud nodded. "There you go. You're taking Max's place. You're working with us now, Danny boy." St. Cloud stopped. Like he was thinking he had made a *faux pas* someplace, couldn't put his finger on it. He scowled. "So just shut the fuck up."

I held up my free hand. "Sorry, boys. Just wanted to clear that point up." We were silent awhile, then I said: "Who's taking me down to the airport tonight?"

The two killers watched me. "Dayton's got a driver lined up for you."

"Who?"

Johnny Kono stood. "What time is it? We better get some sleep, St. Cloud." Johnny Kono went over to the bunk and lay down.

St. Cloud stayed at the table. He looked me over,

almost looked concerned. "Personally, I'd rather jump into a sink of snakes than fuck around that lady. Dub Dayton's a man of possessions."

St. Cloud dragged the table and chairs back to the living area and took the first waking shift.

The afternoon passed with one killer sleeping, the other sitting at the table, watching me. When it started getting dark, St. Cloud went out, came back in ten minutes. He crossed the loft to the bunk where Johnny Kono was lying. St. Cloud looked at the dark blue square of evening framed by the door. "Let's get this thing started, J.K."

Johnny Kono looked at his fingernails. He'd been scraping dried blood from under them the last hour. Sucking one fingertip at a time. "Thirty minutes we'll load everything in the car."

Half an hour passed and St. Cloud went down to the alley, backed the Trans Am to the foot of the stairs, opened the trunk lid and came back up to the loft. He and Johnny Kono went into the back room, came out with the plastic-wrapped corpse. They carried the body downstairs, the trunk lid closed, they came back up the stairs. St. Cloud circled the front room, picking up. Johnny Kono went into the back room. St. Cloud came over to me. It was near true night and I couldn't see much of St. Cloud's face. His voice sounded like the voice of a friend. Something I was going to remember.

"That parachute's going to open."

St. Cloud went to the outside door. He called back, "Let's get moving, J.K." He went down the stairs. A door opened, closed, the Trans Am's motor turned over, St. Cloud keeping it quiet as he could.

Johnny Kono came to the door in the partition. He held a rolled newspaper in his hand. He came to me, tossed the newspaper to the floor.

"You fuck off on us, Cox, I'll suck your eyes out."

He crossed the loft and went down the stairs. The Trans Am rumbled down the alley, then there was quiet. I picked up the newspaper, found the front page. It was near dark in the loft, the moon hadn't risen yet, but I had no trouble making out the bold type spread across the front page:

STOKES SHOT IN TEXAS

The evening *Examiner* had pretty much the same story as the *Chronicle* Johnny Kono had left me. More photographs, more details of the shooting, but nothing really new. I read the *Examiner* story in the BMW's dash light as Thea drove me down to San Carlos.

Gerald Stokes had been shot in Waco, Texas, walking along a street, late yesterday afternoon. Stokes was alive, paralyzed by the gunshot, but no longer in critical condition. He had been flown to Houston to undergo surgery. Stokes' assassin had not yet been apprehended, but eyewitnesses had given the police a description of the man and a police artist had done a fair sketch of the assassin. The killer Max and I had flown in from Mexico. What he would have looked like if he had been an ordinary criminal.

Thea and I had left the loft in San Francisco at midnight, a little behind schedule. Thea had brought clean clothes and boots, and in the time before we left I had washed and shaved and changed. We had said little to one another in the loft and had fallen silent in the car while I read the *Examiner* story. They had done what they had set out to do. There wasn't that much to say.

Thea turned off 101 at San Carlos, crossed under the freeway and went along the lateral road till we came to the fence, hangars and parked planes of the San Carlos strip. A light plane was just taking off, looking wobbly. The BMW had a field sticker on the windshield, and the guard waved us through the gate. We drove along a road fronting lines of parked planes and small hangars till we came to the one-plane hangar Johnny Kono had marked on the map he had drawn of the San Carlos field. Thea stopped the car to one side of the hangar. The hangar door was closed but not locked. Thea stayed in the car as I pulled the hangar doors back. The brown-and-tan Cessna 180 I had put no more than a couple hundred hours on in the six years I had had it. I could still feel the plane in my hands. Light as a falling leaf. I had not liked flying it.

I went to the plane and opened the cowl hood. Thea called out from the car: "He's already checked it out."

I closed the cowl hood, latched it and went back to the car.

Thea looked toward the strip. A light plane, a Piper Cherokee, the same plane we had seen taking off when we came to the airport, was landing. Past midnight and somebody was practicing touch-and-goes. The plane touched down, faltered, gathered speed and wobbled back into the air. Thea turned away from the plane, as if she were looking for another incoming craft. There were none.

"You're behind schedule," she said.

"It doesn't matter."

She looked at me closely. "I suppose not." She stopped. "Do you know what you're going to do whenever you can do something?"

"I have a general idea."

She looked at me. "What?"

"I'm going to talk to your father." I waited. "You still think that's a bad idea?"

She shrugged. "I don't know." She stopped. "He's

changing. Something's happening." She reached out her hand and took my arm and lifted it to her. She looked at my watch. She let my arm go. "I've got to get back."

"Have to check in?"

She gave me a searching look. As if we had known each other since childhood, our parents had been dear friends, and now she was seeing me for the first time. "Yes."

"I'll be in touch. Whenever I get free."

She wasn't listening. Looking out across the Bay. The guy in the Cherokee was circling for another landing. "I know I've got to do something," she said. "I can't just sit in that house and paint and do nothing." She looked toward the hangar. "I'll wait till you're away."

I went into the hangar, got in the plane and looked in the back. The plastic-wrapped body and the bottle of gasoline were there. You could smell them both. The manila envelope with flight maps lay on the pilot's seat. I opened the envelope and shook out the key. The Cessna started up first crank and drew easy out of the hangar, running smoother than I had ever known. I pulled past the BMW, onto the apron. The touch-and-go was calling it a night. The Cherokee was taxiing toward the far end of the runway, turning off into a line of parked planes. The radio was set to the San Carlos tower, but I didn't request clearance. Tough to break the habit, but something a guy stealing a plane probably wouldn't do. I turned the Cessna away from the office and the bulk of the field and ran along the apron. Nothing coming in. Wind sock dead on the pole. The tower tried to raise me, but I left the mike untouched, braked the plane sharp left and went onto the runway. Hit the throttle forward and was off the ground by the time I passed the BMW.

The Cessna went up like it had strings. I curled out

over the Bay, as if I was coming around for a touch-and-go, and passed over the strip. The BMW was already moving away. Toward the strip gate. I took the Cessna in an easy climb to five hundred, angling across the Bay. When I made the Dumbarton Bridge, I turned the plane east and up, hard. Put its nose into the night sky.

*L*OSING all that flab, the mustache, little color in your cheeks—Dan, you're starting to look something like a soldier. A team player."

St. Cloud laughed. Johnny Kono just watched. When Dayton's sleepy alligator eyes went over to St. Cloud, St. Cloud closed his mouth. Dayton came back to me. "You understand what I'm telling you, Dan?"

We were in L.A.—Venice Beach—a house three blocks off the sea, on a narrow alley. The house's first floor was a garage and a storeroom. The second floor, where we were, a single room with a kitchenette, bathroom, sleeping closet tucked behind the stairs.

Windows made three of the big room's walls. The kitchenette, bathroom, sleeping closet and stairs were set against the solid fourth wall. There were some bones of furniture strewn about the room. A sofa, where Johnny Kono sat, a beanbag chair that St. Cloud was laid out on, a bed, a couple other chairs, a TV set, a couple of low coffee tables, the kitchen table and chairs where I sat with Dayton. The windows, maybe a dozen of them set in the three walls, were shuttered with venetian blinds. The blind near me had a bent shutter so that I could see down into the alley. An old bag man was working the alley, going through garbage cans, collecting bottles, newspapers, arranging everything he took nice and tidy in a shopping cart.

I turned away from the bent blind and told Dayton I understood I was just another soldier. A team member.

The cowboy clothes, the way I had seen Dayton last, in the motel bar in Montana, were gone. Now he was California. Golf shirt, slacks, socks under sandals. An over-the-hill bouncer, now he had his own club, some topless joint on Sunset Strip.

Dayton smiled, his eyes could have been closed. "Best for everybody you understand that, Dan." He cocked his head toward St. Cloud and Johnny Kono. "The boys tell you anything about the job?"

"That it would be flying."

Dayton leaned forward, his forearms on the table edge, clasping his big weathered hands together, fingers interlocked. "You flew a 727 with Northwestern, right, Dan?"

"Yeah. It was my plane."

"Think you could fly one without any help?"

I leaned back in the chair, away from the stream of sunlight coming through the crack made by the bent blind. "Might be a little tricky getting it off the ground."

"How about landing?"

"That might be tricky too. Depends on the conditions. What the strip is like."

"The conditions could be anything. The strip ain't going to be much."

I pushed the bent blind up, closing out the light. I took my hand away and the blind snapped back bent. "That would depend on whether you just want to get it down or you want to get it back up again."

"Down will do just fine."

"I can get it down."

Dayton looked over at Johnny Kono. Johnny Kono was still cleaning his nails, a week after the body switch and jump and crash that, so far, were looking good. The *Chronicle*, anyway, had reported Dan Cox dead. "Let's get this thing started, J.K. You got everything together?"

Johnny Kono didn't move. "Downstairs."

Dayton watched Johnny Kono. "Then get it."

Johnny Kono sucked a finger, got up and went down the stairs. Making a little skip going down, rattling the venetian blinds. When the door to the storeroom below creaked, Dayton came back to me.

"We don't know when this thing is coming down. Could be tomorrow. Could be a week."

The election was tomorrow. Stokes was paralyzed from the waist down. Out of it, most of the papers and news magazines and TV pundits said. Stokes' assassin had been identified—Marcus J. Creesy. Nothing much about his past, nothing like what they had had on Oswald. Creesy's picture, an old snapshot blown up, had been in all the papers. Creesy had been seen leaving the scene of the shooting in a white Mustang, New Mexico plates, but as of this morning he hadn't been caught.

Dayton looked over at St. Cloud. St. Cloud splayed over the beanbag chair, looking vacant. Dayton looked back at me. "You're going to be taking over a plane like the niggers who flew to Cuba last month. We'll get into that when J.K. gets back. You'll be flying to Mexico. We'll get into that later too. You'll be flying some friends out of the country. You'll know who when you get on the plane. Any questions before we start?"

"Yeah." I looked at St. Cloud, looked back. "These two morons told me something that has kind of upset me. They said Creesy killed the wrong guy in that crash in Arizona. They tell me I'm second-string. Being groomed to take Max's place. Now that he's dead."

Dayton's sleepy eyes opened. "There weren't any mistakes made, Dan. Max died because he wasn't a good soldier. He was cut by the team." Dayton kept his eyes wide, so I could see into him. St. Cloud was right. You didn't want to get into that sink of snakes. "Got it?"

The door creaked below and Johnny Kono came up the stairs. He crossed the room and tossed a couple of fat manila envelopes onto the table.

Dayton looked at the envelopes. He looked at Johnny Kono. "I thought you said you had everything downstairs."

Johnny Kono moved his mouth. "Yeah."

"Then get it."

Johnny Kono went back down the stairs. Dayton opened one of the envelopes and spilled some maps and overlays across the table. Mexico. Dayton went through the maps till he found one of the coast. The long narrow knife of shale sand off Puerto Peñasco. Where Max and I had picked up Creesy. Dayton turned the map to me. "Think you can take it down there?"

"Not a 727."

Dayton looked at me. "Max said he could."

I leaned back from the map. I looked at St. Cloud, I looked at Dayton. Johnny Kono's heavy footsteps were on the stairs. "Why don't you fly it, Dub? You're good. Better than Max. A hell of a lot better than me. How about St. Cloud? J.K.? They can put a 727 down in a sand pile."

"We might play around with a 727, Dan. But you're the only one who knows how to take it up, get it down." Dayton fanned the maps across the table. "What's your first choice, Dan?"

"The desert outside of Ciudad whatever the fuck it was. If it hasn't rained."

Dayton took out the Ciudad de la Libertad map. "And a backup."

"The beach."

Dayton took the coastal map in front of me and put it with the first map. Johnny Kono came back into the room. He was carrying a suitcase and an attaché case. Dayton reached the two maps to Johnny Kono. Johnny Kono put the suitcase down by the table. He took the maps with his free hand. "Third choice."

I stayed back from the table, looking at Dayton. "Your pleasure, Dub."

Dayton kept his eyes on the table. "Choose a third landing site, Dan."

I picked up a third map, any map, and tossed it on the table near Johnny Kono.

Dayton's sleepy eyes came up to me. "I hope you're taking this seriously, Dan."

I sat forward, drew the maps to me, made a serious choice, probably not any better than the one made at random, and gave the map to Johnny Kono. Johnny Kono tucked the maps under his arm. He still held the attaché case with his other hand.

Dayton looked at Johnny Kono, at the attaché case.

"Would you stop mothering that fucking thing." Dayton swept the rest of the maps to one side of the table and Johnny Kono put the attaché case on the table. He snapped the latches and opened the case. A dozen or so sticks of dynamite taped to the bottom of the case, what looked like the guts of a small transistor radio, an electric light switch set in a block of wood, the wood taped to the case, a dry-cell battery, a lot of wires running from the switch to the radio guts to the dynamite to the battery. Everything taped down. Tidy.

Dayton watched me. "Relax, Dan. We've got to make it look good. No telling what the stewardess might know. She's got to believe you're serious." Dayton nodded and Johnny Kono closed the case, fastened the latches and took the case away. Dayton took the second manila envelope and shook out some maps. Ordinary road maps, a map of L.A. International, another airport I didn't recognize, a plan of a 727 passenger and flight deck. He took up the map of the L.A. airport. "You're going to be taking a PSA 727 out of L.A. International. You know L.A. International, Dan?"

"Yeah."

He put a finger to the map. "PSA terminal. What security they have can't really handle the traffic. We'll probably go for a San Francisco shuttle, but that depends. Anyway, it's going to be a short hop. Lot of folks coming and going. Security overworked. No assigned seats. Fucking chaos. Just what we want." He put down the map. "How long's the hop down to Jalisco going to take, Dan?"

"Couple hours from L.A."

"OK. We'll try and get you out around noon. So you'll have plenty of light for landing. What's the one hundred series' range?"

"Depends on fuel load. Passengers. Baggage. Cruising altitude. Say five thousand miles."

"Good enough. Now we'll get you all set up, looking executive-class with your case." Dayton turned to the plan of the 727 passenger deck. "We want you in the back seat of the plane if possible. If those seats are taken, you take the farthest seat aft available—where both seats are vacant. We don't want any off-duty cop sitting by you. Got it?"

"Yeah."

"Put your case or a raincoat or something on the seat by you. Now once the plane is in the air, you're going to be working quick." Dayton unfolded a road map. Greater L.A. "You're going to take the plane back down at the Burbank airport." He pointed at the L.A. map. "As soon as you can, you give the stewardess a note we'll have fixed up for you. This note will say you have a bomb and the captain will be taking the plane down at Burbank. And if he doesn't you will be blowing the fucking plane out of the sky. Now when you get on the ground the crew, except for the stewardess you're dealing with, and the passengers, except for our friends, will leave the plane by the forward door. The tail ramp, back where you are, stays shut tight. Once this is done, there's nobody on the plane but you, the stewardess and our friends, you go forward to the flight deck. Now our friends all know who they are, so you don't have to worry about any of that. They'll take care of everything back in the cabin. You get in the saddle and once the last stewardess is off the plane, you take the plane off and fly to Mexico." Dayton smiled. "Simple as that. Think you can do it, Dan?"

"Well, I had been thinking of something even simpler."

Dayton sat forward. He looked really concerned. A boss who was having to let you go, he didn't like putting a family man on the street, but things were tough for everybody. "Can you do it, Dan?"

I thought, really thought, for what seemed like the first time in my life, that I didn't know. That I probably couldn't. But what I said was that it would be a piece of cake. A little surprise I was going to be baking and slicing myself.

Then we waited. The election was the next day. Dayton stayed around for that. The crook in office beat the crook trying to unseat him by a landslide. With the maverick candidate paralyzed, America had stuck with the two-party system. One pundit, the dean of the network's analysts, mourned, sort of, Gerald Stokes' absence from the race. How might have things been different, this sage intoned, had the maverick congressman from Missouri not been snatched from the political stage by an assassin's bullet? As the old guy droned on about the threat made by the lone, deranged assassin's bullet to democracy and freedom and a host of other things held dear by TV analysts, I watched Dayton and the boys for some reaction. Maybe elation at a job well done. Nothing. The trio sat watching the TV screen like it was halftime, they were waiting for another closeup of the leggy baton twirlers.

Dayton left the house in Venice that night and didn't come back. St. Cloud and Johnny Kono stayed on to guard me. Sitting was closer. No handcuffs, no threats, no theatrics. The venetian blinds were kept closed day and night and I wasn't allowed out of the house. But even these precautions seemed more for my protection than to prevent escape. I was treated merely as a very valuable member of the team. During those next few days—St. Cloud and Johnny Kono taking turns at the house, the one disappearing while the other was on duty—I spent most of my time thinking forward to the hijack, my hijack, and making out a shopping list.

The following morning, the third full day at the Venice house, Johnny Kono didn't show to relieve St. Cloud. St. Cloud retaliated by sleeping in. I waited till nine, when the local stores would be opening, then wrote St. Cloud a note—gone for cigarettes and coffee—and went out. I walked over to Venice's main drag, a couple of blocks of dingy shops and ice cream parlors and roller-skate rental shacks, found a drugstore and bought an alarm clock and some electrical tape. All that the local store had on my list. I was going to have to get over to Santa Monica, to some big hardware/supply complex, to assemble my own flight kit.

I went back to the house and stood in the small landing at the foot of the stairs. Nothing from the apartment above. Two doors flanked the landing. One to the garage, one to the storeroom. I opened the door to the garage. St. Cloud's yellow Trans Am. The door to the storeroom was locked. I put the clock and tape in a box of crap in the garage and went upstairs. St. Cloud was awake, sitting on one of the couches. A beer and the note I had left sat on the coffee table. St. Cloud's eyes were fixed on the coffee table. Not looking at anything, just staring. He picked up the beer, tasted it, put it back on the coffee table.

"I'm sick of being shut up in these goddamn dumps. Let's open a blind."

"Pretty gray out there this morning, St. Cloud."

St. Cloud was quiet. Then he said: "They're always landing me with this kind of crap. What the fuck are they waiting for, anyway?"

I got a beer from the fridge, sat on the couch across from St. Cloud. "You tell me."

St. Cloud looked at me. Eyes red, face swollen and gone off, hair twisted. St. Cloud needed to move, bad. He drained his beer. "Who the fuck knows? They don't know what they're doing. Everything's all screwed up."

I sipped at the beer. "What's screwed up?"

St. Cloud looked at me. "Get me another beer."

I got St. Cloud the beer and we drank in silence. St. Cloud picked up the note I had written, put it back on the coffee table. St. Cloud gave me a sidelong look. "Are you two split? Like, I mean for good?"

I didn't, for a second, know what he was talking about. I sipped at the beer and watched St. Cloud's morose, ravaged face. Killer in love. And maybe an ally. A neutral anyway. "She took my money, credit cards, driver's license and gave them to you. What do you think?"

St. Cloud brooded some, got another beer, came back to the couch and brooded some more. Once he gave me that look again—he was on the first team, why was the cheerleader going out with me?

I finished my beer, then took to pacing around the apartment. Just enough to drive St. Cloud near the edge. Then I stopped. "You know what I'd like to do this morning?"

St. Cloud was looking toward the fridge. One can of beer left and a bottle of tequila. "You want to go out it's fine with me. I don't give a fuck. You're a fucking human being, right?" He downed the beer and crumpled the can.

I got St. Cloud the last beer. "Maybe this afternoon I wouldn't mind getting out. But right now I'd like to take a look at the device. Whatever you call it. Look, I'm going to have to carry the goddamn thing. I'd like to get familiar with it. I'm going to have to look like I know what I'm doing."

St. Cloud sat looking across the room, looking at nothing, getting more pissed off as he worked through the last beer, getting closer to the tequila. "Why the fuck not? You are doing this shit, right?" He crumpled the last can. "The key's on the key ring. In the car. Hand me the tequila." I got the tequila from the fridge, put it on the table in front of St. Cloud and started down the stairs. St. Cloud called out: "Get some fucking limes the next time you go out. And don't blow us up, Cox. I think that crazy pineapple has got that thing hooked up."

I went down to the garage, got the key ring from the Trans Am, crossed to the storeroom and unlocked the door. The attaché case sat on a table in the storeroom, centered and squared like a case of jewels on display. The small suitcase I would be carrying on the plane sat on the floor by the table. I examined the suitcase. A cheap plaid-and-plastic job, not too difficult to match if I could get the plaid right in my head. I put my hands on the attaché case, snapped the latches and opened it. What I had thought was the guts of a transistor radio was a compact radio receiver. Taped under that was a bank of capacitors. A timing device much more accurate and reliable than a clock, a receiver that could activate the capacitors by remote control.

So my bomb would be a little old-fashioned, just a clock and a light switch taped to the case frame, but then I knew the six or seven flares I would be taping in a bundle wouldn't be blowing up. I eased the lid of the case down, closed it, locked the storeroom, returned the keys to the Trans Am, and went back upstairs.

St. Cloud was sitting where I had left him. Blowing across the mouth of the tequila bottle. He had a hit. "You know the word going around, Cox? You're taking us all to Mexico. That's the backup plan on hold. Dub, even his old lady. Maybe even Blackmuir." He tilted the bottle and looked for the worm. "I don't want to go to fucking Mexico. I *ain't* going to fucking Mexico." St. Cloud reached behind him and opened the venetian blind. It was still gray out. A couple hours before the morning fog would burn off.

Johnny Kono came in that night, but he only stayed for a couple minutes. He swaggered around the apartment like a junior exec whose boss had remembered his name. St. Cloud remained slumped across the beanbag chair, malevolently following Johnny Kono's progress from fridge to table to couch, where I sat trying to stay out of the way. Marching orders hadn't come down yet, but Johnny Kono let us in on the lay of the land.

The contingency operation would come down in a couple days. Nothing firm. Not yet. The chief—not Dayton, the way Johnny Kono said *chief* you had the feeling Dayton was not the one giving Johnny Kono delusions of grandeur—was waiting for something to happen. Johnny Kono didn't say what this thing that was going to happen was, but again, the swell in his neck, the distant look over our heads, to places of power that St. Cloud and I could only dream of, let us know it was going to be something big. In the meantime, we were to sit tight. Observe strict security precautions, go over the hijack plans and maps and timetables and keep fit.

After Johnny Kono had left, St. Cloud blew a low note on the tequila bottle. "I been thinking about something."

"Yeah?"

"This plan. You're supposed to hijack this 727. We're—all of us, you know who I'm talking about—

we're supposed to be on this jet. Then you fly us out of the country. Mexico. Someplace safe. Where we can cool it for a while. Let this Stokes thing die down."

"That's the plan."

"It fucking stinks."

"I don't know. What's on your mind?"

St. Cloud belched, drew his eyes to a point. "All this hijacking crap is going to call more heat down on us than fucking take it off."

"Could be."

St. Cloud looked at me. Like he really wanted to know. "Why can't we just disappear on our own. Everybody go his own way. Mexico. Canada. Wherever. Things cool down, there's another job to do, we come back. Get together again."

"Food for thought, St. Cloud."

"Yeah. Yeah, it is." St. Cloud was quiet for a while. "I ain't getting on that plane. Nobody in his right mind is." He stopped, looked at the tequila bottle. "There's something going on with Dub. Normally he'd be in charge of an operation like this. Wouldn't let J.K. get near it." He stopped. "I got this feeling—I don't know, maybe Dub is getting out." He drained the bottle, tossed it to a couch across the room. His lips went down, as if he had made a serious mistake in judgment. Should have bounced the bottle off something. "You're liable to be the only one of us on that plane, Cox."

"Maybe." I poured out beer. "I think I might go through with it anyway." St. Cloud watched me. I sipped the beer, put the glass on the table. "I've been thinking about doing some shopping."

St. Cloud watched me. "What kind of shopping?"

"Few things for the trip. You couldn't loan me a little money, could you?"

"How much money?"

"I don't know. Most of the stuff's not going to cost that much. Plaid suitcase thirty bucks. The attaché case—that's going to be the main expenditure. Two, three hundred bucks. I'll bring the change back."

St. Cloud took out his wallet, tossed three hundred-dollar bills on the table. He took the Trans Am keys from his pocket, tossed them next to the bills. "Put some gas in it, will you?"

The next two days I shopped. St. Cloud gave me all the freedom I wanted, more money than I needed, and use of the Trans Am. Buying for the fake bomb was a simple matter. Well, finding an identical attaché case took a little legwork. But what I would carry aboard the 727 in the cheap plaid suitcase—that demanded planning. Thinking ahead. After takeoff there wouldn't be any running down to the corner store for the duct tape or alligator clips or vise-grips or epoxy glue that might mean the difference between a quarter of a million tax-free and forty years in jail. But by the end of that second day, when I had the fake bomb assembled, the suitcase packed, both stored in the garage, I felt I had everything I would need. Anyway, I decided to stop thinking about failure and that night got drunk with St. Cloud. Mused about success.

Johnny Kono woke me at dawn the next morning. In a couple minutes we had St. Cloud dragged out of the sleeping closet and dressed. Johnny Kono was in a state of excitement. While St. Cloud and I sat at the kitchen table and drank coffee, Johnny Kono strode about the room giving us the details.

"It's the one o'clock flight out of Burbank. That's different. Got it, Cox? You fly *out* of Burbank. Not *into* it. Now, you're set to go into Frisco. That's where we'll dump the passengers. Then back to Mexico. We're going for the desert floor outside of Ciudad de la Libertad. Like you wanted. OK? Out of Burbank. Into Frisco. The one o'clock flight. Got it?"

I said I had it.

Johnny Kono gave St. Cloud a look, then went across the room. He came back speaking. "Now, Cox here has already got a prepaid ticket waiting for him at the PSA counter, but St. Cloud, you got to buy your own. Things have been moving too fast to get everything set. But that's OK," Johnny Kono said, explaining to us what had been explained to him. "It's better this way. Everybody arrives at the airport. Buys their own tickets. Gets on the plane separately. That way we won't raise any suspicion. Got it?"

St. Cloud sat hunched over the table, looking bad. He pushed the coffee away. "Everybody?"

Johnny Kono swelled some. His eyes darted around. "That's right. The whole team is going. Everybody."

St. Cloud yawned. "That's going to be real nice." St. Cloud looked to me. "Maybe Cox wants to go over the plan one last time, J.K."

Johnny Kono widened his eyes. "You got it by now, right? I'm a busy man."

I put a finger to my temple. "I got it all down, J.K."

"Yeah. Right." Johnny Kono came over and put a square brown hand on the table. "I gotta go down and check the device one last time. The keys still downstairs?"

St. Cloud yawned more. "Cox has them."

Johnny Kono looked at me. Back at St. Cloud. "What the fuck's he doing with them? You ain't let this fucking jerk in the storeroom?"

St. Cloud stretched, scratched. "I been letting him use the car, J.K."

Johnny Kono looked at St. Cloud. Me. "Where's he been going in the car?"

St. Cloud drew the cup of coffee to him. He looked into it. "The beach."

Johnny Kono turned to the west windows. Sea showed down the alley. Johnny Kono turned back. "OK. Well, I'm going down and check everything out. OK?"

"Yeah. Fine," St. Cloud said.

Johnny Kono went down the stairs. There came the creak of the storeroom door opening. Then silence.

St. Cloud looked across the room, his eyes focused small and raw and angry. I didn't say anything.

A couple minutes and Johnny Kono came banging back up the stairs. He tossed the key ring onto the table. "Everything looks OK."

St. Cloud reached out and pulled the key ring across the table. He left the keys on the table, looking at them. "That's good. Wouldn't want that fucker not to work, would we?"

Johnny Kono looked at St. Cloud, at me, back at St. Cloud. Like we had a good rally going. "Yeah, well, I gotta split. Got a meeting." He stopped. "See you at the airport. On the plane anyway. Burbank. One."

"Burbank at one, J.K.," I said. "Be there or be square."

Johnny Kono looked at me. Some code, a joke maybe—he couldn't handle it. With a last look around the room, Johnny Kono turned and went down the stairs and out of the house.

St. Cloud sat for a while, staring at the keys on the table. "I want a beer and some tomato juice. And get some lemons."

I put on my shoes, got my wallet and went down the stairs. I tried the storeroom door. Locked. The door to the garage stood open. I went into the garage, took the fake bomb and the cheap plaid suitcase loaded with my gear from where I had stashed them, put the fake bomb and the suitcase in the Trans Am trunk. Johnny Kono's bomb, the real one, the one that would go bang, would stay in the locked storeroom.

At the corner liquor store I bought beer, tomato juice, lemons and a copy of the *L.A. Times*. The story was spread across the front page. Creesy, the killer Max and I had flown in from Mexico, Stokes' assassin, had been caught. In Utah, on his way north, the story said, going toward Canada.

The contingency the chief had been waiting for.

*T*HE BURBANK AIRPORT—the terminal, strips, parking area—was small. The traffic heavy. Five, six flights an hour, couple hundred people about the terminal, the parking lot, even near noon, near full. Five, ten minutes to the Warner lot, MGM, Universal, fifteen minutes over the hills to Hollywood, half an hour to downtown L.A.—the hideaway airport for movie, TV, business types who weren't interested in having their pictures snapped at LAX. Not a bad place for a man with a bomb, what would pass for one, to board a plane.

I sat in one of the back stalls in the lot facing the terminal building. Limos, rent-a-wrecks, Jensens and

Maseratis and De Loreans swirled past the terminal drop stations. I watched the incoming and outgoing flights, so many PSA 727s I could only guess which was mine. When the clock on the face of the terminal building showed twelve-thirty, I put St. Cloud's keys in the ashtray—he'd pick up the Trans Am later—and took the attaché case and the plaid valise from the trunk and went across the parking lot toward the terminal.

Standing just inside the sliding doors, I thought out what I would do next. How it would, with luck, all end two, three days from now. By the time I got through the operation, I saw that what I had to do in the air would be easy compared with what I had to do now. The first step. Convince the young lady at the PSA ticket desk across the terminal that I was not a man frightened out of his mind.

I went back in my log of fears. A port engine flaming out in an Idaho snowstorm. A forced landing at a jungle airstrip held by a Pathet Lao company. My first solo flight at seventeen. Watching Kat walk down the aisle fifteen years later. I found myself smiling as I went across the terminal toward the PSA counter. There shouldn't be that much to hijacking a plane. Like soloing in a flaming jet on your wedding day.

There was a passenger ahead of me at the counter—a stocky, hairy guy in a serape and tread sandals, some Hungarian film director, I would learn, thinking he was going to be the star of our flight. It was twelve-forty by the time the clerk got him ticketed and cleared away. I gave the clerk my new name—Napier, a British prime minister, some French historian, I couldn't remember—and she looked through the prepaid ticket list. She looked through the list a second time. She shook her head.

"I'm sorry, sir. There's nothing for Napier. N-a-p-i-e-r?"

The clerk let me take a look at the prepaid list while she checked in another passenger. That done, she came back to me.

"The computer printed it out as Namier. C. W. That's me."

The clerk looked at the list. She smiled. "Sorry, sir. Smoking or nonsmoking?"

"Smoking. Assigned seats?"

"Not on this flight, sir. But you shouldn't have any trouble finding a seat in the smoking section." She looked at the plaid suitcase. "Would you like to check your bag?"

"I'd like to carry it on. It just fits under the seat."

The clerk smiled, I signed for a ticket, was given a boarding pass and told to have a good flight.

The Hungarian director had made the security check at the gate. He had been joined by a towering blonde carrying a Huichol yarn painting. The security cops were going over the painting, the director's luggage—a vintage mustard-yellow Mexican valise with belts—and the blonde's handbag. One of the security cops glanced at my boarding pass and went back to the Mexican valise. X-ray, metal detectors, that would come later, post—C. W. Namier, as he came to be known.

I entered the PSA 727, flight 188 to San Francisco, by the tail stairs. The two right rear seats of the craft were vacant. A woman about forty, forty-five, in the seat across the aisle. I fitted the plaid case under the aisle seat, put the attaché case on the aisle chair and took the seat by the window. I breathed for a minute, then looked across the aisle. The woman had long painted nails, rings on every finger, a worn face, short gray-streaked hair, empty eyes, fake lashes dripping mascara. She leaned her face against the cabin wall, stared out the window at the strip. Longing for a drink and a smoke.

Other passengers came into the cabin by the front door, coming down the aisle, all of them looking for seats forward. The nonsmoking section was near two-thirds full. Still only a handful in the rear, smoking section. There came a clatter from the aft stairs and the Hungarian director and the starlet burst into the cabin, struggling with the bulging Mexican valise, the yarn painting. The couple threw cameras, the starlet's handbag on the seats two forward from me. They took to trying to fit the valise and the yarn painting into an overhead baggage compartment, all the while discussing whether the dogs should have been put in the kennel. The stewardess who had been working the rear door came into the cabin. She took the Mexican valise and the yarn painting to the large forward cloakroom. The director and the starlet worked awhile with their cameras and purses and shoulder bags, then settled in, dogs and kennels forgotten, laughing and gossiping. There had been a good party in Brentwood last night.

Having stashed the Mexican valise and the yarn painting forward, the stewardess came back down the aisle, not looking happy with Hollywood. The stewardess went to the rear of the cabin and spoke to the flight deck on the intercom, the in-plane phone in the corridor just behind me. Finished with the flight deck, the stewardess came forward and surveyed the cabin. She looked at my attaché case on the aisle chair.

"That will have to go under your seat during takeoff, sir."

I put the attaché case under the seat in front of me. The stewardess smiled. She was dark and pretty. Named Dominique. Smart, junior in grade, didn't mind having a good time—not a bad girl to work with. After she got used to the idea, a bomb wouldn't be that much more trouble than a yarn painting or a yellow Mexican valise.

One more passenger came onto the plane from the tail stairs. He took the vacant seat just in front of me. A couple more entered through the forward door. To this point I had seen no member of the team, no one I knew. Nor, as St. Cloud had said, would I. Now Dominique was back on the intercom to the flight deck. Then she disappeared into the short passage between the passenger cabin and the aft door. There came the hydraulic whine of the tail stairs being drawn into the plane's belly. The stewardesses forward closed the port door, locked it, and the generator truck stationed by the starboard wing uncoupled and pulled away. The idling Pratt-Whitneys came to life and the plane eased forward, turned onto a lateral strip and taxied toward the east/west runway. One of the forward stewardesses got on the cabin phone and told us what flight we were, where we were bound, what time we were due in San Francisco. The weather we would find there, the captain's name, thanking us, finally, for flying PSA. As Dominique and another stewardess moved along the aisle seeing that all seats were forward, belts fastened, carry-on luggage stashed under the seats, meal trays clamped to the seat backs, the two forward stewardesses went through the emergency drill. Oxygen masks, emergency exits amidship, how the seat cushions could serve as life preservers if we had to ditch in the Pacific. A bell came from the flight deck, followed by the captain's voice asking the attendants to take their seats. Three steward-esses sat forward. Dominique came to the rear of the cabin, pulled a jump seat from the wall just behind me and buckled up. The 727 had come to the east end of the runway. The captain held our position on the lateral strip as an incoming plane swept by, touched down five hundred yards down the runway. Then the captain turned the 727 onto the runway, hit all three throttles ahead full thrust, and we were pushed back into our seats by acceleration. Five thousand feet of concrete and vibration and the machine rotated. The cabin pitched back, steep, and we were in the air.

Two chimes came over the cabin speaker, the seatbelt and no-smoking signs went off, and two stewardesses, Dominique from the rear, another stewardess coming from forward, were in the aisle, taking orders for drinks. The two remaining girls disappeared into the forward caterer's galley to prepare the drink trolleys. Dominique came to the rear of the cabin, writing orders on a pad. As she spoke to the woman across the aisle, I reached under the seat and drew out the attaché case. I put the case on my lap, opened it so that the lid shielded the flares and wires and batteries and transistor radio guts from view. When Dominique turned to me I said I would like a beer and handed her the note I had typed on one of the display machines in the Santa Monica Sears. If Dominique had looked at the note, she would have read:

"I have a bomb. Sit down beside me and do exactly as I say."

But Dominique gave me an icy smile, put the note in her skirt pocket and turned to take drink orders from the passengers sitting in front of me. And I stared without hope at the San Fernando Valley falling away below. That I would be taken for some airborne Romeo was not one of the contingencies I had planned for.

Dominique worked the aisle forward to amidship, where she met the other stewardess taking drink orders. The two went to the head of the cabin and disappeared into the caterer's galley. There then passed five of the longest minutes I had ever known. If Dominique took the note from her pocket now, read it in the caterer's galley, where she could not see me, see the case and the fake bomb, any number of things could happen. All of them bad. The five interminable minutes passed, then Dominique, with drink tray in hand, came from the caterer's galley. Her lips were set in a professional smile. No fear in her eyes.

Dominique came to the rear of the plane. She served drinks to the director and the starlet, those across the aisle, working her way aft till only my beer and the double gin for the woman across the aisle remained on the tray. Dominique handed the woman her large gin, then turned to me with the beer. I did not take it. I spoke to the stewardess as evenly as I could:

"Dominique, would you please read the note I gave you."

The professional smile was gone. "Sir, I'll be with you as soon as I serve the other passengers."

I held the case in my lap, the lid cocked so that she could not see into the case, my hand inside the case. "Dominique, put your hand in your right pocket. Take the note out and read it. Now."

The girl's eyes went to the case on my lap, the open lid, my hand inside the case, and her eyes went dull. Her hand went into her pocket, she brought out the note. Her eyes went to the words I had typed. She looked at me. The hand holding the note was trembling. Just slightly, just enough. And Dominique sat in the seat by me, the beer in one hand, the tray and the note in the other.

I said to the girl: "Dominique, I'm going to tell you many things in the next few minutes. You don't have to remember everything. I'll be repeating it all so that you won't forget. The first thing I want you to do is remain calm. I am a very serious man, but I am not here to harm anyone. As long as you and the captain and the rest of the crew do exactly as I say, no one will get hurt. Is that understood?"

The girl replied in a small dry voice: "Yes."

I turned the case on my lap and pulled back the lid. "I have a bomb in this case, Dominique. Look at it." The girl's head turned. She looked inside the case and I turned it away. "Now, if you follow my instructions exactly, no one will get hurt. But if you or anyone else in this plane does not do as I say—*exactly*—then I will blow us all from the sky. Is that clear, Dominique?"

"Yes. It is." The girl licked her lips. She looked forward, fighting back panic, her mind clearing so that she would do exactly as I said.

"Now, I am going to tell you this twice. Once now, and once when you get on the intercom to the flight deck. All right?"

The girl nodded. "Yes."

"All right. I have a bomb and I am taking control of this plane. No one is to leave the flight deck. No member of the crew other than you is to come to the aft section of the plane. If anyone leaves the flight deck or any crew member approaches us, I will blow us up. The captain is to turn on the seat-belt sign and all passengers are to be told to remain in their seats. And the rest of the cabin crew are to be told to remain in the forward section of the plane. That done, the captain is to stay on course for San Francisco. I will be passing on further instructions as soon as the captain acknowledges by turning on the seat-belt sign and making the announcement I have just told you. Now, you don't have to remember all this. I will be repeating it to you as you speak to the captain on the intercom. All right?"

"Yes."

"Good. Now reach behind you and bring the intercom phone forward. You can do it without standing."

The girl reached back and brought the intercom phone forward. She held it to her ear. "What's the captain's name again?"

"Frank Hightower."

"Good. When Frank comes on the phone, you repeat after me, word for word: Frank, there is a man on the plane with a bomb. If we do not do exactly as he says, he will blow us from the air. Got it?"

"Yes," said the girl. Then she tensed, looked forward toward the flight-deck door. Then she said into the phone: "Frank, it's Nicky. Frank, there's a man on the plane. He has a bomb. If we don't do exactly as he says, he will blow us from the air."

Five seconds passed, ten, then the seat-belt signs flashed on. Another ten seconds and the captain's voice came on the cabin speaker. We were encountering some clear-air turbulence. The passengers were asked to remain in their seats.

The plane was mine.

PSA flight 188, Hollywood-Burbank to San Francisco, landed at San Jose International at two thirty-five p.m. The San Jose tower had been radioed in flight and runway 3 was cleared of all traffic, incoming and outgoing, for the landing. The captain brought the plane in from the south and ran it to the north end of runway 3. Beyond the runway, to the north, were the tiered approach guide lights and a chain-link fence. Beyond the fence lay a plowed field. No roads, buildings, trees or any other obstruction or cover or diversion. Just a hundred acres of turned earth.

At the end of runway 3, the captain swung the 727 ninety degrees west and stopped. He kept the door to the flight deck closed, the Pratt-Whitneys at throttle back, as he had been instructed. Holding ninety degrees across the foot of runway 3, I could see the plowed field from the starboard windows and, to the left, a half mile away, the San Jose terminal. During the flight the captain had announced to the passengers that flight 188 was being diverted from San Francisco, and would be landing at San Jose. At San Jose all passengers would be departing the plane. They would leave all carry-on luggage behind. Nothing to worry about, the passengers had been told, flight 188 would be continuing to SFO after a short delay. Maybe some of the pros on board, salesmen, businessmen who put in a couple hundred flight hours every year, knew something was not right with flight 188, but most of the passengers seemed to think that the problem, the emergency, lay at SFO, forty-five miles to the north.

Once the 727 had made the foot of runway 3, holding ninety degrees across the strip so I could see the length of runway 3 through the port windows, Dominique lowered the tail stairs. An announcement came, telling the passengers they would be departing by the aft exit. Aside from some bitching about leaving yarn paintings and Mexican valises, the passengers went off the plane quickly and quietly. By now, with the plane parked as far from the terminal as possible, with the man with the attaché case in his lap and the frightened stewardess sitting in the last row, the pros among the passengers had taken control and were able to convince the Hungarian director, the starlet, a couple other loudmouths, that they were well off the plane, no matter how far they had to walk, what they left behind.

When the passengers had gone off the plane, hiking along runway 3 toward the terminal, Dominique spoke to the other stewardesses on the cabin speaker. They were to come to the aft of the cabin one at a time. Joyce came down the aisle first. She was told to go down the tail stairs and follow the passengers as they straggled up runway 3 toward the terminal. Then came Pam and she went down the stairs and off the plane. Then the last stewardess, Roberta, chief of crew, came down the aisle. Roberta was told to sit across the aisle from Dominique, in the seat vacated by the woman who had drunk her gin neat. I told Dominique to hand the intercom phone across the aisle to Roberta. When Roberta had the phone to her ear, I said:

"Roberta, you are going to be the intermediary between the terminal and the plane. Dominique and Frank and the first officer and the flight engineer will be staying on the plane. Roberta, if you and the people in the terminal do exactly as I say, no harm of any sort will come to Dominique or Frank or any of the flight crew. I want to show you something, Roberta. Dominique, I want you to stay perfectly still. Keep your hands in your lap and do not move." I turned the case so that the stewardess across the aisle could see the fake bomb, then turned the case away. "If you and the people in the terminal do not do exactly as I say, Dominique will die for certain and, since we will be moving forward in the cabin after you have left, it's very likely that the three officers in the flight deck will be killed as well. Roberta, I am not a madman or any sort of lunatic. I am, in fact, a very reasonable man—*so long as I am not fucked with.* Do you understand what I'm saying, Roberta?"

The stewardess across the aisle nodded. "Yes, I do."

I looked at the stewardess sitting beside me. "Dominique, you can breathe now." No one was amused. I returned to the senior stewardess. "Roberta, I am in this simply for money. Except for a short hop, which I will be explaining in a minute, I don't want PSA's plane. I'm not going to Cuba or Mexico or anything like that. And, except for a brief employment of Frank and the boys on the flight deck, I don't want to have anything to do with any of the crew. Once the people in the terminal have done exactly as I have said and you have brought me exactly what I want, Dominique will be released. Once Frank and the flight crew have done exactly as I say, they will be free of me. Are you with me so far, Roberta?"

"Yes, I am."

As Roberta spoke, Dominique turned her head toward the senior stewardess. She looked past her, out the port windows toward the terminal. A red emergency vehicle was coming along runway 3, toward the plane. Not coming full out, but coming fast enough to scatter the stragglers among the passengers. If I hadn't been upset at the sight of the emergency vehicle, I would have faked it. My fear brought us together. When I sat up in my seat to follow the approaching red truck, Dominique flinched. When I spoke to Roberta, quick and edgy, she hung on every word.

"Roberta, get on the phone to Frank—*now*! You tell him I want that fucking truck stopped—*now*!"

Roberta's voice cracked on the intercom phone: "Frank, tell them to stop that goddamn truck!"

The red truck came another hundred yards toward the plane, then the driver hit the brakes, sliding the truck to a stop across the runway. Maybe the driver hadn't intended to run all the way to the plane, he had been instructed to stop just where he stopped, three hundred yards short of our position, but still his timing was good. Roberta, Dominique, we all felt better. That what we said might have some control over the real madmen—the San Jose TAC Squad, the FBI, airport security—who had by now gathered in the terminal, aching to unleash their high-powered rifles and dogs and tear gas and who knew what other tools of terror they had accumulated to deal with hijackers.

With the truck stopped, I sat back in the seat. Dominique breathed and Roberta took the phone from her ear. She held it to her chest.

We waited, no one moved, then I said: "You see the problem we face, Roberta. We have to convince the people in the terminal that they are not in charge. I am. We have to make them understand that they are the ones endangering Dominique's life. That she's going to be fine if they do exactly as I say. When you go to the terminal, Roberta, do you think you can get this point across? That they have to do exactly as I fucking say."

"Yes, I can."

"Good. Now, Roberta, I want you to get on the phone to Frank and thank him for stopping the truck. And now I want the emergency vehicle to turn around and go back down the strip to the terminal. Runway three is going to remain clear of all traffic. There will be no more vehicles of any sort entering runway three. There will be no aircraft of any sort landing or taking off from runway three. As of now, runway three is closed." I turned my head to the window behind me, the plowed field beyond the chain-link fence. "And there will be no FBI agents out riding tractors this afternoon. That field remains clear. Now get on the phone, Roberta, and tell Frank to pass that message on to the people in the terminal."

The senior stewardess raised the phone and gave the flight deck the message exactly as I had given it to her. Then she took the phone from her ear. We sat without speaking till the emergency vehicle turned and went back as it had come, down runway 3 toward the terminal.

"Perfect. Now, Roberta, this is what I want. Three parachutes. Pull-cable-activated. I know there's a sky-diving club at the airport, so I don't want any stalling on this. And I don't want any funny stuff with the chutes. I will check out all three chutes once they are aboard. All three chutes had fucking better work. Understood?"

"Yes."

"Now, in addition to the chutes, I want two hundred and fifty thousand dollars in twenty-dollar bills. These bills are to be placed in a lightweight suitcase. Twelve thousand five hundred bills—it doesn't have to be that large. And I don't want any tricks with the case the money will be in. You will be opening the case, Roberta, before you bring it on the plane. If anybody has any cute ideas about putting a tear-gas canister in the case, you will be the first to know. Is that understood?"

"Yes."

"Good. Both Bank of America and Crocker have branches at the airport. Between them they will have more than enough money here, at the airport, to meet my demand. I don't want any stalling. No running downtown to find marked bills. I don't want any fucking around on this point. All right?"

"Yes."

"I want you to give this message to Frank now. And when I release you, I want you to give the same message to the people in the terminal. Just to be sure that either you or Frank don't get something wrong. All right?"

"Yes. Do you want me to tell Frank now?"

"Yes, I do."

Roberta raised the phone and spoke to the flight deck. She told them about the parachutes and the money. Then the senior stewardess stopped. Her face went hard. She paled. Her eyes stayed dead on the case in my lap. "No. Please, don't. Frank, this is very, very serious." She paused, listened, then took the phone from her ear. "I think I had better talk to the people in the terminal soon."

"We'll get you there as quick as possible, Roberta. But there are a few more details to go over before you go. Now, the people in the terminal will have one hour to get the chutes and the money together. Plenty of time. It's three o'clock now. Let's make the deadline four-thirty. OK?"

"Yes."

"At exactly four-thirty, Roberta, you will emerge, alone, from the terminal. You will be pushing a baggage cart. The three chutes and the case with the money must be visible in the cart. No guns or anything funny stashed in the cart. You will push the cart along runway three to the plane. You will stop the cart just behind the port wing, so I can see you from any of the rear windows. You will then take off your jacket and turn full circle. Sorry about this little striptease, Roberta, but I can't take any chances you might try and bring a weapon on the plane. Oh yeah, and your hat. You will take your hat off too. That done, you will bring the chutes, one by one, up the tail ramp and into the plane. Then the case. And don't forget to open the case on the strip—where I can see it. These items delivered, you will leave the plane and go back as you came, down runway three. I will then check out the chutes and the money. If everything is exactly what I have asked for, Dominique will leave the plane. And Roberta, no lady FBI agents in PSA uniforms. It had better be you."

The senior stewardess nodded. "It will be."

"All right. Now, when you leave the plane, Roberta—in about two minutes—Dominique and I will be going forward. I am going to take the bomb I have in this case and fasten it to the flight-deck door. The trigger in this bomb is a circuit-breaker device. Do you know what that is, Roberta?"

"No, I don't."

That was good. I had been counting on hubby not being an electrician, that the stewardesses weren't handy around the house. "It means, Roberta, that the bomb is activated by breaking a circuit, rather than completing one. In simple terms, if Frank or anyone on the flight deck attempts to open the door while the bomb is fixed to it, the circuit will be broken and the bomb will detonate. I will also have wires running to where Dominique and I will be sitting and I'll be able to detonate the bomb from there. If I hear anyone on the flight deck opening a cockpit window, I will detonate the bomb. It also means that if anyone is so fucking foolish as to try and shoot me, and I fall or make any sudden moves, the circuit will be broken and the bomb will detonate. It's a very sensitive device, Roberta. It has a hair trigger. It will be advisable not to get me excited about anything. For any reason. OK?"

"Yes. OK."

I looked at my watch. "All right. Three-ten. Call Frank. Tell him you're leaving. Everything's OK here. Dominique is staying here with me. She'll be fine as soon as everything I want is delivered. Any questions? Got everything straight?"

"Yes, I think I have."

"All right. Go on. Call Frank. Tell him see you later. Nobody fucks up, I'll have you all back together before the bars close tonight. Go on."

The senior stewardess put the phone to her ear and did exactly as she had been told.

During the afternoon a bank of storm clouds rose from the Pacific. The sky to the west had gone like night by four-thirty. That hour—riot squads, military vehicles, fire and emergency and crash trucks gathering at the terminal—had gone long. Too long. Too much time for the madmen in their terminal to grow madder. But I had to have dark for what I would do.

After Roberta left, Dominique and I went forward in the cabin. I put on surgical gloves, took the device from the case and taped it to the flight-deck door. I ran wires here and there, taping everything, the tape and wires squared and efficient, looking lethal. That done, I taped the peephole on the flight-deck door and Dominique and I settled down. I put Dominique in a forward aisle seat. I took one of the jump seats in the forward bulkhead wall. I had told Dominique to have the captain cut the number two engine. To keep the starboard and port engines running. Leave them at idle for a quick spool-up and takeoff if the waiting got to be too much for the madmen at the terminal. The 727 had been tanked up at Burbank. I ran the figures through my head. Ten thousand nine hundred gallons from the get-go. The engines sucked a thousand plus per hour in normal flight. By now, after the hour-and-a-quarter flight from Burbank, we had at least eight thousand gallons left. An hour idle on the ground would bring it down another five hundred. Plenty left for the short ride I had planned.

Dominique took up the forward intercom phone every ten minutes and spoke to the flight deck. She told them that she was fine, that the hijacker was calm, that she would remain fine and the hijacker calm as long as the riot squads and snipers and armored personnel carriers and emergency vehicles were kept back, well away from the plane and runway 3. No planes or vehicles came onto runway 3. No one came near the plowed field beyond the runway's end. Little men in camouflage and olive drab dashed about the terminal, brandishing rifles and bullhorns, their vehicles of war and disaster circling and forming and reforming, but no one came near the plane or runway 3 and we waited for four-thirty and dark.

At four twenty-eight a figure in a PSA stewardess' uniform came out of the terminal building. The figure pushed a bright yellow baggage cart. As the figure came onto runway 3, I saw a dark bulk in the yellow baggage trolley. The figure came along runway 3. It was a woman. Then, a hundred yards or so short of the plane, I saw the woman was Roberta and that the cart carried an overnight bag and three parachute packs. Roberta wheeled the cart to a point just aft of the port wing. There she took the three parachute packs and the small bag from the cart and placed them on the runway. Forgetting her pirouette and striptease, forgetting to open the suitcase, Roberta took up one of the chute packs and came to the rear of the plane and came up the tail stairs and placed the chute pack just inside the cabin rear door. Roberta looked forward, the length of the cabin, and saw that Dominique was there. That the device was taped to the flight-deck door. She spoke the length of the cabin to us. The chutes, the money, everything I had asked for was there. Then she turned and went down the tail stairs and in three trips brought the two remaining chutes and the small bag with the money onto the plane. That done, Roberta stood by the aft bulkhead. She looked toward us, as if she had something to say, but I called out before she could speak and Roberta turned and left the plane and walked back up the runway.

The sky beyond the runway and the terminal was like night. The lights from the terminal and the men and the vehicles gathered around the terminal showed against the black wall of the storm like players on a stage, a dress rehearsal in a vast empty auditorium.

When Roberta had gone down the runway, I turned

to Dominique. She was more afraid now than she had ever been. Even at the first.

"Dominique, I want you to remain calm. We're almost home and you're almost off the plane. The only thing left for you to do is to check the bag with the money. I'll take care of the chutes. Now, go back and open the bag with the money. Have a look and tell me what you see. Then close the bag. And Dominique, don't even think about leaving the plane before I tell you. We're all so close to getting out of this unharmed, it would be foolish to lose it now. Ready?"

"Yes," the girl said.

"All right. Go on. Let's get this over with."

The stewardess rose and walked the length of the cabin. She knelt by the overnight bag, worked the latches and opened the bag. "There's money in the bag," she said.

"Twenties?"

"Yes. What I can see."

"Anything else in the bag?"

The girl shook her head. "Not that I can see."

"Good. Now close the bag and latch it." The girl closed the bag and pulled the zipper shut. "Now go to the rear intercom phone and tell Frank you are leaving the plane. Tell him to restart the number two engine. When you leave the plane, Dominique, I want you to walk off the runway. There. So that Frank can see you from the starboard window. When Frank sees you, that you are clear of the afterthrust, I want him to turn the plane onto the runway and take off. Immediately. I'll take care of the ramp and rear door. All right. Go on."

Dominique went to the rear intercom. She spoke to the flight deck. She put the phone back in the wall, turned and went to the rear exit and went down the tail stairs without looking back. As she touched the runway, the number two engine came to life.

I went quickly to the rear of the plane and hit the tail ramp lever. The rear stairs pulled up into the belly of the plane. I closed the rear bulkhead door, locked it. With the surgical gloves still on, I went to the rear intercom. When Dominique appeared off the end of the runway, I spoke to the flight deck:

"Turn the plane, Frank, and take off."

"Roger," said the voice on the phone. "Where we going, buddy?"

"Up. Get this fucking crate moving."

"Right," said the voice. "San Jose, this is PSA one eight eight clearing for takeoff—"

"You don't have to clear. Just get this fucking thing in the air!"

"Right."

The plane's engines rose and the plane revolved slowly left till it was in line with the runway. The three Pratt-Whitneys were pushed full thrust and the plane surged forward. As the plane ran down the runway, I looked to the north. A couple dozen San Jose squad cars, CHP black-and-whites were lining the highway beyond the field. Dozens of men came from behind the cars, rising to follow the plane with their rifles. The plane was accelerating, hurtling down the strip. The San Jose terminal passed on our left. More men crouched behind jeeps, squad cars, crash trucks, all tracking us with their rifles. The plane eased off the ragged strip and went smooth and quiet into the air. Its nose turned up, sharp, pointing into the black wall of the storm to the southwest.

I stayed flat on the floor, holding onto a seat armrest, till the cabin began to level. Then I rose and went to the phone.

"Good job, Frank. Now I want you to take us up to five thousand and enter the normal San Jose holding pattern. Keep us there till you hear from me."

The voice came over the phone: "Damn, buddy, you got us a little low on fuel this afternoon. We're down to twenty-eight percent. Where the hell we going?"

"Frank, don't bullshit me. You've got sixty-five percent if you've got an ounce. Plenty to get us all where we're going. Now, I want you to depressurize the cabin, Frank. I'm going to be opening the tail ramp in a couple minutes. I don't want any pressure locks in the cabin making it hard on me. I'll be jamming open one of the sink drains, Frank. It's going to be singing if the cabin's not depressurized. All right?"

"Right," said the voice from the flight deck.

"And just the cabin night lights on, Frank. Switch off the overhead strips."

"Right."

"What's the weather front doing, Frank?"

"Coming in."

"Good. Now get us up to five thousand and hold, Frank."

"Right."

I put down the phone, blocked open the rear toilet door with one of the chute packs and jammed a pencil in the spring sink drain. Air whistled from the cabin down the sink drain. I went back to the phone.

"Frank, there's a lot of air sucking down the sink drain. Now you tell your flight engineer I want the cabin depressurized now and I don't want any more bullshit out of any of you."

"She's coming down now, buddy. Take just a minute."

I listened. The whistling had stopped. I went back to the phone. "Good job, Frank. Now I'm going to be off the phone a couple minutes. Got to check the chutes. When I come back on, I'll have a flight plan for us. Tell the boys in the chase planes they can have another cup of coffee."

The voice laughed, a bit. "Buddy, be a lot easier on San Jose if we held at seven thousand. They got a lot of traffic backed up they got to be moving in."

"Seven is fine, Frank. I'll be back with you in a couple minutes. And Frank, don't try to open the flight-deck door."

"No problem with me there, buddy," said the voice and then the captain spoke to San Jose tower, telling them we would be holding at seven thousand feet till further notice.

I put the phone in the wall, reached under the rear seat and took out the cheap plaid suitcase. I opened the case, took a small tool kit from it and went into the aft toilet. The toilet lights were on, the toilet's wiring tied into the cabin night lights. I unfolded the tool kit and placed it on the washbasin shelf. I took my shoes off and stood on the toilet seat. Head hunched against the low ceiling, I braced one foot against the washbasin shelf and reached up to my door to the sky.

The ceiling panel was a simple tetragon. The forward side wider than the rear, as the toilet tapered back with the curve of the fuselage. An intercom speaker, a foot-by-foot-and-a-half rectangle, was set in the ceiling panel. Two overhead lights, round, about three inches in diameter, were set into the speaker frame. I took a blade screwdriver out of the tool kit, forced the screwdriver into the slot to one side of the speaker frame. I moved the screwdriver up, gently—not to scar the frame or the ceiling panel—and the speaker frame popped free of the ceiling panel. I put the screwdriver in my pocket and eased the speaker and the speaker frame away from the ceiling panel. The speaker and frame came down two feet before the speaker and lighting wires held. I let the speaker and frame hang from the ceiling panel. The ensemble swayed with the banked turn of the holding plane. I took a pair of vise-grip pliers and a penlight from the tool kit. I held the vise-grips in my left hand, switched on the penlight and reached the light into the speaker opening in the ceiling panel. I twisted my body, put both feet on the washbasin shelf and forced my head into the opening. But I could not get both my head and arm far enough into the space above the ceiling to see the ceiling panel latches. I took my head and hand from the hole. I dropped the penlight into my pocket, took the vise-grips in my right hand and reached them into the hole. I felt along the interior edge of the ceiling panel with the fingers that held the vise-grips. I guided the vise-grips onto the first ceiling panel latch, set the vise-grips on the latch, and snapped it open. Then the second. Then I reached as far as my elbow would turn and freed the third latch. I transferred the vise-grips to my left hand and reached into the hole and released the fourth latch. There were two latches remaining. I could not reach them with either hand.

Keeping my head and shoulders steady against the sagging ceiling panel—it could not bend or buckle or show any mark of my entry—I lowered myself slowly from the speaker frame hole. I supported the sagging ceiling panel with both hands and eased the panel down till it was held to the ceiling frame by the two remaining latches. The panel warped away from the ceiling, but it did not bend or crease or show any mark.

I got down from the toilet seat. The ceiling panel had pulled away from the ceiling frame where the two latches held. A sixteenth-of-an-inch crack between panel and frame. I shined the light in the crack and saw the aluminum latches. A wire saw would have cut through the soft aluminum in a matter of seconds. But I didn't have a wire saw or anything like one. In all my shopping I had not dreamed I would ever need one.

I looked at my watch. Seven minutes in the toilet. I had wanted the panel away from the ceiling and the money case stashed in the headspace above the ceiling in ten. I left the toilet, went quickly forward, the length of the cabin, to the closet where the stewardesses stashed their purses. I tore open the four purses and dumped the contents on the floor. I pawed through the crap on the floor till I found a metal nail file. I went back to the toilet, stood on the toilet seat, fit the nail file into the crack between the panel and frame and began sawing into the soft metal of the latch. Fifty, sixty strokes and the nail file cut through the first latch. I twisted the ceiling panel against the last holding latch, stressing the aluminum, and sawed through the last latch in half the time. The ceiling panel was released from the overhead frame.

I lowered the panel till it hung by the light and speaker wires, two feet below the ceiling frame. I then stepped off the toilet seat and breathed. My heart pounded. My hands were shaking, my face and arms, even in the chilled, depressurized cabin, washed in sweat. Ten minutes exactly to free the panel from the ceiling.

I went back up on the toilet seat. I reached up into the hole in the ceiling and pulled myself into the interior of the aircraft. I braced my elbows against the ceiling frame and shined the penlight around the guts of the plane. There was about a cubic meter of space directly above the toilet ceiling. About the same space forward of the ceiling, half of that aft of the toilet where the skin of the plane curved to meet the housing of the number two intake duct. I played the light along the cramped space, looking for handholds. Wire looms and hydraulic lines were fixed to the interior of the airframe, the wires coiled and twisted like ganglia of a gigantic beast. Breaking any of the wires would spot my sanctuary, maybe even bring the plane down. I turned the light directly overhead: a section of the airframe—a strip of aluminum bracing holed like cheese— made the ceiling of the headspace. The airframe was just wide enough to carry the money case, strong enough, I hoped, to hold my weight when I finally pulled myself up into the skin of the plane.

I lowered myself from the hole, went down from the toilet seat and returned to the cabin. Twelve minutes. I took the money bag, returned to the toilet, stood on the toilet seat and fitted the case into the headspace forward of the toilet. I lifted my head and shoulders into the headspace and, bracing one elbow against the ceiling frame, lifted the money bag with one hand. I pushed it inch by inch, till the bag was wedged into the shelf made by the airframe. I lowered myself into the toilet. Fourteen minutes and the money was stashed. Four minutes behind schedule.

I went into the cabin, took up the intercom. "Frank? You still there?"

The voice on the phone laughed, a bit. "Sure am, buddy. You know, we ought to be getting somewhere. Front's bearing in. Going to be getting wet and bumpy in half an hour."

"OK, Frank. One hundred and fifty degrees. Like you're running to Santa Barbara. Keep it at seven thousand. That's fine."

"One five zero. All right."

"Set the flaps at fifteen and ease her back to two hundred and fifty knots."

"Two hundred and fifty knots. Got that."

"I'm going to be opening the tail ramp now, Frank. There's going to be a little drag."

"We can handle it. Sounds like you know this plane pretty good, buddy."

"Yeah, I'm a buff. Frank, I'm going to want to see the light of King City in about twenty minutes. You should be over Watsonville in seven."

"We'll get you there. You thinking about jumping back there?"

"I'm thinking about it."

The voice laughed. "Well, take care. Tail ramp hanging down's going to kick up a lot of turbulence. Might get hairy going out."

"I'll watch it. One five zero, Frank. Back to you in a minute."

"Right," said the voice and I broke the connection.

I went to the starboard windows. Nothing but dark below. Then in the distance, thirty miles to the northeast, were the lights of the East Bay. The lights of San Jose showed through the port windows. No sign of any chase planes. Keeping above us. Maybe somebody below. The western horizon was a black wall. Thirty minutes and there would be enough night to cover a jump, if I had been going to jump. The plane continued its gentle holding bank till its nose came south-southeast and then the cabin rolled level and we were set on course to Santa Barbara.

I went to the aft bulkhead door. Beyond the door was the cave made by the retracted stairs and the hydraulic switch that lowered and raised the stair ramp. I took hold of the safety lever in the bulkhead door. The handle didn't move. I stood away from the bulkhead door,

fighting panic. I went to the rear toilet. The jammed sink
drain was quiet. The cabin was depressurized. No air-
lock holding the door closed. I went back to the
bulkhead door and tried to think. A drag vacuum in the
rear of the fuselage, where the stairs came up into the
plane's belly. Not much maybe, but then forty, fifty
pounds of pressure around the door gasket and ten men
wouldn't have moved it. I went forward through the
cabin to the emergency hold, found an ax in the hold,
and went back to the bulkhead door. I swung the ax at
the window in the bulkhead door. The plastic cracked
and air whistled from the cabin into the rear fuselage. I
took the safety lever in both hands, put both feet against
the bulkhead wall and pulled. The lever popped back,
the bulkhead door sprang open and I was thrown to the
floor. Struck full now by the roar of the engines and by
the cold.

I moved away from the bulkhead door, into the cabin,
away from the screaming jet engines. I tried to warm my
hands, tried to think in the noise and the cold. I didn't
know how far the air turbulence from the stairs, once
they were lowered, would reach into the plane. Not far. I
would probably be all right at the bulkhead door, but
beyond that I didn't know. Only that wherever the
windstream pulled up into the plane's belly there would
be a claw of boiling, sucking wind that would snatch me
out of the aft door.

I took the safety belt from the jump seat in the
bulkhead wall and knotted the strap end of the belt
around my wrist. I gripped the strap and went as far as
the strap would play out, into the cave made by the
raised stairs. I stretched my hand to the hydraulic
switch. My fingers had gone numb in the cold. I had to
watch my hand grasp the switch, then pull it down. I
could not hear the hydraulic ram for the scream of the

jets, but the stairs began to move. They fell away from me like a room shifting on a rolling ship. Then the noise and the cold—what I had known before was nothing—struck me. The windstream came up into the plane and snatched me and threw me to the floor. Everything went dark and quiet, everything falling away, as if I had been pulled out into the night.

I didn't know how long I had been out. Five seconds maybe. The stairs were just lowering into place, the plane lugging down, yawing, being pulled toward earth by the drag made by the lowered stairs. I stayed hard on the floor till the stairs were fully lowered and the turbulence was gone from the cabin. There was a strange stillness in the tail assembly now, where the stairs had been. The stillness pulled at me, drawing me more surely than the turbulence of the windstream toward the black portal in the tail of the plane.

I went on my hands and knees away from the door made by the lowered stairs. I tried to unknot the safety belt from my wrist, but my fingers would not move. I took the knot in my teeth and tore at the strap around my wrist, like a beast caught in a trap, till the strap came away from my wrist and I could crawl back into the cabin.

I forced my hands under my arms. I beat them against the floor. Nothing. I tore my shirt open and put my hands against my flesh and went forward to the caterer's galley. I took both dead hands and turned the dial of the electric coffee warmer. When the plate had heated, I held my hands to it. I warmed one till I could not stand the pain, then the other, till my fingers moved. I then went to the forward intercom, took the phone with both hands and fitted it between my ear and shoulder.

A voice came on the phone: "How's it going back there, buddy?"

"Little chillier than I thought it'd be. Got any mittens up there?"

"Warm as toast here. Open the door and we'll have you peeled down to your skivvies in a couple minutes."

I laughed, a little. "How's the plane flying, Frank?"

"No problem there. Little bumpy when the ramp first came down, but we got it sorted out."

"Still on course?"

"One five zero. We ain't going to make Santa Barbara, but we figured you probably didn't really care."

"You're doing just fine, Frank. What's the altitude?"

"Nine thousand. We can take her down to seven, but it's a little smoother up here."

"Nine's fine, Frank. I'm going to be leaving your company in a couple minutes. Give me a quarter hour. Got to test the chutes."

"We'll probably feel you go off." Somebody said something in the cockpit, then the voice came back: "Pretty rough country down there. Coming up on Big Sur."

"That's fine. Seen any chase planes?"

"T-15 drifted by couple minutes ago."

"OK. Give me fifteen minutes, Frank, then I'll be out of your hair. Frank, I'll be defusing the bomb before I go. So you don't have to worry about hitting a bump coming down."

The voice laughed. "I'll be walking this baby down."

"All right. I guess that does it. You won't be hearing from me again. Thanks for the lift."

The voice laughed. "Listen, buddy, everybody here on the flight deck, all three of us would like to say we hope you break your fucking neck."

We laughed and I hung up the phone.

I went to the caterer's galley, warmed my hands on the electric plate, then went to the rear of the cabin.

To the parachutes. One was a blue-green nylon backpack—Air Force. The other two were skydiving sports packs. One orange, the other black. I took the Air Force chute to the bulkhead door. Except for swirling bits of paper and debris, a haze of dust in the air, the cabin, as far as the bulkhead door anyway, was free of turbulence. I placed the Air Force chute on the floor at the bulkhead door, went to my knees behind the chute and pushed it to the head of the lowered stairs. When I saw the windstream grasping at the harness, I stopped. I tore the safety cable from the back of the chute, turned the chute up, its back toward the open bay. I pulled the ripcord. Nothing. I pulled the ripcord handle again. A third time—still nothing. The bastards, they were willing to chance losing a four-million-dollar plane and three crew members for two hundred and fifty thousand dollars.

I reached over the top of the pack, opened the snaps running down the pack center and yanked hard at the sides of the pack. The silk canopy exploded from the pack. The windstream yanked the chute from my hands. The canopy twisted madly into the black void.

I went back into the cabin, working quickly against time and cold. I opened the plaid case I had brought on the plane, took out a blanket—a blanket when I needed a thermal jumpsuit—and a small kit containing epoxy glue, a plastic water bottle that I would empty and refill, and the other things I would need in leaving the plane and went into the toilet. I stood on the seat and reached the blanket and the kit into the headspace above the toilet ceiling. I warmed my hands under my arms, then returned to the cabin. I took up the orange skydiving pack and went to the stair portal. I faced the chute pack to the door, pulled the safety pin from the ripcord and pulled the ripcord. There was an explosion, the chute was torn from my hands by the windstream. The chute canopy blossomed five hundred feet below. One dud, one good one.

I kicked the third chute away from the toilet door, leaving it packed and on the plane, took the plaid suitcase I had brought on board and flung it out the stair portal. I left the fake bomb and the attaché case as they were and went into the toilet and closed the door, not locking it. I took the tool kit from the washbasin shelf, closed it, took my shoes from the floor, stood on the toilet seat and reached the tool kit and the shoes into the headspace above the ceiling. I went off the toilet seat, wiped the washbasin shelf and searched the toilet. I could not leave anything I needed, any evidence of my work, behind. I wiped the toilet seat, looked around the toilet a last time, saw nothing, went up on the toilet seat in my socks and pulled myself up into the space above the ceiling.

I fit the blanket, water, tool kit and escape kit into a niche in the headspace, then twisted my body and took hold of the wires to the toilet lights and the speaker and pulled the ceiling panel into place against the ceiling frame. I worked the ceiling panel with my free hand till it fit solid into the ceiling frame. Holding the ceiling panel in place by the wires with my left hand, I snapped the nearest panel latch with my right. I closed the second latch on that side of the panel. I felt along the next nearest side of the panel, found the latches in the dark, closed them. I took the wires in my right hand, twisted and reached my aching left arm across the panel, stretching, not placing any weight on the ceiling panel, and closed the first latch on the far side of the panel.

I took my hand back and breathed. I rested my arm, still holding the panel by the wires. I shifted my weight toward the edge of the ceiling panel, reached out, stretched, felt the latch with my fingers, brought the latch up, then toward me, then down against the clasp on the panel. I rested, my numbing fingers still on the latch, then I eased the final latch back, back—till it snapped in place. Firm. Then I released the wires and the speaker frame lowered two feet into the toilet. I took the twin tube of epoxy glue from the kit, twisted the caps off in my teeth, reached the tubes of glue down through the hole in the ceiling and carefully spread glue around the speaker frame, where it would come flush to the ceiling panel. When the glue was spread, I took the speaker wires and pulled the speaker frame up to the ceiling panel, fitting the frame into the hole in the ceiling panel. When I felt the speaker frame fit firm into the hole, I pulled hard, up, on the speaker wires and held the speaker frame tight against the ceiling panel. One minute, two, three—I pulled on the wires till my arms burned, then pulled till they began to shake, then pulled till I could no longer hold the wires. Then, as my hands were slipping from the wires, I prayed. When the speaker frame stayed firm in the ceiling panel, I leaned back in the headspace and breathed.

A razor of light showed on the far side of the panel, where I had cut the latches away, but the other three sides of the panel were closed tight against the ceiling frame. How it looked from below I did not know. But then there was nothing I could do now but wait and see.

The plane landed, was searched and searched again. The first to come was the bomb crew. The sirens of their crash trucks surrounded the plane. Then there was silence. Then came the soft sounds of the bomb crew entering the plane. Half an hour and the bomb crew left the plane. Quiet, slow, knowing they had a fake in their steel box, still moving as if it were real. The bomb cleared, the plane was overrun. FBI, local TAC squad, airport security—they stormed the aircraft, their military commands and countercommands carrying into my niche in the skin of the plane. The first search was made and the men left the plane. The plane was moved and the searchers came again. Now they had dogs. The animals whined as they went through the cabin. I thought of dogs and how foolish I had been to think that no one else would imagine my plan, that I would not jump, that I would stay on the plane.

The men and the dogs came to the aft toilet. The door opened. The dogs' whining came to me clearly now. They had my scent, the aft toilet reeked of it. Now one of the searchers would stand on the toilet seat. He would reach up, push against the ceiling panel. Feel the sixteenth-inch give in the panel, where I had cut the latches. As I waited, not breathing, I thought of the man somewhere, in the command center in the airport, who was thinking as I thought. *He hasn't jumped. He has stayed on the plane.* But then the dogs, trained to scent bombs, not men, were taken from the toilet. The dogs and the men left the plane and I was alone again. And there was no one anywhere who thought as I had. That I would stay on the plane. That I had not jumped.

I waited an hour. Sixty minutes of silence from the plane. Then I shifted my legs, grasped the airframe above my head, pulled myself up, and eased my legs out over the ceiling panel, careful not to touch the panel. I reached my feet to the far side of the panel, till my heels touched the frame, still not touching the panel. I eased myself down, my weight on my buttocks on the airframe forward of the panel. And I leaned back in the head-space. I moved my shoulders and arms back inch by inch, till I was lying flat in the headspace. Midnight. I had been in the headspace five hours. It had passed like a minute. I had felt nothing. But now that my fear was gone, I began to suffer. My legs cramped from being pressed five hours against my chest. My head was cleaved. My ears throbbed from the altitude change. And now the heat and the foul air in the headspace smothered me. And time, of all the things I suffered in the headspace, it was the lengthening of time that near drove me mad. That near made me kick out the ceiling panel, run from the plane, anything to escape the grinding down of time, till the hands on my watch did not move, till I was begging for them to find me, that these twelve hours would end.

I must have slept sometime near the end, for the plane's movement came to me in a dream. Before I slept I remembered every event in my life. The women I had known, friends, enemies, family, strangers I had passed on the street. I remembered parties, holidays, what we had eaten, what we had drunk. I remembered every year in my life, going back till I remembered flying. The first plane that had taken me into the sky. My Uncle Bob and the old biwing he kept in a shed on his farm. How the plane wound up, hard, the prop before me disappearing but for the blurred circle made by the warning strip. The brakes released, the plane lurching forward, bounding down the dirt road. A house and barns swept off to my right. My father stood at the edge of a plowed field, laughing, waving, calling out something we could not hear. Bob took us into the air. We flew higher and higher. Banking, turning, diving. Then there came a shout from the rear cockpit. I turned and saw Bob laughing, both hands in the air. And I turned forward and put my hands on the stick between my legs and, as

my uncle behind me worked the rudder with his feet, I
flew.

The plane moved. The waiting was over. I would
finish, be free of what I had begun. As the plane was
being towed I brought my knees to my chest, one leg at a
time, till my thighs burned. When the plane stopped I
rested and was quiet. The maintenance men now came
to the plane. Two men worked below me, repairing the
smashed plexiglass in the aft door. Others opened the
access panels to the three engine cowlings. The crew on
the number two engine worked only feet from where I
lay, only the skin of fuselage between us. The maintenance crews left the plane and there was a time of
silence. Then the plane moved again and I exercised
and massaged my legs. The plane stopped and a
cleaning crew came into the cabin. I worked my legs
under the sound of the vacuum sweepers. I stopped only
when a member of the crew came into the aft toilet. The
cleaning crew left the plane, and when the cabin was
quiet, I reached up to the airframe and pulled myself
away from the ceiling panel. Till I was crouched in the
cramped headspace. I waited there thirty minutes, an
hour, fighting down panic. That the plane would not be
put into service for hours, days. That the plane would
never fly again and I would be trapped in this tomb
forever. But then the plane moved again and I knew that
after eighteen hours on the ground the plane would be
back in the air.

The plane was towed a great distance—L.A. International maybe, maybe the flight crew had turned the
plane back to San Francisco. Wherever, the airport was
large and we went for what seemed like miles. The
plane stopped and refueling began. The murmur of the
wing tanks filling passed through the skin of the plane.
The generator truck came and the lights in the toilet

below came on. The crew entered the plane, the stewardesses laughing, and the caterers came. The men
joked with the stewardesses. They all laughed. The
Pratt-Whitneys were started, three beasts waking howl-
ing from their slumber.

Under the noise of the engines I reached up and took
the money case from the airframe, brought it down,
reached the case across the ceiling panel and fit it in the
small headspace where my feet had been. Then came
the hydraulic whine of the tail ramp being lowered. The
rear stairs rumbled and the first passengers came onto
the plane.

And I reached up to the airframe and pulled myself to
my knees and there, like a penitent in prayer, waited for
the three-minute window, from takeoff to leveling at
cruising speed, when I would force my atrophied arms
and legs to action, remove the latches from the ceiling
panel during the acceleration of takeoff—the Pratt-Whitneys screaming—lower myself and the money bag into
the toilet, lock the toilet door, glue the ceiling panel
back in place and pray again that the epoxy glue would
hold. And when the ceiling panel did stay in place, I
would wait again, till the aft stewardess went forward,
then I would enter the cabin, slide my bag under a seat
and join a garrulous passenger. The plane we were on,
the man would say, was famous, the plane C.W. Namier
had hijacked. And the stewardess would come with the
drink trolley, not pleased with the exhausted, unshaven
passenger, so sick he had been in the toilet during
takeoff, who had brought a suitcase aboard he should
have checked, who now had changed seats and now
wanted a beer and had nothing on him smaller than a
twenty.

9

*T*HE NORTH WINDOW showed the Golden Gate, the east the Bay Bridge. It wasn't the Fairmont's penthouse—an Arab emir had that—but it was close. A corner suite on the nineteenth floor. Maybe a proper hijacker would have kept a low profile, taken his battered body and two hundred and fifty grand in twenties back to the Tenderloin, checked into some dump and lived off beer and hamburgers for a couple days, but after twenty-one hours in the skin of the plane, I needed luxury, comfort, the best money could buy. Off the plane at SFO, I had gone to a phone booth and booked the suite at the Fairmont, given them Smith as a name, and a Miami address. The cabbie who took me to Nob Hill got a twenty for his trouble, the only cash I would spend my first day off the plane. I went straight to the Fairmont barber shop, got the works, then checked into the suite. I was in bed as the door was closing on the bellhop. I dialed room service eight hours later, soaked in a bath, ate and drank something that, in my state, could just as well have been hamburgers and beer and slept again, till late afternoon the following day. I ate and drank and bathed for that day, then sent out for newspapers, as many out-of-town editions as Harold's on Geary carried, from the first day the hijack hit the news to today. When the papers arrived, I found the article in the *L.A. Times* that concerned me now, four paragraphs buried in the back pages, then turned to the adventures of C. W. Namier.

The *Chronicle* and *Examiner*, the *L.A. Times*, the *Seattle Post-Intelligencer*, the *Washington Post*, every paper I read and scattered about the floor had C. W. Namier jumping. Not one writer or investigator imagined that, like the purloined letter, the hijacker might have been right under their noses, or in the toilet over their heads, all along. On this, the third day since the hijack, the search for C. W. Namier was tearing through Big Sur. Fifteen thousand square miles of roadless wood and ridge and canyon and mountain, uninhabited but for lone-wolf okies and mountain men, burned-out hippies squatting in canvas lean-tos, and a party of lost backpackers grateful to be come upon by the swarm of search parties, even if they had to endure twelve hours of interrogation proving they weren't C. W. Namier or any of his friends. State cops, FBI, park rangers, the National Guard—an army of two thousand men had converged on this wilderness and were scattered across it and now, into the third day of their search, had found no trace of C. W. Namier but a single parachute.

But then maybe America didn't want to find C. W. Namier. An airborne Robin Hood, Jesse James in the sky, the Scarlet Pimpernel in a 727—the American press, anyway, had taken C. W. Namier to its cold heart. Two recurrent questions were posed by the press. What had happened to C. W. Namier, and, maybe the greater mystery, who was he? The answers to the first were fairly simple. Namier had jumped and was dead or injured in the Big Sur outback or he had, with help from confederates on the ground, escaped. As for Namier's real identity, police switchboards had been flooded with calls from cranks who claimed they were Namier or they knew who he was. A lot of ex-husbands and brothers-in-law sounded just the ticket for some no-account who would lift a jet. I'm sure if Dan Cox had still been alive, somebody in San Mateo would have been on the horn about the Northwestern pilot who had let a soured land deal in Montana lead him to drug smuggling and murder. But even with the testimony from the PSA pilots and stewardesses that the hijacker knew jets and flying, maybe he had been a commercial pilot, there was not a trace of Dan Cox in any of the accounts I read.

When I saw that I was safe for the time being, that no one had come close to solving the mysteries of who Namier was and how he got away, I cracked a bottle of champagne and went through the hijack stories a second time. For amusement. The physical descriptions weren't bad. One paper had me five-seven, another six feet. A pleasant man, said one story, with a nasty smile, countered another. Polite and ruthless. Considerate but cold. And on and on. Of all the bullshit that was printed about C. W. Namier the first two days after the hijack, what amused me most was the pass I had made at Dominique, the stewardess who had remained aboard the plane. I tossed down the paper, lit a cigar, poured champagne and toasted American journalism. Dominique had indeed been a very attractive young woman. Pity I hadn't thought of it at the time.

It was near dark by the time I had finished reading the dozen or so C. W. Namier stories. I sat on the sofa, where I could see both bridges, the Bay and the Berkeley hills beyond, North Beach, Chinatown and the financial district spread below. The bridges sparkled with evening traffic; a freighter eased around Alcatraz, bound for the open sea. When dark came, the lights across the Bay reaching from shore to horizon, I took up the *L.A. Times,* the brief story I had found in the local news pages. Explosion in Venice. House destroyed. Vacant at the time, no casualties. Gas-leak conflagration now believed to have been caused by a bomb. The time of the explosion one thirty-two. About the time PSA flight 188, Hollywood/Burbank to San Francisco, had been riding twenty-two thousand feet over San Luis Obispo.

I reread the *L.A. Times* story, tore it from the paper and considered the view. There was that business unfinished. That Thea and I, Dayton, St. Cloud, even Johnny Kono—he would sooner or later outlive his use—were all living under a death sentence. And there were those already executed. They must be avenged, their killer put down. But there was something beyond vengeance, justice and survival that troubled me. Something else left undone.

I went to the window, looked down on the city. C. W. Namier was everywhere. A hero. A legend. A myth in three short days. Why didn't the man who had made him share this celebration? I went to the bed, opened the suitcase, looked at the stacks of twenties. Two hundred and fifty grand. I closed the case and went back to the window. A 747 was climbing north over the Bay. Arched back steep, as if it might be bound for a star. It wasn't the money or the fame or infamy I wanted. A case of unmarked bills—what should C. W. Namier have asked brought to the plane? I went to the phone and dialed the number of the graceful house in Atherton.

The number rang for five minutes. Nothing. I read the *L.A. Times* story again. I dialed the number a second time, laid the receiver on the table before the couch and let it ring. A little after nine the ringing stopped. I put the phone to my ear. I said Thea's name and the woman released her breath:

"Dan, she's dead."

I saw the dog and the woman frolicking in the yard, the chain lying on the drive, the woman and the dog turning as I spoke from beyond the gate.

"Kat," Thea said. "I'm so sorry, Dan. I'm sorry."

I replaced the phone in its cradle. He wanted us all.

We were in the basement of the Atherton house. Refitted as a den, trophy and game room. Plump buff canvas furniture, a sofa and chairs, thick dark carpet, on the walls photos of Dayton as a flier, the planes he had flown, group portraits of the outfits he had served with. One wall was given to pictures of Thea and her horses. Thea, young, twenty in some of the photos, trim, in English riding habit, her hair tucked under her helmet, jumping her horse over barrier, hedge and fence. A bar in one corner, TV screen set in a bookcase, a pool table, nearly full-size. The heavy glass-top table near us strewn with newspapers, magazines, Mozart playing some-where, the light in the room low, gooseneck lamps curved so that their cowls spotted on the carpet, as if the room had windows and we might be seen.

Thea sat near, on the floor, smoking one cigarette after another. Bits of smoke came from her mouth as she spoke. "I've never heard St. Cloud so—upset. He called this morning and said she was dead. Now he's called back. Just after I talked to you. Now he says she's not. It's not her body in the grave." Thea stubbed out the cigarette. "He seems to think they faked her death. Like yours."

"How did it happen?"

"Her car went into a river somewhere south of Butte." Thea lit a cigarette. Flicked it toward an ashtray. "St. Cloud said she was frightened. She called St. Cloud while you were in L.A. She was at the ranch. Daddy was having her—what? Looked after. I guess she was trying to get away when her car went off the highway. The Gallatin. That's the name of the river."

"When?"

"Three days ago—I think. There was an autopsy. She was buried in Butte. St. Cloud's hometown."

"So St. Cloud has a hometown." I drained my glass, put in on the table, glass touching glass. "This happened three days ago and he just called you this morning."

"He's been somewhere out of touch. Somewhere in the mountains. He's got a friend, a bush pilot who's got a place—the Bitterroots, I think."

"Any way I can get in touch with him?"

"He was in Missoula when he called. Said he would call back when you got here." She stopped. "He's on his way to Kill Devil—Daddy's ranch. He wants you to go with him." Thea looked at me. "Do you think it's possible? That she's not dead." She looked away. "It's just that you don't seem—"

"Upset?"

Thea shrugged. She looked at my empty glass on the table. "Would you like another?"

"One more."

Thea took the glass, went to the bar, made the drink and came back. She put the drink on the glass-top table and sat on the floor. She lit another cigarette and looked at the newspapers on the table. C. W. Namier had even made the front page of the *New York Times*. Thea spoke, looking at the story.

"St. Cloud said another strange thing. That that was you."

"Did he?"

Thea shrugged, smiled. "I thought it might be." She turned the paper to me. "Something about the hijacker being a gentleman."

I smiled. "I didn't read that one."

Thea turned the paper away. "There's something I don't understand. We could have been on that plane. We were in L.A. I don't know the flight number, but we were supposed to take a one o'clock flight from Burbank back to San Francisco."

"You and Dub?"

"Yes. And Daddy too."

I sipped the drink. Put it back on the table. "Daddy too. That's interesting. And you didn't make the flight."

"No. I've never seen Dub drive so crazy. He's usually, well, something of a granny in a car. He tail-ended somebody on the Hollywood Freeway. I don't know, he was upset about the meeting he and Daddy had had the night before."

"The night Creesy was captured."

Thea looked away. "Yes. But it was something else."

"Like what?"

Thea looked across the room toward the wall of flying

photographs. "I think Dub told Daddy he wanted to quit. They had an argument. I don't know—Dub never tells me anything. But when he came in that night, he said something. About us leaving the country."

"And the next morning you had a crackup on the way to the airport."

"Yes. That's right."

"And your father—why didn't he make the flight?"

"I don't know. We had arranged to meet at the airport. When we didn't arrive, maybe he waited. Then took another flight."

"Maybe. Did you know that we were all supposed to be on that flight? PSA one eighty-eight to San Francisco. The whole team."

"No, I didn't know that."

"You didn't know I was supposed to hijack the plane and fly us all to Mexico? Dub didn't tell you that?"

"No."

I took the *L.A. Times* clipping—explosion in Venice—from my pocket and handed it to her. "You see this?"

Thea looked at the article. "No. What does it mean?"

"The address—84 Speedway. That's where St. Cloud and I were holed up the week before the hijack."

"I don't understand."

I turned to the *New York Times* hijack story. "Did you read that the bomb was a fake? That C. W. Namier did his hijack, everything, with nothing but a half-dozen flares and the guts of a transistor radio taped together. That nothing worked."

Thea looked at the headline. C. W. NAMIER STILL MISSING. "Yes. I read that."

"There was another bomb. The one I was supposed to take on flight one eighty-eight for San Francisco. J.K. made that one. It was supposed to be fake too, but I thought it looked just a little too real. So I made my own dud and left J.K.'s device in the house in Venice. In a ground-floor storeroom. Where the L.A. bomb squad say this explosion occurred." I turned the *L.A. Times* article. "You see the time of the explosion? One thirty-two. The flight I was on, the flight you and Dub were supposed to be on—the whole Stokes team was supposed to be on it—PSA one eighty-eight Burbank/SFO was just about over San Luis Obispo at one thirty-two."

Thea took the clipping, held it as if it were a relic that might crumble in her hands. "He was going to kill sixty people to kill us."

I went back. "Looks that way." I waited. "It's nothing new. A guy I knew, a pilot, flew for Allegheny. He went down like that. Except his mad bomber only wanted to ditch his wife. And there was some insurance." I took the clipping from Thea. "At least this has to do with treason. Things like that."

Thea lowered her hands. If I had expected something—fear, panic, disbelief—there was none. She was calm when she asked me what we were going to do.

I went back in the cushions. I had never been so tired. "I don't know. For some reason there doesn't seem much point in going to the FBI, say. People you'd normally contact with a little problem like this. Does there?"

Thea shook her head. "No. We can't go to any of them." She looked across the room. "I've been in touch with a friend in the east. He writes for a newspaper." She looked away. "But I haven't talked to him. I probably won't." She stopped. "There's so much more to tell than this operation."

"Stokes wasn't the first."

Thea lowered her head. Her hair fell across her face. "No. The first was the man we wept for. Remember

those days? When we wept over the men they murdered?" She stopped. I could barely hear when she
spoke again. "I didn't believe my mother at first. I
couldn't believe her. That Americans, respected, respectable men, would kill their own leader. Plan it like a
hunting party. My mother, she was a drunk, mad, anything, I told myself to keep from believing her. But then
later, after my mother was dead—" She stopped, looked
at my glass. "I think I'll have a drink. Want another?"

"If I can have a cigarette. I kicked them on the
plane."

We exchanged pack and glass and Thea went to the
bar. She made the drinks and came back and sat on the
floor. She stubbed out a cigarette she had left burning in
the ashtray.

"There were three teams. The Dimitri team—what
they called the man everyone thinks pulled the trigger.
The B team. The ones who shot him—the man we wept
for. Then there was the executive team. They coordi-
nated the two field teams, kept them separate—not
touching. That was the hardest part. Keeping Dimitri
isolated from what really happened. Daddy did that. He
was also in charge of Fat Boy. The pimp who shot
Dimitri in the police station. Daddy kept Fat Boy quiet.
Cancer. Everyone was quite pleased with how that
went. Cutting the last link between Dimitri and the B
team. It was very, very good. After that, Daddy was
given charge of cleaning up the B team. So many of them
were freaks. I guess it nearly got away from him during
Watergate. Some of the B team members were in that
operation. But Daddy handled all that. Another very,
very good job." Thea stopped, looked at the newspapers
scattered over the low table. "There was one incident I
didn't understand at the time. One of the Watergate team
members, his wife was threatening to talk. She wanted

money. If her husband went to jail, she wanted them all jailed. And then she said something about Dimitri. And then there was a plane crash in Chicago." Thea looked up, at me. "As you said. Nothing really new."

We did not speak for a time. Then: "Your mother knew about this?"

Thea shook her head. "Mother never knew the details." She stopped and did not say anything else.

"Dub?"

"Dub has never told me anything."

I waited. "So you worked for him too."

Thea kept her eyes on me. "No. I just listened." Thea took up a cigarette pack. She crumpled it. "I've got some cigarettes upstairs. Be right back."

Thea left the room. I made another drink and went to the wall hung with her photographs. I made my way from there to Dayton's trophy wall, the display of the planes he had flown, pilots he had flown with. To one side of the display, in the most recent section, the Vietnam War, I found a shot of Dayton and Lane Blackmuir, in borrowed Air Force jump suits, helmets cocked under their arms, standing in front of an F-110. Both men were smiling at the camera. They had just flown or were about to fly.

Thea came down the stairs into the room. She glanced at me standing at the wall of photographs, then sat on the floor near the sofa. She opened a pack of cigarettes, took one out and lit it. I turned back to the photograph of her husband and her father.

"They met in the war?"

Thea smoked, her voice heavy from the smoke. "They met in World War II. To the left. Keep going," she said as I went along the wall. "Second row. About midway down. The Flying Tiger squadron." I found the photograph. Eight pilots standing before a P-40, its cowl carrying the gaping shark grin of the Tigers. I did not see Dayton in the photograph, but Lane Blackmuir was there. The thirty-odd years had scarcely touched him. Except for the eyes. His eyes were bad then. Cruel. He hadn't worked up the suffering yet.

I looked to the other pilots. "Which one is Dub?"

"The boy with the blond hair. Looks white in the picture."

I found the kid with the white hair, kneeling in the front row. It didn't look anything like Dayton. "Where was it taken?"

"China," said the woman.

I turned from the picture of the eight pilots and crossed the room to the couch. I lifted the glass from the table, put it back. I didn't want the drink.

"I didn't know they'd known each other that long."

Thea looked toward the wall of photographs. "Daddy was the squadron leader. Dub was the hotshot. I guess he was very, very good."

I turned from the trophy wall. "They were great pilots."

Thea put out the cigarette. "Yes. Aces."

"So you knew Dub when you were a girl?"

Thea smiled. "No. I had nothing to do with my father while my mother was alive. When we all met—after her death—my father was as much a stranger as Dub." She looked away. "More. Odd how things have been with us." She looked back. "Dub has always been more a father to me, and my father," she said, looking at me, "more like a lover. Possibly the reason that Dub couldn't find the brakes on the Hollywood Freeway." She turned away. "It's all right." She took her glass, rose and went across the room. She made her drink and came back. She put the glass on the glass-top table and sat on the floor. "It doesn't really matter anymore."

I went back in the cushions. Looked toward the dark ceiling. I closed my eyes. I heard the woman say she would wake me when St. Cloud called and I slept.

The room was dark. I was lying on the couch, a blanket over me. The phone was ringing. Thea stood by the phone, her hand on the receiver. The ringing stopped and Thea turned to me.

"St. Cloud," she said. "It's his signal. He'll call back." She came to the couch and sat near me.

"How long did I sleep?"

"Not long."

I put my feet on the floor and sat up. My body ached, burned, was heavy, old and hard. I went back in the cushions.

Thea was quiet, then she said: "Do you want something to eat?"

"No. When will St. Cloud call back?"

"Soon," Thea said, and the phone rang. She lifted the receiver and waited. Then she said: "He's here now. Missoula? All right. I think an afternoon flight might be better. No. I haven't asked him. No. I haven't heard from Dub. He should be calling tonight. I don't know what he has planned. We'll keep in touch the usual way. Yes, that's right. Are you all right? St. Cloud, tell him about it tomorrow. I really don't want to know. There used to be a noon flight to Spokane. Missoula about four. Yes. All right. Bye."

Thea put down the phone and came back to the couch. "I didn't think you could make anything earlier than noon."

"Noon is fine."

"All right. Do you want to stay the night here?"

"I've got to get some things from the hotel."

"I'll get them."

"Just the suitcase. My money." I took the Fairmont

suite key from my pocket and gave it to Thea. "I'm Mr. Smith. I couldn't think of anything else."

Thea turned the plastic paddle in her hand. She looked at the couch. "Are you all right here?"

"I'm fine."

"Do you need anything?"

I said I didn't need anything.

"You should eat something."

"In the morning."

"Do you want to watch TV?"

"Yeah. The news. See if they've found me yet."

Thea smiled. "You do need to sleep." She stood, reached over and tucked the blanket around me. She straightened. "I'll be back in an hour or so." She went to the far wall, turned on the TV and brought a control box to the sofa. "I won't come down when I get back."

"All right."

She stood over me a moment, then went to the stairs and left the room. There was no sound on the TV. I left it silent and was asleep in minutes, long before the ten-o'clock news and the latest word on the C. W. Namier mystery.

"What the fuck you mean you didn't jump?"

"Just what I said. I didn't jump."

"How did you get out of the plane then?"

"I walked off it. Like a paying passenger."

"Bullshit. You jumped. Who'd you have working with you on the ground?"

"Nobody. Look, I stayed on the plane. When all the passengers were off the plane, after I got the money and the parachutes, I took the ceiling panel out of the toilet, climbed up into the headspace above the toilet. I stayed there till the plane was put back in service, then when the plane was in the air, I went back down into the toilet, put the ceiling panel back, walked out into the cabin and joined the passengers."

St. Cloud snorted, cackled. "Unh, not bad. Hunker over and get smart."

What a traveler passing through the Missoula airport men's room would have thought was going on in the end stall—four legs showing under the door, spasms of teletype ticking intersperced with snorts and cackles and wild talk of hijacked planes—I was loathe to imagine, but it was, in fact, nothing stranger than two over-the-hill pilots heating up on badly tramped down cocaine. I leaned over the toilet resevoir and inhaled one of the lines. I leaned back against the stall door while St. Cloud sucked up what was left. St. Cloud swabbed his finger over the toilet top, sucked the finger and the end of the plastic straw, sat on the toilet seat and closed his eyes.

"Crap for cocaine in this town. Fucking crank. Right nostril's sealed up." A smiled worked out on St. Cloud's face. He opened his eyes, red as torn meat. "So J.K.'s bomb went off right on time."

"I put it we would've been about thirty minutes in the air."

"And nobody showed but you."

"That's right, St. Cloud. Seems like everybody knew the plane was never going to land again."

St. Cloud massaged his gums with a forefinger. He eyes rolled over and focused on me. By his own account he had snorted an ounce of coke or speed or whatever white powder you could buy for one-ten a gram in Montana and drank a mixed case of Beam and Smirnoff since Kat's death. The only sleep he had had was a nap he had caught yesterday while he was taking a piss. St. Cloud let his red pig eyes brood on me awhile, like he was wondering what my life would be like with my nose turned upside down, would I drown in the shower? "Don't you fucking miss her?"

I shifted into the corner of the stall. "Yeah. I miss her."

St. Cloud looked at me a full five seconds, then put a hand to one eye, got some moisture and spread it around his face. He then breathed hard and pitched forward. "Shit, let's go kill somebody."

I eased away from the stall door, pulled back the latch and pushed the door open. A traveler was standing at the wash basin, looking at me and the end stall in the mirror. I closed the door. "Maybe we ought to talk about this somewhere else, St. Cloud."

St. Cloud wiped his face, breathed in most of the air in the stall, and stood. "Yeah. We got other matters to tend to. Step at a time. Right? Let's get moving. Make a pitstop in Missoula, then drive over to Butte. They got her buried there. Maybe." St. Cloud pushed past me out of the stall, giving the traveler watching him in the mirror a look to freeze steam.

The traveler wisely made no response and we left the airport terminal and drove into Missoula, the chubby mountain backing the town dusted with snow, the snow burnished and gilded by the setting winter sun. The first stop on St. Cloud's itenerary was more drugs, then we'd see about getting some guns, shovels, maybe a gravedigger or two. See if Kat was really dead. Then we'd talk about driving over to Kill Devil Ranch and skinning Lane Blackmuir. We parked the Trans Am in downtown Missoula and went to a bar that could have been a Hell's Angels rest home. A black plastic cavern with a bar and about forty aging bikers and their mamas fitted in the back corner. The bartender, a round-faced young woman who mixed drinks with the élan of a juggler, tumbled four glasses in front of St. Cloud and me, a pair of double bourbons and a couple of light scotches, this being Happy Hour, two of everything for the price of one. St. Cloud swallowed one of the double bourbons, ordered another, got two, finished the second, got two more and, with glass stacking up in front of him at an exponential rate, looked about at all the muscle, leather, scars, eyepatches and tattoos. "These fairies frighten me to death," St. Cloud observed and had another drink. When the lady bartender went past, St. Cloud sent a gorilla arm over the counter and stopped her. "You seen Rodney the Rat? I'm gonna break his fucking back."

The pretty bartender wheeled around, put her pretty face on the bar. "You mad today, St. Cloud?"

"I'm tired of getting Drāno for one-ten a gram."

The pretty bartender bit her gum and smiled. "I told you everything around here has come a long way."

St. Cloud finished a double. "Yeah. Well, I need something to keep me up. Maybe something to loosen me up. I been tense lately. I think my girlfriend just died in a car crash." He jerked his head at me. "His old lady."

The pretty bartender smiled. "Oh, we're going to have a party." The bartender raised herself from the bar and went into the walk-in cooler. She came back with her purse. She put the purse on the bar in front of St. Cloud and leaned over close, elbows on the bar, looking into the purse. St. Cloud leaned over the purse, as if there were a chess set inside. "The black ones are real nice if you gotta stay up. I made those little purple tabs myself." She smiled at St. Cloud. "It's going to be better than ever, St. Cloud."

St. Cloud scooped his hand into the purse. He stopped. "How much is this gonna hurt?"

"Five bucks a pop," said the bartender.

"Jesus. Five bucks for a fucking pill." St. Cloud took

his fist out of the purse, put it against his mouth and sucked a half-dozen pills off his palm. He finished off another double bourbon and burped.

The pretty bartender looked into the purse and smiled. "This is going to be a very good night for you, St. Cloud."

St. Cloud wiped his mouth. "All right. Trot that goddamn Rodney out."

The bartender put her chin to the bar. "Rodney's out of touch, St. Cloud. A couple nights ago a Ford blew up across the street from Eddie's Club. Rodney did it or was in it. They're not sure yet."

St. Cloud burped again. "OK. Anybody else around here can get me some M-15s and a couple gravediggers? And maybe some dynamite."

The pretty bartender tossed a capsule into her mouth. "You got to go to Butte for dynamite, St. Cloud. You know that. What do you need gravediggers for?"

"I am personally going to kill somebody. Nah, it's a personal matter." St. Cloud started rotating his head, like a helicopter warming up. "Yeah, and I need to get hold of some doctor. Somebody who can do an autopsy."

"You know Doc Blue in Butte, St. Cloud. He can do that."

"Jesus," St. Cloud said, hanging his head. "That one was a couple g's." He pulled his head up. "Yeah, Doc Blue. I'm gonna break his fucking back too." St. Cloud went back on his barstool, the room pitching forward. "Forget it. Just an idea."

The bartender came over the bar close to St. Cloud. She spoke low: "St. Cloud, you've been in California the last couple weeks, right?"

St. Cloud eyed the bartender, swayed forward to stay up with the shifting room. "More or less."

The pretty bartender looked at the drinkers left and right, came in closer. "Are you C. W. Namier?"

St. Cloud jerked his head toward me. "Nah. He is."

The bartender looked at me, smiling. "Really?"

"No," I said. "Not really."

"Shit," St. Cloud said. "Take a look in that suitcase he's mothering. Two hundred and fifty grand in twenties."

The bartender looked at the suitcase that I was clutching rather close, then at me. "How did you get away?"

"He didn't," St. Cloud said. "He stayed on the plane."

The bartender looked from me to St. Cloud. "How did he do that?"

"He took the ceiling panel from the toilet. Climbed up into the airframe. When all the searching was done and the plane was back in the air, he climbed back down and took a seat. Easy as pie."

The bartender smiled, halfway, looked from me to St. Cloud and back. "You guys really are weird tonight."

"You ain't seen nothing yet, sugar," St. Cloud said, peering into the purse.

The bartender turned to the bikers and mamas gathered at the bar. "Hey, this guy is C. W. Namier!"

There came a bored growl from the bikers and mamas and much lifting of glass and the pretty bartender went off to pour a round of hijack doubles on the house. St. Cloud turned his back on the C. W. Namier party and addressed me: "Listen, I hate this shit. When we get over to Butte, maybe you can look at her. She was your wife."

"Let's see if we can do it some other way."

St. Cloud looked at the suitcase in my lap. "All right. Got a dime in there? I'll call Butte."

I took a coin from my pocket, put it in St. Cloud's
hand. He looked at the coin as if it was another pill. His
hand closed over the dime.

"Sometimes I miss that fucking J.K. He would have
gotten off on this shit."

St. Cloud rose, steadied himself, and went toward the
phone.

We left Missoula after seven, well dark, the freeway
lonely as a country lane. St. Cloud drove awhile, then,
when he began questioning how many lanes the freeway
had, I slid under the wheel. An hour, little more, the
freeway curled around Anaconda and its dormant
smelter stack and began climbing toward the Continental Divide. Leaving behind the forests and rivers and
snow-capped peaks of western Montana, the way you
saw the state on a postcard, to enter a landscape of ice
and rock and withered scrub pine and larch that no
traveler in his right mind wanted the folks back home to
know about. The moon rose and the country spread
away. From the height of the freeway it seemed we had
come to a place once inhabited by giants, the wall of the
Divide standing like the rubble of a massive fortress laid
waste by siege. Then the freeway topped a ridge and
pitched down and there lay Butte, rising files and
scatterings of shanty dwellings and derelict factories and
warehouses clinging to the sides of a great rock, the
summit of which had long since been carried away by
the Anaconda Mining Company for the few pounds of
copper salted in every ton of ore. A profound despon-
dency might have fallen over a man who had lived most
of his adult life in California, but the native among us,
his eyes brightened and blood came to his cheeks.
Couldn't you just feel the nasal cartilage, St. Cloud said,

peering nostalgically through the windshield at his hometown, spreading out soft under your knuckles.

We went off the freeway in the Flats, where most everybody who had a job or owned something lived, and went toward Uptown, a grid of gritty streets and dark-brick buildings that would have looked more at ease set in the mining districts of Pennsylvania or Yorkshire. We parked the car in an icy gutter before a café with a front like an armored truck, everything steel and gun portals, stuffed a paper bag with twenties from my suitcase, and locked the rest in the Trans Am's trunk. The café's front room was flanked by two counters, bar to the right, short-order cuisine to the left, both packed, a lot of cross traffic between bar and café. We found the game room in the rear of the café—a keno and basketball pool board and counter against the back wall, a half-dozen poker tables set about in the foreground. Two games were in progress, a big one and a little one, the big table surrounded by a dozen onlookers. St. Cloud had a word with the night bar manager and we joined the crowd around the big table. Play here went along quiet and brisk. Hands folded, cards dealt, bets made and raised and called, somebody winning, somebody losing. As the winner of a modest pot was drawing chips to him, the dealer working up the pack, one of the early folders, a man in his fifties with cold tired eyes strangely magni-fied by rimless glasses, hair slicked back like a twenties matinee idol, looked up at St. Cloud, turned away from his rack of chips and spoke to one of the men behind him. The backup took the player's chair and Doc Blue came out of the crowd and followed us into the bar. Doc Blue saw no problems filling any of our needs, so long as the money was there. All we had to do was tell him what we wanted.

St. Cloud ordered drinks and when they came started

from the top of our shopping list. "There's a body out in the cemetery we want to take a look at. See who it is."

Doc Blue rolled bourbon around the shot glass. "Catholic or Jewish?"

St. Cloud looked away. "Catholic, for fuck's sake."

Doc Blue took a pen from his pocket and reached over the bar for a napkin. "Two diggers two hundred bucks. Five hundred to pay off the cops." Doc Blue wrote down the figures. "What then?"

"If it's the right person we want an autopsy. See how she died."

Doc Blue tapped the pen against the bar top. "How long ago she die?"

"A few days."

Doc Blue watched St. Cloud. "This the woman they pulled out of the Gallatin last week?"

"Maybe."

Doc Blue put the pen back in his pocket. "Too hot for me, boys." St. Cloud put his hands around the bar rail. Doc Blue looked at the brass tube running along the bar, it could have been his neck, and took out his pen. "All right. We'll start over. Five hundred for the diggers, a thousand for the cops." He wrote in the new figures. "A p.m.'s been done on the woman, so an autopsy's out. Her vital organs are over in Helena. Maybe destroyed by now."

"What can you do without the guts?"

Doc Blue put the pen in his pocket. "Take some tissue and hair tonight. I can detect something basic like arsenic. But that's about it. You want to do it right"—he looked at the figures as if they were something crawling on the napkin—"I can talk to Jim Lister. He did the p.m. But that's going to cost you."

St. Cloud looked at Doc Blue. "Fuck money."

Doc Blue took the pen from his pocket. "All right. A

thousand for me. Four for Jim Lister." He wrote the figures down, noting each.

St. Cloud watched the man write. "How long is this going to take? We got to make some moves tomorrow."

"I'll talk to Jim tomorrow morning. Should know something by noon."

St. Cloud turned the napkin and looked at the figures. "For four grand, call the fucker tonight." He turned the napkin back. "All we want to know is whether they murdered her or not. Got it?"

Doc Blue looked at the napkin. "All right. We got five for the diggers, a thousand for the Butte Police Department and a grand for me. Four for the coroner." He looked up. "Sixty-five hundred dollars."

I took a wad of twenties from the paper bag and counted out the sixty-five hundred. Doc Blue took the bills and put them in various pockets. He tossed down his shot. "Be right back."

St. Cloud watched Doc Blue pass into the game room, thread through the crowd at the keno counter. Doc Blue knocked at a door set in the game room's back wall. The door opened, and Doc Blue disappeared inside the café office. St. Cloud turned back to me. "I got an idea how we can deal with Blackmuir, but it's gonna cost money. We're gonna need an airplane. Make it two airplanes," St. Cloud said. "One for me. One for you."

I looked toward the game room. The office door opened. A man, not Doc Blue, pushed his head out of the door, looked toward the bar, his eyes came to St. Cloud and me, the head withdrew, the door closed.

"Two planes are fine with me," I said.

St. Cloud was smiling at himself in the backbar mirror, nasty, as if the reflection was about to make his first and last mistake. "Yeah, right. Get some maps in the morning. See if I can get on the VHF out at the airport."

St. Cloud grinned at himself in the mirror. "Blackmuir thinks he's some kinda great white hunter. We'll let him hunt us." St. Cloud rocked back, forward. "I got a pal, an old bush pilot, he's got a place with a strip in the Bitterroot wilderness. No way in or out this time of year short of flying in. I'll get some topos in the morning. Make some overlays in case we get split up." St. Cloud looked toward the back of the café. "Yeah. That's the ticket."

The office door opened again, a second head, not Doc Blue, not the first man, came out, looked at us, went in, the door closed. I turned back to St. Cloud.

"You ain't got a thing to worry about, Danny boy." St. Cloud grinned. "I'll take care of old Doc Blue." St. Cloud became pensive, tapping the bar top with a finger. "What's the name of that game they play in England? You know, some kinda fairy baseball."

"Cricket."

"Yeah, that's it," St. Cloud said. "Jesus, they got these fucking clubs. Saw one in a sports store in Frisco once. Don't bust off at the handle like baseball bats."

The office door opened a third time. Doc Blue emerged and made his way through the milling keno players toward us. Doc Blue came up to the bar, ordered a round. He smiled, looked us in the eye. It was going to take a couple hours to get things set up, he said, find a couple diggers, get straight with the Butte cops. After Doc Blue had told us how long all this was going to take, the hand on his shot glass was shaking like it was breakfast.

Doc Blue looked at me, St. Cloud, he looked away. "You boys going to stick around here or you going to wait out at the graveyard?"

St. Cloud turned back to his drink. He looked at it, picked it up, drank it, put the glass down on the bar, looked at the glass. "We'll wait out at the graveyard. I'm driving a yellow Trans Am." He looked at Doc Blue. "Shouldn't be that hard to find."

"Right. Right," Doc Blue said. "Yellow Trans Am. Catholic cemetery, right?"

"Yeah. The Catholic graveyard," St. Cloud said. "You Catholic or Jewish, Doc?"

Doc Blue looked at me. He swallowed but there was nothing to swallow. "I'm not anything."

St. Cloud smiled. Like a scalpel had opened his mouth. "Now you're talking, Doc." St. Cloud jerked his head toward the game room. "Think your chair might be warming up, Doc."

Doc Blue looked back toward the big poker table. He raised his empty shot glass and tossed back nothing. "Right. Right. Let's say the Catholic cemetery at midnight. Right?" With that Doc Blue backed away from the bar, turned and went into the crowd around the poker table.

St. Cloud studied himself in the backbar mirror. "I'm amazed how much I've matured in the last couple years. Don't get upset like I used to. Now I'm more philosophical about somebody selling me down. Subtle—that how you say that word?"

"The *b* is silent."

St. Cloud took a deep breath and stood tall. "Yeah. Sub-tle. That's me these days." St. Cloud turned and surveyed the crowd in the bar. "All right. Let's get some flowers and go out there." St. Cloud came in close. "And I mean right now, you heartless bastard."

We drove down off the shattered hill of old Butte, toward the Flats, new Butte, leaving the ghosts of Uptown behind. St. Cloud drove in silence awhile, then he looked across at me, expressing profound interest:

"Want to see Evel Knievel's house?"

"No."

St. Cloud looked back at the road. "Cold. Cold as a fucking fish." St. Cloud drove in silence. Then he said: "You want to know about me and Kat?"

"No."

St. Cloud watched me long enough for the Trans Am to stray across the center stripe. A dump truck, air horn blasting, brought him back. We went under a railway bridge and came up onto a wide straight street, the strip, lined with shopping centers and gas stations and bars. St. Cloud drove easy, hitting every red light. "We were going to run," he said at the first light. "Change our names. Start up a new life somewhere else. That piss you off?"

"The light's green, St. Cloud."

When the Trans Am had eased through the intersection, St. Cloud said: "We were going to a place in the Bitterroot wilderness." He was quiet for a while. "I know people up there. Ranchers. Bush pilots. Guides. They all got strips. We'll get a couple planes with skis. Get him up there in his hot little Foxjet and fix his little red wagon there. Ain't nobody can touch me in a dogfight." St. Cloud turned to me. "You in or out?"

"It's something we can think about."

St. Cloud turned back to the road. "Yeah. Maybe we can dynamite a strip or something. When he comes in for a landing—blooey—or maybe we could fly him into a rock wall. Some canyon, see, and he can't get out. I know those mountains, nobody knows those mountains like me. Except Dutch and he's getting old." St. Cloud was quiet. "Yeah. Got to get some maps and do some thinking. Get a deal on some dynamite. That's it."

After a couple of miles, the strip gave way to empty spaces, vacant lots, the fields of the Butte airport, until we came on the hedge wall of the Catholic cemetery. We turned through the entrance and went into the old, wooded section of the cemetery, the gothic statuary— Mothers of Christ, winged angels, saints in prayer— looking in the deep night shade to be figures risen from their graves. St. Cloud stopped the car at the border of the woods and we walked out onto the plain of the new cemetery. Kat's plot was not yet marked by granite, the metal rod and disk of a pauper's grave standing at the head of a mound of fresh-turned earth. St. Cloud went off in search of a spray of flowers left by an anniversary mourner. When he returned I had almost done with my mourning. St. Cloud placed the flowers by the metal marker and stood by me at the foot of the grave. I turned away for a time and watched a plane, a Western 707, float down from the ridge of the Divide, sweeping wide to the flats south of Butte, to approach the airport low and steady. When the plane had come to earth and taxied to the terminal, I turned back to the grave. We were silent, then St. Cloud said:

"Tell me something about her. Anything. Tell me something she liked."

I looked about us. "Well, she was fond of cemeteries at night."

Which was true. Before we got the San Mateo house, there had been an old cemetery near us. Great eucalyptus and redwood, winding roads, the graves scattered here and there. Kat had liked to go out at night into the cemetery and wander about studying headstones, oddly, it had seemed to me, at peace among the dead.

St. Cloud did not see the seriousness in my recollection. "Christ, can't you think of something else!"

There was how Kat and I had met. On a flight to Mexico. I had been going down to Acapulco for a little time on the beach. Kat was working first class. Running it like a private party. Champagne for breakfast. Caviar.

There was this crazy guy, a writer, passing a joint around. Kat let him go. Maybe she smoked herself. Disappeared into the can with the guy for a while anyway. When we landed in Mexico, Kat found a manuscript the writer had left behind. We dropped the manuscript by the hotel where the writer was staying. We went out that night. Ate, danced. When we came back to the hotel, there was a bottle of champagne waiting in the room. And a note from the writer. Only the guy's first name and a couple digits of a phone number legible.

Not much, maybe, but it seemed to satisfy St. Cloud. He was quiet for a while. Then he said: "She didn't come over here because she gave a shit about me. She was scared. Wanted a place to hide from Blackmuir." He stopped. "There wasn't anything between us. Nothing."

St. Cloud raised his head, turned away, looking toward another section of the cemetery. The 707 that had landed a few minutes earlier was now drawing away from the terminal. We watched as the plane taxied to the end of the runway, turned without holding and ran back north along the strip. The plane swept into the air, banked sharp west, away from the heights of old Butte, climbing hard to clear the Anaconda-Pintlar Range. When the plane had gone into the night, St. Cloud turned back.

"Shitty place to work out of. You ever fly in here?"

"Couple times."

St. Cloud looked to the dark ridge of the Divide. "That's one way we could do it. Play hide-and-seek in the Bitterroots. Get him into something real short. Let his power throw him into a rock wall." St. Cloud turned away from the mountains and spat on the flowers at Kat's grave. "Ah, we'll figure something out."

I had heard nothing, but now I saw the second car in

the trees, its long black silhouette drawn in behind the Trans Am. Two men were moving away from the cars and the trees, coming toward us.

"The gravediggers," St. Cloud said and went forward, in front of me, as if to shield me from the approaching men. "I'll get the maps and an overlay to you soon as I can," St. Cloud said and moved away toward the two men. "He went for it," St. Cloud called out. And then the shaded forms of the two men came close. The squat bulk of Johnny Kono and next to him Blackmuir. I saw that Johnny Kono was carrying something—a shovel. Then he hit me with it.

HE HANG GLIDERS floated in the air like kites without strings. Brightly colored wings soaring against the sky. Men hung from the wings—as the kites wheeled and turned in the wind—like prey caught in the machines' talons. The house Blackmuir and I stood before was so large I had no sense of its boundaries. Beyond us a wide tawny lawn stretched toward a range of mountains, their faces near-vertical walls. Scattered about the lawn were more hang gliders at rest. Their fliers were gathered in small groups watching other gliders soar down from a lesser mountain in the foreground. Blackmuir spoke as a glider drifted down to the lawn, its pilot attempting to land on a bull's-eye chalked in the grass.

"I hear you passed an easy night," Blackmuir said. "I wanted to put you in the Livingston clinic, but Dr. Hurt, one of my guests, assured me it was unnecessary. He seemed to think you were suffering from nothing more than exhaustion. And there was the blow you received from J.K." Blackmuir's lips curled around the name. "He can be a vicious man. The reason I keep him on."

Blackmuir stood transfixed for a moment, as if his mind had gone out of him. Then he said: "Forgive me if I appear overly solicitous, Cox. I don't give a shit about your health. I merely want to keep you well long enough to get a few of our problems sorted out." Blackmuir removed his glasses and cleaned them, keeping his eyes closed till the glasses, like a mask, were again in place. He turned his magnified eyes full on me. Having fixed me, he looked away. "I have killed many things for many reasons in my life. As a boy I killed without thinking. Since, I have killed for sport, pleasure, for food, to save my own life and the lives of others. I have killed to mete out justice, to serve my country, and for business. I have killed for love and I have killed for hatred and I have killed merely to see a live thing dead. But," he turned his gaze to me, "I did not kill your wife."

Blackmuir made no gesture of rage, but without movement or bombast he was transformed to a man near losing control. In a moment his fury had receded. "People like you, Cox, have very rarely killed anything in their lives. A bird, game animals. If you've killed men, it's been in war. And even then you've rarely watched them die." Blackmuir smiled. "You're like the vast majority of mankind. You devour the beast on your plate, while despising the men who have killed these things for you. A modern man. Weak, middle-class, ignorant. A fool with his eyes closed to the killing about him. But you are going to change, Cox." He spoke softly, with intimacy: "It's only a matter of time before you turn to what is inside you. One day, soon, you are going to look a man in the face and kill him." He smiled. "I promise, I will bring you to it."

Blackmuir looked beyond me, toward a canopied pavilion, bandstand and dance floor set on the lawn and the thirty or so people who had gathered there. From their dress they were local businessmen, bankers, ranchers, their wives—pretty much the same crowd as in the Missoula restaurant the night I had met Blackmuir. "I'm afraid we'll have to postpone our discussion till later. My guests seem to be arriving." Blackmuir turned from them, toward the fliers who had collected around two ultralights—motorized hang gliders—and St. Cloud and Johnny Kono, who were working at the ultralights' engines, tuning them for flight. He smiled toward the fliers. "And I think the boys are to give us some sort of entertainment. After this nonsense is finished, the four of us will meet upstairs and sort out a few things." He looked at me. "I haven't told you the occasion of this gathering, have I? I am celebrating a birthday." He laughed as he went across the winter grass. "A birthday! These people are mad."

As Blackmuir moved away, the sound of motors starting came to me—a furious whine, like bottled insects—and the two ultralights, Johnny Kono and St. Cloud seated in their frames, began to lift and straighten. The fliers turned the ultralights and ran them into the wind. The ultralights were caught in the updraft and the winged machines were airborne. The two ultralights— the wings of Johnny Kono's machine black with scarlet markings, St. Cloud's a glossy, metallic green—went away from the house, rising gently toward the peaks beyond. The ultralights went fifty, a hundred feet in the air, then turned, the black wings leading, the green glider behind, and came back toward the house. The ultralights passed in formation over the lawn. The squat form of Johnny Kono in the black glider, St. Cloud flying the bright green wings. The ultralights turned into the wind, toward the peaks, and long red streamers unfurled from their wingtips. The gliders parted, breaking formation. The black wings turned, climbing to the north. The green glider banked east. The gliders rose to three hundred, three hundred and fifty feet. There they turned and came toward one another. From the ground it seemed the gliders would collide, but there was ten feet, maybe, between them and the two gliders passed without harm. Johnny Kono turned his black wings sharp. He slid into a dive, while St. Cloud took the green glider into a gradual circling climb. Johnny Kono tracked St. Cloud, rising under the green wings. The black glider came up quickly behind the green wings. Johnny Kono maneuvered his machine, its rearfacing prop rising toward the streamers flowing from the wingtips of the green glider. But as the prop of the black glider came onto the green glider's streamers, St. Cloud banked his machine hard, ninety degrees. The green wings were emptied of lift and St. Cloud and the green glider dropped toward earth. A cry rose from the fliers on the ground—the green wings spiraling to earth—but at fifty feet St. Cloud turned the glider's frame with a hard rudder, and at twenty feet the green wings caught air and the machine was jerked out of its dive, ten feet above the ground.

Now St. Cloud tracked the black wings from below, rising slowly beneath them. St. Cloud followed every maneuver Johnny Kono executed, as if the green wings were a shadow of the black glider. Johnny Kono took the black glider up—three hundred, four hundred feet—and still St. Cloud came with him, closing on the black glider as his wings took the updraft from Johnny Kono's machine. Then Johnny Kono banked his wings sharply, as St. Cloud had done, to escape his pursuer in a dive. But Johnny Kono did not have the nerve for St. Cloud's fall to earth and St. Cloud was quickly on the diving black wings. When Johnny Kono pulled his glider from its dive, St. Cloud sent his shining green wings in behind the black glider—close—and the right wingtip of the green glider cut into the streamer flowing from the tip of the black wings. St. Cloud kept his glider in its dive till near the ground, then he pulled the stick back hard and righted the machine a few yards above the dusty winter grass. A cry of relief and applause came from those on the ground. St. Cloud turned his machine, gliding it, without power from the motor, and brought the wings to rest dead on the chalk bull's-eye. And as those on the ground surged toward St. Cloud's green ultralight, the black wings circled above, the red streamer from the wingtip now no more than a rag fluttering in the windstream.

I went away from the house and saw the size and scope of Blackmuir's ranch, called Kill Devil, after the hill at Kitty Hawk where modern aviation began. The bit of lawn I had seen from the house was but part of a landing strip that went on for three-quarters of a mile to the south, away from the granite wall rising over the ranch. A half-dozen light planes, among them a Foxjet, Blackmuir's private craft, were parked at the distant end of the strip. Another light plane, a two-prop Aztec, was approaching the strip from the southwest. The Aztec came into the light north wind, touched down and taxied toward the house. At the end of the Aztec's run, three passengers left the cabin and the pilot turned the plane and taxied back to where the other aircraft were moored. The passengers, two women and a man, went to the southern side of the house, where another party of guests were gathered around a heated pool, steam rising from the water. I recognized the man who had left the Aztec, William Chance, the son of a famous movie star who had become almost as famous as his father. And that was how Blackmuir's winter fete was divided—Hollywood, locals and fliers. I joined the fliers.

A dozen or so people were circled around St. Cloud and Johnny Kono and their bright wings, the fliers instructing them on the most dangerous of all the ways there are to fly. For a time I listened to the pilots' instructions, watched as beyond the strip two of Blackmuir's ranch hands, men wearing blue baseball caps and starched Levi's as if they were uniforms, took to stepladders to string a HAPPY BIRTHDAY LANE banner across the pavilion canopy. Blackmuir stood in front of the banner, making sure the men on the stepladders were getting the banner high and straight.

When the guests who had gathered around the ultralights had heard enough to know never to get near one, turning to move off toward the birthday preparations, I joined St. Cloud. He was tightening a cable under the green wings. St. Cloud came out from under the green wings. He tilted the light aircraft. Took about the same effort as picking up a Sunday newspaper.

"You ever drive one of these things, Cox? Ain't nothing like it. Like flying. Really flying. Like you was a bird or a bug." St. Cloud straightened the ultralight and went under the wings. "Come on, Dan, I want you to know how to fly one of these things." St. Cloud looked from the canopy and banner hanging to the house and pool to the strip and the half-dozen light planes parked at the distant end. He turned back and reached up to the ultralight engine. "It may be the only way we have of getting out of this fucking place. Myself, I'm making a move. Soon." St. Cloud turned to me. "Sorry about the shovel in the graveyard last night. I had to cover myself. You too."

St. Cloud pointed to the padded harness and seat fitted in the frame. "You got a stick and pedals to play with. The foot pedals are spoilarons. Like ailerons. Cloth panels on the wing tops. Make nice stall flaps if you need them. OK. Hop in, buckle up."

St. Cloud did this for me. He then stood away, licked his forefinger, held it to the air. "Couple knots due north. Just right for a solo. Keep her nose into the wind till you get up to where you can glide out of trouble. Nothing fancy, Cox. You got low stall speed. Good glide ratio. Next to no power. Fifty horses. Take it real easy till you get the feel." He pointed to the frame. "There's your throttle. Full, half, and glide. Let the motor take you up. When you get where you want to go, cut her back and glide down. Couple feet off the ground, stall her, and you come walking in." St. Cloud pulled the rope above my head and started the engine motor and turned the wings facing north. He called over the motor noise: "Full throttle and up you go."

With that, I moved the throttle to full and the machine rolled away from St. Cloud, down the strip, past a couple of fliers dismantling and packing their wings.

The machine took me down the strip, the speed increasing. At thirty knots, I hit up elevator and the machine lifted into the air. I flew straight along the strip, the machine easing up—twenty, fifty feet—the strut cables humming in the airstream. The crowd around the canopy and dance floor, Blackmuir among them, turned to watch my flight. The machine cleared the end of the strip at seventy feet. I kept the machine flying straight, rising over a pasture and a band of horses who observed my passage, then sprang into an easy gallop. I waited till the machine had lifted to two hundred feet, then I put the stick left, left pedal, and the machine banked gently away from the granite wall to the northeast. I kept the machine in its turn till it had come three-sixty, nose back into the north breeze, still rising. At four hundred feet or so—with nothing between me and the falling ground but air—I banked the machine again and made a down-wind run over the strip, the machine leveling now that it did not have the headwind lift. I passed over the canopy, a gaudy red-and-cream-striped toadstool, the bright wings set on the lawn, the house and pool. Minute cries and applause came from the ground. Some wit at the pool tracked me through the sky as if the furled pool umbrella he held to his shoulder were a rifle. I flew down the strip, toward the light planes parked there. As I went I saw that the valley was long and tight. Another range of mountains rose quickly against the western horizon, their gray walls sheer, veined with ice and snow. A blacktop road went the length of the valley, the road, so far as I could see, running straight to the mountain walls and ending there.

I passed over the aircraft at the end of the strip, banked the machine and turned to run back north into the wind. As I made the turn, the machine rising with the headwind, the air chilled and from five hundred feet I saw the black mass of a storm gathering behind the north mountain wall. As the ultralight came over the pool and house, tiny cries came to me, and I banked to see Lane Blackmuir go under the black wings Johnny Kono had flown. The black wings ran along the lawn, lifted into the air, and now rose swiftly and steadily toward me.

I tracked the black glider for a time, then lost sight of the machine as it came up behind me. I turned in the frame, saw nothing, then turned forward—and there was nothing but stone before me. The granite walls of the northern mountains. I had run far over the pasture. Too far—no way to cut power, to glide to earth. No way to escape the black wings coming relentless for me.

I banked the machine west, away from the walls. With the turn away from the wind, lift went from the wings and the machine dropped. The dive was gentle, just a swoop as seen from the ground, but for two eternal seconds I felt stripped of all support. Wings, power— there was nothing that would stop my fall to earth. But with the dive the green wings caught air and the machine came level, flying light but steady with the tailwind.

The fliers on the ground were looking up. Not at my machine but behind me. At Blackmuir, as he brought the black wings to me silently, the sound of his motor trailing away in the slipstream. I turned in the ultralight frame to find Blackmuir. I banked my machine, stick forward, and the green wings fell—and I saw the black ultralight was directly under me. I put the stick back hard, to pull away from the black wings, but it was Blackmuir who saved us. He turned the black ultralight into a steep bank, emptied his wings of lift, and fell away from me. The tips of our wings cleared by a yard.

Blackmuir's turn took him thirty feet below me. But now he was climbing again, quickly, bringing the black wings and his prop directly beneath me. Ten feet, five, Blackmuir rose till the propwash from his machine grasped at my legs.

We came to the end of the strip, but still Blackmuir would not go from under my machine. I banked to go back into the wind, my machine dropping to within inches of the black wings' prop and top cables, and still Blackmuir would not release me. As we went into the wind, I pushed the throttle forward and pulled back hard on the stick, but Blackmuir drove his machine up, still only feet under me.

We went over the house and pool and the gathered fliers and their gliders, now too high to hear anything over the whine of our engines. We came to the end of the strip and went over the pasture beyond the strip toward the mountain walls. There, with the sheer granite face rushing toward us, I saw our maneuver and its end as it would be seen from the ground. The two machines in elegant formation challenging the mountain. At the last moment the flier below would turn away from the wall, to safety. While the flier above, because of his greater altitude, his inexperience, would bank his wings too late. Strike the wall and plummet, his wings scraping, tearing against the face, to his death.

Now the mountain wall was only yards away. Nothing left but to go down. To drive my machine frame and landing gear into the black wings. To rip the stretched nylon, send Blackmuir and his machine—both of us— hurtling to the valley floor. I pulled stick and throttle back hard, spoilarons up, like full flaps. The nose of the ultralight went up in a power-back stall and the air became still under my wings. Nothing moved. And then I dropped.

I didn't strike the black wings. Didn't see them. They were gone. There was only the swirling earth below. Green, brown, gray, green again—a sickening kaleidoscope rushing to me. The airstream choked me. I went blind from tears. The wing cables vibrated, the nylon rattled overhead. The weight of the frame and wings and motor was crushing me. Against everything that seemed right, I pushed the stick and throttle forward—*hard*—to drive the machine toward the earth. I did not think the wings would ever grasp air. Two, three, five seconds— then the dive snatched the wings out of the spin, the nylon snapped with air, and I was yanked back as if a parachute had opened, and the craft came right. And we floated gently in the air.

While ahead, above, were the black wings, banking toward me. Blackmuir turned in his frame. He gave me a sign—well done, I had escaped for now—and I turned my machine and soared toward earth.

The birthday celebration was done. The speeches, the gifts, the country music and barbecue cut short by the snowfall drifting off the mountains north of the ranch. St. Cloud, Johnny Kono and I had been led from our places among the hired help at the foot of the table to an octagonal room set like a turret high in the back of the house. Four alternate walls were glassed, a good part of the ceiling was skylight, the colors in the room leached by the pale light made by the falling snow. Now only the base of the north mountains could be seen, their summits cloaked by the storm. Below lay the pool, steaming from the snow, and beyond that the part of the strip where earlier the fliers had gathered their gliders. Now only the two ultralights remained assembled. The gliders' nylon had not yet cooled to hold the snow. Their brilliant green and black and red wings were set like gems in the collecting white.

While we waited for Blackmuir's appearance I went about the room. There were model planes, various certificates of flying qualification, photographs like those

on the walls of Dayton's den, one the same shot of
Blackmuir and Dayton as young men in China, standing
with their squadron before a P-40. Most of the photographs were of an older Blackmuir, in Hollywood with
stars, in Washington with politicians. One of the photographs was Blackmuir standing with Jack and Bobby
Kennedy, Bobby Kennedy looking toward Blackmuir as
if he would eat his heart out. Jack didn't appear so lethal,
but then he was smiling for the camera.

After a few minutes, the door opened and Lane
Blackmuir came from an elevator, the only entrance to
the room. Blackmuir crossed to a desk, took the chair
behind the desk and turned to a phone console. He
pressed a button on the console and said:

"Find some chairs, Let's see who we have first."
Blackmuir put the receiver to his ear and turned away, to
look toward the storm-bound mountains. The three of us
found chairs and brought them to the desk. When we
were seated, Blackmuir turned to us, speaking on the
phone: "All right. Put him through. Buzz me when you
contact the coroner." Blackmuir sat forward, pressed a
button on the console and put the receiver in its cradle.
Blackmuir leaned back in his chair, glanced toward the
north window and the snow falling against the glass,
then looked at St. Cloud.

"Not that bad."

St. Cloud looked at the north window. "I've seen
worse."

Blackmuir waited. "Probably pretty nasty in Butte by
now."

St. Cloud made no answer.

Blackmuir kept his eyes on St. Cloud. "What have
you got going with Cox or whatever he calls himself
now?"

St. Cloud let his malevolent gaze come to me. "Not a fucking thing."

"That's better." Blackmuir went forward over the desk. He sorted through a stack of folders there. He took one folder from the others, opened it and withdrew a map. He looked up. "Our operation is over. The team is disbanded." He looked at each of us, then opened the map. "We'll be turning our attention to tying up loose ends. I will be directing field operations personally, till you all are safely out of the country." Blackmuir turned to St. Cloud. "Didn't you fly some people into the Bugaboos for me once?"

St. Cloud nodded. "Skiers."

"Fixed-wing aircraft?"

"A chopper. Nothing but a pad there."

Blackmuir looked at the map. "Do you know a secure mountain strip in Canada?"

St. Cloud went back in the chair. Leather creaked. "Yeah."

Blackmuir closed the map and returned it to the folder on the desk. "All right. When we're finished here get the maps from the file." Blackmuir turned to Johnny Kono. "Sorry we can't make it to Mexico, J.K., but we're all here now, close to the mountains, and that's where we'll go." Blackmuir turned to another file on his desk. "Now to take up the reason we are not all in Mexico." Blackmuir opened the file and went back in his chair. He looked at me. "Cox, I don't understand your attitude. After all I have done for you." Blackmuir went forward, to the file open on his desk. "Your former friend and associate Max Hubbard was to do a job for us. Hubbard had a simple mission. He was to fly to Mexico, investigate several strips there, for a possible resort development my associates and I were contemplating investing

in. Hubbard chose you as his copilot. At the time we saw
no reason to veto your employment. You were, we
thought, a simple man in some sort of financial trouble.
Our trust in you and Hubbard was, it turned out,
misplaced. You and Hubbard flew to Mexico, made an
arrangement with a heroin manufacturer there and attempted to smuggle this drug back into the States."
Blackmuir put down the paper and sat back. "On your
return trip your lack of flying and navigational skills,
your abandoning the detailed flight plan we had drawn
up, caused you to crash the plane. Max Hubbard was
killed in the crash—or so it was thought at the time. The
authorities found you alive at the crash site, your craft
loaded with heroin. You were taken into custody, to a
hospital. It was there that you concocted your first wild
tale. That you had flown not heroin, which was found
stashed in the plane, but an assassin into the country.
And that you had been hired to do so by my
associates"—he swept his hand toward St. Cloud and
J.K.—"and by Dub Dayton and by me." Blackmuir's
hand came down hard on the desk top. "My God, man,
how did you ever manage to come up with such crap?
Don't you understand you are among heroes?"

Blackmuir went back in his chair, swiveled toward
the wall hung with his political photographs. He looked
at the picture of Jack and Bobby Kennedy and himself.
"Unfortunately, there were people in power, in Washington, willing to believe your lies. People who would
like to see Lane Blackmuir crawl. These people managed to cover your smuggling enterprise and arranged
for your release from custody in Arizona." Blackmuir
turned from the Kennedy wall, to the folder on the desk.
"You returned to California, there to string together
more lies. These lies you pressed upon my daughter.
Fortunately for us, the authorities in Arizona examined

Max Hubbard's body. The coroner in Tucson ruled that Hubbard was dead before the plane crashed. That he had been killed in flight. That his murder had probably been the cause of your crash. As the authorities in Arizona, one young district attorney in particular, did not believe your bullshit about there being a third man in the plane, preparations were made to indict you for Max Hubbard's murder. You returned to Arizona to face these charges. On the surface, the behavior of an innocent man. But you did not surrender yourself into custody upon your return to Arizona. Instead, you lured the young district attorney, the man who was drawing up the charges against you, to some seedy motel. There you killed him. But then once again you botched your scheme to bring Lane Blackmuir to his knees. As you failed to make the murder of Max Hubbard look like an accident, now you failed to make the young district attorney's death appear a suicide. Now not even your powerful, corrupted friends in Washington could save you. You were charged with this, your second, murder."

Blackmuir turned from the folder. He looked toward a framed photograph on his desk—a studio portrait of a pretty young woman and a small girl. By the clothes and hairstyles of the woman and the girl, the picture had been taken in the late forties, early fifties. Blackmuir gazed at the photograph of his dead wife and his daughter as he spoke.

"After your second murder, you fled Tucson. You returned to California. There, again with aid from your Washington friends, you disappeared for a time. You surfaced only to renew contact with my daughter. To commence your plan to lure this tragically unbalanced young woman to your cause. When Gerald Stokes was shot by a lone, deranged assassin, you went to this unfortunate young woman with your theory of conspir-

acy. Madder still: you had her believe that her husband
and her father were the secret leaders of this conspiracy.
In spinning this gargantuan lie, you had the young
woman believe you were a small, innocent man, alone in
a world of killers. Under your seductive persuasion, the
young woman fell in love with you. In love, the young
woman agreed to put you in contact with me and my
associates. That you might infiltrate some sort of assassi-
nation 'team,' disrobe our alleged conspiracy and prove
your innocence." Blackmuir turned from the photograph
on his desk, to face the wall hung with flying mementos,
among them the picture of Blackmuir and Dayton
grouped with their China squadron before the Flying
Tiger. Blackmuir turned from the wall hung with flying
photographs. He lifted a page in the folder. "The fault is
mine. My judgment has been flawed." He turned the
page, lifted the paper beneath it, scanned down the
page, replaced the paper in the folder and faced me. "I
hadn't done proper investigation of you, Smith, Namier,
Cox, whatever your name is today. I thought you were
what you appeared to be. A fool drawn into this cabal.
First by greed, by Hubbard. Then later, after the crash
and Hubbard's death, that you compromised yourself
merely to save your own skin. It wasn't till much later,
till now, that I have seen you are an agent of my
enemies!"

Blackmuir stood, came from behind the desk and
went to the wall of political photographs. He took the
picture of himself and the Kennedy brothers from the
wall. He gazed at the photograph. "I didn't understand
that it was you, Cox, Smith, Namier, and your murderous
friends in Washington who were set on destroying one of
the greatest friends of democracy this nation has ever
known!"

This bit of business done, Blackmuir replaced the

Kennedy photograph and returned to his desk. Blackmuir closed the folder and went back in his chair. He
smiled. "A bit rough, I must admit, but you may rest
assured that it will be polished to perfection if you ever
try to go public on me."

Blackmuir turned to the telephone console. He
pressed a button and spoke without lifting the receiver.
"Is the call to California ready, Dale?"

A voice came from a wall speaker behind Blackmuir.
"Yes sir. We've been holding."

"Good," Blackmuir said. "Put the call through."

In a moment a second voice came over the speaker.
Dayton's easy country drawl. "What's the weather doing
up there, Lane?"

"Little snow, Dub. Probably get a couple inches
tonight."

"Sounds like good elk hunting tomorrow. Wish I
could be there."

"It would be good to have you here. Maybe the two
of us can go out when we get things settled in California.
Dub, we have you on the box here. I'm upstairs with St.
Cloud and J.K. and a man at various times has called
himself Dan Cox. You did some work together recently
in California."

Dayton's voice had some edge. "How'd you ever run
him down?"

"St. Cloud brought him in."

"That's good."

"Dub, before we get into the problems we're having
with Cox, I'd like an update on the California situation."

There was a pause. Then Dayton said: "We got some
problems here, Lane. Nothing we can't work out, but it
might take a day or two."

Blackmuir waited, not moving. "What exactly is
happening down there, Dub?"

"Well, we got Thea to the sanatorium, the usual place, and everything seemed to be going OK. Seemed like she was responding to medication—"

"What was she on, Dub?"

"That zinc crap. What she used to be on."

"What she should be on the rest of her life, Dub. These drugs have to be used methodically if they're going to be of any use."

"I understand that, Lane, but I can't watch her every minute of the day."

"The point of the nurse/companion I've been trying to get you to engage for years."

"Yeah, but there are as many problems with that as something like that solves."

"I doubt that. She'd been drinking again?"

"Yeah. She'd been drinking again."

Blackmuir went back in the chair, looked at the photograph of Thea as a girl on his desk. "And now she's left the sanatorium."

"Yeah. She's walked on us. We've checked the usual places. Nothing yet. I got a couple men down in San Jose. Seems like that might be where she went."

"How many men do you have working on this, Dub?"

"The boys from the sanatorium. They know her patterns pretty well. And I got two PIs checking out San Jose."

"I don't like anyone outside the team working on this, Dub. You know the problems we've had before when somebody from the outside hears her bullshit. She can appear quite lucid to someone who hasn't worked with her before. One of the problems we're having with Cox."

"I understand that."

"All right. If you can personally oversee the San Jose

search—and that means being there with the proper medication when they find her—maybe we can keep the damage done to a minimum. I want you to report to me, day or night, as soon as you find her."

"Right."

Blackmuir turned to the folder on the desk. He opened it. "Have you received my report on Cox?"

"Got it this morning. I haven't had a chance to read it yet."

"I'd like you to read the report, Dub, as soon as this conversation ends. We want to make a decision on Cox today." Dayton said nothing. Blackmuir continued: "We're considering terminating Cox's contract with the team, Dub."

Dayton waited. "I got that impression."

"Do you have any problems with letting Cox go from the team, Dub?"

"Well, I'd like to read the report first, Lane, but offhand I think I would."

Blackmuir waited. "Can you explain, Dub?"

"I don't know, Lane. Just seems like we got to stop somewhere." Dayton waited. Blackmuir did not speak. Dayton said: "Let me read the report and get back to you."

"We're going to need your yes if we're going to move on this."

"I understand that."

"I hope you do, Dub. Now, anything else on your end?"

"Can't think of anything, Lane."

"Call me as soon as you hear anything about my daughter."

"Will do," Dayton said and the connection was broken.

Blackmuir pressed a button on the console. The

operator's voice came over the speaker. Blackmuir said: "You have my call to Jim Lister ready, Dale?"

"He's on the line now, Mr. Blackmuir."

"Hold it one second, Dale." Blackmuir pressed a button on the console and held it. He looked at me. "This is Jim Lister. Coroner for Silver Bow County. The man who performed the autopsy on your wife's body." Blackmuir released the button. "Put Coroner Lister through, Dale."

A gravelly voice came over the speaker. "Jim Lister here on this end."

Blackmuir went back in his chair. "Jim, this is Lane Blackmuir over in Yellowstone County. What's it like in Butte this afternoon, Jim?"

The coroner chuckled and coughed, sucking in breath. "Spitting snow and down around ten. But they say we got a cold front coming in."

Blackmuir smiled. "Have you been able to do the exhumation I requested, Jim?"

"Well, Lane, we can get the jackhammer out if you want to, but I don't see the point in it. I went through my files and what they got over at the cop shop, and for the life of me, I don't care what that investigator says, that's Katherine Cox buried in that grave."

"Could you be more specific, Jim. The investigator is here with me now."

The coroner coughed, sucked in cigarette smoke. "Well, the photographs we took at the autopsy, now granted the body was pretty fucked up after being dragged two miles down the Gallatin, but the shots we did get, they're the same woman whose picture is on the license we found in the car. Katherine Cox of San Mateo, California."

"If I send this investigator over to Butte, Jim, could he look at these pictures?"

"No problem there, Lane."

"And if he's not satisfied that it's Katherine Cox buried in Butte, could you then perform the exhumation I've requested?"

"If that's what you want, Lane, we'll do 'er."

"Now have you had a chance to look into the other matter I mentioned to you?"

The coroner cleared his throat. "I did that myself this morning, Lane. Personally went to the yard where the car's impounded and looked it over. The front end's all messed up from going into the river, but there's not a mark of any kind on the rear bumper. Or on the left-hand side. I just don't think Katherine Cox's car could have been forced off the road like your man suspects. When he comes over to look at the autopsy shots, I'll take him over to the yard and he can see for himself."

"That would be very kind of you, Jim. The man's name is Smith. He probably won't be able to make it this afternoon. Say tomorrow morning?"

"Damn, Lane, tomorrow looks like it's going to be a fine day for tracking."

"Maybe we can get out next week, Jim, when we both have our desks cleared away."

"Next week sounds fine to me, Lane," the coroner said, and the connection was broken.

Blackmuir wheeled his chair from the desk, stood and went to the window. He looked out on the silent, swirling snow.

Blackmuir's pose was broken by a sound behind us. The elevator doors opened, displaying Chance, the famous actor's near-famous son, a girl under one arm, a magnum of champagne under the other. Chance and the girl came into the room singing happy birthday. When the song was done, Blackmuir held out his arms to Chance, the girl, the champagne.

"You are such good friends—all of you. I had forgotten, I had truly forgotten."

Chance shucked the girl and started wrestling with the champagne cork. "Lane, you've never forgotten a thing in your life." The cork blew off and champagne spilled over Blackmuir's desk. "Shit, sorry, Lane," the actor said, reaching the spilling bottle across the desk. "Forgot the glasses." Blackmuir raised the bottle to his lips, gingerly, like a politician lifting a soiled baby. Chance recovered the girl, scanned the room till he saw his photograph on the Hollywood wall. Then he made a cool appraisal of the three hired hands. "Sorry to interrupt your little powwow here, Lane, but some of us are thinking about flying out under this before it gets too thick. We got you a toy down in the game room. Took us a little while to get it off the truck and set up. Come on, let's unwrap it." Chance had maneuvered the girl so he had Blackmuir under his free arm. The trio moved toward the waiting elevator carriage. "Now what we got wired up ain't as good as the real thing, but it's a kick. Shit, I've already wasted two hundred and fifty souls." The trio fitted into the small carriage and the door closed.

The three hired hands sat looking at the vacant chair behind the desk. No one moved or spoke. Then St. Cloud yawned and said: "Fuck." An observation that had many distinct meanings for Johnny Kono. In this case it was the word for snow: Johnny Kono looked toward the white veiled window. "Yeah. Fuck," he said.

St. Cloud looked at the window, looked back. "Maybe we ought to go downstairs."

Johnny Kono looked at St. Cloud, me and the snow, then back to St. Cloud. "What are we gonna do with him?"

St. Cloud reached his legs out as if he was going to

rest his boots on the desk corner. He brought his feet back to the carpet. "I'll look after him, you want me to."

Johnny Kono thought this over. Then he said: "Maybe I better."

"Suit yourself," St. Cloud said. He scratched his knee. "Lane wanted me to check out those Canada maps."

"Right. You check out those maps." Johnny Kono looked at the folders on the desk. "Maybe we ought to lock that shit up."

St. Cloud looked around the room. "This whole place is a lockup, J.K. There ain't nothing or nobody getting out."

Johnny Kono looked at the snow. "Right." He looked at me. "On your feet." I stood. Johnny Kono stood. St. Cloud didn't move. Johnny Kono said: "Downstairs. The game room. Soon as you get the maps."

St. Cloud looked out the window, at the snow and the mountains. "I wonder how old that fucking lunatic is?"

Johnny Kono looked at St. Cloud, looked, dumb-struck, to me.

I said: "I don't know. Fifty-five, sixty."

Johnny Kono propelled me toward the elevator. He pressed the call button, then stood looking up at the wall. Like there was a floor arrow above the door. The carriage came, the door opened and we went into the elevator. The last thing we saw as the door closed on us was St. Cloud sitting in the chair, gazing out toward the snow and the mountains, his boots propped on the corner of Lane Blackmuir's desk.

Blackmuir's birthday toy was a DC-10 flight deck. One of the Hollywood gang had picked up the flight deck for a couple grand when MGM sold off their backlot props.

Only the basic stuff was wired up—making everything work would have put the price tag up to fifty thousand dollars, a little steep even for Lane Blackmuir's birthday—but every gauge, dial, lever and tape instrumentation was there. Well, the automatic checklist was missing, but then ACLs probably hadn't been around whenever this rig had flown.

Blackmuir was in the right seat, Chance in the pilot's chair. Blackmuir had talked the actor through the flight-deck layout, the actor a quick study in the ergonomics of instrumentation, and had then talked him through a smooth takeoff, complete with noise-abatement procedures. A man who knew office and business, Blackmuir took Chance and the simulator through a flight instructor's list of problems—Dutch roll, yaw, directional and lateral trim, spiral and speed stability, stalling and high Mach numbers. If the flight deck didn't simulate buffeting near the speed of sound, the stick shakers rattled when Blackmuir took Chance to stall speed. After they had gone too fast and too slow, gone through every unstable condition a big jet might encounter, Blackmuir took the simulator up to forty-two thousand feet, the craft's heavy-weight ceiling. Blackmuir talked Chance through the high-altitude drill, working with the actor to trim a big jet at forty-two thousand feet. That done, Blackmuir turned to a high-altitude emergency descent.

"Now let's assume some maniac, some madman," Blackmuir said, his eyes on the TV horizon screen, "has brought a bomb on board. The bomb explodes, tearing a hole in the passenger cabin. Cabin pressure goes. No oxygen. At our permitted ceiling of forty-two thousand feet, the average person will be unconscious in fifteen seconds. And your ability to fly will be reduced sooner than that. Now, the emergency descent drill varies with the aircraft, but it always involves three things. Reduction to idle thrust, operation of your craft's high-drag devices, and a steep descent. You have to get down to oxygen fast, while at the same time not exceeding your Mach number. Now in the real world, if the plane's skin is ruptured by a small bomb explosion, everything in the passenger cabin would be chaos. There would be those killed and maimed by the explosion. There would be those fools who fly unbuckled who would be sucked out of the hole in the fuselage. Others would be thrown about the passenger cabin, human missiles battering those strapped in their seats. A sudden and complete decompression at such an altitude would fill the cabin with a mist that erupts like boiling smoke. There would be the cries of the injured. There would be terror and panic. The aircraft would be a hell soaring at forty-two thousand feet. Your job is to get down to breathable atmosphere, say fourteen thousand feet, as quickly as possible."

Blackmuir eased the column forward, trimming the imaginary aircraft's pitch, and continued: "On the flight deck, at loss of pressure, you and your first officer have divided responsibilities. One of you gets on oxygen, while the other immediately begins the descent. For both pilots to attempt to fly the plane will be deadly. Neither of you will remain conscious through the initial steep dive. In this drill, Chance, let's say I'll start the initial pushover, while you get on hundred-percent oxygen. Once you get your mask on, I'll give the plane over to you. It should take no more than ten seconds for both pilots to be breathing oxygen.

"Now the duration of the initial steep dive will be determined by your craft approaching, as it gathers speed in the dive, your Mach ceiling number. Let's say three hundred and eighty knots, which on a good day will be about twenty-four thousand feet. Remember that some airplanes can descend at fourteen thousand feet a minute. And nine thousand feet is common. You have to be very careful to hit your twenty-four thousand feet on the nose. Where you begin reducing the angle of your dive. If you overshoot twenty-four thousand, your craft will be in severe Mach-number trouble. If you undershoot, you will bring your craft level well above breathable atmosphere. Not doing anybody any good." Blackmuir smiled at Chance. "Ready Captain?"

"Oh Lord," Chance said. "I guess."

Blackmuir half turned to those of us standing behind the simulator. "We have any madmen back there? Somebody who's brought a bomb on the plane?"

One of the Hollywood gang said, "Bang!" and Chance and Blackmuir went through their emergency descent drill, leveling out at fourteen thousand feet three minutes later. Right on target, right on time.

As Blackmuir went on to take Chance through a landing, a good one—the craft trimmed tight, well-flown approach, gentle glide slope, descent rate smooth into the heart of the threshold, nose pitched up at two hundred feet, gears down, thrust eased to near stall speed, firm touchdown, stick forward and nose gear put on the pavement, aileron and spoilers up, reverse thrust and brakes to a dead stop—I went away from the simulator, to a bay of windows that looked out on the strip and the mountains beyond. The snow looked to be thinning now. A dusting, no more than a quarter inch, had collected on the grass. As the snow wasted in the air, the ceiling had risen, maybe a thousand feet. The light gathered beneath the gray cover was a pearly blue.

While Blackmuir and the Hollywood gang played with their toys, I stood by the window, watching the snow, the blueing light, trying to puzzle a way out of this mountain trap and what I would do if I did escape. I was at the window for ten minutes, maybe, and having discovered no solutions, was turning away when I saw out of the corner of my eye a green wing floating past. Then from another window along the wall one of Blackmuir's cowboy soldiers called out: "Chief! Somebody's up in one of the ultralights!" The crowd gathered behind the simulator came to the windows to watch the green wings turning against the snowy sky.

We went out of the house, led by Blackmuir and Johnny Kono and the cowboy who had warned him of the flier. The crowd cheered and called out, waiting for the flier to turn at the end of the strip, to come back to us, so that we might see what fool would take his frail machine into the snow. But the glider did not turn back at the end of the strip. The green wings went on, beyond the pasture at the end of the strip, toward the mountains. As the green wings were fading into the veil of snow, someone nearby said: "We've got a runaway."

I turned to see Blackmuir running Johnny Kono along the strip, toward the planes moored at the far end, Blackmuir talking close to Johnny Kono as they went. Blackmuir released Johnny Kono and came back to the crowd. He called out to one of the cowboys: "He's going into the mountains. Probably up through Elkhorn Canyon." Blackmuir turned to the actor. "Chance, we don't know what we've got. A drunk, drugs, we don't know. You go with Dale. Get the ground search team organized. You'll have to go back up behind Crazy Mountain. Dale and the fliers know the road. We'll follow the glider in the Foxjet." Blackmuir turned to the cowboy. "We'll be on the ranch frequency. Keep it there. This stays ranch business. You've got a thirty-minute climb in the snow. Get moving."

Chance and Dale and two other cowboys and a few of the Hollywood gang went off toward the house. Blackmuir turned to the planes at the distant end of the strip and the rising hiss of the Foxjet's two Rolls-Royce turbojets spooling up. Then the small tight craft came down the strip toward us, taxiing at near takeoff speed. Blackmuir turned to me, taking my arm. "You take the right seat. We'll put J.K. in the back with the maps."

Johnny Kono hit the brakes and reverse thrust hard, sliding the plane to a stop. The snow billowing from the locked gear and the reversed engines enshrouded the craft. Blackmuir and I ran into the silken whirl of snow, Blackmuir making for the left door. By the time I had climbed onto the wing, slipping hard on the icy surface, Johnny Kono had gone into the back, Blackmuir was strapping into the pilot's seat. Blackmuir had the plane moving toward the end of the strip before I was tied in. Blackmuir brought the plane up easy to the fence marking the end of the strip. At the fence he took the plane in a tight circle left, wheeling to run down the strip away from the mountains. Blackmuir gave me throttle and brakes as he set the radio to the ranch frequency. That done, he took the plane from me, pushed the throttle forward slow, warming the engines, holding the brakes hard. At 80 percent rpms he went off the brakes a fraction and the plane crept forward. At no more than five knots, maybe forty feet of runway gone, Blackmuir released brakes and the plane jumped forward. After the initial acceleration, Blackmuir went full forward on the throttle, smoothing the run across the snow-dusted grass. He kept ignition on, that the snow kicked up by the gear wouldn't flame out the turbojets. At one-ten knots he went back on the stick and the small jet near stood on its tail getting us into the sky. Blackmuir banked twenty degrees right as the gear came up. We were into the snow cloud quick, Blackmuir holding the bank. When the compass came to two hundred degrees, the azimuth of the valley, he trimmed the plane till the artificial horizon came level. He then eased back on the stick, taking the plane up at thirty-five, forty degrees. "We'll go up and see what it looks like on top." He spoke to me: "Give me altitude when we come clear. We want to know how much cover we're working with when we go back in."

The Foxjet climbed steep as easy as flying flat. At eighty-five hundred feet we jumped clear of the gray clinging to the windshield, were thrown above a dazzling sea of cloud, the sky blinding blue, the sun fixed well above the horizon. To the south a massive range of mountains stood above the cloud. Another range was strung along the western horizon. "Yellowstone and the Madisons," Blackmuir said. "What do the Crazies look like, J.K.?"

Johnny Kono turned in his seat, toward the range that rose north of Kill Devil Ranch. He reported plenty of rock showing.

Blackmuir leveled the plane, bringing the nose down smooth. "We'll go up the valley a bit, so we can come back down under the cover nice and easy." Blackmuir scanned the instrument panel, trimmed nose down a couple of degrees. He looked out over the shining, rumpled field of cloud, toward the looming Yellowstone Range. "You've got the maps, J.K."

"Right. Right, chief."

"The map is marked. North two miles from Kill Devil headquarters you'll find the foot of Elkhorn Canyon. Most people think it's the only way through the Crazies, over to Boulder Valley. But about three miles upstream there's another pass breaking off from Elkhorn Canyon. Angel Pass. Nasty chute. You got that, J.K.?"

"Got it. Angel Pass."

Blackmuir smiled. "Good. If I were St. Cloud and I

were running, that's how I would go. Very difficult to track a man through Angel Pass."

Blackmuir banked the Foxjet hard right, putting the jet into a steep, sliding dive. We had come around one-eighty, nose north, toward the Crazies, the mountains St. Cloud had gone into, when we went into the cloud. The windshield went gray, blank. Blackmuir kept the nose down thirty degrees, the altimeter needle whirling. The Foxjet hurtled blind toward earth. "You worked much on the deck, Cox? Where the greatest pilots love to fly. As near the ground as they can get." Blackmuir turned his head a bit, the altimeter reeling off five hundred feet every fifteen seconds. "That's how Dub Dayton got his start. Crop dusting in Texas." Blackmuir looked at the altimeter, the compass, the pitch gauge. "We should be through the cover in thirty seconds. Take the wheel, Cox. I'll give you a call in twenty-five." Blackmuir reached his hands from the wheel, to the windshield, wiping away the fog collecting at the windshield edge. Twenty seconds went, the altimeter tumbling toward forty-eight hundred feet, the valley floor elevation. I found my hands tight on the wheel, not pulling back, not yet. Blackmuir looked at me, smiled, looked to the gray windshield. "Should be getting close," he said, twenty-five seconds into the dive, the altimeter showing fifty-five hundred. The muscles in my shoulder had gathered, ready to pull back hard on the wheel, when holes of light and color tore in the windshield. "Closer, Cox," Blackmuir said, looking down. "Let's see where we are."

We came through the cloud, a field of snow spread five hundred feet below us. I took the Foxjet out of the dive, leveling the plane two hundred feet above the valley floor. Blackmuir peered through the windshield, watching the roads and fences and houses that rushed under us, searching for some sign of where we were. He went forward, close to the windshield. "There we are. Kill Devil." Blackmuir sat back. "Lower my wing a bit, Cox, as we pass over the headquarters. Don't be afraid to kick her in the ass if you have to."

I made a roll that took the left wingtip fifty feet over the headquarters' radio antenna.

"Nobody around. Must be on their way,'" Blackmuir said as the ranch-house roof swept under the left window.

I rolled the Foxjet to level, eased the nose up and throttle back as we flew toward the face of the Crazy Mountains, no way through the mountains that I could see.

Blackmuir took the wheel, trimmed the plane, pulled the throttle back to half. He hit the landing flaps once, backed the throttle a touch, trimmed the nose down as the plane's airspeed dropped to one-twenty knots. A ragged granite buttress reaching from the mountain wall rushed up on our right. Blackmuir curled the Foxjet around the rock talon and slid the plane into a round-bottom tunnel that rose through the mountains. Blackmuir inched the throttle forward, put the nose up ten degrees, following the rising canyon floor. Rock stood a hundred feet off the wingtips, the cloud cover maybe five hundred above. Ahead: the narrowing, rising, twisting chute of Elkhorn Canyon. "Maps ready, J.K.? We're going to have to fly the needle out of here." Blackmuir took one hand from the wheel, looked at his watch. "I make St. Cloud about eighteen minutes into the canyon." Blackmuir dropped the airspeed, then put the throttle hard forward as we went through the canyon's first twist. "Just might overtake him before he reaches Angel Pass. Maybe get him in the air." Blackmuir turned his head a bit. "What have we got, J.K.?"

Johnny Kono had his nose in a map. "Forty-five degrees left to seventy-five coming up."

Blackmuir leaned forward, looking up through the windshield to the cover—two hundred feet above.

The forty-five-degree twist Johnny Kono had read out came up, Blackmuir made the turn. We were faced with a straight, rising tube of rock that ended, maybe two miles away, in the lowering gray wall of cloud. Blackmuir strained forward. "I think we're just going to make Angel Pass. Time, boys, to start looking for a green wing."

As this was said, Johnny Kono came forward hard against the back of my chair. "There it is! To the right! Up there!"

Blackmuir rolled my wing up and there, fixed to the granite wall like a moth, was the green-winged ultralight. As the green wing flashed by, Blackmuir spat out: "Get a position! Did you see the flier?"

Johnny Kono was turned back, pressed against the rear window. "Fuck, nothing! Could be trapped under the wing." Johnny Kono turned back. "Didn't see him on the wall."

Blackmuir had his eyes forward, on the gray ceiling closing down on us. "He could have fallen free, to the canyon floor." Blackmuir reached to the throttle, pushed it full forward as he brought the column back. "No point in risking Angel Pass now. Maybe another day." And the plane was yanked up into the blank silent snow.

The house and grounds of the ranch headquarters were floodlit, though it was not yet true dark. Blackmuir had, during our harrowing return through the snow cloud, gone on the radio and raised Chance and Dale, the leaders of the vehicle search team, and ordered their mission to reach Elkhorn Canyon by the back door aborted. By the time we landed, their convoy was returning to the ranch. To the vast garage at the rear of the house where the vehicles were stored. Men were offloading the snowcats from the pickup beds, for the search that would now proceed directly up Elkhorn Canyon. The search team would go as far up the canyon as the snowcats would pull, then the party would dismount and continue on foot to the site of the crash. If no body was found on the canyon floor, the party would camp there for the night, to wait for dawn to scale the wall to the crashed ultralight. Chance and Dale and the other leaders of the team had gathered in the headquarters operations room, to detail men for the search.

The operations room was located in the basement of the headquarters. The subterranean room was divided and fitted out much a like a battalion field headquarters. At the hub of this warrish activity stood Lane Blackmuir. One moment Blackmuir was at a large wall map of the Crazy Mountains, briefing the snowcat drivers. The next in the radio shack, establishing emergency frequencies for the VHF sets mounted on the snowcats. From there he went to meet with the campsite personnel. He spoke briefly with the security guard, six men with high-powered rifles and sidearms. Then he returned to the wall map, where Chance and Dale and Johnny Kono were studying the terrain of Angel Pass and Elkhorn Canyon. That done, Blackmuir went alone into a small glass-walled office and spent some time on the phone. By the time Blackmuir had done with his calls, the leaders of the various divisions of the search team had done with their planning and had formed themselves in a briefing area near the wall map. Blackmuir stood before the search team leaders, spoke briefly and, when no questions were offered, dismissed the team and the leaders. There were, after these men had mounted the steps to the waiting snowcats, maybe a dozen of us left in the operations room. Blackmuir sent these men off to various parts of the room to their operations posts. With the last man put to his business, Blackmuir turned to me. "Let's see what becomes of the first stage of the search, Cox. Then we can discuss what can be done about you." He turned away. "Wait in my office. I'll join you in a minute. We can monitor the radio transmissions there."

A speaker on the wall crackled as I entered the glass-fronted office. The ranch operator's voice came into the room. The operator identified himself and hailed the search party. A reply from one of the snowcat radios reported that the search party was ten minutes from the head of the pass, maybe another thirty minutes, if all went well, to the spot below the wreckage site. "We're on lights now," the snowcat operator said. "Got enough snow on the valley floor for the cats, but we may have to pack 'em when we get into Elkhorn. Pretty rocky in there. May have to pitch camp lower down and proceed to the glider on foot."

Lane Blackmuir's voice came over the speaker: "I want a party at the site tonight. A search for the body on the canyon floor must be made tonight."

"We'll pack a team in if we can't run all the way," the snowcat operator replied. "Should have somebody there in half an hour."

"That's fine," Blackmuir said. "Let me know what the going's like once you get into the canyon."

"Right, chief," said the snowcat operator and the wall speaker went dead.

Fifteen minutes passed and the snowcat operator's voice came over the speaker. He reported that light in the canyon was bad, not enough snow cover to operate the cats. They were pitching a main camp about a quarter mile into Elkhorn Canyon. A small climbing party would be backpacking into the crash site. "Don't think we'll be able to do much good tonight, chief, but we'll have everything set up to start work come first light. If it keeps snowing tonight, we'll be able to take the cats all the way to Elkhorn Pass tomorrow morning."

Blackmuir said: "Is there any chance of getting a party of climbers up the wall to the ultralight tonight?"

"We could try it, but it'd be a lot better to wait till morning."

Blackmuir paused. "All right. But let me know what you find on the floor beneath the crash site—I want that tonight."

The snowcat operator promised that and signed off.

Blackmuir emerged from the radio shack, passing before the office glass wall. He crossed the operations room to the wall map, spoke with a man there, then went to the foot of the stairs and conferred with one of the security guards. Blackmuir crossed the operations room and came into the office. He took the chair behind the desk, pushed his glasses up his forehead and massaged his eyes. He let the glasses come back in place and turned to me.

"Your wife's death was an accident, Cox. Sorry I couldn't have been more candid with you this afternoon, but not even my closest associates know the truth. I was there." Blackmuir turned from me. "After Kat left you in San Mateo, she came to me. Here, to the ranch. Max's death had frightened her. I tried to reason with Kat. That she was safe with me. She agreed, but then she escaped. I located her in Butte. St. Cloud has a place there. He was in L.A. baby-sitting you. I guess the plan was he was going to come back, they were going to run. I tried to convince her this was mad. She was safe with me. But she ran again. I followed her car south of Butte, into the

Pintlars. I overtook her on the Gallatin River. She was slowing when the accident occurred. She saw me in the rearview mirror. The brake lights went on. She was going to come back to me. But there was ice on the road. The car spun. She couldn't control the car. It went into the river. The car was submerged in seconds. I went into the river. The driver's door had been torn open on impact. Kat's body had been swept downstream. There was no point searching for her body. I drove back to Butte and reported the accident without identifying myself. I didn't even go to the funeral. Five days ago there was so much, so many things that seemed important to me."

Blackmuir stopped. "Cox, you are indeed a fortunate man. I got a call from Washington about thirty minutes ago. Creesy, the man you and Max flew in from Mexico, the man who shot Gerald Stokes, has been transferred from Utah to a secret federal penitentiary near McLean. He arrived about an hour ago. The transfer was made without incident. With Creesy alive, beyond my control, I am finished. It's all over. Everything. That, Cox," Blackmuir said, reaching toward a pegboard on the wall behind him and taking down two keys, one to an automobile, the other to a motel room, "is why you will soon be free to leave."

Blackmuir placed the keys on the desk. Twirled them about. "Since we have a few minutes, perhaps you'd be interested in the real story. What has brought your life into mine. My original plan seemed, if not simple, then elegant." He looked at me, smiled and looked down to the keys. "So, we go back to, what, last October when you were just a normal little man. The plan was for you and Max to fly Creesy into the country. You were to be shot in the back of the head. Max set up for your murder, forcing him to work deeper for us. His death then was to

be faked, a new identity made for him—generally to put
Max in such a state he would do exactly as we said. All
that"—Blackmuir lifted a hand, dismissing that part of
his plan—"much as has happened to you. After the
Stokes assignment, Max was to fly Creesy out of the
country. A bomb would be on the aircraft, it would
explode in midair—end of Creesy, end of Max. Everything clean. Tied off.

"But things didn't work out so"—Blackmuir
smiled—"elegantly. It started with Creesy. He killed
the wrong man. Max instead of you. Looking back, it
seems that first fuckup was probably the worst. Having
you"—Blackmuir nodded toward me, a slight bow—
"involved in our operation instead of Max. The crash put
Creesy off his head—maybe the reason he got you and
Max confused. At any rate, he still wasn't right when
Luke Air Force security picked him up wandering the
test range the next day. It took a great deal of effort, you
might say, to cover Creesy. I considered letting him go,
but then Creesy had worked for me before and I couldn't
chance what he might say if I sold him down. So, Creesy
stayed and everyone who wouldn't be silent about him
had to go. The assistant D.A. in Tucson, his death was
something of a fuckup. It turned out all right, but we
probably could have lived with him. After you had
spotted Creesy at the Stokes rally at Desert Mall, Creesy
doubled back to your motel room." Blackmuir stopped.
"You had left the motel number with our lawyer in
Washington." Blackmuir shook his head, smiled. "According to one of my men, the motel room was dark.
Creesy thought the D.A. waiting in your room was you.
You've led a charmed existence, Cox. So we had to make
you the prime suspect in this man's murder—more
work. Then there was the lawyer's friend at the test
range. That man was a real problem. He was the admin-

istrative officer in charge of the Luke security force that found Creesy. It was tough getting rid of him. If it mattered any longer, you might be pleased to know his wife is still after us.

"Then the next fuckup. You escaped us in Tucson. How you got back to San Francisco—well, if we ever have the time and opportunity, I'd like to hear that story. If we wanted to take care of you in Tucson—you were just a little man causing me nothing but trouble—by the time we ran you down in San Francisco our plans had changed. Or rather"—Blackmuir smiled—"they had stayed the same. We could have easily eliminated you at your Tenderloin hotel, arranged something with one of the rental cars you shuttled. But we decided to put you to work for us. Give you the false death we had planned for Max. A new identity. Get you so deep in shit you could never go public on us. We would carry on as planned, with you doing Max's job for us. At this time I still thought you really were a fairly simple man. I knew you flew by the book, so I thought—" Blackmuir laughed. "Well, I never dreamed you had such spine and imagination.

"But at this point you were the last thing on my mind. Fuckups were raining down on me. Creesy didn't complete his Stokes assignment. A crippled Stokes may have been put out of the presidential race, but with Stokes alive, the men I work with in Washington lost their nerve. They were under great pressure. They panicked. They turned on the Stokes operation. They turned on me. If I could not eliminate Creesy, I was told, tie off that end of the Stokes operation, then my participation with our group would be terminated." Blackmuir leaned forward, stretching his mouth as if that might be a smile. "Which is exactly what has come to pass—with Creesy beyond my control."

Blackmuir went back. "So. While you were undergoing your metamorphosis in San Francisco—" Blackmuir stopped. "No. You were already in Venice when I took to the hunt for Creesy." Blackmuir stood, went around the desk, looked out the glass front to the operations room. He spoke looking toward the wall map of the Crazy Mountains. "When I started out in this sort of thing, we were all fairly well organized. If not a single operation, we had such contact among us that we more or less acted as one. That changed after—I think it was Hoover's death that sprang everyone." He turned to the room. "Something about the old fairy kept everyone together. Under tight rein, anyway." Blackmuir went behind the desk, sat. "Now everyone seems to have his own operation. FBI, CIA, the Pentagon, White House, NSC, and on and on. At least until recently." Blackmuir went back, hands clasped behind his head. "There has been a consolidation going on. Everyone outside the White House anyway. Probably my worst mistake," Blackmuir said, thinking aloud. "Not seeing that the cowboys were being rounded up." He came forward. "At any rate, my hunt failed. Another operations group got to Creesy before I did. In Utah. The penultimate fuckup. Stokes alive, Creesy in custody, time was running out on me. My only chance with Creesy alive, I was told, was to clear away the rest of the Stokes team. My group was going out of business. It would be wise if I did the same. So, men I had worked with for years— Dayton, St. Cloud, eventually J.K., even my daughter— they all had to go. You as well, Cox, even if you were a minor detail.

"There was no real way to go about this piecemeal. One at a time. If, say, St. Cloud met with an unfortunate accident, the others wouldn't wait around for their mishap to occur. The bomb on the plane, as I think my daughter may have told you, was not an idea unknown to me. But I had never attempted anything this elaborate. Using you, the hijack, the supposedly fake bomb, having the entire team on the same plane, the fact that word had leaked that I was in trouble and looking for a way out—I'm sure Dub knew what was happening—despite all this, I was desperate and I drew up a desperate plan to be rid of you all. It really was my only chance to survive. And we know what happened. You alone were on PSA flight one eighty-eight to San Francisco. Not even the bomb that J.K. had so carefully crafted made it. So. That ended my chance of cleaning up the team. I had some idea of dealing with you all here at the ranch, but my daughter has escaped me and Dub, he's unstable these days, and now St. Cloud has run. And in any case, with Creesy at McLean, none of you matter any more. The end of that."

Blackmuir pressed a button on the phone console. "One point I would like to make in my own defense. If you think bringing down a plane, causing the deaths of sixty, seventy people to silence three, two, even one person—even one's daughter—is, shall we say, surely excessive, you must know that there are men in the White House now—and they have their counterparts in the Kremlin—who are quite capable of destroying so many more to retain their power. Really, Cox, the only reason that I may seem mad to you is that I work on such a small scale."

Blackmuir released the button and went back in his chair. The radio operator's voice came over the wall speaker. The search team had reached the head of Elkhorn Canyon and was establishing a base camp there. A team of climbers had gone ahead. They should, the operator said, reach the canyon floor below the crashed ultralight in a matter of minutes. Blackmuir thanked the operator and the speaker went dead.

Blackmuir looked at his watch. "They should be near the crash site now. A few minutes more." Blackmuir halted. A man came from the radio shack, crossed the room to the wall map. When the map had been marked with the position of the base camp and the progress of the team of climbers as they went toward the crash site, Blackmuir turned back to me. "I began my career as a technician. I was, of course, different from men like Dub Dayton and St. Cloud and J.K.—I had from birth and wealth close connections to the men who ruled the nation—but still, it was not who I was but what I could do that brought me to power. I could fly and, as I have told you, I could kill. It should come as little surprise that those in power, the very men who would with a touch of a button plunge the planet in darkness, that very few of them have killed another man. They are generally aghast at the notion of putting a bullet in an animal's head. That I was rather good at such field work gave me a mystique among the men in power. I soon moved out of the field, into an executive position, but the aura was still there." Blackmuir smiled. "I did take some pleasure in this reputation. But then as time passed, as I climbed near real power, I saw this image as a stigma. I was an outcast among my own kind. An untouchable. It became apparent I would rise only so high. That I would never realize my true ambitions. And now, only today, I understand that my reputation will be the end of me.

"The idea of eliminating the entire Stokes team was nothing new. It was born in my first operation. I gather that my daughter has told you something about the Dimitri operation. Fat Boy and so on." Blackmuir smiled. "These fools were only two of the many members of that first team who were silenced. We couldn't, of course, quiet everyone. The operation was too vast. But still, twenty people close to the operation met timely ends. During the years I was in charge of cleaning up the Dimitri operation, I thought I was immune to elimination. But then as I saw my path to power blocked at every turn, I realized that I would someday be a marked man. That they couldn't let anyone who knew as much as I go free."

Blackmuir looked away. "When I understood my predicament, I turned to others in the same danger. I put myself in league with these men. Men I generally would have shunned. I fought to save myself on many levels. I bought this ranch, built these headquarters, established a paramilitary organization to protect me. From here I went into the country. I made contact with survivalists, vigilantes, posses comitatus—by whatever name, outlaws. But there are many other such outlaws—men who are far from cranks who would take rifle, knife and rope and go into the wilderness. Many of these men were close to power. A few in power. Take the man who is now in the White House. From the day of his election, this small dirty man knew he was not meant to be President. That he had gained office without the proper imprimatur. This dirty little man and I met before his inauguration. We spoke in private. The two of us. Even as President-elect, he had drawn up plans for an alternate government. Even then he dreamed of remaining in office beyond his elected terms. It was a simple matter to be recruited to the President's team, as the head operations officer of, oh, you might call it his shadow CIA. At first I worked with the White House, but it soon became clear that the Oval Office was not a safe place to conduct our operations. The President hadn't been able to purge the White House. There were too many old boys close to the Oval Office. I left the White House and became part of the President's personal team. An elite group of men who worked privately, in great secrecy, for the President. Of the many offices I performed for the President, by far the most crucial was that of securing his reelection. And of all the operations we conducted to secure the President's reelection, the most crucial, more important even than discrediting his rival, was the elimination of Gerald Stokes. It was this assignment I was given and which I have performed so poorly. But really, the Stokes operation was just the final nail in the coffin. In the words of another man whose death I saw, the chickens had come to roost long ago." Blackmuir stopped. "Looking back over it all, it seems a strange place for me to have come. All I ever wanted was to fly," he said as the wall speaker crackled, "and now the wax is melting."

The radio operator's voice came over the speaker. "Chief, we've made contact with the climbers. Shitty read—the base camp is transmitting the climbers' walkie-talkie."

"I'd like to speak to the climbers directly if we can pick them up."

"Right," said the operator and there came a frying static over the speaker. "Big, we've got Mr. Blackmuir here at the headquarters. Can you read?"

A faint voice came under the static. "We've made the canyon floor under the site. Nothing on the floor so far. We've got two men going on up the canyon. We got a portable spot on the ultralight. Pretty hard to say for sure, but it don't look like there's a body under the wings. Still snowing some."

Blackmuir said: "Any tracks?"

The radio operator repeated the question. The climber answered: "Nothing here. We might find something upcanyon. Hang on." The climber's voice went under the static, then came back. "Tobe went up the wall a ways. Nothing under the wings. Nothing on the canyon floor. Looks like he might have survived the crash and gone on upcanyon. You want us to go after him tonight?"

The radio operator spoke to the climber, again repeating Blackmuir's question: "How hard is it snowing? Any chance of finding tracks tonight?"

The climber replied: "It was easing up some at the trail head. Still coming down here. Won't find much by morning for sure."

Blackmuir did not speak. The radio operator said: "Come back, chief?"

Blackmuir turned to the wall speaker. "What do you think, Jerry? Looks like he's got away."

The radio operator said: "Maybe. But it's going to be tough up that canyon tonight. Even if he had a tent and a bag."

Blackmuir said: "He knows mountains. He'll go up into the snow and dig a cave."

The radio operator cut in: "We've got something coming in from the climbers, chief. I'm going to have to take it on the head set." Blackmuir toyed with the keys on the desk the fifteen seconds the radio operator was off the speaker. The voice of the radio operator came back on the wall speaker. "Chief, they've found some tracks going up into Angel Pass. Probably be covered up in an hour. Doesn't look like there's much chance of running him down tonight."

"Yes. They would have to carry lights." Blackmuir waited, then turned to the wall speaker. "Jerry, let's hold everything in place tonight. See what things look like in the morning. We may have to bring the outside in."

"Whatever you say, chief."

"Jerry, I want the climbing team to stay in place at the crash site for the night."

The radio operator laughed. "No problem. This is an outing for them."

Blackmuir smiled. "Jerry, I want you to clear a Mr. Cox from the compound. He'll be leaving in a matter of minutes."

"Cox. Right, chief."

"And Jerry, if Dub Dayton's call from California comes in, let me know immediately."

The wall speaker went silent. Blackmuir took up the keys from the desk. "There is one other thing you should know. Might make what you are going to do easier. When I was following Kat, when her car went into the river and she drowned, if she had stopped the car for me, as she seemed to be doing, I would have killed her. Five days ago I had a cardinal rule. Nobody ever left me."

Blackmuir tossed the keys across the desk. "The car and the motel room are both yours. The car is in the lower lot. Your luggage has been put in the trunk, along with some maps St. Cloud wanted you to have. The motel is in Livingston. The name and room number are on the key." Blackmuir stopped. "I think that's all there is to say, Cox."

I picked up the keys, dropped them, picked them up. "Now let me get this straight. Let's forget about all your civic-minded activities—murdering presidents, blowing up planes, setting up secret governments within governments—let's just deal with my small ordinary life. You have set me up as a murderer and a smuggler. You have seen taken from me my ranch and my house and my job and my name. You have murdered a friend and a man who probably would have been a friend if he had lived long enough. You have tried to murder me and your daughter and her husband and a man who has worked for you for years—not to forget sixty or so people you have never set eyes on. Have I forgotten anything? Oh yeah. You have fucked my wife and maybe even killed her too. Now, after all of this, you sit there and you say it's over. Finished. I am free to leave now. To go back to leading my small ordinary life. Is that what you are saying?"

Blackmuir didn't move. Then he smiled. "Yes. That's exactly what I'm saying."

"And you think I'm actually going to lie down for this? Walk away from you like nothing has happened. That one way or another I'm not going to come back for you."

Blackmuir had not moved. He still smiled. "I would suggest you drive carefully into town, Cox. The roads are very slippery tonight."

The snowy road to Livingston was empty. No one followed me, no one was waiting at the motel. I passed a quiet night. Even my dreams were peaceful. There were no nightmares of being trapped in a shining winged coffin far above the earth, no madman's tale of a nation ruled by murder and intrigue, no reiteration of the deaths I had known. Only a cabin near-buried in the snow, a light glowing from within, a figure at the window.

I rose early and showered and dressed. I went through my valise again. The money was there and a manila envelope with maps of the Bitterroot wilderness and an overlay that showed the location of St. Cloud's bush-pilot friend. I closed the case and thought of the mountains and what I would do now. Buy a plane and fly into the strip St. Cloud had marked on the map. Wait for Blackmuir, he would come. But that night's dream held me. The cabin in the snow. I tried to see Thea as the figure in the cabin window, but I couldn't. Maybe that was the nightmare.

I ate at the motel coffee shop, called the car rental agency and arranged to have the car returned to Kill Devil Ranch. I went to the room, packed what little I had besides money and maps and checked out of the motel. The clerk called a cab to fetch me at the car rental agency and take me to the Bozeman airport. These things done, I stood outside the motel office. The winter morning was bright and cold. The sky the blank, searing blue we had seen above the snow clouds yesterday. The parking lot had been plowed. Low, ragged ridges of snow banked the sidewalks. The snow crystals on these miniature ranges glittered like tiny pieces of electricity.

I stowed my case in the trunk and started the car. As I waited for the motor to warm, the motel clerk stepped outside the office. He looked toward me. I left the motor idling and went across the lot to the office. The clerk directed me to a booth across the lobby, then transferred the call. A man's voice came on the line:

"Mr. Cox, this is Dale White. At Kill Devil Ranch. I'm sorry to bother you so early, sir, but Mr. Blackmuir left instructions to contact you before you got away. There has been an accident. Mr. Blackmuir felt you would want to know."

I saw St. Cloud's body somewhere in a steep mountain pass, neck broken, the body covered with snow. I waited, then asked where they had found St. Cloud.

The man hesitated. "I'm sorry, sir, but this is another matter. The tragedy Mr. Blackmuir wanted you to know about has happened in California. During the night."

11

*D*AYTON stood before the wall where Thea's photographs had been. All but two of the photographs had been taken from the wall. Dayton held a third in his hands. He turned when I came into the room, laid the photograph on a sheet of newspaper spread over the table, folded the paper around the photograph and placed it in a box. He took the remaining photographs from the wall, wrapped them and put them in the box. This done, he turned from the blank wall and went to the bar. He poured whiskey into a glass and came to the couch. He sat and sipped at the drink.

"You want something," he said, "help your fucking self."

I had followed Dayton from the cemetery. It hadn't been a full funeral, just a memorial service. The coffin, hole and cut marble would come later, when the body was found. Dayton and Blackmuir had both been in attendance. Neither had mourned that much. The priest had said a few words and we had gone away from the grassy patch where Thea would be buried. Dayton and I had been the last to leave. Dayton had waited in the parking lot till I got to my car, then had driven easy back to the Atherton house. Marking every turn with blinker signals as if I did not know where he was leading me.

Now Dayton sat on the couch watching me, shoulders bunched, eyes bad, as if he was grieving now. Then the tension went out of Dayton and he leaned back in the couch. He brought the drink to his mouth, reached forward and put the drink on the glass table before the couch. "You want a drink?"

"I'm fine for now." I sat on the couch, away from Dayton. He put his hands to his face and pushed them up through his hair. I waited, then said: "Where is she?"

Dayton tensed, then let the muscles in his arms and shoulder go. He said nothing.

I waited. "You know, it seems a little strange, Dub. A one-car accident, the car goes into the sea. No witnesses, no body, no skid marks. Nothing." I moved on the couch. "Where have you got her?"

Dayton looked away. "Some pump jockey in Bolinas saw her a couple minutes before the accident. She stopped for gas. He says it was her. She was drunk. Fucked up on something. She was driving bad when she left the station."

"Maybe I will have that drink." I stood. "You want another one?"

Dayton looked at his glass. It was empty. "Bourbon."

I took his glass, went to the bar and poured two bourbons. I came back to the couch, put the two drinks on the glass table. I took the glass from the table, sipped the drink.

"Lane Blackmuir, he didn't seem suitably distraught either. For a man whose daughter has just died."

Dayton waited. "Maybe he's just not showing it."

I put the glass back on the table. "You know I've been up at Blackmuir's ranch in Montana. We had a couple chats. Just the two of us. He let his hair down. I got the impression he didn't give a shit if his daughter lived or died."

Dayton rose and went to the phone. He punched out a number and waited, looking at the wall of flying photographs, Blackmuir and himself standing with their squadron before a Flying Tiger. He turned from the display and spoke into the receiver. "Jay? Dub. Right. That Mojave job still on? Yeah. I need something to take my mind off it. Right. The Hyatt on El Camino. Right. Soon as I can get there. In the bar. Fine." He put the receiver down and came to the couch. He stood over me. "I got to see a man about work."

"You leaving the team, Dub?"

"It's over, Cox."

"Not as long as he's alive."

Dayton looked at me, then turned, looked around the room. "You want anything, take it. There's some good cognac there. She liked it." Dayton put his glass on the table and went to the stairs. He looked at the room, at the wall where Thea's pictures had hung. "She and I have a chance to get away from all this shit. If you fuck it up, Cox, I will kill you." He turned and went up the stairs.

Dayton was backing through the drive gate by the time I reached my car. I followed the paired ruby lights of Dayton's El Dorado as they sank into the Atherton woods. Dayton turned east toward the Bayshore Freeway, as if he were going to the Hyatt Hotel in Palo Alto. He drove slowly, signaling every turn, till he came to the last traffic light before the freeway. There he hit the El Dorado hard, accelerated through the yellow, moved into the right lane that would take him onto the southbound ramp. I waited till cross traffic had cleared, then went through the light. By the time I had made the on-ramp, the El Dorado had disappeared into the evening commuter traffic. I went bumper to bumper with the traffic, letting Dayton run. The El Dorado was parked on the Willow exit overpass, lights off. I moved my car to the right lane, passed the Willow off-ramp, went under the Willow bridge, going south toward San Jose. The El Dorado showed in the rearview mirror, lights on. The car passed over the Willow bridge, turned left to make the northbound on-ramp, turning toward San Francisco.

I left the freeway at the next exit, crossed the overpass and went back onto the Bayshore, north toward San Francisco. In forty-five minutes I left the freeway, Army Street exit, turned west to Folsom, then north to 16th Street. I parked my car beyond the alley and walked the two blocks around 16th and Folsom. I found the El Dorado parked on Capp. The car was locked. There were maps on the dash and a flight bag on the rear floorboard.

I went back to the alley. The warehouse and top-floor loft were dark. The smell of bread baking lay sweet in the air. I went up the stairs, the old wooden building creaking with my weight. No sound or light or movement came from the loft. I turned the knob, pushed back the door and went into the loft. Thea stood at the window at the back wall, looking out over the surrounding warehouse rooftops. As I came into the room she turned to me. Her body held stiff, cold, her hair pulled tight at the back of her head. I started toward Thea, she raised her hand, as if I should not come near, then something moved out of the shadows and everything was dark.

"OK, maybe I overdid it there, but I couldn't take any chances. Didn't know it was you."

"Bullshit."

Dayton made a fist before my face, but he was just being friendly. A forefinger extended near my nose. "I said I was fucking sorry, Cox."

Thea's voice came from the dark: "Do we have to keep him like this?"

I was back in my old suite. Handcuffed to the pipe that ran the length of the loft.

Dayton turned to the dark. "Till we figure out what he's up to, yeah."

Thea came near. "We could take him with us," she said, standing away, Dayton between us. "We'll be safer if he's with us."

Dayton watched me. "How do we know he ain't working for Lane? Like what the hell was he doing up at the ranch?" Dayton took my chin in thumb and finger and tugged it, as if I had a beard. "What were you doing at Kill Devil, Cox?"

"I was invited by Johnny Kono. Believe me, it was his idea."

"Yeah?" Dayton looked at his wife, back to me. "What happened with St. Cloud up there? I hear he disappeared."

"He took an ultralight. Went up some canyon. Crashed it on a wall and went into the mountains on foot.

He's running." I waited. "Look, my car's parked a couple blocks away. There's a case in the trunk. There're some maps and overlays in the case. St. Cloud has a friend in the Bitterroot wilderness. Bush pilot. He has a mountain strip. No roads. St. Cloud wants me to meet there. He thinks we can deal with Blackmuir there."

Dayton straightened. "Yeah. I heard about it."

"You talked to St. Cloud?"

Dayton looked at his watch, turned to Thea. "I've got to go through with this meeting tonight. We'll figure out what to do with Cox when I get back from Lane."

Thea moved to the bench. She lit a cigarette. "Be careful, Dub. You know Daddy doesn't believe I'm dead." Thea dropped the cigarette to the floor, put her foot on the coal.

Dayton looked at me. He turned away. "I've got to call Lane now. I'll come back before I go. You be all right here?"

"We'll be fine, Dub," Thea said.

Dayton waited. "Where's your car, Cox? I'll take a look at the maps."

I gave Dayton the keys and directions to the car. Dayton took another set of keys from his pocket. "I'll leave this here." He tossed the handcuff key on the bench between Thea and me. "All right. A couple minutes," he said, turned and went out of the loft and down the stairs.

When he was gone, Thea said: "You can take those things off if you want."

I took up the key and unlocked the handcuffs.

Thea shook another cigarette from the pack, lit it, and blew smoke into the dark. "Dub's more afraid of you than of any of the others." She looked at me. "You know that, don't you?"

Thea went across the room. She stood before the

window, looking out across the warehouse rooftops toward the lighted towers of the financial district. "What happened at the ranch?" She turned from the window. "Besides St. Cloud."

"There was a birthday party for your father."

"Really? I had forgotten." Thea came across the room. She stopped away from me. "Did you talk?"

"We talked."

"What did you talk about?"

"He said his world has collapsed. His friends in Washington want his head. That's what he said."

Thea came to the bench. She sat and took out another cigarette. She offered me one and lit them both. "I'm curious about something," she said. "Do you like being dead?"

"It does have its dangerous side."

The woman turned to me. "Really? I've never felt so secure in my life."

"Well, if we ever do die again—really die—there won't be many questions asked."

Thea smiled. "That doesn't bother me. Anyway, shouldn't we both consider the last week borrowed time?" She stopped. "I'm sorry. I just don't see how you or St. Cloud or Dub or anyone can beat him."

"St. Cloud seems to think we might be able to arrange for him to beat himself."

Thea turned away, toward the window where she had stood looking over the rooftops toward the spires of the financial district. I heard nothing, but there was some slight movement in the old building. Thea faced the door as it opened. Dayton stood framed in the doorway. He held a case in one hand. He looked across the dark loft where we sat, then went to the small kitchen at the front of the loft and put the case on the table there. He reached to a light hanging over the table and pulled the string. A tight circle of light fell over the table.

"Unlock the bastard," Dayton said, "if you haven't already."

Thea and I went to the table and sat. The light showed Dayton's face set hard. He reached to the case and opened it. He took the maps and overlays from the case, looked at the stacked twenties, then closed the case and put it on the floor. "My meeting with Lane is set up for tonight. Eleven o'clock. It's going to be public. I should be OK." Dayton stopped. He looked at the maps on the table, then looked at Thea. "We can only run so far. We'll go on and make it look like we're running. Then I'll go along with Cox. Once I get you set up somewhere safe. See if Cox and I can hook up with St. Cloud in the mountains. If that doesn't work out"—he raised his eyes to his wife—"we can always go into Canada from there." He looked back to the maps, still folded, on the table. "I've got a light plane ready at the San Carlos strip. I don't know how long this thing with Lane is going to take, but I should be getting to San Carlos with plenty of dark to work with. Four, five hours till daylight. I'll fly to the Mojave strip. The San Carlos plane is an old Aerobat. They won't have any trouble following me. I've got a Turbo 310 waiting at the Mojave strip. I'll switch planes there. The Turbo 310 is pretty hot. I should be able to shake them. Whatever happens, if I'm not back at SFO at flight time tomorrow, you go ahead without me. I'll catch up later. Cox can use my ticket. I'll buy another one at the airport." Dayton took a letter-sized manila envelope from his pocket. He shook a set of car keys, a couple of credit cards and two airline tickets onto the table. "In a couple minutes I'll go out of the alley. The front way. I'm figuring they'll only have the head of the alley covered." Dayton looked at his wife. "You remember how to get out the back way? Through the bakery."

Thea looked at the maps, keys, the airline tickets on the table. "Have you talked to the man at the bakery?"

"I've got it set with the night floor boss. He ain't expecting the two of you, but he's getting paid enough to cover the extra traffic." Dayton picked up the car keys. "There's a yellow Datsun on the other side of Mission. Twentieth and Valencia. The tag number's on the keys." Dayton tossed the keys onto the table. "Take two-eighty out of town, then cut over to the airport. Check into a motel, somewhere near the main terminal." Dayton stopped. He took one of the maps from the table. "Check into one room. Husband and wife." He put the map down. "Probably going to work out better this way. They won't be looking for two people." Dayton unfolded the map of the Bitterroot wilderness. "It's United flight eight oh seven. Noon to New York. It's got a stop in Salt Lake. The tickets are booked through to New York, but we'll get off at Salt Lake, make connections there to Montana. Our baggage will go on to New York for cover, so don't check anything," Dayton looked at my money case, "that you want to take with you." If I don't see you at the United terminal, I'll see you on the plane. Probably better that way, no contact till we get on the plane." Dayton looked at Thea. "Got the money with you?"

"It's in my purse."

Dayton turned to me. "I'm paying for this trip. I don't trust those fucking twenties you got."

"They're all right, Dub."

"Maybe," Dayton said. "Any questions?" No one spoke and Dayton unfolded the onionskin overlay. He fitted the overlay onto the map of the wilderness. "All right, let's take a look where St. Cloud is going to be."

*   *   *

The room had no windows. Twin beds. TV. Dresser. Luggage stand. Night table between the beds. A phone and lamp on the night table. Any motel room anywhere but for the roar, the vibration that came every minute or so. The big jets from SFO lifting off the north runway, climbing hard under full throttle to clear the San Bruno Mountains, on their way to Portland, Seattle, Hawaii, the Far East.

I unpacked what little we had brought with us. Thea stood at the wall near the door. When I had done with the cases, Thea turned back to the room. She came to the bed. Her valise lay open on the luggage stand. She touched a blouse folded in the case. "I want to go out tonight. I want to go to the terminal. I know we shouldn't. Daddy may have someone there at the terminal. We should stay here, watch TV and be good. But I can't." She looked up. "Not tonight." She went to the wall where there should have been a window. "Let's go out, Dan, and watch people come and go."

A courtesy shuttle took us to the main terminal. By now Thea was in good spirits. She laughed, chatted with the orange people pushing dried flowers and damp philosophy near the terminal entrance. We went to the main cocktail lounge and took a table by the windows overlooking the United parking bays, the black expanse of the field beyond marked only by strings of runway lights. While I ordered champagne, Thea went back onto the main concourse. She returned with a loaf of sourdough bread, magazines, the *New York Times* for the crossword. We nibbled at the crisp, tart bread, drank champagne and watched the great jets lowering from the sky. Thea opened one of the magazines, a thick journal touting the latest fashions, and read our horoscopes.

There did not seem to be any problems we could not overcome.

As the champagne went, I told Thea of the time I had spent in the San Francisco Tenderloin, after I had fled Arizona and started a new life from the bottom. The hotel on Taylor, the job I had found shuttling rental cars to the airport. I turned Thea to look across the vast field, to the north, and told her about the plane watchers with their binoculars and charts and schedules and airline identification books.

We watched as an Alaska Airlines 747 landed and ran down the runway, spoilers and flaps up, engines reversed, braking hard. Then Thea rose and said she wanted to go where the runway freaks had gathered.

The cab stood waiting as we went to the fence at the edge of the landfill, to look across the bay inlet toward the north runway. For a time we watched the massive jets come to earth, lift into the sky, then Thea came under my arm, huddling away from the chill mist rising from the Bay. After a time, we went back to the cab. The cab's dome light was on, the driver was reading a paperback. He turned to the back, Thea huddled under my arm. The driver looked at me. "Your lady friend OK?"

"She's all right. Just cold."

Thea turned her face into my shoulder. "I'm afraid."

The driver looked forward, across the bay inlet, toward the north runway. A jet's landing lights were suspended like twin stars far to the south, the jet easing into its final approach. "Yeah, I know how you feel," the driver said. "Sometimes I get a little jumpy getting on one of those things." The driver turned back. "But you got to remember, lady, it's a lot safer than what I do for a living. Driving a frigging cab."

Thea smiled. "It's all right. I'm all right."

The driver looked at Thea, at me. "Anywhere you want to go, pal?"

I turned to Thea. She was looking away, into the dark. "Are you hungry? We could go back to the terminal."

She turned. "No. Let's go back to the room. I just want to sleep."

I gave the driver the motel name and he started the cab and drove back the way we had come. I got the key from the office and we went to the room. Thea sat on the bed, looking toward the TV as if it were on.

"We should have brought the champagne. I don't really want it now, but it would have been nice in the morning. I like still champagne in the morning."

"I could go out."

Thea shook her head. "I don't want you to leave me. Anyway, there's no place to buy a bottle at the airport. There is duty-free, but then you'd have to buy a ticket to a foreign place. Rather a lot for still champagne."

"We could both go to duty-free. And keep going."

Thea shook her head. "Where would we go?"

"We could go to Europe. Australia. Anywhere. Just the two of us."

Thea looked about the room. "I'm sorry. I really don't know how to leave him. I've never done it before." She put her hand on the bed. "I'll give you a fuck tonight, Dan, if you want it, but I don't feel anything. It's not that I can't love you. It's that I don't want to. It's the best I can do."

"Maybe it will come."

"Turn off the light," she said. "Maybe that will make it easier."

*　　*　　*

United flight 807 for New York, with stops in Salt Lake
City and Chicago, was scheduled to depart SFO at noon.
The clock on the main terminal tower read eleven
forty-five when the cab dropped us at the United departure landing. The crowd before the United check-in
counter was so large that for a moment we thought we
might miss the flight. But Thea turned us to a shorter
line, the position for passengers without luggage to be
checked. Our tickets were pulled and we were assigned
smoking seats in the rear of the plane, a DC-10. I took
our tickets and boarding passes and turned from the
counter, but Thea stayed back. She spoke to the clerk:

"I'm sorry to trouble you, but I wonder if you could
tell us if my husband's brother has checked in on this
flight."

The clerk looked at Thea. "I'm sorry, ma'am, but we
can't give out that information."

Thea said: "Yes, I know. I used to fly for Pan Am. But
it really is important for us to travel together. If he
doesn't make the plane, we have to wait for him. Please.
Shaw. He may be forward, in the no-smoking section of
the cabin."

The clerk turned to the computer terminal and
punched up the passenger list. The clerk looked at the
display. "Mr. Gerald Shaw and his luggage have been
checked onto flight eight oh seven for New York." The
clerk looked up. "Your plane is boarding now, if you care
to proceed to gate eighteen."

We turned onto the main concourse and went north
toward our boarding gate. At the head of the concourse,
we came to a security check, installed since the C. W.
Namier hijack. Our bags trundled past a metal scan; we
went through a metal-detector threshold. Beyond the
security check we claimed our cases and went along the
concourse toward our gate. The gate waiting area was

empty. Those who were taking flight 807 for New York were already on board. It was one minute till twelve when we entered the mobile tunnel that led to the United DC-10.

The McDonnell Douglas jumbo was a hundred and eighty feet long, sixty feet high, wingspan a hundred and sixty-five feet, maximum takeoff weight, with three hundred plus passengers, their luggage and cargo, over half a million pounds. Modest compared to the 747, maybe, but large enough that Thea and I did not see Dayton when we came onto the craft. We entered the DC-10 by the forward door and made our way along the port aisle the length of the passenger cabin to the rear smoking area. The aisles were crowded with passengers stowing luggage in overhead compartments, making last calls to the toilet before takeoff, those who wanted to watch the inflight movie jockeying for seats near the two screens on the interior cabin walls. Dayton could have been seated forward of the door, in one of the toilets, on the starboard side of the cabin, screened by the passengers still arranging themselves and their luggage.

Our seats were five forward from the rear toilet bulkhead, 56A and B, window and aisle on the port side of the aircraft. Thea took the window seat and turned to watch the last luggage train being loaded into the cargo hold directly below us. I stowed our luggage overhead and went forward to look for Dayton. I had gone as far as the rear interior cabin wall when the whine of the plane's three turbofan engines rose and a stewardess asked me to return to my seat for taxiing and takeoff. I returned to the rear of the cabin and strapped in. Thea sat at the window, looking out. The rear cargo door had been lowered and shut. The empty baggage train was moving off, crossing the runway toward the baggage hall. In a few moments the plane eased back from the dock and the stewardesses took their places in the aisles near the interior cabin walls and began their emergency drill. Few passengers aboard flight 807 listened to the rote listing of the DC-10's eight emergency exits. Rather, as the plane moved along the lateral taxi strip, we turned to newspapers, magazines, books, those, like Thea, by the windows looking out, watching the ground traffic, the departing jets moving to takeoff position, the incoming planes taxiing from the end of their landing runs toward the terminal.

We came to the foot of the runway second in line, behind a Thai Royal Orchid 747. The Thai jet was cleared for takeoff and wheeled onto the runway. Thea watched the dramatically marked 747 begin its roll to takeoff, our aircraft turning onto the runway behind the Thai jet. "Have you seen the Braniff Calder? It must be strange for the crew—working inside a painting." Thea did not speak again till we were airborne, climbing over the Sierra foothills toward cruising altitude. She turned from the window and smiled. "When I was working I never looked out at the ground. Most of the time I forgot where I was."

Thea was quiet for a time, then asked if I had brought the newspaper. I gave her the copy of the *Chronicle* I had bought at the motel and, as she turned to a back section of the paper, rose and went to one of the aft toilets. When I returned to my seat, Thea's eyes were closed, her head resting against the cabin wall, the *Chronicle* laid across her lap. I went forward from our seats, along the port aisle to the head of the tourist section of the cabin, then returned to the rear of the cabin along the starboard aisle. I did not see Dayton anywhere, I'd check first class later. I sat by Thea without waking her and passed when the drink trolley came along the aisle. The drink trolley was followed by a stewardess handing out magazines and newspapers. The stewardess smiled at Thea asleep and asked the man sitting across the aisle if he would like anything to read.

The man looked up from the work papers spread over his tray. "You got the *New York Times?*"

The stewardess smiled. "I'm sorry, sir, only the afternoon *Examiner.* It does have the noon stock prices from New York."

"That'll do."

The stewardess gave the man the newspaper and smiled. "Have you had a successful trip to California, sir?"

The man took the business section from the back of the paper. "It's been OK."

The stewardess continued down the aisle, passing out magazines and newspapers. The man across the aisle peered after the stewardess, then said to me: "To tell the truth it's been a wreck." The man went back a bit, looked at me over his reading glasses. "You from California?"

"I've been living in Montana recently."

The man studied me, as if that might be a foreign place. "What do you do there?"

"I'm retired."

The man looked at me. "You? Retired?"

"I got lucky."

The man turned to the front page of the business section. "Yeah. Luck. That's what you got to have." He opened the section to the New York Stock Exchange quotes. The man moved a finger down the stock quotes. He stopped on a share price, shook his head and folded the paper shut. "Retire. That's what I ought to do. Give my wife the shock of her life." The man picked up a work paper from the tray, looked at it, put it down. "But I'm good for just one thing. Work. And dead. This thing falls down, she'd be sitting pretty. Jesus, you ought to see the premiums I pay." The man took the folded *Examiner* and held it across the aisle. "You want this rag?"

I was about to decline, then saw the lead headline on the folded front page:

AT SAN CARLOS AIRPORT

I took the paper and unfolded the front page. The full headline read:

FREAK ACCIDENT AT SAN CARLOS AIRPORT

There was a photograph of two men standing by a light plane, the plane an Aerobat. A covered form beneath the plane's prop. The story was brief. An as yet unidentified man had been struck by the plane's propeller sometime after midnight. The man's age was listed fifties. Airport authorities theorized that the man had backed into the plane's prop while removing a wheel block.

The drink trolley had neared the forward galley. The stewardesses there were preparing the meal trolley. I folded the paper closed, put it on my seat and went forward to first class. No Dayton. I returned to tourist. One of the stewardesses who had served drinks came along the aisle, looking overhead, for a call button that had been lighted. I asked her the name of the chief stewardess and was told to ask for Nancy Taylor in first class. I went past the galley into the plane's center cabin. I had not see Dayton anywhere. I returned to the front of the plane, to the forward galley that served first class and asked for the chief stewardess. The center cabin stewardess said that Nancy Taylor was occupied on the flight deck. Could she be of any assistance?

The stewardess was drawn into the forward galley— there was some problem with a request for a salt-free meal. When the stewardess came from the galley, she was harried, out of temper.

"I'm sorry, sir, but can't this wait till after lunch service? We really are in over our heads today."

I stood in the aisle before the stewardess. "This will just take a moment. I'm a captain for Northwestern. I was supposed to meet a friend, a pilot, on the plane. I can't find him. Did your passenger count come up short today?"

The stewardess looked past me. "He probably simply missed the plane, sir."

"No. I asked at the check-in desk. My friend and his luggage had been checked through."

"Your friend still could have missed the plane after check-in, sir."

I put my hands on the seatbacks next to the aisle. "Look, all I want to know is if your headcount came up short. Tell me who was at the door and I'll waste her time."

The stewardess turned away, toward the galley. "Jane, who was at the door today? Ginny? Did she come up short?"

A voice came from the galley. "Yes. Ginny. I think she did come up short."

The stewardess turned back. "Ginny's working first class, if you want to talk to her." The stewardess moved past me. "Sorry, but this saltless woman is driving everybody up the wall."

I went forward, into first class. I found Ginny in an easy mood. She and her partner were working only thirty

people, not having to deal with cash for drinks. I gave
Ginny my story, that I flew for Northwestern, was
looking for a friend, a pilot. She smiled. "That explains
it. I thought I'd made a miscount." Ginny was tall, leggy,
with a long face and what could have been an authentic
smile. "Do you know Jeff Knudsen? First officer. Flies
the Pacific out of Seattle."

"We've gotten pretty big these days."

Ginny smiled. "So I hear." She moved out of the
aisle. "Would you like to upgrade?"

"I'm with someone."

Ginny shrugged, smiling. "Well, I hope your friend
catches up with you."

I went back to the rear of the plane. I thought Thea
was still asleep. Her head rested against the cabin wall,
her face turned toward the window. But as I came to my
seat, I saw that her eyes were open, that the front page of
the *Examiner* lay over her lap. I sat by her. She did
not turn to me. She looked out the window as she
spoke.

"Did you find him?"

"No, I didn't find him."

Thea turned. She looked at the paper's headline.
"His luggage, Dan. They checked his luggage on board
the plane."

Ginny was not pleased to see me a second time. She
smiled when I said I had to speak to her privately, but it
was work. We left first class and found two empty seats
in what United called executive class. Ginny put me in
the window seat, she stayed near the aisle. I held the
Examiner, the front page folded shut, in my lap and
began to tell a story that, I hoped, would save our lives. I
said I really was an airline pilot. I was not a drunk, a

Lothario, or a crazy. "Ginny, we've got to act quickly. As soon as we've finished you've got to go forward to the flight deck and tell the captain that he must land the plane now. At the nearest available strip. Anything long enough to handle the plane. Ginny, there may be a bomb on board the plane. I didn't bring anything on board with me. I am not a hijacker. I had nothing to do with the bomb being on board." I unfolded the newspaper to the front-page headline. "There was a man my wife and I were supposed to meet on the plane. According to the check-in clerk that man and his luggage were checked onto the plane. That man is not on the plane." I held the *Examiner* front page to the stewardess. She looked at the headline, at me. "He was killed last night at the San Carlos airport. He was murdered. The people who murdered him came to SFO this morning, checked the man and his luggage onto our plane. In one of the bags is a bomb. The bomb could go off at any moment. We've got to take the plane down immediately. You've got to help me, Ginny. We must get this plane out of the air *now*."

Ginny looked at the headline. "Is the baggage in the cabin?"

"No, Ginny. You've got to listen. The bag was checked through at the terminal. It's in one of the cargo holds."

The stewardess had gone rigid. The smile was gone. She kept looking at the headline. "What do you want me to do?"

"I want you to go forward to the flight deck. Tell the captain to begin emergency descent immediately. Tell him there is an emergency and to get the plane down. Do you understand, Ginny?"

Ginny raised her eyes. She did not look at me. "Yes. I understand."

I went back in the seat. "All right. Get up and go. I'll wait here."

Ginny stood. She remained in the aisle by the seat. "What is your seat number, sir?"

"Ginny, tell the captain to get this fucking plane down now!"

Ginny went forward, disappearing into the first-class cabin. I looked back. The executive-class cabin was near vacant. No one sitting near. I turned to the window. Below lay desert, an endless tan blanket torn by gorge and dry riverbed. Far to the north stood a mountain range, the peaks shining white, icy, under the winter sun. We were over Nevada somewhere, the Sierras behind us, Utah and the Rockies three, four hundred miles ahead. Reno was probably the nearest strip that could handle the DC-10. A harbor that was ever falling to our rear.

I went to the aisle seat and looked forward. The stewardess had closed the curtain to the first-class cabin. I went forward in my mind to the flight deck. I put myself in the left seat, captain of the plane. What story would the stewardess tell him? There was a drunk, a crazy, on board. And the captain's reaction—he would keep the plane on course, raise the crew in the rear of the craft on the intercom. They would be coming forward now, maybe a United security man, an off-duty cop, to deal with the madman who said there was a bomb in one of the cargo holds below.

I did not know how much time had passed. A minute, minute and a half. The plane flew steady, toward the mountains to the east, away from the strip at Reno. I rose from my seat and went forward. I pulled back the aisle curtain and went into the first-class cabin. The door to the flight deck was closed. The first-class cabin was quiet. A man stood in the aisle talking to another passenger. People read, slept, looked out the windows toward the mountain range to the north. Neither Ginny nor her partner was in sight. I went forward through the small, plush cabin. The first-class galley was empty. The two stewardesses were forward, on the flight deck. I went to the flight-deck door, stood to one side, away from the peephole, turned the knob, pushed the door back and went into the flight deck.

The DC-10 flight deck was a ten-by-twelve-foot cubicle crammed with panels and consoles and tables of gauges and dials and instruments and controls. Two chairs forward for the captain and first officer, a third to the rear right of the cabin for the flight engineer, a fourth supernumerary seat to the left rear, directly behind the captain's seat. The flight-deck crew members were in their seats. Ginny sat in the supernumerary chair. The other first-class stewardess stood near the door. The captain and the first officer were turned in their chairs, looking back at me. I took the standing stewardess by the arm and moved her away from the flight engineer's console. I spoke to the flight engineer:

"What's the nearest strip we can land on? Is there anything closer than Reno or Salt Lake?"

The flight engineer watched me. "We're probably closer to Salt Lake now."

"Is there anything else? A military base? Anything."

The flight engineer glanced at his desk, then back. "It would probably take more time to clear. Salt Lake's probably quicker."

"How far to Salt Lake? How long?"

The flight engineer turned in his chair. He looked forward, toward the first officer. "Thirty minutes to Salt Lake. Maybe less."

I turned to the captain. "Radio Salt Lake for emergency landing. And take the plane down."

The captain turned to the first officer. "About time to start descent anyway. Right, Doug?"

The first officer remained turned back, looking at me. He was a short, stocky, hard man, about thirty-five. He worked out, maybe had played college ball. He looked ready to come for me. "What the hell is your story, man?"

The captain reached across the pedestal between the pilots' chairs. He put a hand on the first officer's shoulder. "Start the Salt Lake descent, Doug, and radio emergency landing. I'll see what the gentleman wants from us."

The first officer turned his chair forward. He reached to the panel beneath the glare shield and disengaged the automatic pilot. He eased the wheel column forward and the plane's nose went down. The captain turned back to me. He moved his feet as if he were about to come out of his chair. I took the stewardess' arm and moved her between the captain and me.

"You stay in your fucking seat. If something happens, it's going to take two of you to fly the plane."

The captain went back in his seat. He kept looking at me, nothing else. "Fine. Fine. We'll do just what you say. All right? Now." He looked toward the two stewardesses, then back to me. "I'm afraid Ginny might not have gotten your story right. What sort of danger are we in?"

"Someone has put a bomb on the plane. It's stored in one of the cargo holds. We've got to get down. The bomb goes, we're going to lose cabin pressure—at least. Fuck knows what else."

"That sounds like a good idea to me," the captain said. "We should be in breathable air in five minutes." The captain cocked his head toward the flight engineer. "You know, we could send you and Jerry down into the nosewheel compartment. You could work your way back into the cargo holds and see if you could find this bomb."

"Don't give me that shit. There's no way from the nosewheel hold back through the forward bulkhead."

The captain looked at the instrument panel, the first officer pushing the plane over into descent, then back to me. "Ginny says you fly one of these things."

I moved the stewardess back, gripping her arm hard, so that her fear of me was seen by the captain. "I want you to turn in your seat and get Salt Lake on the radio and tell them to prepare for an emergency landing."

The captain did not turn forward. He smiled. "Who do you fly for?"

"Look, you're playing with our lives. I don't have anything in the passenger cabin. Taking me is not going to solve a fucking thing."

The captain spoke to the first officer, not taking his eyes off me. "Doug, call Salt Lake. Tell them we have a problem." To me: "Mind if we tell them we have a hijack in progress?"

"Whatever it takes to get the emergency equipment in place."

The first officer took the mike from the panel and began calling Salt Lake control. The captain smiled. "Actually, we've already done that." The captain waited till Salt Lake answered the call, then he turned to me. "So who do you fly for?" A light flashed on the overhead between the two pilots. "The intercom," the captain said. "Mind if I take it?"

"The flight engineer."

The captain looked at the flight engineer. "Jerry, see what's going on in the back."

The flight engineer reached for a phone under his table. He listened, then said: "Yeah. All right." The flight engineer put the phone back under the table. He turned to the captain. "He's got a friend."

The captain said: "Fucking C.W. Namier. Now everybody wants to have his own plane."

I put an arm under the stewardess' throat. "What's going on back there?"

The flight engineer slowly turned his chair to me. "Nothing."

I pulled the stewardess back to the flight-deck door. "I'm going back. If my friend is all right, she will be all right."

The captain smiled, his eyes blank. "Not a bad idea. We can get down to getting the plane out of the air."

I reached back, turned the knob and pushed the door open. I backed into the threshold, keeping the stewardess between me and the flight engineer. I looked into the hall that led past the forward galley into the first-class cabin. No one in the hall or the aisle beyond. I turned back to the flight deck just as the first officer was pulling back on the column, twisting the wheel. The floor pitched under me. I grabbed at the threshold, trying to keep my grip on the stewardess, but the floor went back sharp and the stewardess twisted from under my arm. I lost hold on the threshold and went down on the hall floor. Then a man came from the forward galley.

United security, off-duty cops, whatever, both were big, hard men. One of them, the one I could see, had a gun. His partner was behind me, his forearm tight against my throat, twisting my right arm behind my back. As the man behind me pulled me back and up, I saw the stewardess along the aisle, rising to her feet, and, out of the corner of my eye, the captain standing in the flight-deck door. The plane was leveling, coming straight. The first officer's voice came on the passenger intercom, apologizing for the turbulence, asking all passengers to remain belted in their seats till further notice. The man behind me got me to my feet, pushed my face against the bulkhead wall.

The captain looked toward the rear of the aircraft. "You got the woman under control?"

"She's secured," the man behind me said. "No problem with her."

The captain turned to the man behind me. "Check their bags?"

"Everything but one case. Locked. Everything else is clean."

The captain looked at me. "Maybe we can get this joker to open it."

"Leave it be," the man behind me said. "You open it, it might go."

The captain waited. "All right. Get this guy somewhere he won't cause any trouble. We'll get us down quick as we can." The captain looked at me. "You guys handle everything?"

The man behind me pushed my face hard against the wall. "We got it under control. You guys just fly the plane."

The captain spoke to the stewardess down the aisle. "You OK, darling?"

The stewardess looked at me, her face drawn. "I'm OK."

The captain said: "Ginny's still a little shook. We're going to keep her up here with us. Can you get everybody settled down?"

A passenger had come forward along the first-class cabin aisle. The stewardess turned to the man, blocking his way. The man moved his head left, right, trying to see past the stewardess. "Hey, what's going on with the plane?"

The stewardess stood her ground. The security man with the gun kept his back to the passenger, shielding the gun from view. The stewardess said: "We've encountered some clear-air turbulence, sir. Will you please return to your seat and fasten your seat belt."

The passenger's head bobbed over the stewardess' shoulder, the man looking toward me. "What's with that guy?"

The stewardess began backing the man down the aisle. "Sir, the captain has turned on the seat-belt sign. Will you please return to your seat."

When the stewardess had cleared the passenger into the first-class cabin, the security man reached back and pulled the curtain across the aisle. The security man put his gun away. The guy at my back took my face off the wall. The captain turned in the flight-deck door, looked back at me.

"All right," the captain said. "Get him out of here." He looked at the security man. "Keep the gun out of sight. We want to keep everybody quiet."

The captain closed the flight-deck door. The security man came close to me. "You ain't going to cause any more trouble, are you, pal?"

The man behind me said: "Got your cuffs?"

The security man jerked his head back. "They're on the woman."

"Fuck," the man behind me said.

The security man came close. He grinned. "That's all right. We'll take him to one of the rear toilets." He took my face in his fingers. "You're going to keep quiet, aren't you?" The security man stepped back. "All right. Let him go. See if he's interested in walking back."

The man behind me released my arm, took his forearm from my neck and pushed me toward the security man. The security man spoke to the man behind me. "Go first, Eddie." He came close. "And I'm going to be right behind you, pal."

Eddie came from behind me and went to the curtain across the aisle. He looked back at me, the security man. "Ready?"

"Let's go," the security man said.

Eddie pushed the curtain back and the three of us—Eddie ahead, the security man behind—went into the first-class cabin. The first-class passengers who had heard the scuffle looked frightened, others queasy from the plane's roll; a few smiled at the drunk who had tried to upgrade from steerage. Those in the two aft tourist cabins scarcely noticed our passage. They were all in their seats, strapped down, a few looking out the window at the engines, looking for trouble there, something to explain the plane's sharp roll. As we went back along the starboard aisle, I looked across the cabin toward Thea. The seat beside her was vacant. A coat lay across her lap and hands and whatever part of the plane she was handcuffed to. Thea looked toward me, then turned her eyes toward the window.

There were five toilets in the rear of the DC-10. Three positioned in line against the rear bulkhead wall, two larger toilets, starboard and port, forward of these, snugged against the plane's fuselage shell. The three of us went through the passenger cabin and stopped in the short hall by the rear galley. Two crew jump seats were set against the fuselage wall, an intercom phone against the forward wall of the starboard toilet. A stewardess came from the rear galley. Eddie told the stewardess he wanted the starboard aisle to the rear toilets blocked. The stewardess pulled a drink trolley from the galley and turned it across the aisle just to the rear of the last seats in the cabin. The passengers in those seats turned to watch the drink trolley being placed across the aisle. Eddie went into the hall that ran across the rear of the plane, fronting the three rear toilets. He came back and reported those three toilets empty. The occupied light in the forward starboard toilet was on. Eddie pointed at the starboard toilet door and spoke to the stewardess:

"Who's in there?"

The stewardess knocked on the toilet door. "Ma'am, can you please return to your seat now? The captain has put the seat-belt sign on. We're encountering turbulence."

A toilet flushed behind the door and a woman unlocked and pulled back the door. Eddie took her arm and drew her from the toilet. "I'm sorry, ma'am. Can you use the other aisle?" He led the woman to the hall that ran across the rear of the plane.

The security man pushed me into the forward starboard toilet. He stood in the hall before the toilet door. He told me to sit on the toilet seat. He turned to the stewardess: "We think there's just the two of them, but we don't know. Keep everybody away from this side of the plane."

The stewardess had gone back into the galley. I could not see her, only hear she was close. "Should I close all the rear toilets?"

The security man looked at me. "Yeah."

The stewardess' footsteps passed through the galley to the other side of the cabin. The security man pulled a jump seat from the wall. He sat on the jump seat. "So where you got the bomb? In the locked case?"

"There's no bomb in that case. The bomb is in one of the cargo holds."

The security man leaned forward on the jump seat,

toward the toilet door. "You got the fucking thing set to go off?"

"I don't. But the people who put the bomb on the plane do. Look, my lady friend's husband put it on board. You got that? He's willing to blow everybody up to get the two of us."

The security man looked at me, as if my story was entering regions he understood, then his attention was drawn to the cabin. The security man rose. The jump seat banged up against the galley wall. The security man went to the drink trolley blocking the aisle and looked into the passenger cabin. "What the fuck is happening, Eddie?"

I could not see into the passenger cabin, only hear his partner's voice as he came down the starboard aisle: "The word has got out. We got a woman going crazy up there. Half the fucking plane forward is about to riot."

The security man said: "Get those people back in their seats and tied down. Tell that jerk who flies this thing to get everybody ready for emergency landing. This guy's story might have something. How far we from Salt Lake?"

"I don't know. Twenty minutes. I don't know."

"How's the woman doing?"

"She's all right. Quiet."

"I don't like this, Eddie," the security man said. "These people ain't hijackers. Go on Eddie. Move it."

There came a woman's voice crying out from somewhere forward in the plane and I did not hear Eddie's voice anymore. Just the woman's scream and other passengers calling out, the voice of a stewardess asking the people to return to their seats.

The security man stood at the trolley blocking the aisle, looking toward the panic sweeping the passenger cabin. I rose from the toilet seat and went to the door and looked beyond the security man into the passenger cabin. A half-dozen people were in the aisles. A woman was coming along the starboard aisle toward us. The woman was crying. Eddie had reached the woman and was forcing her back to the forward cabin. The security man turned and saw me standing at the toilet door. The security man reached his hand inside his coat, toward his gun. He started to speak, but he did not finish. There came a muffled explosion from under us. A soft, harmless sound. A shock wave passed through the shell of the aircraft. The cabin floor vibrated, the superstructure shuddered. The security man turned forward, his mouth open, his hand held toward the drink trolley to gain support. There came a scream of metal shearing, a splitting explosion from where the security man stood, and the wall of the cabin and the floor where the drink trolley and the security man had stood and the trolley and the man were gone. Then I could not see. Bits of debris, air fouled by the loss of pressure in the cabin blinded me. I only felt the abyss before me, the powerful suction of the air in the cabin roaring through the hole in the plane's skin. I pulled at the doorframe and went back into the toilet, onto the floor, grasping the toilet seat so that I would not be sucked out of the hole torn in the fuselage wall.

I held on to the toilet seat till the rush of pressure from the hole in the fuselage wall no longer pulled me toward the door. I freed one hand and cleared my eyes. A roar came from just beyond the door, and beyond the roar made by the hole torn in the fuselage wall came the cries of terror from those left in the cabin. Now I felt myself being pulled toward the door, then I was pushed back—the plane was rolling, the tail of the plane yawing. I let go of the seat and pushed myself across the toilet floor to the door. I worked my hands up the door threshold till I stood at the door, just inside the toilet. Then, holding to a safety grip on the toilet wall, I eased beyond the door threshold and looked forward, into the passenger cabin.

The earth showed a few feet beyond the toilet door. The smooth, scalloped hole began where the drink trolley had stood and arced forward, along the starboard aisle, five or six seats into the cabin, where the tear turned up the cabin wall, the plastic baffle shredded as if rent by great teeth. The tear reached no higher than my line of sight. It was the floor, mainly, and the dozen or so seats that had been there and the people strapped in them that were gone. The scene below was mountains, like a model landscape for a miniature train set. So distant, detached from the hellish world of the plane's cabin.

At first I saw nothing in the cabin but smoke or what looked to be smoke—a boiling caldron of fog made as the frigid atmosphere rushed into the warmed cabin. As the warm air was sucked through the tear in the fuselage, the fog cleared and I saw the chaos I had only heard. The screams nearby were from those who had been mutilated by the exploding floor and cabin wall, their limbs torn away by the seats sucked through the hole in the plane wall. One of those nearest the hole, a man still strapped in his seat, was dead, his neck broken. Beyond were more cries of pain, from those who had not been strapped in their seats and had been thrown about the cabin by the force of the suction. The cabin was filled with swirling debris. Oxygen masks hung from the overhead luggage compartments like entrails ripped from a wounded animal. Two stewardesses, sublimely calm it would seem from their deliberate movements, went along the aisles ministering to the injured, comforting those stricken by terror. Other passengers seemed resigned to their fate. Some were leaned forward in their seats, their heads bent to their knees, as if this posture would save them. Others sat upright as if nothing had happened or worse was about to happen. Some were frozen by fear. Some, a few, maybe they were thinking they would live, that the plane could be brought to a landing.

The plane yawed, rolled and dropped flat. The tail slid from side to side, the cabin pitched left, then right, the floor felt weak beneath my feet. The explosion and the collapsing floor and wall had torn through the plane's electrical and hydraulic systems. What control the pilots had came from the thrust and idling of the two wing-mounted engines. For now the pilots kept the nose of the plane above the line of the horizon, but still, even in trim, the plane sank toward the earth and wandered through the sky. The plane made a sharp bank right and I thought for a moment that the pilots had turned the plane to approach the Salt Lake runway. That we might survive an emergency landing. But then the plane's wings did not level, the bank steepened, and the plane's nose began to drop. The plane was out of control, sliding into a wide, circling dive.

Still holding to the safety handle inside the toilet, I went into the hall. The turbulence in the hole in the fuselage reached up and near yanked me into the sky. I pushed forward as far as I could reach and looked into the passenger cabin. I could not see Thea. I could not remember where she sat. Fifth, sixth row from the back. I thought of going along the hall that passed before the three rear toilets, making my way up the port aisle to her, but then I remembered she was handcuffed to some part of the seat or the plane. There was no way I could save her. I pulled myself away from the sucking hole in the plane and went into the toilet. I closed and locked the door. I went to the floor, curled around the toilet seat, my back braced against the front wall of the toilet, my feet and knees against the rear wall. I wrapped my arms about my head and waited for the concussive darkness of the impact.

12

*B*UCK LLOYD was the first person to arrive at the scene of the crash. Or so he thought when he came on the charred ruin the DC-10 had cut through the cedar-and-jack-pine forest fifty miles west of Dinosaur National Monument. Buck Lloyd ran the ore crusher at the Neola Silver Mine set in the Uinta foothills. By noon on the day of the crash Buck was four hours into his second shift, ready to go sixteen, twenty hours straight to keep the crusher rolling, but the day crusher floor boss, the juicer who hadn't made it in that morning, finally showed and the BYU engineer who read the dials and thought he ran the place told Buck he could knock off.

Get a little sleep before his regular shift at midnight. It was one o'clock by the time Buck showered and changed and turned his Dodge Ram pickup toward Vernal, the small town thirty miles to the south where Buck lived.

The day had begun clear and bright, but now, at a little past one, high cirrus clouds had washed over the sky, leaching color from the earth. As Buck drove south, he thought the mountains and ridges and formations he passed through looked like the petrified remains of the spined and armored beasts that had given Dinosaur National Monument its name. Buck hadn't got through his first Coors when he saw the column of black smoke rising to the east, maybe ten miles away. Buck stopped, got out of his rig and looked toward the smoke. Too black for forest fire. Buck reached into the cab and put out a call on the rig's CB. He raised a park ranger at Dinosaur. The ranger reported he had just got a call from park headquarters. A plane had gone down somewhere between the park and the Uinta Mountains to the west. The ranger didn't know the type of plane that had gone down and, until Buck had raised him about the smoke, had figured the site of the crash could have been anywhere in the thousand square miles that lay between the north gate of Dinosaur Monument and the rearing, snow-clad Uinta Mountains.

Buck Lloyd gave the ranger the position of the smoke, turned his hubs to four-wheel drive and went off the asphalt onto a track leading east, more or less toward the column of smoke. Maybe it had been the ranger's bare, toneless transmission, whatever, as Buck Lloyd drove east along the track, he thought it was a light plane that had gone down, even if there was a lot of smoke. Black as Buck had seen since the war.

*   *   *

The aircraft's tail assembly and rear engine pod stood among the rocks and low forest. Shorn clean from the fuselage, unmarked, a gleaming white construct set down in the wilderness. Buck Lloyd got the ranger on the CB, gave him his new position, then left his vehicle and approached the tail assembly. One of the elevators had been torn away and the engine intake cowling was crumpled, but there was little other damage to the assembly. Looking into that rear section of the craft, Buck felt he could have pushed open one of the exposed toilet doors, gone in and found the flush working.

Buck left the tail assembly and climbed a low ridge, moving toward the haze of smoke rising from beyond the ridge. At the crest of the ridge he stopped. Buck could only imagine what the valley had once looked like. Low hills and ridges strewn with rock and small boulders, cut by ravine and gorge, tangled stands of dwarf pine and cedar and birch—that had been cleared and burned. Buck Lloyd looked across the low valley, toward the crest of the next ridge, five hundred yards distant. A swath of carnage and destruction and burn, near a hundred yards wide, lay between the two ridges. Nothing stood at the center of the path of the crashed plane. Trees, brush, rock, everything had been swept away. The scorched earth was littered with bright pieces of metal, tangles of tubing and wire, bits of clothing and pieces and objects from the interior of the craft, seats and luggage, bottles and meal trays, and among them were bodies and pieces of bodies, some burned and charred, others showing pink and red, glistening slick as fresh-butchered meat, against the blackened earth. Nothing moved here but the haze rising from the burn.

Buck Lloyd went down into the burn. At first he made his way with care among the pieces of metal and machinery and wiring and objects from the interior of the craft and the bodies and pieces of bodies. In time Buck saw that whole bodies were rare. A row of three seats, a woman strapped in one of the seats, the woman leaned back in the seat, her hair and clothes scarcely disturbed. Then a doll or a baby. Then a man who might have been sleeping but that his legs below the knee were gone. Those were the only near whole humans Buck Lloyd saw. The rest—arms, legs, heads, trunks of bodies scattered everywhere. He noted the surgical precision of much of the butchery—brains plucked from skulls, spines and rib cages carved from trunks, viscera scooped undisturbed from bellies, nerve ganglia and arteries and veins tangled like the bright wires and hydraulic tubing of the aircraft. Buck Lloyd walked among flesh and brain and bone and viscera and genital, so much everywhere, that in time he quit taking care where he trod, not looking at what might be underfoot.

By the time Buck Lloyd reached the far ridge, the end of the burn, and turned to look back over the devastation, he had noted the pattern of the crash. The near-pristine tail assembly beyond the first ridge. The dense carnage where the rear of the fuselage had ground into the earth. The charred midsection of the plane where the fuselage fuel tanks had been. Then, where he stood, the shattered remains of the nose of the craft and what had been the flight deck. Fifty yards beyond the burn Buck Lloyd saw one of the DC-10's engines, stripped of its aluminum cowling, its hardened steel and nickel machinery looking as if it might be fitted direct to another plane, ready to run. But as his eyes swept over the wreckage, it was the tail assembly to which his gaze returned. He could not imagine how, amid such destruction, any part of the craft save the engines could have remained whole, practically untouched by the awesome force of the plane striking the ground at three hundred miles an hour.

It was when Buck Lloyd looked back over the crash site that he saw he was not alone. Another man had come upon the wreckage. The man moved through the wreckage, searching for survivors or bodies that might be identified. Buck Lloyd could tell little of the man from this distance. Only that it wasn't the ranger Buck had raised on the CB, the man wore civvies—maybe a camper or rancher or hunter who had seen the troubled plane in the air or seen the smoke rising from the wreckage. Buck Lloyd went down into the burn and saw the man close. The man's disheveled, wounded look, his grief as he went searching through the wreckage, Buck Lloyd thought these were the reactions of horror at coming on the hell made by the crash. The man did not look away from the burn when Buck approached. Even after Buck had told the man it was hopeless, there were no survivors, the man continued his search. The man went on, going from body to body, turning even the most disfigured and burned, as if he were hoping he might see a face, someone he knew. In time the man took to searching through the passengers' belongings scattered by the crash. Like a looter or a graverobber, Buck Lloyd thought, except that the man took nothing with him. He cast away cameras, jewelry, wallets as if he were searching for a single thing. Something that had been his.

Three men came onto the crash site next, arriving at near the same time. Brad Hollis, a traffic cop in Vernal, the only one of them who had seen the plane in the air; Mel Cooley, an insurance investigator from L.A. who had been climbing a deserted fire tower when he had seen the fireball made by the crash; and Roger Billings, the park ranger Buck Lloyd had raised on the CB.

When Buck Lloyd saw the three men standing at the edge of the burn, he left the man he had come on first and went up toward them. The park ranger was speaking of his last transmission with park headquarters when Buck came up. The dispatcher, the ranger said, had been in touch with Salt Lake air control. "Salt Lake received some kind of emergency call from the plane," the ranger was saying. "Bomb threat. Hijacker on board."

Mel Cooley, the insurance investigator who had seen the fireball, said: "If it was a bomb, it went off when it hit."

Hollis, the Vernal traffic cop, said: "Yeah. I saw the plane. It looked OK. I didn't see any explosion or anything in the air. It was flying funny—" Hollis moved his hand like a fish twisting through water. "There wasn't any smoke, any explosion in the air. Nothing I could see."

The ranger turned and looked down into the burn. Toward the man Buck Lloyd had first seen. The man had stopped his search. He was kneeling in the wreckage, behind a twisted sheath of aluminum. It looked like the man was reaching down into the wreckage, but you couldn't be sure. The piece of aluminum blocked the view. The man came to his feet, looked around, saw the four men on the ridge above, and came toward them. As the man drew near, Buck Lloyd saw how bad he was. Eyes dead, empty, how Buck had looked after thirty-six days at Khe San.

"Jesus," said Mel Cooley as the man came up to them. "He looks like a fucking ghost."

Buck Lloyd watched the man, turned to the others. "It ain't pretty down there."

The park ranger spoke as the man joined them. "You see the plane in the air?"

The man looked away. "No. I didn't see anything."

The traffic cop looked hard at the man. "Yeah. Well, remember that's private property down there. All that stuff still belongs to somebody."

The ranger turned to the others. "We probably ought to keep people away from the crash for now. There's a chopper with some FAA guys coming in from Salt Lake. Just keep things the way they are till they get here." Billings touched a coiled rope at his foot. "Got enough line to cordon off the path coming from the road. It's not going to be just us for long."

Buck Lloyd looked to the south, the direction of Vernal. "Maybe we ought to get somebody from town to doze a road in here. So the emergency trucks can get down close."

"Not a bad idea," the Vernal traffic cop said. He looked at Buck Lloyd. "You work out at Neola Mines, right?"

Buck Lloyd turned back. "Yeah."

The traffic cop looked at the others—the ranger, the insurance investigator, the fifth man.

"I'm a fucking tourist," Mel Cooley said. "I got my wife back in the car."

The traffic cop looked at the fifth man. He wasn't dressed like a local or a miner or a tourist or a hunter or a backpacker or anybody who would be out in the badlands between Vernal and the Uinta Mountains. "You nearby when the plane crashed?"

"Yeah," the man said. He turned to the ranger. "How far is Salt Lake?"

"Probably take the chopper forty-five minutes to get here," Billings said. "Depends on how long it takes them to find us."

Mel Cooley looked toward the wreckage. "Yeah. No smoke now. You'd think one of these things would burn longer than that."

"The fuel vaporized at impact," the man said. "There was a fireball, not much else. Look under the surface, there's not much burn."

The men were quiet, then the ranger said: "I don't guess there's any point of us going back through the wreckage."

"Shit, no. There ain't nobody alive in this," the traffic cop said.

"I don't know," Mel Cooley said. "How about that Jap stewardess that survived that 747 crash on Mount Fuji, wherever? That had to be as bad as this."

Buck Lloyd had walked a couple steps away from the others. He could see the tip of the tail assembly showing over the first ridge. "Looks like the tail broke off when the plane hit." He turned back to the men. "If somebody'd been in one of those toilet's they might've made it."

The traffic cop said: "I looked in the toilets. There ain't nobody there."

"Yeah, Jesus," Mel Cooley said, "who'd be taking a piss at a time like that?"

The ranger moved to the center of the group. "All right, let's do something." He turned to the traffic cop. "Maybe you ought to get on the radio back to Vernal. Get a bulldozer in here, start making a road." He looked at the others. The insurance investigator wasn't looking good. "Maybe you and I can string up a little line here."

Mel Cooley grabbed one end of the rope. "Fine with me."

The ranger turned to Buck Lloyd and the fifth man. "Why don't you guys take it easy. No point in going back."

Buck Lloyd didn't say anything. The fifth man turned toward the burn. "No," the man said. "There's nothing alive down there."

Within an hour the mob had arrived at the crash site. Government inspectors and airline personnel and emergency workers and a National Guard unit from Salt Lake City. Firefighters and local cops and officials and medical workers followed by a horde of sightseers, souvenir gatherers and looters drawn by the smoke and the choppers and the stream of emergency vehicles coming over the desolate terrain to the wreckage of the United DC-10. By dark several hundred men and soldiers had descended on the site. A road was cut into the burn and the emergency and firefighting vehicles came to the wreckage. These men scoured the wreckage for survivors and put down the few low fires scattered about the site. That done, the government officials and airline personnel and the soldiers from the National Guard entered the burn. A few of these men began a painstaking search to learn the cause of the crash. Others began collecting, identifying and marking the personal belongings of those who had died in the crash. A larger group headed by doctors and morticians and forensic experts began collecting and identifying the bodies and the pieces of the bodies of the dead. The few corpses that had remained whole were gathered first. Then came the grisly task of piecing together the dismembered bodies. The experts in these matters attempted to match bits of clothes still clinging to the pieces of flesh, the pigmentation of that flesh and the gender of the dismembered. The experts soon saw the futility of this and turned to collecting the severed heads and hands of the dead. Some identification could be made by fingerprint and dental records.

A temporary morgue had been established in the Vernal high school gym and Buck Lloyd saw stretchers laden with heads and hands and arms carried from the site. The belongings of the dead were taken to a Vernal church, to be stored and protected from souvenir hunters and looters, eventually to be matched with the pieces of bodies being gathered in the gym. The wreckage of the aircraft was for now to remain in place at the site. Experts from the FAA and the NTSB and the airline and the aircraft manufacturer went among the torn pieces of the plane, identifying and tagging and charting the position of each bit of the plane. Later the wreckage would be reconstructed at another site. As dark came, vehicles from Utah Power arrived at the site and emergency lights were erected about the wreckage and the task of collecting and identifying and marking bodies and belongings and the pieces of the aircraft went on into the night.

Of the five who had first come on the crash, the three nonuniformed men—Buck Lloyd, Mel Cooley and the fifth man—had been given jobs beyond the cordoned perimeter of the site. Buck Lloyd worked with the crew dozing the road into the crash. They had a road graded to the wreckage well before dark. That done, Buck Lloyd went to the cordon around the wreckage. There was no further work for him anywhere and he stood for a while at the rope, looking down into the burn, watching the soldiers and officials and experts collecting belongings and pieces of bodies, the men stuffing anything that looked like meat into black plastic garbage bags. Dark came and Buck Lloyd remembered he was tired. He had had maybe five hours' sleep in the last two days and he went back on shift at the mine at midnight. Buck Lloyd went along the cordon, looking for Officer Hollis or Ranger Billings, someone who thought he was in charge, to report he was calling it a day. Buck Lloyd came on Mel Cooley, the L.A. insurance investigator, standing among the sightseers at the rope. Mel Cooley came away from the crowd of ghouls and joined Buck Lloyd. Mel Cooley had had enough. He was packing it in too.

Mel Cooley lit a cigarette, offered the pack to the miner. "Yeah, the wife is back in the car. Going nuts." Mel Cooley looked back toward the burn, then turned and walked with Buck Lloyd away from the lighted wreckage. If you didn't look close it could have been a small-town football field on Friday night. "They got these stretcher loads of heads going right by the car. Got to get a couple drinks down the lady. Couple down yours truly as well." The two men came on the Cat parked off the graded road and stopped there. Mel Cooley lit another cigarette and for a time the two men watched the traffic move along the road. "Something about things like this, accidents, they bring out the Napoleon in people," Mel Cooley said as a Salt Lake City fire chief's car passed, dome light flashing. "That traffic cop, what's his name—Hollis? The fucking guy's been stamping around like a field marshal." Mel Cooley tossed the cigarette to the ground, lit another. "Some of these people love it. It's like war except you don't have to worry about getting your ass shot off." Mel Cooley looked away from the road. "What they have you doing?"

"Working on the road."

Mel Cooley looked back at the road. "Good job. Me and that other guy, we been running around like ants. Coffee, those goddamn plastic bags they're shoving meat into, that sort of shit." Mel Cooley was quiet, then he said: "You know, that guy's a strange bird. Told me he used to be a pilot. Seen something like it before up in Alaska. Well, I thought he was taking it all better than any of us. You know, being a pilot maybe, he'd seen it all before. Looked real calm anyway. But then about an hour ago he fuck near collapsed. I put him back in your pickup. Didn't want to upset the wife any more than she's already upset. Hope you don't mind."

"Fine with me," Buck Lloyd said.

"There's something wrong with that guy. I mean really wrong. The guy is hurt. There's something busted inside him." Mel Cooley looked around. He turned back to the miner. "Awhile back, we were working together, we take a piss break. I look over, the guy is pissing blood. And then when he fell down and he couldn't get back up. That guy is more than just tired. He's sick or hurt." Mel Cooley shook a cigarette out of the pack, looked at it, didn't light it. "There's another thing strange about this guy. I don't think he's got a car out here. When I got him back on his feet and told him he should knock off, he gave me this song and dance about his car breaking down somewhere. Not around here. A guy out in the middle of nowhere, right after the crash, and he ain't got a car. There's something ain't right."

"Maybe."

"And the way the guy is dressed. You notice that? Lightweight suit. Street shoes. The only thing I could think of he was some kind of salesman bugging out. But then I got to thinking. That he was a looter or something like that. You know, when he was down there. When we all first showed up. The guy was acting real strange. I figured he was searching the wreck for survivors, but the guy didn't move more than twenty yards away from one spot. You notice that?"

"Nah, I missed it."

"Yeah?" Mel Cooley looked around the Cat, then came back to the miner. "Well, I've been thinking. I've been thinking maybe this guy is a survivor of this crash." Mel Cooley held up a hand. "OK. I know. Crazy. But I've been thinking about the tail section of the plane. How it looks like new. I know, crazy after what we've seen, but I've been thinking maybe this guy was back in that part of the plane. Maybe he lived through the crash." Mel Cooley held up both hands. "Listen, it's happened before. I saw a thing on TV about plane crashes. This plane comes down in Florida, the tail section breaks off, it acts like an escape capsule. Everybody else in the plane is killed. The twelve people sitting in the back, by the tail, they live. So it ain't like it's never happened before. OK. I ask myself, if this guy is a survivor of the crash, why doesn't he say so? Then I started putting deuces together. You know what that park ranger said? Remember? That there was a bomb on the plane. A hijacker. I heard a couple guys from Salt Lake talking. The Salt Lake field got a call from the plane. The field was all set up for an emergency. And there's been bodies found scattered around sixty miles away. There was a hijacker, a bomb, the bomb exploded. That's a fact." Mel Cooley leaned back against the dozer, looked up at the sky. "The only thing wrong with that theory is that if our friend was the hijacker with the bomb, he wouldn't be here right now." Mel Cooley looked toward the lights in the wreckage. "He'd be soup come now." Mel Cooley pushed away from the Cat and stood. "I got to get out of here." Mel Cooley moved away. "I'm starting to freak out. I've seen some bad shit. I had a hotel fire last year, I thought it was the worst, but I never seen anything like this."

Buck Lloyd stayed leaning against the Cat for a while after the insurance investigator had gone. He saw the

unlit cigarette Mel Cooley had left on the dozer tread.
He picked up the cigarette, held it in his teeth, then lit it.

With the reopening of the Neola Mines, housing had
gotten short in Vernal. The trailer park on the outskirts of
town had filled, expanded, and was filled again. Buck
Lloyd had lived in a one-room crackerbox for a while,
then he began trading off hunting rifles and chain saws
and front-end winches till now he occupied one of the
largest trailers in the park. More like a real house. Living
room, kitchen, bedroom and a den with a foldaway bed.
On the foldaway, that's where Buck put the man who
had been the first or second person to come on the crash
site. Buck thought he was going to have to carry the man
from his pickup to the trailer—the ride over the dirt
track into Vernal had almost done the man in, the man
clinching his body tight every bump the Ram hit—but
once Buck got the man out of the cab, he made it into the
trailer on his own. Buck got the foldaway stretched out
and made up and put the man to bed. The ex-pilot or
whatever curled away from Buck, dealing with the pain,
whatever was busted inside him, like he was alseep, and
Buck Lloyd let him be. Maybe they'd have a talk later.
   After Buck had showered and changed, he looked in
on the man again. The man hadn't moved, still curled
tight on the bed, his back to the door. Buck Lloyd pulled
the door to, went out to the Ram pickup and drove into
the Clover Café on the main highway, where the locals
hung out. Buck decided to have a drink before he sat
down to eat. The bar next to the restaurant was packed
tonight. The most people Buck had seen in the place
since Vernal had won the state B basketball champion-
ship couple years back. But tonight talk wasn't about
putting a round ball through a hoop, tonight everybody

was worked up about the big plane crash north of town. Word had got around that Buck had been one of the first to come on the wreckage, and Buck was grilled some about that, but more often people told Buck about the crash. Rumors about the bomb on the plane, the pilots had a couple stewardesses in the cockpit, there was even some talk about somebody surviving the crash. Buck drank a couple whiskeys and listened to all this talk, not saying much, since everybody in the bar knew more about the crash and the causes of the crash than Buck or the FAA or anybody who had actually been to the site. Buck tossed back his drink and was about to go next door and eat when one bullshitter, a rancher who usually had only wild horses and the government who ran them on his place on his mind, brought up a line of talk that kept Buck Lloyd at the bar.

"What I heard from Dave Ebert," the rancher said. "He's got a cousin in the National Guard. What Dave said, he got it from his cousin, was that the National Guard was going through the wreck, some of them picking up bodies, some of them picking up personal effects, and one guy picked up this suitcase. The crash had busted the lock and when this guy picked up the case, it fell open and a fucking pile of money fell out. Hundreds of thousands of dollars. According to Dave, there weren't no name on the case. They ain't got no idea who it belonged to. Next of kin. Anything like that. Hundreds of thousands of dollars, Dave said. There's a line a block long at the Salt Lake airport, people claiming they had next of kin on that plane."

Buck Lloyd went next door, ate, then went back to the trailer. He put on a pot of coffee, then went into his bedroom and set the alarm for eleven-thirty. Maybe he could get an hour sleep before he went to work. Buck went into the kitchen, had a cup of coffee and thought about the man on the foldaway. Maybe he had been hurt bad, like the insurance investigator said. Maybe he should see a doc.

Buck Lloyd pushed open the door to the den. The man still lay curled on the bed, his back to the door. Buck thought about taking the man to the hospital, but then he thought maybe a night's rest would do more good than a doctor. Let him sleep, then see how bad he looked when Buck got off shift in the morning. Buck was pulling the door to when the man spoke from the bed. He said a single word:

"Thanks."

Buck stayed at the door. "Feeling better now?"

The man turned on his back. He moved with great care. "I've got to get out of here."

"Maybe you ought to take it easy tonight." Buck said. "See how you feel in the morning."

"What time is it?" the man said.

"Ten."

"Ten at night?"

"That's right." Buck came into the room, took a chair and sat straddling the back. "Where you going?"

"Montana."

"You live there?"

"I've got a place there," the man said. "I used to." The man stopped. "There's somebody there I'm going to kill."

Buck Lloyd waited. "You want a drink? Something to eat?"

The man raised his head, pulled himself back on the bed. "You got a cigarette?"

Buck shook a cigarette from a pack, lit it and handed it to the man. The man drew on the cigarette and coughed, bending down in pain.

Buck put an ashtray on the bed. The man put the

cigarette out. He leaned back in the bed. "I've got a favor to ask. I need a car. Just something that'll get me to Montana. I've got some money, but not a lot."

"There's a Datsun pickup out in the yard. Guy came through last summer and broke down outside of town. I towed him back in. Thought the motor had froze up. You know, this high desert eats those low-compression motors up. The guy left it and went on. Turned out it had just overheated. Started up fine the next morning. The guy never came back for it."

The man reached into his jacket pocket and took out a stack of twenty-dollar bills. He tossed the bills on the bed. "Take whatever it's worth."

Buck Lloyd looked at the twenties spilled over the bed. "Well, it's not mine to sell. Why don't you just take it. The guy ever shows up, I'll deal with him."

"All right," the man said. "I'll get back to you. When I get up to Montana."

Buck Lloyd waited. "You know, maybe you ought to check into a hospital. Least have some pictures taken. You might have something bad busted inside. I could always tell them we had a little accident. The way I drive, they'd believe it."

The man turned his head. He looked at Buck Lloyd. "I'll be all right. A couple broken ribs. I'll have it looked at in Montana."

The man turned away, like he didn't want to talk anymore. Buck Lloyd stood and went to the door. He looked back at the man on the foldaway. "I'll leave the Datsun keys on the phonograph. By the front door."

"Thanks," the man said. "I'll get back to you. One way or another."

The man didn't say anything else and Buck Lloyd went down the hall to his bedroom. He stretched out but couldn't sleep. He got up at eleven and drove out to work early. The man and the Datsun pickup were still there when Buck got off shift the following morning. But by four in the afternoon, after Buck had slept, the man and the truck were gone. Buck found a note on the phonograph, where he had left the truck keys. The note said the man had taken and was responsible for the Datsun pickup. The note was signed Don or maybe Dan Cox, Buck couldn't read the writing.

Buck Lloyd never saw this Don or Dan Cox again, but two months later, when he came home from work one morning, he would find the Datsun pickup parked behind the trailer. Keys in the ashtray, gas tank topped up, a bottle of first-rate bourbon under the seat.

13

*Y*OU LOST the whole two hundred and fifty grand?"

"I got some of it. Maybe a thousand. Less now."

"Shit. We needed that money, Cox." St. Cloud gentled the little Super Cub out of the climb. The altimeter rode around eight thousand feet, not more than twenty or thirty peaks in the wilderness rising above that. "We'll have to improvise." St. Cloud looked at me. "Where'd you lose it? Maybe we can go back and get it."

"It's been found."

"Yeah? How do you know that?"

"It was in the papers. They found it in the crash."

"Let's go back three squares. What crash? You fuck up another plane, Cox?"

"I was a passenger. The DC-10 crash down in Utah. A week ago. You read about it, St. Cloud?"

St. Cloud dropped the left wing below the horizon. He looked down into the ragged field of mountains we had come to. Now that we had crossed the Bitterroot Range there was nothing but mountains, range after range, as far as we could see. At eight thouand feet we were still in the lowering sun and the teeth of the peaks we moved through burned red, but below us night had come. The plane drifted into the shadow of a peak ahead and the valleys and gorges below turned a deep blue where there was snow or ice, the blue field scarred black by the timberline. St. Cloud kept the plane in its gentle bank and we passed through the mountain's shadow. When we had curled around the peak that had blocked our path, St. Cloud took his hands from the wheel and went back into the seat.

"Yeah, I read about that crash, Cox. I read no survivors."

"I was on the plane. I survived the crash."

St. Cloud put his hands back on the wheel. The bank indicator swung as St. Cloud dropped the right wing, looked beyond me to the black valley below. "There ain't a fucking scratch on you, Cox. Anybody else make it?"

"Not that I know of."

St. Cloud eased the wheel left, trimmed the plane, setting a course 290 west. "That your bomb that brought it down?"

"It was Blackmuir's."

"Jesus fucking Christ," St. Cloud said low and was quiet. Nothing in the cabin but the drone of the engine behind the firewall and the hiss of the airstream passing

through the wing struts. "Anybody else on the plane we
know?"

"Thea."

St. Cloud looked at me. "Thea," he said, then:
"Dub?"

"No. Blackmuir got him the night before."

"Dayton is dead."

"That's right. Dayton is dead. Thea is dead. I think
you're up on the others."

St. Cloud looked over to the instrument panel. Nothing needed doing. He had the plane trimmed and
smooth. "Just the two of you?"

"Yeah. The three of us were coming up here to meet
you. Dayton was supposed to join us on the plane. He
didn't make the flight because he was dead. Blackmuir
had killed him the night before."

St. Cloud changed course. Winding the plane west
and north through the Bitterroot wilderness. He gave me
a searching look. "Listen, Cox, I ain't religious, supersti-
tious, any of that shit. But this surviving the crash—you
ain't bullshitting me now."

"No. I lived through the crash."

"You're the only one."

"I was the only one."

St. Cloud looked up through the windshield. He
scanned the sky. "One guy out of three hundred something lives and it's you."

"I wasn't in my seat. I found a place. Then I was
lucky."

St. Cloud twitched the wheel, not bothering the
plane's trim. "What kind of place?"

"One of the rear toilets."

"You survived the crash in the can?"

"That's right."

St. Cloud made a sarcastic laugh. "I'll say you were

lucky." Then he grew solemn. "Maybe Dutch can fix us up with something to fly." He banked the plane hard left, standing it on one wing. He looked down into the night pooled among the mountains. "I want to keep Dutch out of it. He's getting old. This ain't none of his concern." St. Cloud looked up at me. "You tied in OK? I want to take a look at something."

St. Cloud cut the throttle back to idle and the plane fell into the darkness beneath the peaks. A couple seconds into the slip stall, St. Cloud kicked left rudder and punched the throttle. The plane shuddered, its nose came down and the plane tucked into a full-power dive. St. Cloud peered out his side window. The altimeter needle spun, the airspeed indicator edged toward the red line, and the sky about us grew black. Then St. Cloud saw something in the night below, eased the throttle and wheel back as one and, when most fliers would have been pulling g's, had the Super Cub gentled and trimmed, skimming treetops. We sailed between two trees and passed over a white oval plain that St. Cloud identified as Emerald Lake.

"Not as big as I thought it was," St. Cloud said. The end of the lake, a rising forest and beyond that a sheer mountain wall rushed toward us. "Might have a hard time getting out if the wind ain't right. Best time to fly up here, at night. Good smooth air." St. Cloud brought the Cub's nose up, went near full throttle a second, then throttled down as he kicked left rudder and banked the plane tight over a fifty-foot pine. He stood the plane on one wing, rolled one-eighty and turned back over the lake. Like he was dusting cotton. "Get a good bright sun on this snow and ice—real squirrelly air." The Super Cub went quick across the lake. Snow-covered ice passed five feet below our skis. "We might get in here all right. But the weather shifts, warms up, might be hairy getting out. Got to think about things like that." St. Cloud eased the wheel back as the end of the lake and the forest and mountain wall beyond came up on us. "We got a lot of things to think about, Cox. A lot of thinking to be done."

The Super Cub cleared the stand of pine at the lake's end and St. Cloud hit full throttle and put the small plane in a circling climb. St. Cloud watched the steep, forested slopes till we had cleared the timberline. Then, angling the plane across an unmarked field of snow, he turned to me: "Like, we got to be thinking about landing planes on mountains. You ever land on a mountain, Cox?" St. Cloud grinned as the Cub circled higher. "Well, you're going to learn."

The Super Cub came clear of the ridge towering over the lake we had inspected and St. Cloud gave the wheel over to me. He pointed a course a few degrees north of the evening star, said we had fifteen minutes' running time and closed his eyes. The sun had gone from the horizon now and the wilderness was cast in a deep, still blue. Then in a short time, maybe a quarter hour, there appeared below the horizon a light as bright and singular and steady as the planet to the west. I woke St. Cloud by pointing the nose of the plane toward it.

It had taken me twenty-four hours, sleeping more than I drove, to reach Montana. The maps of the Bitterroot wilderness and the overlays that showed where St. Cloud would be had been lost in the crash. But I remembered from the maps the small town of Darby in the Bitterroot Valley, the nearest civilization to the mountain strip, where St. Cloud and I would meet. I checked into a motel a block off the highway and slept off and on for another day and night. Whatever was broken inside me was bad—when I could piss there was blood and there was no way I could lie or sit or move without pain—but my mind and heart hurt worse. My dreams were filled with the horror of the crash, but I longed for sleep. Anything to escape the room where I was alone. Then the second day in the room there came a knock at the door and a maid, a woman with sparse teeth and ample arms, let herself into the room. The woman went about opening blinds, chattering, she made me leave the unturned bed so she could smooth it. I had overstayed checking-out time, I was told, and followed the maid into the hall. I settled with the desk clerk and was about to go back to the room when I saw a bank of snow beyond the door. I went out. Beyond the banked snow were trees. I went into the trees and the snow and there, fifty yards beyond the motel, found a river. Much of the riverbed was exposed. A sluggish icy stream wound through the rock. The banks were crusted with ice and old snow. I walked over the riverstone—dry, white, smooth as eggshell—to the water. The river held no life that I could see, but farther along, upstream, a man was casting into a pool, hunting whitefish. The fisherman did not seem to take much interest in his sport, but he was out of the house, flexing his rod, placing the bait with little mark on the water's surface. Waiting for spring when the river would come up, the water warm, and the trout in the stream—brown, cut-throat, rainbow—would rise from their winter sleep and feed.

If the river had given me reason to live, now, as St. Cloud flared the plane over the snow-packed runway, I had found a place where it might be done. St. Cloud set the landing skis to snow and ran the Cub toward a hangar at the end of the strip. He cut throttle short of the hangar and an old-fashioned handle gas pump, the kind I hadn't seen since I was a kid. I went across the stiff, crackling snow and pulled back the hangar door. St. Cloud revved the engine and eased the Cub into the hangar. St. Cloud found an electric blanket, wrapped the motor cowling and plugged the blanket lead into an extension socket.

Dogs barking and the methodical bite of ax into wood came to us as we went through the trees behind the hangar. St. Cloud gave a shout and something between a yodel and an exclamation of welcome came in answer. We soon came to a cabin, its windows coppery from a light within. We entered a short hall cluttered with winter gear—parkas, knit caps, sweaters, boots, skis, snowshoes—and passed into a low-ceilinged room. A kerosene lamp turned low hung over a table. On the table sat a cat. The dark room seethed with movement, other cats, maybe a dozen of them, their copper-bright eyes following us. A purring roar rose from the shadows, a lazy meow came from somewhere beyond the room. St. Cloud tossed his flight bag on the floor and sat at the table. He stared at the cat on the table. The cat stared back. St. Cloud thought, searching through his vocabulary.

"Scat," he said finally.

The cat yawned.

The hall door banged open and a man wearing a lumberjack shirt, suspenders, yellow boots came into the room. The man's face was obscured by a stack of firewood. "Gonna snow tonight, boys." The man crossed the room and dumped the wood by a small black barrel stove. The man recrossed the room and went into an adjacent kitchen. "Have a good flight?" he called out.

"Yeah. OK, Dutch," St. Cloud said toward the kitchen. "Anything new here?"

There came the rattle of dried cat food being spilled into dishes, a chorus of mewing, a hiss or two, then the clink of glass. The man came back into the room and placed a bottle of whiskey and three glasses on the table. "Nothing new here." The man reached to the lamp over the table, turned it up and sat under the circle of light. Dutch Genet, as St. Cloud introduced the man, pronouncing the last name in a way that would have got you fined in France, had a pink face round and plump as a pie, a twinkle for eyes, a sooty briar pipe stuck in a grin. It was not till the pipe needed refilling that I saw three fingers and some of the fourth on the bush pilot's right hand were missing. Dutch Genet got the pipe going, poured out three stiff whiskeys and leaned back in his chair.

"You check out Emerald Lake?"

St. Cloud tasted the whiskey, coughed. "We didn't touch down, but it looked all right. The Cub didn't have any trouble with it. Not tonight anyway."

"I lost an Aeronca Sedan on that little green lake. Back in 1950, I think it was." Dutch poured out whiskey and began a tale that St. Cloud would tell me he had heard a good twenty times. On the other hand, you want to fly in the snow and cold and mountains, St. Cloud instructed me later, your first mistake was being bored with Dutch Genet and his stories. But then as Dutch wound up the flying part of this tale—a float landing on the tiny lake to pick up an elk hunter and his kill, weather change while butchering and packing the elk, stiff turbulent winds stalling the plane when Dutch couldn't clear the eight-hundred-foot wall around the lake and had to turn downwind, the nosedive into fifty feet of icy water—and went into his twenty-five-mile tramp through knee-deep snow, St. Cloud's head went down to a couple of inches of the tabletop. My attention was stalling as well. Dutch gave St. Cloud's chair a kick that brought both of us up.

"A pair to draw to." Dutch squinted at the match flame sucking into his pipe bowl. "Even odds which of you boys gets the first ride into Missoula General Emergency."

I looked at St. Cloud. Saw the grayish-black patch that spread from his nose across one cheek, the gloves on his hands, he hadn't taken them off even now inside the cabin. Remembered the way he had walked from the plane, like his toes were curled against the ends of his boots, the cough that had torn at his lungs. And understood what St. Cloud had suffered, exposed that night and the next day in the mountains above Kill Devil Ranch.

St. Cloud came back enough to help Dutch get me to a room down the hall, undressed and into a bunk bed. Maybe St. Cloud stayed awake awhile longer, maybe the bush pilot was talking to the cats. Whatever, the last I remembered of that night was the sound of Dutch Genet's voice in another room.

The storm had come in from the north. The lower panes of the windows on that side of the cabin, the room where I had slept, had been blanked out by the drifting snow. The cabin was quiet but for the sounds of the cats, the rumble from one under the eiderdown at the foot of my bunk, the talking cat still complaining in the kitchen. For a while I lay looking at the ceiling and the model planes hanging from it. World War II fighters mainly, a P-38, a Flying Tiger, a Spitfire, carved from balsa. One of the walls was hung with photographs. More planes, ancient biplanes, ex–military trainers that Dutch had flown in his early days as a bush pilot. And a picture of a girl, twelve or so, pigtails sprouting from her head, her face showing a tomboy grin.

In time I rose and dressed and joined the cats. The table in the main room was cluttered with the whiskey bottle, empty now, and glasses from last night and two sets of greasy, egg-smeared dishes. I found warming coffee and milk and honey in the kitchen. From the kitchen window I saw three paths had been stamped through the thigh-deep snow. One to the hangar, another to a line of well-mixed huskies on a run chain, the third leading to some sheds on the far side of clearing. When the coffee was gone, I went into the hall, found pac boots and an anorak and went out.

Of the three paths tramped in the snow, I took the left, to the hangar. There was no one about there, but I saw Dutch in the distance, at the end of the runway. Dutch was moving the length of the strip, like a man plowing a field, packing down the strip with snowshoes. I followed the path back to the cabin, a half-dozen fur-ringed muzzles watching me from their snow caves, and went along the right path toward a stand of pine and the sheds beyond. Voices came from one of the sheds. I pushed back the door, on which was fastened a CAUTION: MEN WORKING sign that had been altered to read CAUTION: MAN TALKING, and saw a large VHF radio. The radio was monitoring the emergency frequency. I thought that St. Cloud might be nearby and continued along the path as it wound through the stand of pine, away from the radio shack, cabin and hangar. In fifty yards the woods gave way to a rounded field of snow. The tramped path ended at the crest of the low hill. It had begun to snow again, the light gone flat, dull, and I saw the panorama through its mist.

Dutch Genet's homestead and strip sat on a high

mountain plateau. The ground dropped sharply from the prow of the hill where I stood to a crested bowl whose bottom I could not see. A gently slanted ridge formed the far boundary of the chasm. I could not see beyond that for the new storm coming toward me. I was about to turn back, return to the cabin, when a black dot appeared in the field of drifting snow. The head of a man on skis or snowshoes climbing the far side of the ridge, that ridge more than a mile away. When the man had made the ridge I raised an arm and called out across the bowl. It seemed the man saw me, but he made no response. In a few moments he skied along the crest of the ridge and then disappeared down the slope he had climbed. I thought that St. Cloud knew a way to come around the bowl to the cabin and I turned and retraced my steps along the path.

Dutch Genet had made the foot of the strip near the hangar when I got back to the cabin. He called out, unstrapped his snowshoes and leaned them against the hangar wall. Dutch was not pleased with his machinery, his snowmobile in particular, when he came banging into the cabin. "Goddamn coolie work," he said and poured a trace of whiskey in one of last night's glasses. "Take about fifteen minutes to pack that strip with the snowmobile. Carburetor." Dutch took a chair and eyed the dishes strewn over the table. "Had to fly into McKinley once. Emergency rescue. Team of Japanese climbers—girls, about ninety pounds a head—got themselves all messed up. Lost four of them. Made a glacier landing not too far from their base camp. Fly out the survivors. You can land on unpacked snow, but to take off—it's got to be hard. No snowmobiles up there. You pack a strip a step at a time. One of the little girls, bless her heart, said climbing McKinley was easier." Dutch looked at his empty glass, the empty whiskey bottle with the same suspicion he had viewed the dirty breakfast dishes. "Where you been this morning? Thought you'd sleep in."

"I wandered around a bit. Went to the bowl out past the radio shack. I saw St. Cloud skiing over on the far side of the bowl. How do you get back around to your place? He went off the back side. Was he going somewhere else?"

Dutch clicked his pipe stem against his teeth. "St. Cloud on skis—don't think so. Not unless he learned since yesterday. Anyway I put him back to bed right after breakfast. Paws are still hurting him." Dutch leaned back in his chair and called out: "St. Cloud! You in there?"

There came a noise from down the hall. Dutch Genet rose and disappeared into that part of the cabin. There was the sound of voices, then Dutch came back into the room. He picked up the whiskey bottle, looked at it, put it down. "Mmm, visitors. There ain't nobody twenty miles around here." Dutch stopped. "They didn't look like they were in trouble, did they?"

"No. He didn't look like he was having any trouble at all."

"On skis," Dutch said. "An enigma. Must have landed somewhere around here." Dutch went to a desk, came back with a topo map. He spread the map on the table, moved his finger over the map, northwest from his cabin and strip. "Probably where he put down. High meadow along this rockfall," he pointed to the map. "Never used it myself, so near the house, but it could be done. Next-nearest place would be three, four miles on the other side of Rocky Boy." Dutch leaned back from the table, looked at the fine misting snow drifting against the window. "Maybe we better get St. Cloud up and go have a look."

Dutch ran the small plane the length of the strip, the skis smoothing a trail over the path he had tramped down this morning. He turned the plane at the end of the strip, eased the throttle forward. The throttle, all instrumentation on the panel was fitted with pull rings that Dutch operated with the stub finger on his right hand. "Visibility looks poor in all quadrants, boys, but have no fear. I know the first name of every rock twenty miles around here." Dutch let the motor warm ten seconds, then pushed the throttle full open and the Super Cub leaped forward. A cloud of snow kicked up by the propwash enveloped the plane. Dutch went forward, his nose against the whited-out windshield, till the plane had gathered speed to outrun the swirling snow. The hangar, the trees beyond the hangar appeared through the snow and Dutch pulled back on the wheel. The Super Cub went nose up and we rose into the snow mist. The trees, hangar, cabin and sheds faded into the white. "Got to fly trees and rock today, boys, so keep your eyes peeled for anything dark."

St. Cloud studied the map spread over his knees a couple minutes, then looked at Dutch. "We ought to be coming up on Bench twelve forty pretty soon."

"Yep. Yep, there it is now," Dutch said, and a gray pyramid of rock appeared above the left wing. "We'll go around on the Idaho side and come upslope on it."

Dutch banked the plane away from the peak. Dark spires and slashes of trees and more rock showed in the side window. Dutch circled the plane wide, letting the nose drop. When the peak turned to a faint blur in the white, he brought the nose level, banked, and came back dead straight into the peak. The peak came to us fast, looming over the plane like a granite tower. When there was nothing but rock in the windshield, Dutch hit the rudder right. He pulled the plane's nose up and the Super Cub peeled away from the wall.

"He's gone now, but he's been here," Dutch said. "You see them?"

St. Cloud was staring out the right window, at the snow-hazed slope we had just skimmed. "I saw them."

Dutch turned to me. "Pine branches. Trick I learned in Alaska. You got flat light, it's whited out, you got to put something on the snow so you know where it is. Used to carry spruce boughs myself. Anything'll do. I've had passengers disrobe. Throw anything out. Caps, jackets, anything that'll tell you where the snow is." Dutch put the plane in a wide circle, coming back around nose into the peak. "One thing about this guy, whoever he is, he knows what he's doing."

Dutch had the Super Cub back on the peak, but now he was throttling back. He brought the nose up, coming down to stall speed. Dutch tipped the left wing, looked down at the white slope rising quick beneath us. "You want it, St. Cloud? Get a little practice in." St. Cloud took the wheel, tipped his wing, looked down at the snow. Dutch Genet turned back to me. "Got to have an upslope of at least eighteen degrees. That's to shorten your landing uphill and to shorten your takeoff going down." Dutch glanced at the instrument panel, saw that St. Cloud was easing the throttle to the firewall, turned back. "Got to have a full-power landing. That's the only tricky part. You got to run as far up your slope as you can, so you have as much run as you can for takeoff."

The Cub's skis hit the snow. Propwash boiled snow over the windshield. St. Cloud kept the throttle near full, running the small plane up the steep slope. "The problem is, see," Dutch said, "most of the time wind is going to be coming downslope. Fine for a landing, but then you got to take off downwind. Got to have plenty of room to run to get up airspeed. Don't want to just drop off the side of the mountain." Dutch turned to St. Cloud. "How you doing?"

St. Cloud had his head pressed against the right window. "What d'you count—four? Five branches?"

Dutch put his face against the left window. "Something like that."

The Cub nose went up suddenly, sharp. Dutch reached out for air. "Jesus, St. Cloud! Don't drive us all the way to the top of this fucking thing!"

St. Cloud laughed, pulled the throttle back to idle. Dutch kicked open the door, dragged me out of the back and tossed me under the tail of the plane. "Get hold of the wing strut. Push like hell when we come around. I'll take the upslope wing." I went under the tail, grabbed the right wing struts. Dutch shouted from the far side of the plane: "All right! Bring her around right—easy! Easy, St. Cloud, you fucking maniac."

St. Cloud gentled the throttle forward, rudder full left and, with me pushing up hard on the right wing, Dutch clinging to the left, brought the Cub around one-eighty, facing down the slope. Dutch and I went away from the wings and St. Cloud ran the Cub forward a few yards, to a point where the slope leveled a little, still eighteen, twenty degrees. There he cut the throttle back to idle and tossed a couple of parking blocks out of the cabin. Dutch and I fit the wooden wedges under the ski tips as St. Cloud cut the motor and crawled out of the cabin, grinning.

Dutch laughed. He wrapped an arm around St. Cloud's shoulder, and the two of them strolled down the slope like boulevardiers out on a Sunday morning. "Damn fine landing, St. Cloud. Couldn't've done better myself. I'm telling you, boy, you're missing your calling.

Learn how to think on the ground, you'd be a good one.
I'm getting old, getting out. You could work yourself
right in. Three, four years, you'd have yourself a good
little business up here. What with all them hippies going
back to the land, living year-round, like down around
Call, things are going to be booming."

St. Cloud broke out of Dutch's grasp and knelt in the
snow. "Maybe." He brushed his hand across the snow
and looked down the slope. "I'm thinking about getting
out of flying."

Dutch went on one knee in the snow. Like St. Cloud
he looked at the tracks the skis had cut. "Well, think
about it. Peggy's coming back. Getting shed of that New
York lawyer, whatever he was. She's going to be needing
a man around. Can't do it all herself."

St. Cloud gripped snow in his gloved hand. He
opened his hand, the snow drifted away. St. Cloud stood.
He looked downslope, at the ski tracks disappearing into
the snow mist. "What do you think it was?"

Dutch stood, brushed snow off his knee, looked at
the tracks at his feet. "A lot heavier than the Super Cub.
Skis set wide. Pretty big plane to be bringing in here."

There came a sound from behind us, from the plane.
A metallic crack, a ping, like a rifle bullet striking the
plane's aluminum shell. Dutch sucked on his dead pipe,
felt for matches in his pocket. He looked back toward the
plane. "Engine's cooling down. Maybe we ought to be
getting back to the house."

We went up the slope to the plane. On our way St.
Cloud found the rutted circle where Blackmuir, Johnny
Kono, whoever had stopped and turned the plane. He
stayed back to examine the tracks in the snow while
Dutch went to the Super Cub to check the prop, be sure
it hadn't been nicked landing. I went to the tail of the
Cub and looked up toward the peak—a solid gray

pyramid in the falling snow. Then a pool of light came through the mist and a ragged gap formed in the rock wall. The fissure that Dutch had slipped the Cub through on our first pass over the slope. With the faint, swirling light spilling down the rock wall, there came a roar, then a crack, and for that instant a shadow passed over me. The wings of a plane. Then the shadow was gone into the snow, now nothing but the whine of its engines. That faded and the mountain was quiet.

St. Cloud came running up the slope, shouting: "The Foxjet! He's got the fucking Foxjet up here!"

Dutch stood at the nose of the Cub, a parking block in his hand. "He couldn't have landed a jet here." He looked at me as if he were just starting out, knew nothing. "Could he?"

St. Cloud had reached the Cub. He kicked at the second block still wedged under the landing ski, he shouted at us. "Get the hell out of here! He's coming back!"

Dutch half turned. He held the wooden block toward me, still looking into the whited sky. "Wait. Listen." He went to one knee. He looked down the slope, toward a hiss rising below us. "Jesus H. Christ," Dutch said, so low I could barely hear. "He's going to land that jet here."

St. Cloud had freed the parking block. He stayed on his knees, turned downslope, facing the rising hiss of the oncoming jet. I felt Dutch's hand on my arm, then saw on the slope below the wasp snout of the Foxjet, the gun barrels of its twin engines, the jet not moving, it seemed, but to grow larger. I went down in the snow. The crack of jet passed a few feet overhead. Then came the trailing boom of the jet, its echoing roar as it twisted through the gap in the rock above.

I was on my feet, yanked up, being hurled into the

Cub's cabin. When I got turned upright, Dutch and St. Cloud were strapped in front. Dutch punched at the ignition switch. The engine came to life and Dutch had the Super Cub bounding down the track we had cut landing. The Cub jolted down the slope, taking once to the air in a great leap. Dutch brought the plane down, St. Cloud called out airspeed—fifty, sixty. Then both pilots' hands went to the throttle. Both pushing to keep the throttle open. Lose groundspeed now, with half the takeoff slope covered, and the plane would be impossible to stop, impossible to fly, and we would tumble into the canyon below. With both pilots yelling—I didn't know what—I went forward and saw the evil snout, the gun-barrel intakes of the Foxjet hovering on the track below, buzzing the slope again. Dead ahead. On collision course. Still the jet did not seem to move but to grow larger, spreading across the windshield at an incredible rate. If we cut power or changed course now, the Cub would end in the canyon below. Then, as it seemed we were to be sucked through the intake cowlings, the Foxjet went up. It passed feet, inches maybe, over the Cub's wings. There followed the crack and boom of the jet and the Cub went up. Dutch fighting the Foxjet's vortex as we rose.

Dutch wheeled the plane low, staying close to the canyon walls beneath the peak where we had landed. St. Cloud studied the maps with one eye, the other on the milky sky pressed against the right window. I saw nothing, heard nothing but the roar of the Cub's engine. Dutch kept the plane in the treetops. We curled through the canyons that led back to the cabin, but then, when we had begun to think the danger gone, the air around us was split by the Foxjet, a shadow passing a few yards above our wings, our small plane near turned upside down from the jet's pass. St. Cloud cursed, he screamed at Blackmuir, he pounded the windshield. Dutch turned the Cub's nose up sharp, banked the plane left, away from a rising wall of snow. He kept the plane in a tight, climbing circle. Then the surrounding walls of snow fell away and I saw we had come up the tunnel of the bowl where I had seen the skier. Dutch grazed the trees surrounding the cabin and settled the Cub on the packed strip.

Dutch ran the speed out of the plane and turned, maybe halfway down the strip, and taxied back to the hangar. By the time I had dragged myself out of the back of the plane, Dutch had the hangar doors open. I went into the left seat and taxied the plane into the hangar. When we had got the plane put to bed, we went out on the strip. St. Cloud had gone a hundred yards beyond us. He had stopped, was looking up into the sky. Dutch and I had gone a few paces onto the packed snow, moving toward St. Cloud, when a hiss came from the far end of the strip. A white shadow moved in the white sky. The Foxjet glided over the distant trees, coming down to the strip low, rushing toward us, the snout and gun barrels of its engines growing like a cancer. Dutch and I went on our knees, then our bellies. Then as the jet cracked over us, we put our faces in the snow.

The roar of the jet faded and we rose. Dutch wiped snow from his face. He laughed. There was nothing else to do, with St. Cloud, who had stood his ground against the onrushing jet till the last moment, now lying on his back in the snow, shaking his fist, cursing the sky, like a boy taunting a bully to fight and fight fair.

The following morning Dutch and I packed the Super Cub. The day was bright, cold, and St. Cloud stayed in the cabin, nursing his hands over the stove. There wasn't that much work in loading Dutch's supplies anyway. Whiskey, matches, tobacco, a can of white gas, half-dozen frozen steaks, milk, oranges, nuts, food that freezing wouldn't ruin—Dutch's hideaway, the mountain house, he called it, was stocked with just about everything else. Dutch tossed in some pine boughs in case the light got flat later in the day and we went into the cabin for a farewell drink. We found St. Cloud standing over the stove, still smarting from losing last night's argument. Dutch poured himself a good drink and sat at the table, the usual clutter of maps and dishes about. Dutch sipped the bourbon and fired up his pipe.

"Look, St. Cloud, it's the only way to do this. If you boys ain't going to cut me in on this crazy bastard, you worried about my health, then it's you boys stay. I leave." Dutch glanced over the map. "There ain't no other place in these parts you're going to find outfitted like this. You got the radios, you got the aviation gas, the strip, the planes—I don't need any of that shit. You got to have it."

St. Cloud came to the table, scowled at the maps. "We're going to pay for whatever fuel we use."

Dutch spilled whiskey in a glass. "All right. You pay for the gas. You fuck up a plane, you pay for that. Pitch in on the insurance premiums anyway."

St. Cloud looked over the map. "You got a good radio up there? We want to keep in touch."

Dutch turned the map. "No problem there. I took an old Narco transceiver up to the mountain house last summer. We'll make contact on one twenty-one point five every day. Fair enough?" Dutch put a finger to the map. "I'll be about forty-five miles southwest of here. Mount Paloma. I ever take you there?"

St. Cloud looked at the map. "Long time ago. Back before you built the house."

Dutch leaned back from the table. "My God, it's fine up there. Pristine. Whenever Peggy comes back, that's where I'm going to be. Year-round, year in, year out. Get away from this rat race over here." Dutch went back to the whiskey and the map. "Now I thought it'd be best to have Cox fly me over later today. When the sun gets low, we'll have a better look at the snow. Been having some avalanche problems on Paloma, so we want to check it out before we land. You can stay close here, take care of yourself, monitor the radio. Your friend might be calling back today."

St. Cloud pushed the map away. "I don't like it, Dutch. You out there on this fucking mountain top. No plane, nothing, no way to get out of there."

"I got skis and snowshoes, St. Cloud. Somebody comes looking for me, I'll lead them a merry chase. There're places around there there ain't nobody but me going in and coming out." Dutch sucked fire into the pipe. "Maybe next week I'll ski over and get the dogs and sled." Dutch tossed the burned match onto a breakfast plate. "If you boys ain't got yourself sorted out by then." St. Cloud said nothing. Dutch watched him, sucking hard on the pipe. "You still ain't going to tell me who this fucker is?"

St. Cloud looked at me. "No."

Dutch shrugged. "Suit yourself. You ever need a third hand, I'm available." Dutch came close to the table, with some interest. "One thing I want you to find out, you get this guy back on the radio. See if he landed that Foxjet up where we were yesterday. Looked like he had skis on the jet. That'd be some kind of flying." Dutch knocked the pipe against the palm of his hand, looked around, put the ashes on a breakfast plate. "Maybe they got two planes. Landed something prop-driven up there."

"There's two of them," St. Cloud said. "They probably got something else. Something a little slower."

A cat came into Dutch's lap. He rubbed its ears,
ruffled its fur. "Well, you got the Super Cub and the
Cessna 180. Two of the best bush planes ever driven.
Now I don't know what you got in mind for whoever
you're having this little war with, but I'm going to give
you some unasked-for advice. With the Foxjet, whatever
else they got, more'n likely they're going to be flying
circles around you. But up here that's all right. Going
slower than the other guy ain't necessarily a bad thing.
The stall speed on the Cessna is around sixty, the
Cub—little over forty. Add ten for the thin air, you'll still
be coming in slower than a ruptured duck. You're going
to be getting into a place and getting out of it when the
Foxjet is sucking rocks. You got the weather on your
side. Best air is cold at sea level. Worst is up high on a
nice sunny day like today. You get a plane in someplace,
say one of these little bowl lakes, on a cold morning,
overcast, then the sun comes out, heats up the snow and
ice—you ain't taking off where you landed. I ever tell
you boys about that Aeronca Sedan I busted up on
Emerald Lake?" Dutch said, launching into the story he
had told a couple nights before. How the Aeronca had
stalled, Dutch being forced by rising rock to turn downwind, the plane's wide fuselage stealing lift from the
upwind wing.

When Dutch had run down, St. Cloud turned toward
the window. You could see a bit of the hangar and the
strip through the trees. "I been thinking about something," St. Cloud said, yawned. "I been thinking about
getting that goddamn snowmobile running. Fuck if I'm
packing down that strip by foot."

Dutch and St. Cloud spent the rest of the day, till
early afternoon, in the hangar. St. Cloud disassembled

and cleaned the snowmobile carburetor, while Dutch
went over the Super Cub, tuning its hundred-and-fifty-
horse-power Lycoming engine. I passed most of my time
in the radio shack, monitoring the emergency frequency,
waiting for Blackmuir to call again. I had missed last
night's transmission. It had been brief, St. Cloud said.
Couple words, but then that had been enough. Our little
war, as Dutch called it, was on.

Midafternoon we pushed the Super Cub from the
hangar, filled its tanks with red aviation gas, filtering the
fuel through a piece of chamois. "That's rule one up
here," Dutch said. "Don't want that little molecule of
water in your eighty/eighty-seven gas turning into a little
molecule of ice in your carburetor at fifteen thousand
feet. Rule two is to keep your engine warm," Dutch said
and fitted me into the Cub's left seat. "Get her started
up, Cox. I forgot something in the house."

Dutch went into the trees, came back a minute later
with a gray Persian cat rolled under his arm. Dutch
tossed the cat in the back, got into the right side. He gave
St. Cloud thumbs-up and I turned the small plane down
the strip. The Cub jumped into the air at seventy-five
and, after a pass over the cabin, Dutch pointed me
southwest, toward his mountain house.

It went against everything I had learned in thirty years
of flying. Low-throttle glide to a flat, hard, usually
well-tended strip, cutting power at touchdown, ending
your landing run pretty much anywhere you chose—it
was all gone up here in the mountains where everything,
landing a plane anyway, Dutch said, was turned on its
head.

We made a low pass over the glacier strip, the
mountain house that sparkled like a jewel in the slanting

light, and the snowcap of Mount Paloma. Dutch thought
the snow looked good, maybe a couple feet cover, he
judged from the banks against the glass-walled house,
laid over one of the few glaciers left in the Bitterroots.
On our second pass, Dutch tossed a red surveyor's
ribbon out of the cabin and then, the third time around,
he talked me through a full-power, upslope landing. I
didn't cut the throttle till the Super Cub was within a
few yards of the door of the mountain house.

Though there was not a breath of wind, Dutch went
by the book he had pretty much written, and we tied the
plane down. Dutch lashed rope around two pine boughs,
we dug pits beneath the Cub's wings, stamped the
boughs in the snow, covered them, stamped the snow
cover and tied the ropes to the wings. Dutch packed the
skis with stamped snow that would freeze in minutes
and the Cub was secured. We unloaded cat and provi-
sions, then Dutch tossed me a pair of snowshoes. While
Dutch tinkered with his solar panels and the batteries
they charged, I went out and tramped a path to the
storage shed and two fifty-five-gallon drums of aviation
fuel. The sun had dropped behind Mount Paloma, the
light gone blue and icy, by the time I had finished the
path. When I went back into the house a cloud of steam
rose about the door, the sun-warmed air of the house
condensing in the cold. Dutch had found the batteries fit
and was tuning the small Narco transceiver to the
emergency channel. That done, he sat me and a glass of
whiskey in a soft chair before the windows that made the
south walls of the house and went about doing something with the frozen steaks. I sipped the whiskey and
watched night creep up the peaks to the south and east.
The snow and ice went from a glittering gold and white
to pink to red, then blue as the shadow line rose over
them. In time Dutch finished with hacking and simmer-

ing the frozen meat and brought more whiskey and the cat and joined me before the windows. He settled into another tale about flying in Alaska, a yarn that, though it began well—Dutch backing a float plane down a spring-swollen river, the current so swift he had to push the throttle near full to keep from being swept downstream—I did not hear the end of. When I woke the panorama before me had gone dark. Black where the mountains had been, above that a field of stars so bright and close they might have been dazzling fruit hanging from a tree. Dutch's voice came from behind me, from the transceiver desk. Dutch broke off the transmission and came back to the window.

"St. Cloud's all right. Nothing much happening." Dutch turned from the window. "He got another call from your friend. Wouldn't tell me what. Said it would wait till tomorrow." Dutch came up from his chair. "Guess I better make some water. In case we decide to wash up tonight." He looked to the window and the black folds and spires and rumpled fields of the mountain wilderness. "Moon'll be up in about an hour. Maybe we'll take a little hike then. I'll show you a sight you won't forget."

Dutch brought the buckets of snow, put them behind the stove, climbed a ladder to the loft in the rear of the house and returned with a photograph album. During the next hour Dutch talked me through an illustrated story of his life, we ate, and Dutch talked again. Of his tomboy daughter, her marriage to some Wall Street type, her leaving Montana, her divorce, her imminent return. Of his wife, killed in a plane crash in Alaska. Yarn after yarn about flying bush from Peru to the Arctic. Fliers he had known, how the dead had died, and their planes— Dutch spent as much time and affection describing the planes as the men who had flown them. He talked of his adventures in World War II, piloting everything from gliders to General Mark Clark's B-29. He held up the hand with the finger and a half left.

"Battle of Falaise Gap. August '44. Got shot down when the Germans were making their runout. Bailed out, everything OK. Behind enemy lines, if the enemy had any lines. It was dark and muddy—well, lot of what I was slipping and falling in turned out the next morning not to be mud. Anyway, I was going along and I bump into this German officer. He had a Luger, maybe a P-38, and I had my .45. Well, we started waltzing around. Flopping around in dead men's parts. The German trying to get his pistol into my ear, me trying to get the .45 into his. I finally got the .45 up next to his head but couldn't turn the muzzle in where it'd do much more than give him a haircut. We were rolling around like so, my arm hit something, the .45 went off. Exploded like a hand grenade right next to the Kraut's ear. The .45 barrel had got jammed with mud or something. The Kraut's ear, most of the fingers on my right hand went flying off into the dark." Dutch laughed. "Peggy used to say that wasn't the first ear I'd ever taken off, though I usually did it by talking."

Dutch worked on his pipe for a while. "Falaise was where I gave it up. The lunacy of man destroying man. And nature. And everything else he can get his hands on. What's it all about?" Dutch twisted his head, shook the match out. "Who's going to rule a burned-out rock. No point in it. Just like there ain't no point in you and St. Cloud and this other fella, however many of them there are, destroying each other." Dutch turned to me. "Look, I know St. Cloud's been in some bad company. Maybe once he was a bad man. Maybe you're a bad man. I don't know, it's hard to tell by looking. But I know you can give it up. You start by changing your way of life. St.

Cloud's told me a little about you. You used to fly commercial. Before that for Air America, people like that. I know it'd be tough to give up the money and glamour and excitement and the big fast planes, but there's something to be said for my way of life. Flying bush. You're your own boss. You got timetables and contracts and obligations and somebody gets in trouble you got to roll out of the rack and go help them out. Still, there's a freedom in that you're not going to find flying for United or the government, no matter how much money they pay you." Dutch stopped, studied me. "In a way, you'd be better up here than St. Cloud. I know—he can fly circles around the two of us, but he's almost too good. A good pilot's got to be quick-thinking in the air, but a good bush pilot's got to put in a lot of that slow thinking on the ground. Cautious. Methodical. Preparation. You do everything by the rules even if you do make those rules yourself. I know all this sounds crazy coming from me. Spent half my life flying in blizzards, landing on mountains, lost twenty-one planes in my career—but you've never met a more careful flier than me. That's why I'm still alive, the rest of them are dead." Dutch put down his pipe. "I watched you during the landing today. You're going to be taking them up and bringing them down a long time after St. Cloud is gone. Think about it." Dutch looked toward the windows, then leaped up from his chair, his manner of rising it seemed even when that was premeditated. "Moon's up. Let's go take a look at this paradise before the outside world comes in and fucks it up."

We gathered up skis and parkas and gloves and went out to a world lit by the cold fire of moonglow. The faces of the east-standing mountains were hung with shadow, black falls spilling from their summits and ridges, but to the west there lay a boundless folded field of white. We strapped on our free-heel skis and Dutch pointed to the summit of Mount Paloma and the curling ridge of snow that led to it. Dutch broke through the snow and I skied easy in his tracks, stopping from time to time to look down into the great bowl carved under Paloma. A lake lay at the bottom of the bowl, Dutch called over his shoulder, no fish in the summer, he climbed down to bathe and swim and think about one day, maybe, stocking the frigid water with native trout. Halfway to the summit Dutch stopped for a breather and I volunteered to break trail for a time. Dutch looked to the snow ridge curling to the summit, to the bowl below.

"All right. But stay right. Ten, twelve yards from the edge. There's been a cornice building up near the top. Could go at any time. Sneeze might do it with all this fresh snow on the old base. I got caught in an avalanche up in Alaska once. Remembered what an old-timer told me. Swim with it. I performed the breast stroke. That day I could've paddled the Atlantic."

I went ahead, breaking through the snow, calf-deep at times. When I started lugging in, Dutch went ahead. He knew a way we could ski damn near to the top of Paloma, only a couple of rocks to climb. We came to that place, stood our skis in the snow and went easy up the last thirty feet of rock. Dutch stopped under the last wall, the rock little higher than his head, and drew me up to him.

"You go first," he said and grinned and with a push on my backside sent me up to what seemed to be the top of the world. The mountains and hanging shadows, the fields of white and the cold, moonlit sky—it was as if I had no contact with earth, floating free in the air. I looked around the high, cold world of snow and stars and felt free. Like I had felt when I first came to Montana, to the land.

Dutch came up, turned full circle, guiding me with him, calling out the names of mountains he knew—Hunter, Burnt Strip, Nipple Knob, the Lonesome Bachelor, Sugar Loaf, North Trapper and Watchtower Peak. Then he took to naming the stars, then he fell silent. We stood without speaking for a time, then Dutch started walking about, looking down to the skis standing in the snow, fidgeting with his shirt pocket. He had forgotten his pipe.

We climbed off the summit and strapped on our skis. Dutch set himself in the tracks we had made climbing. "Now's the fun part," he said. "Stay behind me, stay in track and don't go near the edge." With a whoop and push with his poles, Dutch went down the curling slope toward the cabin.

I gave Dutch a lead, put my skis in the tracks and went down the slope after him. After twenty yards I seemed to be flying off a cliff. The tracks were a blur before me, Dutch a black patch sinking into the snow. My eyes began to tear from the speed and I could not see anything but the white field rushing beneath my skis. Then, at a point that I knew I had gone over the cornice edge, was surely falling into the bowl and the snow-covered lake below, something hard struck my chest, my feet went out from under me and stars appeared beneath my skis.

Dutch lay not far away, on his back in the snow. He was laughing at the sky. Skis were strewn all about us. One of the glass walls of the house stood to my left and when I looked up I came face to face with a blade of the Super Cub's prop. Dutch rose from the snowbank I had bowled him into, came and, still laughing, collected me from the burrow I had made at the nose of the Cub.

"There'll be plenty of time for you to fly out of here

in the morning," Dutch said, leaving the skis where they had fallen, taking me into the house and putting me down before a whiskey. "Anyway, you see how your takeoff's going to be done. Like a little kid going down a slicky-slide."

"I say we shoot the motherfucker right now. You don't want to touch it, Cox, it'll be my pleasure."

"I don't know. J.K.'s story's got the ring of truth to it. Blackmuir is going to get us all, J.K. included. He kills us, J.K.'s next. Maybe he really does want to take his chances with us."

It was dark now and I could just make out St. Cloud's response, a sneer, in night shade. I had landed an hour before, at dusk, having spent the afternoon, as Dutch had suggested, wandering the Cub through the mountains and passes and valleys of the wilderness. I had seen the Cessna 180 parked on Dutch's strip, near the gas pump, from the air and had thought that St. Cloud had wheeled Dutch's plane out of the hangar to refuel it and had forgotten or been too lazy to drive it back inside. But as I landed and ran up to the hangar I saw it was not Dutch's silver 180, unpainted, knocked twenty pounds off the payload, but the same model Cessna painted sky blue. A plane I now remembered having seen at Kill Devil Ranch.

St. Cloud looked toward the blue 180, turned and looked through the trees toward the cabin. Johnny Kono was framed by the window. He sat slumped at the table, head in his hands. St. Cloud turned back. "He's afraid of dying, all right. Dying of me." St. Cloud came close. "Look, Cox, you know why the little bastard's here. A Trojan horse, whatever the hell you call it. He's going to be snooping around, getting the lay of the place, coming in our plans, fucking up our planes, the radios, something. Then he'll run back to Daddy."

Johnny Kono raised his head, turned to look out the window, into the dark where his future, or lack of one, was being decided.

I moved between St. Cloud and the cabin. "Why not let him? We could go along. Let J.K. think he's some kind of superspy. Feed him a little misinformation. I don't know what, but we could figure something out. Keep the radios and the planes locked up. Keep an eye on him. Might learn a lot more from J.K. than he'll get out of us."

St. Cloud pushed me away, so that he could see the cabin. "Yeah. Maybe you're right. Maybe I could just go in and make him think I'm going to shoot him."

I brought St. Cloud's attention around to me. "What they're flying, is this Cessna and the Foxjet all they've got?"

St. Cloud looked toward the hangar and the plane Johnny Kono had flown in. The Cessna was near invisible now. All you could see was the prop, the skis, the windshield and the markings on the tail, its blue the same cool shade as the backing snow.

"Far as I know it's just the two of them, Blackmuir and J.K., and that's the only two planes they got," St. Cloud said. "J.K. swears the Cessna ain't hot." St. Cloud looked the 180. "And it ain't got a STOL kit. Blackmuir don't believe in them any more than Dutch does."

"Was it Blackmuir in the Foxjet the other day?"

"Maybe. J.K. says it was. I think they're switching around in the planes. So we'll shoot at the wrong target."

"J.K. say what plans Blackmuir has for us?"

"Nah, but ain't it obvious after the other day? He's going to fly us into the ground."

"You come up with any ideas what we're going to do?"

"Couple. First thing we got to do is get rid of the Foxjet. Even things up a bit. I got one good idea. Something I picked up in the war." St. Cloud looked down the strip. The moon had not risen, but its glow showed over the stand of pine beyond the strip. St. Cloud turned back. "The next time he buzzes this place, he's going to be mine."

"J.K. have anything else?"

"Yeah. We got a new frequency. One thirty-one point double ought. Blackmuir'll call every day at six."

"That's it?"

"He left a message. We're all dead men. Some of us just ain't got the news yet." St. Cloud pushed air through his nose. He moved toward the cabin. "Give me a minute. I want to sweat the greaser."

I gave St. Cloud the minute, then followed him inside. The look on Johnny Kono's face, when he saw me, showed not relief that he was going to live but triumph—that we were going to die.

Johnny Kono was good the first night. We shut him in Peggy's room and he didn't make a peep, displaying his new loyalty by snoring greatly. I had him the next morning and early afternoon, going over his story like an intelligence officer interrogating a POW. Blackmuir was in trouble, Johnny Kono didn't know what exactly. He had fallen from grace with his friends in Washington and Wall Street. Whatever he had done for them over the years, he wasn't doing it anymore. Maybe there were some money problems. The Hollywood gang, Montana locals who had gathered at the fete a couple weeks ago, now shunned him. Now that Johnny Kono had stolen the

Cessna and escaped, Blackmuir sat alone at Kill Devil. Even the cowboy servants had pulled out and gone back to McLean, Virginia, for reassignment. In California the investigation of Thea's death, the first one, the fake one, had been reopened. Dub Dayton had been identified as the pilot killed in the accident at the San Carlos airport. The faked passports and suspect flight plan found in the Aerobat had sent the cops digging up the garden of the Atherton house, looking for the wife's body. The only other item of interest that Johnny Kono could pass on was that C. W. Namier had earned a T-shirt. Johnny Kono had almost brought me one. The front read:

C. W. LIVES

St. Cloud was out of the cabin for most of the time I spent grilling Johnny Kono. He passed a couple hours in the hangar, fitting the hangar door with chain and lock. St. Cloud left the blue Cessna as it was, parked near the gas pump. Without the engine kept warm, the plane wasn't going anywhere. St. Cloud then put in some time in the radio shack. After a couple of calls and a bit of worry he had raised Dutch at the mountain house. Dutch was OK. He had been out skiing. From now on he would sit by the radio at ten and four and eight when either St. Cloud or I would call. St. Cloud then went out on the strip. He walked its length. Up one border, back along the other. He stopped periodically to peer into the flanking woods. That done, he returned to the radio shack and stayed there, the door locked, till midafternoon, when he came to the cabin. There St. Cloud looked at Johnny Kono, he looked at me, then he looked pleased. That night after dinner the three of us gathered around the table and St. Cloud unfolded a bullshit scheme. The one we wanted Johnny Kono to take back to Blackmuir. The more whiskey that went down the more Butte the evening got.

The following morning I woke to a great crashing. I rose and followed the sounds of riot. A chair and a cat flew past me, going on some distance down the hall. In the main room other cats and chairs and tables and dishes and books and lamps were sailing about. St. Cloud and Johnny Kono were spinning around the room. St. Cloud's head and shoulder were stuck into Johnny Kono's gut, his arms around his waist, like a linebacker driving into a ball carrier. While Johnny Kono had locked his arms over St. Cloud's back—hanging on to his bucking mount anyway he could. The two danced around the room another turn. Then Johnny Kono saw me, looked at my hand and released his grip. I had brought the .45 from under my pillow. As Johnny Kono relaxed his hold, St. Cloud came up, pushed Johnny Kono back a foot and hit him in the face. St. Cloud then fell to the floor. St. Cloud writhed in pain, holding his right hand.

"What the fuck is going on?" I said, sounding, I hoped, like a man holding a gun.

"He's gone fucking berserk!" and "The little mother-fucker's been in the radio shack!" came at about the same time.

Then Johnny Kono: "You're fucking crazy. I ain't been nowhere."

St. Cloud twisted to his knees. He came toward me. "Give me that gun."

I backed into a neutral corner. "I'll keep the gun. Now what the hell is happening?"

St. Cloud turned, tried to rise, went back to the floor. "Just shoot the little fucker. Go on, goddamnit."

Johnny Kono wasn't looking that worried, wasn't

looking that sure of things either. "What the fuck. All I did was go out and take a piss. What the hell's wrong with that?"

St. Cloud came to his knees, then, slowly, to his feet. "We got to check it out, see what else he got into." He turned to me. "I mean this, Cox. If he moves one muscle, blow him away."

I made no response but to level the gun at Johnny Kono. That seemed to satisfy St. Cloud. He went to the door, opened it with his left hand, his right held to his side, and went out. Johnny Kono waited till the outer door slammed, then showed me some innocence. "He's gone batshit, Cox. I went out this morning. Took a piss. Breath of fresh air. That's it."

"Just sit down and shut up, J.K."

Johnny Kono grinned. "Going to shoot me if I don't?"

I moved the gun a couple feet to the left of Johnny Kono's midsection and squeezed the trigger. Nothing happened, the hammer clicked against the empty chamber. I then chambered a round. Johnny Kono righted a chair and sat down.

I went to the window. St. Cloud was disappearing down the path to the radio shack. I turned back. "All right, I'm going to give you one chance to tell me before St. Cloud comes back—why did you come here?"

Johnny Kono near closed his eyes, opened them. "I told you last night."

I found a chair with legs, seat and back attached and sat. "Yeah. You know it is true, J.K. Really true. Blackmuir is going to kill you after he kills us." I raised the gun when Johnny Kono opened his mouth. "No. No more. I'm tired of your bullshit." I came forward in the chair. "You're going to be the last to go, J.K. That's all you're going to get."

The dogs opened a chorus of protest. St. Cloud was

crossing near them, making for the hangar. I turned to Johnny Kono "You get into the planes?"

"The fucking things were locked up," Johnny Kono replied with absolutely perfect candor.

I went back in the chair. "J.K., I've been thinking about you. Something I'm going to put to St. Cloud." I smiled. "Maybe we should just let you go. We'll get your Cessna warmed up and get you into the air. Back to Daddy."

Johnny Kono looked to the wall. If there had been a window there he could have seen the blue Cessna, the hangar, the strip. "He'll kill me," he said as if he believed it.

"You know, J.K., the mood St. Cloud is in, you might stand a better chance back at Kill Devil."

"Yeah. Yeah," said Johnny Kono.

The dogs barked again and the outer door opened. There was a clatter in the entry hall, St. Cloud came into the room. He held his right hand pressed under his arm, a pair of gloves in his left hand. He looked at Johnny Kono. "The planes are all right. Locked up tight. He's been at the radio. Clever little bastard. I left the VHF on Blackmuir's frequency last night—one thirty-one. Now it's back on emergency." St. Cloud stopped. "J.K., take a stroll. Feed the dogs, do whatever you were sent here to do. Just get out of here for a while." He looked at the gun in my hand. "Cox and me have some business to discuss."

Johnny Kono looked at the gun. He looked afraid. "I can't go back. Not now."

I moved the gun. Johnny Kono wasn't seeing it. "You know where the dog food is?"

Johnny Kono looked toward the kitchen. "I think so."

I moved the gun toward the kitchen. "Feed the dogs, J.K."

Johnny Kono rose, went to the kitchen, came out with a black plastic sack. He looked at me, St. Cloud, then went out.

St. Cloud watched Johnny Kono moving along the path toward the dogs. Then to me: "Give me a hand, Cox. One of my fingers is fucked. Maybe we better do it in the kitchen in case anything falls off."

We went into the kitchen, stood over the sink. St. Cloud took his right hand from under his arm. The blackened flesh on two fingers was tearing away from the bone. St. Cloud turned the hand over. Flesh hung free from the bone. He turned the hand back, fitted the flesh back on the bone. "Looks like I'm going to have to get me an instrument panel like Dutch's. One you can work with your teeth."

"St. Cloud, I'm flying you into Missoula Emergency now."

St. Cloud held the glove to the damaged hand. He grimaced. He moved the glove over the bad fingers. He went white, his knees buckled. He held on to the sink, waited, came back. "You're going to have to do this last part, Cox. Take it slow and easy. Try and keep as much finger on the bone as you can."

"All right. But sit down before you fall down."

St. Cloud went to the kitchen table, leaned against the edge. I took the hand and the glove and St. Cloud went white. "Want some whiskey?"

St. Cloud opened his eyes. "Yeah. Good idea."

I got the bottle, St. Cloud drank a cup or so and for the next minute I worked the glove over the hand, gently kneading the bad fingers into the fingers of the glove. St. Cloud made no sound till it was done, then he let out his breath. "Jesus, that feels good." He held the glove hand up, looked it over. He tried to make a fist, winced, and stopped. "That's going to have to do for now. Maybe it'll grow back or something."

"Sure. You want the other one on?"

St. Cloud turned the gloved hand, examining back and front, as if he was admiring the fit. "Might as well."

We got the left glove on. St. Cloud did some breathing, then looked toward the sink, the counter where I had put the .45. "Let me see if I can fit the glove in the trigger guard."

I passed the gun to St. Cloud. He took the gun with his left hand, didn't even think about the right. The gloved finger fitted snug into the trigger guard. St. Cloud held the gun up, admiring that fit. Then he moved the gun, not right at me but close. "It's got to be done, Dan. We're fucking fools playing their game. It's like logic. We don't have to worry about two planes if there's one man to fly them."

I looked to the window over the sink. A shadow passed over the glass. I thought of every humane argument I could come up with on short notice. None of them sounded right. I turned to St. Cloud. The gun and his attention had gone off me. He sniffed the air.

"You leave something on the stove?"

I looked to the stove, the window over the sink. The shadow pressed against the glass. Now it was a cloud that drifted away, now it was smoke.

"Fucking little bastard!"

St. Cloud was out of the kitchen. I went behind him, through the entry hall, outside. St. Cloud had gone into the wall of smoke, toward the hangar. I went into the smoke, was blinded, could not breathe. I ran low, keeping to the path beaten in the snow. The crackle of fire came to me, and the heat, then a chopping, beating sound. I came out of the smoke at the foot of the strip,

near the gas pump. The wind was clearing the smoke
from the hangar, feeding the flames that ate at the side of
the hangar, driving the flames into the hangar, toward
the planes. St. Cloud stood at one wing of the blue
Cessna, the one plane not in the hangar. With the engine
too cold to start, St. Cloud was turning the plane,
pushing it away from the hangar and the pump. As I
went to the other wing I saw Johnny Kono go into the
hangar door.

St. Cloud and I pushed the ski plane as far as we
could onto the strip. St. Cloud went behind the plane,
toward the hangar. He shouted:

"Get the fire extinguisher! Shovel! We've got to save
the pump!"

I went back to the cabin, found the extinguisher, then
a shovel. I ran back toward the hangar. The fire had gone
to the hangar roof now and the smoke lifted. Through the
haze I could see the hangar, the pump and beyond the
blue Cessna. There came a roar from the hangar. The
flames on the hangar roof went wild. Exploding, spraying sparks and pieces of burning timber and shingle into
the air. The silver Cessna, its engine warm, burst
through the open hangar door with Johnny Kono in the
left seat. Sparks and pieces of burning wood from the
roof above the door showered into the snow around the
pump.

I ripped the cap off the extinguisher and began
spraying the flaming hangar. I did not see St. Cloud
anywhere. There came a second roar from within the
hangar. The fire on the roof went wild. I saw through the
boiling smoke and flames that the prop of the Super Cub
was turning, now a blur, coming through the second
hangar door, St. Cloud at the controls.

St. Cloud wheeled the Cub onto the strip, upwind
from the hangar. He came out of the cockpit shouting:

"The pump! Let the hangar go! The fucking pump!"

St. Cloud ran to me, dragged the extinguisher away and began spraying the pump and the pieces of flaming wood and shingle scattered around it.

"Get the shovel! Get snow on the pump! Goddamnit, we can't let this thing go up!"

I took the shovel and, as St. Cloud sprayed the burning debris, began packing snow around the pump's base. We worked hard, a minute, not more, then St. Cloud stopped. He straightened and looked down the strip, toward the silver Cessna, the plane coming at us.

St. Cloud wrested the shovel from me and ran down the strip toward the oncoming plane, waving the shovel. The Cessna came up well down the strip, banked and rose quickly, passing far above St. Cloud and the shovel he sent twirling into the air.

The next hour and a half was spent at Dutch's kitchen table, St. Cloud, his hands too bad for such detailed work, talking me through the construction of three homemade turtle mines that we hoped would take Blackmuir's Foxjet out of the sky. I prized the tops off a case of shotgun shells, dug out wadding and shot and dumped the powder into a bowl. While I worked at this, St. Cloud took a bucket to a rock outcrop near the strip and returned with four or five dozen rocks, none bigger than a golf ball. With about two pounds of powder collected from the shells, St. Cloud directed me to strip the glass off three, twelve-volt light bulbs, exposing the bulbs' delicate filament. St. Cloud found three zip-lock bags under the kitchen sink and filled the bags with powder. Still working under St. Cloud's direction, I taped three lengths of double electric wire to the contact bases of the three broken bulbs. I took the exposed filaments of the broken bulbs and carefully buried them in the powder, one inside each of the bags. I then sealed the zip-lock bags so that the electrical wire extended from the closed bags. I taped the zip-locks and around the wire extending from the bags, making the bags watertight. As I did this, St. Cloud punched a single hole in the bottom of three large coffee cans. I was then told to thread the free end of the double electrical wire through the holes in the coffee cans, so that the zip-lock bags carrying powder and filament rested on the bottom of the cans. We took the three cans outside and set them on the snow. We then carefully poured water and snow into the cans till the bags of powder were covered. We waited till the water began to set, then put the small rocks, our projectiles, on top of the ice-covered bags of powder, our explosive charge. We then went out onto the strip and dug three holes across the landing path that ran the length of the strip. We placed the homemade mines in these holes and covered them with snow, leaving only the free ends of the double electrical wire exposed. We ran a spool of single insulated electrical wire from near the hangar burn out to the three mines. We stripped the single wire in three places and to these exposed sections of wire taped one strand of the double electrical wire leading from each of the mines. Similarly we connected another length of single wire to the second strand from each mine and ran that single wire back to near the hangar, forming a potential circuit. While I was covering the two lengths of wire leading out to the mines with snow, St. Cloud took the battery out of the Cessna and lugged it over to the wire ends near the hangar burn. He waited till I had completely covered the wire and returned to the hangar burn. He then coiled one of the copper wire ends around the negative battery terminal. He took the end of the free cooper wire, smiled and handed it to me. "OK, maybe it's Mickey Mouse, Cox, but it's worth a try. Fucking Blackmuir brings the Foxjet down to buzz the strip again, all we got to do is get the timing right, wait till the Foxjet is over the mines, then," he looked at the free end of the copper wire in my hand, then at the exposed positive battery terminal, "then, whoever's on duty, all he's got to do is touch wire to the positive terminal and—well, the rocks ain't going to do much to wing or fuselage, but if we're lucky, real lucky, if just one of those fucking rocks blown up in the air gets sucked into one of the intakes," St. Cloud smiled, "it's going to be junk city for one nasty little jet." He shrugged. "I seen it work before. Pathet Lao took out one of our Otters in the highlands. Of course they didn't have to fuck with this frozen ground. Little cocksuckers buried a fifty-five-gallon drum of TNT and scrap iron next to one of our strips near Muong Sing. I'll tell you, there was one less Otter in the sky that night. Ah well, if this don't work, maybe we can come up with something that will."

He looked down the strip. The wire was covered, only our tracks showed in the snow and they could not be seen from the air. "Nothing to do now but wait." He turned back. "Listen, can you take the first shift at the battery? I didn't call Dutch this morning. Want to see what's going on over there." He looked at the smoldering ruin of the hangar. "Maybe you could get a rake or something. Fuck around here. Just don't get too far from the battery."

St. Cloud went to the radio shack. I found a rake and returned to the hangar burn. The burn was still hot and I stayed away, trying to keep near the battery and upwind as the smoke shifted in the breeze. In time St. Cloud came back from the radio shack. He had not been able to contact Dutch. Out skiing, he thought, he would try again at two. Nothing on 131.00, Blackmuir's frequency. St. Cloud volunteered to take over the watch, but I sent him inside. He had taken to suffering from the cold. He looked smaller, his face gaunt, the bad spot by his nose gone slick and dark.

St. Cloud passed a half hour in the cabin, then came out. He gave a shout and went back along the path toward the radio shack.

I worked for a quarter hour at the burn, then a sound came to me. Like hearing a shadow. I turned to the strip and the snout of the Foxjet sitting level to the ground two hundred yards off. The jet coming so low at me it might have been landing. I went to the battery. The Foxjet came low and quick down the strip. I waited, then when I thought it was near the buried mines, I touched the copper wire to the positive terminal. Two of the mines went. Two dull thuds, two plumes of snow shot into the air. The Foxjet passed through the snow plumes, came on down the strip, low and quick, directly toward me.

The Foxjet had passed beyond the trees behind the cabin when I came up. Then came the explosion. The Foxjet reared over the trees, tumbling backward nose over tail, a sight that sickened me, like watching a diver go off the wrong end of the platform, twisting elegantly toward concrete. The Foxjet hung still for a moment, then slid back and disappeared beyond the trees. I ran along the path toward the radio shack and the bowl beyond, where the Foxjet had fallen. St. Cloud had come out of the radio shack. He was now running ahead, up the slope toward the bowl. There was a second, larger explosion and a fireball, blossoming black as it rose, came from the bowl. I went past the radio shack, up the slope, toward St. Cloud. There was a third explosion. By the time I had reached St. Cloud a black funnel of smoke was boiling up from the pit of the bowl. St. Cloud grabbed me, he leaned out over the cliff, looked down into the bowl. He came back. Our talk was fast.

"Goddamn, it worked! Did it work?" He looked to the stand of pine that edged the wall of the bowl.

"I don't know. Two mines went. The plane looked OK over me. Then there was an explosion."

"I heard it. Two mines went?"

"Yeah. Two."

St. Cloud looked down the steep slope to the bottom of the bowl. He pulled himself back, breathing hard. "It fucking worked." He looked to the trees, to the sky. "Did you see anything? Who was in the plane?"

"I didn't see. Just one pilot. That's all."

I went to the rim of the bowl and looked down. The smoke was coming too thick, black, to see the plane. St. Cloud took my arm. He pulled me back.

"Too steep here. We'll have to go down on the far side." He looked across the bowl. "Can you do it?" He turned to me, spent, beaten. "Somebody's got to stay up here. By the radio." He turned away from the bowl. "One pilot—it's J.K. Blackmuir sent him back. He'd let J.K. test our rat traps. Better check it out anyway." He went a few paces off. "How long's it been since J.K. split?"

"Three hours. More."

"Plenty of time to land, switch planes." St. Cloud stopped. "Any foam left in the can? Take a shovel. Snowshoes. There's a place over there. You can kick a stair down to the bottom. Both tanks went, so it ought to be all right by the time you get down." He stopped, his back to me. "You remember the little motherfucker's teeth? The gold ones."

I said I remembered Johnny Kono's teeth.

St. Cloud lifted his face to the sky. "Dan. I'm worried." He lowered his head, half turned from me. "I can't raise Dutch."

We made a pass over the mountain house and saw the tracks another plane had cut in the snow. I brought the Super Cub around, set down on the slope and ran up it between the wider, heavier tracks, toward the mountain house. I turned the Cub where the other plane had come about, set the throttle to idle. St. Cloud got out and walked a few yards down the slope. He looked at the tracks made by the plane that had landed before us. Up toward the mountain house. He called out for his friend. The name echoed across the bowl beneath Paloma summit. There were tracks—skis, snowshoes, boots, the small deep holes made by Dutch's cat or some other animal—all about the house, leading in every direction. The door was cracked open. The cat was there, looking out. St. Cloud pushed back the door. The cat rubbed against his leg.

"Puss," St. Cloud said, watching the cat, "where has Dutch gone to?" He looked around the many-sided room. "It probably needs something to eat." He went to the counter by the stove, found a thawed steak and tossed it into the cat's dish. The cat looked at the meat on the tin plate, purred and went to the door. St. Cloud watched the cat. "Maybe not." St. Cloud went to the ladder leading to the loft. "Look around. See if there's any whiskey left."

I went to the table. Dutch's photograph album lay open on the table. There a picture Dutch had showed me, his wife, a small blond woman, standing by a plane. Last night's dishes were stacked on the table, glasses, a bottle of whiskey half gone. Dutch's pipe lay among these things.

St. Cloud came down the ladder. "Not there." St. Cloud sat at the table, poured out a glass of whiskey. "Want one?"

"Yeah."

St. Cloud put whiskey in a second glass. He turned the album to him. "I think that's the plane she died in. Got caught in a storm up around Point Barrow." He turned the album away, picked up the pipe, smelled it, put the pipe down. He looked to the south-facing windows. The glass was burnished by the sun, as if that wall were made by dozens of squares of copper. "No point in going out and looking for him. Not enough time to do that much." St. Cloud turned to the wall by the door, where Dutch stacked his boots and skis and winter gear. "You mind waiting a couple minutes? If he's going to show, it'll be soon. Maybe we'll come back tomorrow." St. Cloud fell silent. He watched the cat, who had taken to licking the steak.

I went to the window. The sun had gone behind Paloma summit now and the glass was freed of glare. I looked to the summit and the blueing slope of snow that went up to it, the smooth curving cornice that formed the top of the bowl. My eye followed this unbroken arc till, near the summit, I saw a niche in the overhanging snow. I called St. Cloud to the window. He looked up toward the summit.

"You take the skis," he said. "There's just one pair. I'll follow in your tracks."

We went out. I fixed the free-heel skis to my boots and pushed up the tracks leading to the summit. St. Cloud came behind. We stopped short of the collapsed section of the cornice. One set of ski tracks led out to the break. I stamped out a place in the snow where we could stand. I laid the skis to the edge of the break and St. Cloud went out on this platform. He looked down into the bowl, then came back. St. Cloud looked around the snow. He went down, dug his hand into three small holes in the snow, and stood. He held three empty cartridge shells in his hand. "Back him over the edge. No fucking need to shoot him."

St. Cloud turned and looked around the bowl. "No way we can get down tonight. Not find him and bring him out." He stooped, drew back one of the skis. He looked over the bowl, toward the ranges to the east, all but their summits gone blue. He turned away, took up the second ski. "I guess we better take that goddamn cat back with us."

"We'll split it. Down the middle. We'll get it back to Peggy. She'll probably get it from us a hell of a lot sooner than she would waiting for these fucking lawyers to settle the will or whatever this crap is." St. Cloud divided the stack of bills in two, leveled the two stacks, pushed one across the table to me. The bills were fives, tens, twenties, hundreds, in no order. The cash divided, St. Cloud peered into the rusted strongbox Dutch had kept under his bed. "I'll go through the rest of this shit and try to make some sense to it. Looks like deeds and stuff." St. Cloud went back from the table. "You take the Super Cub. You can leave it in Missoula. Guy named Stan Lambert out at Johnson Field. Old buddy of Dutch's. He'll take care of it till Peggy shows up. Fair enough?"

"I suppose."

St. Cloud ruffled the stacked bills. "You know something you might think about, Dan, if you want something to do. Peggy's down in Reno, getting her divorce straightened out. You could go down, pay her a visit. Maybe tell her what's happened. She's a good girl. She'll understand." St. Cloud looked across the room. "Just give me a day. Fly down to Reno, have a good night's sleep, break the news to her tomorrow." St. Cloud stopped. "She'll be all right. Every day Dutch went out, she figured he wouldn't be coming back."

"I'll think about it."

"Fair enough." St. Cloud came over the table, looked into the strongbox. "I guess that's about it." He looked up slowly. "Anything else before we get you on your way?"

"What are you going to do?"

St. Cloud leaned back in the chair. A cat came up on his lap. St. Cloud stroked the cat. "I think I'm going to Hawaii. Tired of this fucking cold. Really getting to me." St. Cloud dropped the rubbed cat to the floor. "Well, the first thing I'm going to do is get my hands taken care of. Guess what I end up doing depends on how much is left."

"I meant what are you going to do about Blackmuir."

St. Cloud looked at me. "I told you. It's over. Finished."

I flipped through the bills on the table, maybe two thousand dollars. "When did this call come in?"

"I told you that too. Last night after we came back from the mountain house. When you were washing the dishes."

"Nobody washed any dishes last night."

"Well, whatever the hell you were doing. Lane called in on one thirty-one. Said it was over. He wants to disengage. Something. You know that phony military shit he talks."

"And you're willing to leave it at that?"

"Sure. Why not? What's in it for us now? Nothing. They're all dead and they're going to stay dead no matter what we do to Blackmuir. According to what J.K. said,

the guy's on the skids anyway. End up a wino somewhere. Ain't that good enough?"

I squared the bills, picked them up, tossed them
on the table. "You don't have any ideas of getting me
out of the way, then going after Blackmuir on your
own."

St. Cloud shook his head very slowly. "No."

I picked up the scattered bills, straightened them.
"All right. I'm getting sick of this shit too. You know how
many people have died in this nightmare—not counting
the three hundred in the Utah crash? Well, if we stay up
here and play Blackmuir's game, we're going to join
them. You want to go down a cipher, be another one of
Blackmuir's statistics, St. Cloud, go right ahead. But not
me. I'll tell you what I'm going to do. I'm going to take
the Super Club to Missoula. I'll leave this morning. But
I'm not going to Reno. I'm not going somewhere and
take up yet another name and try to start yet another life.
That bullshit is over. What I am going to do is go to the
cops. Somebody. Newspapers, FBI, I haven't figured
that out yet. But I'm going to somebody and I'm going to
tell them this story. The whole goddamn thing, from
beginning to end. Nothing is going to be left out. Now I
don't care what they do to me. Throw me in jail,
whatever. But before that happens, somebody is going to
know about Lane Blackmuir. That's what I'm going to
do, St. Cloud. Fair enough?"

St. Cloud's face had gone hard, eyes narrow. He
spoke quiet, dangerous. "Just do me one favor. Give me
one day. Tomorrow. Till I get Dutch's body out."

I came over Lolo, the last peak before making the brown
scar of the Bitterroot Valley, hit the toggle pump and
retracted the Cub's skis, lifting them over the wheels. I

flew downriver, over the snarled confluence of the
Bitterroot and the Clark Fork, toward Missoula's Johnson Field. I cleared for landing with the Missoula tower,
set down and taxied to a line of private planes. A
mechanic was working down the line, overhauling the
prop hubs on a twin Beechcraft. I went along the line of
planes to him, asked for Stan Lambert. The mechanic
pointed his wrench:

"In the office." The mechanic looked to the silver
Super Cub. "Dutch Genet's plane?" The mechanic went
back to the prop hub. "You just come from there? Stan
got a call from Dutch's place this morning. Something
about sending the chopper out."

Lambert's operation was housed in a one-story
building, plate-glass window looking onto the field, a
pilot's waiting room, a high counter separating that from
a dispatcher's office. The young woman behind the
counter went to a glass wall at the end of the counter,
tapped the glass and jerked a thumb at me. The man in
the office looked through the glass, beckoned me in.
Lambert had a phone to his ear, writing notes on a pad.
He pointed to a chair, listened, talked, listened, wrote,
laughed, told the person on the line to fuck off and hung
up. Lambert went back in his swivel chair, grinned. "I
didn't do it, I ain't got it and I don't want any. Now what
can I do you for? What's the name?"

"Cox. Dan Cox. I'm a—"

Lambert came forward, looked at the notes he had
just written. "Cox. I know that name. We know each
other?"

"I used to fly for Northwestern. Had a place in the
Bitterroots, kept a plane here now and then."

Lambert read the notes. "That must be it." He tossed
the pad onto the desk. "Now what's happening this
morning, Cox?"

"I'm a friend of Dutch Genet's. Just brought his Super Cub in—"

Lambert came half out of his chair, saw no point in it and went back. "Goddamn, you just come from Dutch's? What the hell is going on out there? Got a call from St. Cloud this morning—" Lambert stopped. He rapped a finger against the desk top. "That's it. St. Cloud. You're a friend of his." Lambert's eyed flickered, as if he remembered who St. Cloud worked for. But then half the people at the smoke jump center just down the road were spooks, and he passed over it. "You just come from Dutch's? What the hell *is* happening out there? St. Cloud calls in this morning. Said Dutch has gone missing up at the mountain house. We couldn't raise Dutch on the radio either. Now I can't get St. Cloud at Dutch's place or at the mountain house or in any of the planes. Just about to get on the blower to Missoula General and get a chopper out there." Lambert had taken to weeding his in-box. "Look—what's your name? Dan. Do me a favor. Radio room's down the hall. See if you can get St. Cloud or Dutch or somebody out there on the VHF. Dutch usually stays on one twenty-one point five— emergency band. Shit, what is that other frequency he uses?" Lambert stopped. "Funny, St. Cloud didn't say anything about you out there. You say you brought the Super Cub in?" Lambert shrugged. "Ah well, fucking St. Cloud'd forget Christmas if they didn't put lights up." Lambert had the phone to his ear. "Dan, see what you can raise on one twenty-one five. I'll call the bank, then maybe we can make a decision on the chopper."

I found a door marked NO ADMITTANCE at the end of the hall. Two walls of the small room were stacked with radios. I sat at the table before the VHF, put on the headphones and turned the tuning knob to 121.5. I'd see if I could raise St. Cloud, then deal with Lambert and

Dutch's death. A transmission from the smoke jump center. I turned to 131.00, Blackmuir's frequency. Soft static. Nothing else for a minute or two, then a transmission came over. Faint, I couldn't make out the words or recognize the voice. I put the volume up, tuned out static. Then from far away came St. Cloud's voice:

"Come on, you motherfucker." Like a cowboy talking to his horse, a pilot to his plane.

I pulled the stand mike to me, pressed the transmit button. I came on with the Super Cub's ID, waited, then another voice, Blackmuir's, came on:

"Delta Hotel one nine seven three six. Over."

"Delta Hotel one nine seven three six, this is Yankee Charlie seven four nine one one. Can you give me your position? Over."

Then St. Cloud's voice: "Fuck off, Cox."

Then Blackmuir's laughter, soft as static: "Forty-six north. One-fourteen thirty west. On the move. Should find us somewhere around there."

"Delta Hotel one nine seven three six, I've got four six north. One one four thirty west. Over."

Then nothing but static. The transmission had ended.

I went back as I had come. Over the north shoulder of Lolo, into the wilderness. I pointed the Cub's nose south, a touch west, passing over Pyramid Butte, St. Joseph, Bass, St. Mary's, Totem and Hidden peaks, Heavenly Twins, Stormy and Packbox and Bear Creek passes, Gash Point and Goat Roost and Sky Pilot, toward the coordinates Blackmuir had given me. The Cub's Lycoming ran well, fuel down but enough to get back to Dutch's. Nothing in the sky, nothing on 131 as I approached 46° north, 114°30' west. I went down there, circled the lakes, ran the ridges, wound through the valleys and passes and mountains, but saw no planes on the ground. I took the Cub up and was about to start a grid search when a fleck blinked silver far to the southwest, deep into Idaho. The plane circled at fifteen, sixteen, seventeen thousand feet. Near as high as the Cessna would go.

I lost sight of the silver Cessna as I came under it. Still nothing on 131, no sign anywhere of the sky-blue plane St. Cloud had been flying. But then as I banked to go up to Blackmuir, I saw a shadow, a blue, winged form brushed on an icebound lake to the west. The bowl rising above the lake was tight and I circled above its peaks. The blue Cessna looked to have broken through the ice near the lake's edge. Its nose and part of the cabin were buried in the frigid water. Then I saw a black curl beneath one of the wings. The curl moved. A man straightened, lifted an arm. I found a break in the bowl's wall, not much, and put the Cub through it. I sent the nose down, skis clipping treetops, back hard on the stick at the small lake's edge. The Cub set down on the snow-covered ice, speed dropping nicely as I ran across the lake toward the downed Cessna. Near midpoint in the run a green bruise spread over the ice. A thaw stretched across my path. I hit the throttle full forward, pulled back on the wheel. The skis jerked at the rotten ice and the water on its surface, but the Cub planed over the thaw, ice and water billowing over the windshield. Then the ice was good and held and the Cub's nose came down, but I had run to within fifty yards of the lake shore. I cut throttle to idle, flaps full out, and aimed the plane's nose between two trees on the steep bank. The Cub bounded up the drifted bank. The last I saw before the explosion of snow smothered the plane was that the nose would go between the trees, but that the wings would not.

After a time I crawled out of the cabin and went on all fours down through the snow to the lake's edge. St. Cloud stood over me. He stooped, reached down. "Great landing, Cox." He took my arm to lift me, but pulled himself down. He curled on the snow and looked toward the Cub and the trees. "No shit. It really wasn't that bad."

I stood. My head rang, but everything else seemed all right. I worked with St. Cloud till we got him back to his feet. It was like grappling with a block of ice. His clothes were set stiff as armor. St. Cloud had me walk him about, till he could keep moving on his own. I then went up through the trees to the Super Cub. The wings were still attached to the fuselage, wing struts, everything structurally sound so far as I could tell. I went back to St. Cloud. He looked up toward the Cub.

"You weren't going that fast. Must've felt like a good ride, but you'd damn near run out by the time you made the trees." St. Cloud looked to the sky. "See Blackmuir coming in?"

"He was circling about fifteen thousand. Marking where you went down."

St. Cloud turned, scanning the sky. Nothing. The silver Cessna was gone. "White of him." St. Cloud looked to the nose-down Cessna. "I forgot to strain the goddamn gas. You know Dutch's rule. It started missing. And this fucking hand. If I'd had Dutch's pull rings—" St. Cloud stopped, looked the length of the lake. The bowl walls rose steep all around. "Probably won't have too much trouble getting the Cub out of here. Too tight for the Cessna. I had to turn downwind. Caught some fluky air turning, sucked the lift off the downwind wing.

Went into a spin. Maybe fifty feet. No way I should've walked away from it. If you call this walking." St. Cloud stopped. "Look, I'm fucking freezing to death. Let's see if we can get the Cub back down on the ice and get the hell out of here. Go back to Dutch's and get thawed out."

"If we do get out of here, we're going to Missoula. To the hospital."

St. Cloud grinned. You could damn near hear the ice crack. "Cox, you fly us out of here, you can take me anyplace you want to. Can't remember how long it's been since it felt like I had toes." St. Cloud looked to the Cub. "Dutch usually carries a little rope in the back. We can tie a line on the tail, dig out the snow down to the lake. Rev up the engine, get a little lift, she should pop right out and slide down to the ice. Try not to fuck up the skis coming back," St. Cloud said, moving toward the bank. "Lose them we ain't going nowhere."

We found a coil of half-inch climbing rope in the Cub, lashed the rope to the tail wheel, then spent twenty minutes clearing the snow from the Cub to the lake's edge. We came to near the bottom of the slope, the ice five feet below. St. Cloud gave a kick at the last snowbank. "Good enough for Forest Service work. Let's get out of here before I turn into a snowman."

St. Cloud took the line tied to the tail wheel, wrapped it over his shoulder and went down to the ice. He pulled the line taut. "Rev it up some," he called out. "Cut power, I'll give a yank. Don't work the first time, try again. Like you was stuck in the mud."

I went up to the Cub, into the cabin. I turned the starter switch. The Lycoming missed, hit, missed, then caught and ran. I pushed the throttle forward. The leading edges of the wings ground against the trees. I cut power. Nothing. The plane did not move. Again power, off, nothing. Again, then again, then the fifth time I took off the throttle, the nose of the Cub came up, then back. The trees that had stopped the plane fell away. I saw nothing but branches clawing the side windows. There came a cry of triumph from below and a crash and the backward rollercoaster ride ended.

The tail of the Cub had hit the ice hard. The small rear wheel was broken, but St. Cloud said we could manage without it on snow. In fifteen minutes we had cleared ice and snow from the plane's tail, lifted it, turned the plane. With St. Cloud hanging onto the downslope wing struts, the pull from the prop brought the Cub around, the plane bumping hard the last few feet to the level bed of ice. I ran the plane a few yards onto the ice, along the lake's edge. Then there came a snap from under the fuselage and the right wing jerked down. One of the skis had come unfixed from its mounting.

St. Cloud peered under the plane. "You're going to have to take off on one ski anyway." He looked toward the center of the lake, the green gash in the ice there. "Going to have to curl around the edge of the lake. Doing it on one ski'll make it easier." St. Cloud grinned. "Don't worry, Cox. I'll talk you through it. Dutch used to make one-ski takeoffs all the time. Cuts drag. Pop that little Cub in the air in five hundred feet." St. Cloud looked up. The sky still empty. "Blackmuir's probably gone back to Dutch's to gas up." He looked to the Cub, right wing tilted down, resting on one ski and the wheel above the broken ski. "How's your gas doing?"

"Down a bit. Didn't have time to get any in Missoula."

"Got a can on board?"

"I don't think so."

St. Cloud looked toward the blue Cessna, nose into the ice. "There's a five-gallon can in the back of my plane. We better do it. It's a stretch to Missoula." St. Cloud went up on the wing strut, reached to the fuel-tank cap on top of the wing. "You mind getting it? I've had enough of that fucking water."

I went over the ice to the Cessna, kicked in the side window and after some struggle got the gas can out. St. Cloud was standing on the Cub's wing strut. He took the can. "You got any chamois on board? Better do it right and strain it this time."

I found a piece of chamois in the Cub. St. Cloud wrapped it around the can nozzle, lifted the can and fitted the chamois-wrapped nozzle into the wing tank.

"Take a look around and see if anything came off besides the ski and the tail wheel."

I walked around the plane. Dents in the leading edges of the wings, scratches on the fuselage wall, but the working parts—rudder, elevator, ailerons—were intact.

When I came back, St. Cloud had done draining gas into the wing tank. He gave the can a heave onto the ice and fell from the wing strut. I got him to his feet and into the cabin. He was shaking bad.

I got into the Cub's left seat, strapped in and worked the starter switch. The Lycoming coughed, hit, caught and ran smooth as it warmed. St. Cloud looked forward. He moved his hand in an arc, as if he were caressing the curved edge of the lake. "You want left rudder. Put you on your left ski. The plane'll go left natural around the lake shore. All you got to do is keep her balanced. You seen it on TV. Those stunt-car drivers going along on two wheels. It's going to be wobbly till you get her up on the left ski. At forty knots, bank it off the wheel. You can handle it." St. Cloud peered up through the windshield, toward the wall of rock and snow at the far end of the lake. "The tricky part's going to be when you get up. You got to stay upwind, Dan. Got to get out in one pass. Turn downwind, you're going to lose altitude. Be like a fly caught in a bottle." He went back, moved his hand toward his seat belt. "Get the buckle for me, Dan. Already starting to stiffen up."

I tightened St. Cloud's seat belt and he closed his eyes.

I eased the throttle toward the firewall. The Cub shuddered and moved forward. Twenty yards and I thought we wouldn't make it. The wheel and broken ski dragged the plane right. The right wing pitched down. But then at forty knots I pushed rudder left, the right wing came up, and the Cub ran smooth on one ski over the snow-packed ice. At fifty the left wing came down, grazed the snow. I eased the rudder right and the plane straightened and at sixty lifted into the air. I put the nose up, into the wind, toward the wall beyond the lake.

I kept the throttle full forward, the Cub's nose up steep, and still there was nothing in the windshield but snow and rock. I was thinking I would turn downwind, stall, be trapped in the bowl before I drove the Cub into the mountainside, when I saw a break in the wall. The gap I had found coming in. I turned the Cub toward the bit of sky at the top of the windshield. The plane climbed toward the sky. But too slow. Then, when I saw we would not make it through the break, that it was too late to turn away from the rock face and fly downwind, the Cub banged hard into turbulent air. The plane bounced up, hit bad air again and then, as if the plane were a model on strings, went straight up and was lifted through the break in the rock.

St. Cloud opened his eyes, looked at the blue before us. He smiled. "Found you a nice little thermal there, Dan. You are a lucky bastard."

We went through more bad air over the peaks ringing

the bowl. The Cub banged hard into these invisible holes and bars, till we passed beyond the sun-warmed snow and the air went smooth again.

St. Cloud made a noise of pleasure. He did not open his eyes. "Damn, I feel better already. Fuck that hospital. Go on back to Dutch's. Toasty in here."

The cockpit was thirty-five, forty degrees. Freezing air seeped through the cracks around the doorframe. St. Cloud lay back, his head turned on the seat. I could have slapped him, to keep him awake and alive, but it seemed his face, gone rotten now, would have come off in my hands. I moved his leg. It was cold and stiff, dead already. I told him to open his eyes, talk to me.

St. Cloud's head moved against the seat back. "Why?"

"Because you're going to fucking die if you don't stay awake."

"No." Then: "Fuck, it's hot in here. Open my jacket."

"You're not hot, St. Cloud. It's cold. You're freezing to death."

"Yeah? The way I look at it, you think it's hot, it's hot." His head went away from me, then he said low: "It's all right. It's cold again." Then: "You know what J.K. used to tell me? She was just using me. I didn't give a shit. Cunt." Then: "Know what Blackmuir said?"

"What?"

"Nothing."

"What did Blackmuir say?"

St. Cloud moved his lips. He couldn't smile. "That you couldn't drive a bus. Just joking."

"What else did Blackmuir say?"

"Nothing. I think his radio is fucked. I took the antenna off with one of my skis." St. Cloud turned his head. "What do you call that when these knights in armor get on horses and run at each other with spears?"

"A joust."

"Yeah." St. Cloud's eyes came open. He came up, tried to. He looked through the windshield, then at the instrument panel. His arm moved as if he were trying to put his hand inside his jacket pocket. "Fuck, Dan, I forgot. I forgot the goddamn—"

A silver flash caught in the corner of my eye. I turned forward. A silver knife was there, slashing across the windshield. The Cessna passed feet over us. The concussion bucked the Cub down, as if we had been kicked.

St. Cloud had come forward. He looked out the side window, up. "Bastard!"

I settled the Cub, banked St. Cloud's wing up. "See him?"

St. Cloud turned hard in the seat. "Lost him. Get this son of a bitch down. We don't have a chance up here."

"Fuck that. We're getting out of here."

St. Cloud had his face to the windshield, looking up. "He's got too much speed. Where is that cocksucker?" He reached toward the panel mike. He couldn't hold it. The mike fell, dangled to the floorboard. St. Cloud went forward, reached down. He still could not hold the mike.

"How much fuel you got?"

I looked to the instrument panel. The fuel gauge showed empty. I hit the panel. The needle stayed down.

St. Cloud pressed the mike between his hands. "I forgot the goddamn gas cap. Airstream's bled the gas out." He turned to the side window. "Got to look for a place to go down."

I banked the Cub a couple degrees. The silver Cessna showed in the right rear window. Sliding toward us.

"Get this son of a bitch straight. See what he wants."
St. Cloud brought the mike to his mouth. "Blackmuir,
you cocksucker!" The mike fell from his hands. "Fuck.
Nothing works!"

I trimmed the Cub. The silver Cessna had come level
with us. The plane moved in close, slow, as if we were to
fly formation. Blackmuir sat in the left seat. He was
looking toward us. Not at St. Cloud or me, St. Cloud
screaming at him. His eyes were on the Cub's right
wing. He brought the Cessna's left wing to the Cub.
Down two feet. In closer. Then he brought the Cessna
wing up hard against the Cub's wing, slapping our plane
off trim. I settled the Cub and Blackmuir came in again.
Still under us. Two feet. Closer. St. Cloud reached to the
wheel.

"Goddamnit, he's going to take out the wing struts!
Go down! Do what he wants. Get him on the ground."

Then, as the Cessna wing came up under ours, St.
Cloud reached forward and with his last strength turned
the wheel and kicked the rudder left. With the Lycoming's first stutter, the Cub banked away. The right
wing lifted from the Cessna and our small plane swept
back toward the wilderness.

I *HAD WALKED* the length of the frozen lake. To the west end, the wall of snow and rock there blocking the sun. I looked back to the Cub. Its silver tail stood high in the air, its nose ground into the ice. St. Cloud dead in the right seat. I had felt no life in him. A hundred yards beyond the Cub I could make out the mound of snow we had caught landing, the bad ski snagging the felled tree, the beaver hutch, whatever, that I had seen too late, had not had the fuel to go over had I seen it. I looked to the western wall of snow and rock, to the ridge leading to the summit, the massive cornice reaching out from the ridge, much larger than the cornice where Dutch had died, and went back to the plane.

I reached my hand in the cabin, to St. Cloud's jacket pocket. The gas cap. In the other I found the .45. I took out the map, tried to find the lake where we had come down, the lake and bowl here much larger than those beneath Dutch's mountain house, but couldn't. I had no idea where we were. I took up the mike, pressed the transmit button. Nothing. The radio had been taken out in the crash. I looked to the sky. The silver knife circled high above the lake. I fitted the .45 into my belt and went across the ice lake.

I had made the west end of the lake when the sound of the Cessna came to me. Blackmuir glided into approach, skimmed the trees east of the lake. The Cessna set down along the north shore, avoiding the weak ice in the center of the lake. Blackmuir ran out the landing and turned the Cessna, maybe five hundred yards from me. I waited till Blackmuir had gotten out of the plane, had seen me, then went into the deep snow at the shore.

For a time I did not think I would finish. The snow had collected waist-deep among the trees. When I could go no farther, I would stop, fight for breath and look back toward the lake. I could see nothing for the trees. I went up, reaching to the branches, pulling myself from tree to tree. I fell, fought out of the snow, foot by foot, digging through the snow till I came to the end of the trees. A slanted field of snow stood before me. The slope curved steep to the ridge I had seen from the lake. The ridge was capped, four, five hundred feet above, by the cornice. The shadow beneath the overhang showed dark as a well. The cantilevered snow so massive it seemed that only a man's step would be needed to break it free from the ridge.

The snow before me was deeper than in the trees,

but to the left, at the foot of the ridge that led up to the
cornice, was rock and once I had gotten there I climbed
easily. After leaving the rock I found the snow along the
wind-swept ridge hard-packed. From time to time I
broke through the crust, but there was a bed of snow and
ice a foot beneath that and I climbed quickly. Half
through my climb to the cornice, I went low to the crest
of the ridge and looked down. For a moment I thought
Blackmuir had already entered the trees. That I would
not reach the cornice in time to kill him. But then I saw
tracks from the silver Cessna skirting the shore of the
lake, avoiding the weak ice in the center. The tracks led
to the downed Super Cub. Now Blackmuir came away
from the plane. He had seen St. Cloud was dead. He
looked toward the trees and the wall of snow and rock
above them. I stood on the ridge. Blackmuir raised an
arm and came along the tracks I had made going toward
the trees. A rifle was slung on his back. He was wearing
snowshoes. He moved quickly. I turned and went up
toward the cornice that bulged like a malignant growth
from the ridge.

I dropped to my belly and eased out on the cornice
platform. I went as far as I thought I dared and still could
not see the trees below. I went forward by inches. The
spires of the trees appeared over the cornice edge, then
their thatched branches, then the bars of their trunks, the
holes they seemed to have bored in the snow. Then,
when I thought the cornice would surely collapse under
my weight, I saw my tracks in the snow. Where I had
come out of the trees. Blackmuir came into view, moving
quickly on the snowshoes. He stopped at the last tree
before the field of snow. He looked up. He did not see
me. He came into full view, away from the trees.

I went back on my belly to a point where I thought
the cornice might break away from the ridge. I took the

.45 from my belt and waited. I imagined Blackmuir
below. He was looking toward my tracks that led to the
rock at the foot of the slope. Now he followed my tracks
into the open field of snow. Away from the trees. I
chambered a round in the .45, lifted the safety. I aimed at
the line where I thought the cornice would break away
from the ridge and fired. Nothing. The cornice held. The
echo of the gunshot moved across the lake. I fired again.
A third, fourth round. Still nothing moved. I went near
the cornice. I kicked desperately at the hard snow. It
held. I looked to the summit rearing beyond the ridge. I
could hide in the rocks there, wait for Blackmuir to
follow my tracks along the ridge. But he would never
come within range of the .45. There was no other place to
kill him but here. I fell to my knees and began hacking at
the snow with the pistol. I struck the snow again and
again, till I could not move my arm. The pistol fell from
my hand. I went down into the snow, finished. The .45
lay near me. Snow and ice were jammed into the barrel.
I tore away my gloves and forced more ice and snow into
the barrel, till the barrel was packed. I rammed my fist in
the snow. I drove my arm down to the elbow, beyond, as
far as I could reach. I took up the pistol and drove it into
the hole in the snow. I pulled the trigger.

The explosion and the pain and a long cracking came
at once. There was a roar and weightlessness and a cry
from below. I went down the slope on top of the snow. I
lashed my arms and legs against the boiling mass under
me. The snow sucked me down. It took my legs first,
gripping them, then my arms. Then my head went under
the surface of the avalanche and the snow all around me
went black.

I could not see. I could not breathe. I could not move.
I knew nothing but that I was being crushed. Then
something came to me. There was something beyond

me. Something other than the immense, blind weight on me. My foot. I felt it and it moved. Then feeling came up my leg. I felt the other foot freed and that leg as well, and something like a soothing wind came over me. I had drawn breath.

I was in the trees. Crawling through the snow. What I had thought was a hideous labor before, fighting through bank after bank of snow, now came easy. I fell, came up, fell, came up again, without effort, it seemed, till I emerged from the trees and the snow and lay on the ice. I lifted my head and saw the plain of the lake. Nothing else. When I came up again there was a silver glint in the distance. The tail of the downed Cub reflecting the last of the sun. I looked beyond the Cub. In the shadows on the far side of the lake, I made out Blackmuir's Cessna. Prop and windshield and the lettering on its side. Cabin empty. I stood. I went toward the plane, not directly to it, circling away from the shine of weak ice in the lake's center.

I did not see my hand, what was left of it, until I was in the Cessna's cabin, reaching toward the instrument panel. A finger and part of another were gone. Flesh hung away from the bone stub. I fitted something into a pull ring on the instrument panel and pulled. The starter cranked and quit, cranked again and then, when the burning from my hand came to me, the engine fired and caught and ran. I eased the throttle forward. The engine wound up smooth. The power of the prop pulled at the plane. I put the throttle half forward, left rudder, and the plane came around. As the plane turned I saw a ghostly white figure, Blackmuir crusted with snow, crossing the ice. His rifle was gone. He staggered toward the Cessna. He fell. His legs went through the ice. He came out of the rotten ice on his knees. He struggled to his feet and looked toward the plane. He came again. Not toward me now. Angling away, where the plane would taxi and run to takeoff. I pushed the throttle full forward. The plane shuddered, moved, then ran along the snow-packed ice.

I thought the prop would take Blackmuir. That he would throw himself into the prop blades, anything to destroy the plane. But the plane had gathered speed and the prop went past him. Then the wing was struck a blow. Blackmuir had caught an arm on the strut. He slipped, then pulled himself back and stayed there, so close he seemed to be in the cabin with me. The plane went hard right, veered off its run. I fought the wheel and brought the plane straight again. Still Blackmuir's weight brought the wing down. When the plane lifted, the wing would drop. It would strike the ice beneath the snow, cartwheeling the plane to destruction. I eased down on the left rudder, as St. Cloud had shown me, and the wing straightened. The plane ran level across the snow, gathering speed toward takeoff.

Fifty, sixty, the airspeed made seventy-five knots and still the plane did not leave the snow. The trees at the end of the lake rushed toward me. Then the plane went light. It came up. The right wing dropped. It struck the snow. I hit left rudder, pulled on the wheel. The plane rose four, five feet, so that when the wing went down again, it grazed the snow but cleared the ice.

The plane gathered altitude. Twenty, thirty, fifty feet. Still the right wing would not level. Blackmuir's weight was forcing the plane to bank as it rose. The plane climbed in a circle, following the shore of the lake.

I looked to the right window. Blackmuir there, feet away, clinging to the wing strut. Then Blackmuir turned his head, face into the windstream. I looked forward, toward the rock wall at the west end of the lake. The banking plane would not clear the rock. Blackmuir would kill us both. I snapped my foot off the left rudder and twisted the wheel right.

The Cessna slid into a hard stall right. All lift went from the wings. The plane cut through the air toward the ice. I saw nothing but a swirling field of white. Then against all instinct, I kicked left rudder and pushed the wheel full forward, toward the white field spread over the windshield. The plane powered into a dive. The wings caught air. I pulled back on the wheel—hard. The plane righted, maybe fifty feet above the lake, now turned east, safe, away from the rock face at the far end of the lake.

Blackmuir had held to the wing strut through the stall and dive and pullout. But that superhuman effort had finished him. His strength was gone. He could not raise his head. He was freezing in the airstream. Dying of the cold.

The plane climbed, still banking right, still trapped in the circle that would take us back to the wall. North, east, south, then west again—the plane circled and climbed. The granite west wall spread over the windshield. But the plane had risen now, maybe a hundred feet higher than before. I kept the throttle forward, wheel back, and eased off the left rudder. The plane banked right. The left wing cleared the rock by yards. The wings did not lose lift. The plane kept climbing. Still circling, but climbing, so that as we came around the third time the plane cleared the rock wall at the end of the lake and went free into the sky.

Blackmuir held to the wing strut another circle over the lake, then the airstream swept him away. He fell for a time like a soaring bird, arms outstretched, but then his body began to tumble and he was gone.

I pulled the stick back and let the plane climb.

Twelve, fourteen, sixteen thousand feet, as high as the craft would fly. To the east lay the Bitterroot Valley, dark, already taken by night. The west: snow, ice and the inferno of the setting sun. I lowered a wing and turned away from the valley, toward a mountain strip in the wilderness. Where I would start a new life, one that will not be taken from me, mend and come to fly again and, now that this account is told, forget who I have been and what I have seen done.

Michael Köepf is the author of *Save the Whale,* a novel published in 1978. He lives in Northern California and is a professional fisherman.

Max Crawford's previous novels are *Waltz Across Texas* (1975), *The Bad Communist* (1976), *The Backslider* (1979), *Lords of the Plain* (1985), and *Six Key Cut* (1986). Raised in West Texas, he now lives in London.